CW00750070

DIRTY DEALINGS

GILLIAN GODDEN

Boldwood

First published 2019. This edition first published in Great Britain in 2023 by Boldwood Books Ltd.

Copyright © Gillian Godden, 2019

Cover Design by Colin Thomas

Cover Photography: Colin Thomas

The moral right of Gillian Godden to be identified as the author of this work has been asserted in accordance with the Copyright, Designs and Patents Act 1988.

All rights reserved. No part of this book may be reproduced in any form or by any electronic or mechanical means, including information storage and retrieval systems, without written permission from the author, except for the use of brief quotations in a book review.

This book is a work of fiction and, except in the case of historical fact, any resemblance to actual persons, living or dead, is purely coincidental.

Every effort has been made to obtain the necessary permissions with reference to copyright material, both illustrative and quoted. We apologise for any omissions in this respect and will be pleased to make the appropriate acknowledgements in any future edition.

A CIP catalogue record for this book is available from the British Library.

Paperback ISBN 978-1-80280-146-0

Large Print ISBN 978-1-80280-147-7

Hardback ISBN 978-1-80280-145-3

Ebook ISBN 978-1-80280-148-4

Kindle ISBN 978-1-80280-149-1

Audio CD ISBN 978-1-80280-140-8

MP3 CD ISBN 978-1-80280-141-5

Digital audio download ISBN 978-1-80280-144-6

Boldwood Books Ltd
23 Bowerdean Street
London SW6 3TN
www.boldwoodbooks.com

1

A NIGHT TO REMEMBER

'What the hell are you doing? Get off me!' Shocked horror filled her. She couldn't believe what was happening. Only a few moments ago, they had been chatting and laughing, but now he was grabbing a handful of her hair and pulling her down to the concrete floor and on to her knees. He kicked her backwards with his steel-toecap boot, which made her cry out in pain. He straddled her, his leering face looming only inches away from her own. Her head was pounding from hitting the hard surface. She felt dazed, but adrenalin and panic drove her on. Reaching up, she scratched his face with her long nails. They dug deep into his cheeks and drew blood.

He grabbed her jaw with his rough builder's hands and squeezed hard. As he shouted at her, spit flew out of his mouth and hit her in the face. 'Try that again, you bitch, and I'll punch you so hard you won't know what day of the week it is,' he rasped.

'Get off me, you're hurting me. Get off me!' she pleaded, doing her best to fight him off, but her resistance seemed to urge him on more. There was a wild look of excitement and expectation in his eyes as he ripped open her silk blouse. A noise filled the air and echoed around the room. And then she realised it was the sound of her own voice screaming and shouting.

'Why not?' he snarled. 'You're a tease. You've wanted this all along and men like me don't like prick-teasers like you. You've asked for this, prancing around in your short skirts. Now shut up,' he shouted through gritted teeth, pinning her down on the cold, hard concrete floor. His heavy body prevented all movement from her as she tried to struggle free. He was panting and sweating, holding her hands tightly in a vice-like grip with one hand and frantically undoing the belt on his jeans with the other.

'No! Leave me alone, you bastard. Please.' Tears rolled down her face as she begged him to stop. He was so heavy she could hardly breathe. He slapped her and the sharp sting across her face threw her head sideways with a thump. Feeling the warm stream of blood running down her neck, she cried out even more.

'Like it rough, do you? That's okay by me, sweetie. You just keep struggling. One more word and you'll get another slap across the face.' His red, sweaty face was only inches above her own and salty drops of sweat ran from his forehead onto her face and mixed with her own tears. She knew there was no way out of this. He was going to rape her.

His rough hands felt like sandpaper against her flesh as he mauled her, grabbing at her breasts and squeezing them tightly, making her wince in pain. 'Please stop. I won't tell anyone. Just please leave me alone.'

Another sharp slap across her face stung even harder and sent her head reeling to the side again. With his dead weight crushing the breath out of her lungs, she could hardly breathe, and she felt exhausted. He put his dirty hand over her mouth and his snarling grin showed no mercy. He was excited; he knew what he wanted and he was going to take it.

'Who are you going to tell, you stupid bitch? There's no one here. Everyone is away for the bank holiday weekend, including me after I've had you.' Drool dripped from his lips as he spat out the words like some crazed madman. He slid his hand down her body, groping her legs, then pulling her skirt up and ripping her knickers away, causing her more pain. His trousers were already undone, displaying his nakedness. His manhood was hard and prominent. Closing her eyes to shield herself from the sight of him, she pleaded once more, but she knew it was useless. She had almost given up.

'Open your eyes. I want you to see what a real man can do,' he rasped, oblivious to her screams.

She did as she was told. His face was red; he was hot and sweaty. Something caught her eye and she blinked harder to see it properly. In her spinning head, a thought of hope formed. Anything was worth a try to end this sordid nightmare. This could be her only chance to get this filthy bastard off her!

'Wait!' she shouted, panting under his weight and forcing her body to relax. 'All right, I give in.' Forcing a smile onto her face, she managed to free one of her hands and reached down to stoke him.

He frowned, confused at her change of heart. 'No fucking tricks, now. There's nowhere to run and you'll only make things worse for yourself if you try. Do you hear me?'

Nodding and still forcing a smile, she turned her head to the right and saw what could be her salvation. She prayed that this might just work. He released her other hand, and watched her as she pulled her blouse further open. His tongue slid along his lips in expectation.

Reaching out to him and pulling his head towards her naked breasts, she saw the smile appear on his face. So far, so good, she thought to herself.

The wetness of his tongue roaming over her made her cringe.

She could feel the acid bile in the back of her throat and she swallowed hard, forcing the vomit back down. Her heart was pounding. If this went wrong, God only knew what he would do to her. She reached her arm out as far as she could away from him. He was far too busy biting her neck and breasts to pay her any attention. He sounded like a pig, making grunting noises as he did.

Her hand scrabbled for the nail gun that lay on the floor just a couple of feet away from her and, grabbing it tightly with all the strength she had left, she lifted it, pointed it directly at his head and pressed the trigger, secretly hoping that it was loaded with the six-inch nails the workmen had been using earlier that day.

In her panic, she couldn't stop. She closed her eyes tightly shut and squeezed the trigger, not daring to let go, glad of the repeated hammer action of the gun, hearing him cry out in pain. His screams, and the sound of the nails firing into his head, were deafening. Blood poured onto her face and body, then she felt him slump on top of her. She could feel his body was lifeless, but still couldn't force herself to let go of the trigger. It seemed like an eternity until she heard the nail gun click to indicate it was empty.

He lay motionless on top of her, his wounds pouring with blood. She held her breath and waited. Finally, she opened her eyes and took in the full horror of what she had done. They were both covered in gore. His head was full of the long nails that had been used to put the plasterboard up on the ceiling. His eyes were wide open. Shock and horror filled her as she tried with all her might to push him off her. Sliding away from underneath him, she started to tremble and shake. Tears rolled down her face as sobs wracked her body. Looking at him, still and motionless, filled her with dread.

What had she done? Oh God, what was she going to do now? She felt she had only one option.

Doing her best to stand, she reached for her mobile and dialled. Her voice was shaky and incoherent. 'Papa! I've just killed a man. I'm at the shop.' Dropping the mobile, she fell to her knees and started to cry again.

'Scarlet! Scarlet, is that you?' A man's voice was shouting on the other end of the phone. She could hear it but didn't have the strength to answer it; she simply sat back and waited for help to arrive...

* * *

Sitting in his office with Jake, Tony Lambrianu held the telephone in his hand. He could hear a woman sobbing on the other end. His face paled as he looked up at Jake.

'Come on, we have to go,' he said and, picking up his jacket, he flew towards the door.

Jake looked at Tony oddly. 'What's wrong? Where's the fire?'

'We have to get to Scarlet's shop; we'll use the back exit. Something's wrong.'

He ran to his car, which was parked outside. His mind was whirling and panic rose within him. What had Scarlet said? She'd killed a man?

'Calm down, Tony. Are you going to tell me what all of this is about?' Confused by this sudden panic, Jake got in the car beside Tony and waited for an explanation.

'I don't know what the hell is going on, Jake.' Tony let out a deep sigh. 'That was Scarlet and she just said she'd killed a man and she's at the shop. That's all I know.'

'She's what?' Jake shook his head, stunned. 'Are you sure you heard her right?'

When Tony nodded, he sat back in his seat and folded his arms.

'If this is a fucking joke, Tony, I'll kill her.' He was at a loss, but hardly surprised that Scarlet had screamed down the telephone. Tony's daughter was feisty and was always arguing with some-body, threatening to start a fight. She was hot-tempered, just like her father.

Tony looked out of the window at the passing traffic, his mind in turmoil. Never mind Jake, if this was some overheated joke, he would kill Scarlet himself!

'Don't park outside the shop, Mark,' Tony instructed his driver. 'I don't want anyone seeing us go in there. I'll let you know when the coast is clear and I've found out what the hell is going on.'

Mark pulled over. Walking quickly, almost running, with Jake hot on his heels, Tony reached the new hair salon that Scarlet was having renovated. Tony and Jake could see the front shutters were down. Exchanging looks, they frowned. This got weirder by the minute. Where the hell was she?

Thankfully, the streets were almost empty. Everyone had their plans for the bank holiday and had gone away for the weekend. Crossing the road and not speaking a word to each other, Tony pointed to the alley that led to the back entrance where the skips were.

It was a tense moment as neither of them knew what to expect. Maybe someone had kidnapped Scarlet and forced her to make the call so that Tony and Jake would walk into an ambush.

Reaching for his trusted gun, which he always kept in the inside of the custom-made false lining of his jacket pocket, Tony noticed the door was ajar. When he touched it tentatively, it swung open. Somebody was in there. Taking the lead, Tony walked to the staircase. The downstairs of the shop was in black-ness, but upstairs the lights were on. He put his finger to his lips and looked at Jake, then they both climbed the stairs as quietly as possible.

As they neared the top of the staircase they could hear muffled sobs. It was a woman crying. Tony started running. 'Scarlet! Scarlet, where are you?' he shouted. He followed the noise then stopped so sharply Jake bumped into him from behind.

Standing in the doorway, Tony and Jake both took in the scene before them. It was devastating. Blood was flowing across the floor, making patterns in the creases of the heavy-duty plastic that had been laid by the workmen. They could see the back of a man who was lying on his side.

Jake ran across the room. There, huddled in a corner, was Scarlet. She was sitting on the floor with her arms wrapped tightly around her legs, rocking back and forth, sobbing. Jake took in her appearance. Her blouse was ripped open, exposing her breasts. Her long blonde hair was matted with blood. Mascara and blood were smeared across her face. A bruise was forming around her swollen eye. It was obvious what had gone on here. Sitting down beside her so as not to frighten her, he reached his arm out and put it around her shoulders. She moved away from him and started shouting for him to get off her. She was clearly in shock.

'It's me, Scarlet, it's okay, it's me, Jake, remember?' Lowering his voice almost to a whisper, he tried getting through to her. 'What happened, Scarlet? Do you remember, love?' Jake looked up at Tony, who was walking around the room taking everything in, ignoring Scarlet's distress.

Scarlet pointed to the dead man on the floor. 'I killed him. He was going to rape me and I fucking killed him!' Then she broke down again.

Taking off his jacket, Jake put it around her shoulders. She was shaking with fear. 'Aren't you going to say something, Tony?

For Christ's sake, she's your daughter!' Jake felt angry at the way that Tony had ignored Scarlet and was walking around the room taking stock. He hadn't said one soothing word to Scarlet.

Trying to calm the emotions he felt surging inside himself, Tony turned to Jake. 'Not now, Jake. I need to know the facts.' Standing beside the man on the floor, Tony pushed him with his foot and the man fell on to his back. 'Do you see this, Jake? He's a fucking pin cushion! How many nails are embedded in his brain alone?'

Jake hadn't thought to look; he'd been far too occupied with Scarlet. Puzzled, he stood up and walked over. 'Fucking hell, Tony, there must be twenty or more nails in his head, never mind that one sticking out of his neck that looks like a bloody coat hanger. Wait a minute. Isn't that one of the builders that's been working on the place?' Jake looked up at Tony and then turned to Scarlet.

Nodding her head, Scarlet looked up at them both and then buried her head back into her knees, pulling Jake's jacket tightly around her.

Tony's voice was serious and stern. 'Scarlet, listen to me. Is that your builder guy? Is Jake right?' The anger was beginning to show in Tony's face. His cheeks were flushed and his eyes were glaring at her. Tony walked over to his daughter, grabbed her by the arm and forced her to stand up.

'Listen to me, young lady. I want to know everything and you had better start talking.'

'Stop shouting at her, Tony; can't you see she's in no fit state?'

Raising his hand, Tony slapped Scarlet across the face then pulled her close to him and held her in his arms. 'Scarlet, you need to come out of this. Do you hear me? I am going to help you, but I need to know all the facts, darling.'

His slap seemed to bring her back to reality. 'It wasn't my

fault, Papa,' she cried, holding on to him. Tony felt like crying himself. Scarlet was his baby and he hadn't been there to protect her when she'd needed him.

'You're right, Jake, he's one of the builders – the one in charge.' Averting her eyes from the body, she continued as best she could. 'All the builders left at five. I left with them and then I realised I'd left my mobile phone here and came back to get it.' Her shaky voice managed to tell the story.

'How long after you left did you realise that you didn't have your phone?' Tony was pushing her. He needed to know every detail.

'Couple of hours. I'm not really sure. I met up with Katie for something to eat and when I took my purse out I realised I didn't have my mobile. Katie was going to come with me but she was meeting Christopher so I told her not to bother. Oh, God, Papa, I wish she'd come.' Again, Scarlet burst into tears and sobbed on Tony's chest. His heart was breaking but he couldn't think about that now. He needed his business head on.

'It's all right, Scarlet. Papa's here. Tell me when you can.' He wanted to hurry her in case anyone came, but he was trying his best to keep her calm.

'I came through the back exit because I knew I must have left it up here and I couldn't be bothered to open up the front shutters. When I came up he was already here. He was finishing tiling the wall over there.' Scarlet pointed to the newly half-tiled wall.

Confused by this and pushing her away slightly to see her face, Tony said, 'Why did he come back to tile the wall, Scarlet? I want to know the truth, now, and I don't care what it is. Did you come back to meet him? Had you planned to meet him and something went wrong? Did it all just get out of hand?'

'No! No, it didn't. If you don't believe me, then the police won't, will they?' She ran to Jake.

'You heartless bastard, Tony. Can't you see what she's been through and you ask her that? Even if she had planned to meet him, no means no. Any woman in the world will tell you that. It doesn't matter how far it goes. If you say no, then that is final.' Jake wrapped his arms around Scarlet and held her tightly, all the while glaring at Tony over her shoulder.

'A stiff prick has no conscience, Jake. This one had no conscience at all and now he has no fucking brains, either. We have to get the full story of who knew he was here if we're going to sort this out. And it needs sorting. Fast.'

'Go on, Scarlet, he's right. No stone left unturned. We need to know the facts.'

'He was surprised when I came back and was acting normal, telling me he'd come back because the cabinets are coming Tuesday and he needed the wall finished and dry before they put them up. He said he was going away for a few days to visit his family or something. I'm not sure. Then he started talking dirty and when I told him to shut up, he started slapping me and pushed me to the floor. He pinned me down and I couldn't fight him off. I tried, Papa, I really did.' Scarlet pleaded her innocence.

Ignoring her outburst and yet more tears, Tony said, 'Carry on, Scarlet.'

'I froze, Papa. Yes, me.' She pointed to her chest to stress the point even more. 'Me! Scarlet who never backs away from a fight. Mad angry Scarlet froze, until I saw the nail gun they had been using to put the boards up. That's when I reached out and pressed the trigger. I couldn't let go; I was too frightened to stop. I just squeezed the trigger until it was empty.' Scarlet fell forward on to Jake's chest. She was exhausted.

'You did the right thing.' Turning towards Jake, Tony grinned. 'The floor is covered in plastic. That has saved us a lot of cleaning up.'

Scarlet's eyes widened. 'Do you think I should go to the police? He was going to rape me; it was self-defence.' She was confused and distraught.

Tony and Jake burst out laughing. If nothing else it broke the tension. 'Scarlet, love, you are entitled to use reasonable force to defend yourself, but this is a massacre. This is murder – at the very least, manslaughter, given the circumstances. But it is your word against a dead man's. No, Scarlet, we do not go to the police.'

'What are we going to do, then?' she asked. They couldn't just make him vanish into thin air.

'Tony! Look what I see. Is that an angle grinder?' A big grin spread across Jake's face.

Looking up to where he was pointing, Tony laughed. 'I'll give you this, Scarlet, you make life very easy. You need to leave now. Burn those clothes; they are covered in blood and DNA. Mark's outside, he'll take you home. Come to think of it, where is your car?'

'My car's parked near one of the skips around the back,' Scarlet said.

'Okay...' Looking down, Tony took in his bloodstained shirt and jacket. 'Fucking hell, Jake, why does everyone bleed over my good silk shirts? Do you know how much they cost?' Tony shook his head and sighed.

'You're a vain bastard, Tony. Even after all these years. Your daughter has nearly been raped. There is a dead man with nails in his head, and you're worried about your bloody shirt. I love you, man, I really do.' Jake couldn't help laughing. It was a crazy situation they had found themselves in and that was the last straw.

Tony drew his attention back to Scarlet. 'Just one more thing, Scarlet.' He felt almost embarrassed to ask. 'Did he erm... did he manage to...?'

'No, Papa, he didn't.' Her tearful blue eyes met his and he nodded.

That seemed to satisfy Tony and he walked over to look out of the windows into the black night sky. 'Right, Jake, let's get this sorted out. Is his van downstairs?'

Puzzled and confused, Scarlett wondered how on earth they were going to sort this out. It was impossible; although she had heard the stories about her father and Jake, she had never really believed them. It was almost disturbing that they were acting so calmly about this. Tony was her father. Loving, kind and funny. Not this cold businessman, weighing up the situation with Uncle Jake and deciding what to do with a dead man. These men were cold and calculating. This was a side to her father she never knew existed.

'I'm not leaving you. If you're going to help me by getting rid of that bastard then I'm going to help you do it.' With her father by her side, Scarlet felt stronger.

'No, Scarlet, go home. Get cleaned up and burn those clothes. Go on, love. Tonight has been bad enough. You don't need to see this.' Tony's words were soft and comforting.

'Yes, I do, Papa. I am Scarlet Lambrianu. I'm staying with you. Just tell me what you want me to do.' She stood her ground. If they could sort this out then she would help them. She was adamant she would see it through to the end, although she didn't know what to expect.

A grin spread across Tony's face. 'Okay, but it's not going to be pretty. If you have the stomach for it, then stay. What do you say, Jake?'

Jake nodded. They could do with an extra pair of hands and she seemed to want to help finish this.

Tony pointed his finger at her. 'As long as you do as you're told without question and if you feel sick, leave. Oh, and just one more thing, Scarlet,' Tony said as an afterthought, looking at her properly. 'Do your bloody buttons up. I never thought I'd tell a beautiful young woman to cover her tits, but I really don't want to see yours!'

For the first time that evening, Scarlet smiled. She hadn't realised her blouse was still wide open. Her cheeks flushed slightly at her father seeing her nakedness. She pulled her blouse around her and tied the bottom in a knot to hold it together, then waited for her instructions.

Rubbing his hands together, Tony now felt on firmer ground and more in charge of the situation. This, he could handle. His daughter being hurt and mauled by a rapist, he could not. 'Jake, start up that saw and get undressed. Scarlet, I want you to take the tiles off that wall carefully, like they were never there. We need to cover our tracks. The other workmen know it wasn't finished when they left. Let's not cause suspicion.' Walking over to the builder lying on the floor, Tony gave him an almighty kick. 'There, I feel better now.' Turning to see the puzzled look on Scarlet's face as she watched Jake taking his shirt and trousers off, he raised his eyebrow and smiled. 'No questions asked, do you hear me? What you are going to see is not going to be pretty. This is your last chance to leave; we need to get on with this fast.'

Scarlet nodded as Tony started undressing as well.

She walked over and picked up a wall scraper, knelt in front of the tiled wall and promptly began levering the tiles off. She was glad of the distraction. Behind her she could hear the saw; it was deafening. She could also hear her father and Jake puffing and panting and giving each other instructions. Although she was on her knees with her back to them, she couldn't help glimpsing over her shoulder. She saw Jake and her father, wearing only their boxer shorts, on their knees at either side of the builder.

Tony's driver, Mark, came upstairs with another man. Scarlet didn't know him and kept her back to him as they all spoke in muffled voices. She continued to remove the tiles and scrape off the adhesive, until the wall was spotless. She went to get some of the heavy-duty rubbish bags to put the tiles into. When she'd cleared the tiling away, she turned around and was surprised to see the dead builder had vanished. All that was left was the blood on the plastic flooring.

'Darren, you take the builder's van and get it crushed, okay?' said Jake, who was as nonchalant about the situation as her father. 'What about CCTV?'

Tony turned and looked at Scarlet.

'They aren't installed properly yet,' she said. 'The men are coming Wednesday. But there are the shops next door.' She swallowed hard to hide her confused state. She couldn't believe it. This was like a military operation.

'Come on, Scarlet, let's roll up this plastic flooring.' Jake was smiling and cracking jokes. 'Bloody good idea, this. Makes life really easy.' It felt surreal, but bit by bit, the room was cleared. Once the plastic was rolled up carefully and a new batch was laid, Tony and Jake started scattering dust and debris over it to make it look worn.

'Take a load of that plastic, Scarlet, and put it in the car before you get into it. Cover all the seats. Your work here is done. No arguments.' Tony's cold blue eyes stared directly into her own and she nodded. Taking a roll of plastic in her arms, she went downstairs.

She opened the car door and, doing as she was told, threw the sheet of plastic over the front seats, smoothing it out. Then she did the same with the back. Following her to the car, Tony handed her a pair of rubber gloves. 'Put these on and then wipe the door handle. Keep them on while you use the steering wheel. I need you to be clever, now, Scarlet, or all of this will have been for nothing.' Tony's voice was nothing more than a hushed whisper. 'Go to the apartment at the club. Go in the back way, and make sure there's no one around. You can't afford to be seen looking the way you do.'

'My long coat is in the boot of the car. I'll wear that. Thank you, Papa.' Her eyes filled with tears.

Tony looked up at the sky. He could handle anything but his daughter's distress. It broke his heart. 'This night is never to be mentioned again, Scarlet. I'm not happy that you've witnessed all of this, but you have done well, Scarlet. Remember one thing if your conscience pricks you. What would he have done with you when he had finished with you? When reality dawned in his sick brain, he would know that I would want revenge.'

That had never crossed her mind. Of course the builder knew who she was and who her father was. What would he have done with her? Dumped her in one of those skips? The very thought of it sent a chill down her spine. She could be dead now. Although a cold wind was blowing, it was nothing like the cold empty feeling she felt inside when she realised what could have been her fate.

She started up the engine and was about to leave when Tony tapped on the car window. Grinning at her in his usual way, he said, 'Go on, drive carefully. I'll meet you back at the apartment. Be lucky.' Blowing her a kiss for good measure, he watched her drive away.

He was freezing, standing in the yard dressed only in his boxer shorts and socks. Pushing his hair back from his face, he gave a big sigh and climbed the stairs.

'You took your bloody time. Well, Tony, what do we do now? What is your plan B?'

'You know that old farmer that lives near Ralph Gold? Well, he has some very strange looking pigs, like nothing I have ever seen before. Wild boars or something, with big horns. Bloody horrible. He's really proud of them because they are prize winners, but he also said they eat anything. And I mean anything.'

'What? Pigs with horns? What the fuck is this, the Dark Ages? Why on earth would you want them near your house? They sound disgusting.' Jake was horrified at the thought. 'Still, you have a point, you sick bastard. Well, let's see if they really do eat anything, shall we?' They both burst out laughing and got dressed.

* * *

'Fucking hell, I can't believe it. It's 2 a.m. and I am creeping around on farmland covered in horse shit and God knows what else. And it's started to rain.' Puffing and panting, Jake stopped. 'God, he's heavy. Couldn't we have parked closer, Tony? This fat bastard weighs a tonne. How come you only got the bags with his arms and legs?'

'Jake, shut up. It's not the first time it's been feeding time at the zoo, is it? Right, here it is.' Putting down his own plastic bags, Tony took the other end of Jake's. 'One. Two. Three,' he counted. Lifting the large plastic bag as high as they could, they threw it over the fencing which contained the wild boars. Then they did the same with the others.

Instantly they heard grunts and a stampede near the fence. They looked at each other and grimaced; the noises coming from behind the pigsty were blood-curdling.

'Time to go, Jake,' said Tony. He began to traipse back through the sludge, raising his knees high as he walked, to stop him from sinking into the mud.

'Hang on, Tony, my bloody shoe's come off.' Jake struggled to pick up his shoe from the mud, then caught up with him at the car.

They could both see the look on Mark's face as the smell of manure hit him. 'Put the bloody heater on and open the windows,' said Tony; he was sickened by the smell.

'My feet are covered in shit,' Jake moaned, as he fell back on the seat. 'I'm absolutely knackered. And you know what? That has put me off bacon sandwiches for life!'

'Good. You're getting fat, anyway. High five, Jakey boy. We haven't lost our touch.' They both burst out laughing as they raised their hands and slapped them together.

grateful. It will give you a break. That old tom cat, Tony, is like a rabbit on steroids when he's home. Sniffing around you and fondling you, thinking no one is noticing.' Pointing her finger at Francesca, Julie warned, 'I told you. You should have taken him straight down the vets when Adam was born. See you later, girls.' Julie burst out laughing at her own joke and left.

* * *

'Why are we in Elle's car? For goodness' sake, Julie, I feel like I'm on a stakeout.'

'Because, you daft cow, don't you think Diana would recognise my Rolls Royce following her? This clapped out old banger is just right for the job.' Julie was determined. She was driving along, watching Diana's car, although holding back slightly. When she saw Diana's car slowing down to park, she stopped and pulled into a space further up the street. Julie's jaw dropped. 'What the hell is she going in there for?' she said.

Sitting closer to the windscreen to take a look, Francesca and Julie watched Diana. 'Do you think she's doing some kind of community service?' They couldn't take their eyes off Diana as she stepped through a doorway.

'Community service? At this time of night? I thought you were here to help me, Fran. Let's wait and see how long she's in there for.' Mesmerised, Julie watched the door. Half an hour later Diana emerged. Stunned into silence, Julie turned to look at Francesca, her eyes wide.

'She's in police uniform, Julie. She's a special constable.' Francesca sat staring, while stating the obvious.

'Well, she's not a fucking strippergram, is she?' Julie snapped. 'I can't believe it. Ralph will go bonkers. Fucking hell, a boyfriend is nothing compared to this. No wonder she's kept it secret, Fran.'

They both watched as Diana, dressed in her black uniform and hat, got into the front of a police car with what looked like a sergeant.

'I thought she was studying languages at college or something,' said Fran.

'I speak languages, Francesca. In fact, I am fucking bilingual. I speak bitch! Oh, the lying cow!'

'Slow down, Julie, it's a very respectable profession. I can see why she hasn't told you and Ralph, though. The police aren't exactly your favourite people, I know that. She must have sat exams or something and passed. But I do agree she should have been honest with you.' Francesca couldn't help but wonder what Ralph's response to this revelation would be when he found out.

'Not just that, Fran, do you really think Ralph would want his little girl patrolling the streets of London at night, when they're full of druggies and drunks? He would have her followed by an armed guard. Jesus, what am I going to tell him?' The thought of telling Ralph set Julie's teeth on edge.

'I know, Julie, and I agree, the streets of London are full of unsavoury types, but they're someone's daughters and sons, aren't they? Let's go home, you've solved the mystery.'

Taking out a cigarette, Julie lit it and took a drag, then exhaled smoke into the car. 'Don't even think of complaining about this.' Julie waved her cigarette in the air. 'I need a drink to go with it. Let's go back to yours, I've seen enough.'

Francesca let the window down a little, but said nothing. She could see Julie's mind was troubled.

When they got back, Elle was eager for the news. 'Well, what happened?'

'I'm going to check on Adam,' said Fran, and she left the other two women to it.

'Oh, she's got a boyfriend all right, Elle. In fact, she has a

hundred of them – the whole of the Metropolitan police force!'
Julie shouted. 'She's only training to be a fucking copper. That's
what all of this sneaking around has been about.' Julie stormed
around the kitchen shouting about what they had witnessed.

'Good for her.' Elle didn't give the shocked, disgusted reaction
that Julie was hoping for. 'Although, why all the sneaking around?
I don't like that part, but they don't just accept anyone, you know.
It's a good career, so what's the problem?'

Julie looked at her. 'You have to ask?'

'Oh,' said Elle, as the penny dropped and knocked the
wind out of her sails somewhat. The problem was Ralph
and Tony. That was what all the concern was about. They
were gangland bosses and known to have their fingers in a
lot of pies. 'Do you think she's some kind of informer or
something, Julie? Because if you do, you're barking up the
wrong tree. She can't help the fact that her father has a
crooked past. That's his life, not hers. Why shouldn't she do
as she pleases?' Elle was going to stand her ground and be
as stubborn as Julie about this. It was a good profession and
Diana had proved herself to be just like her mother. She
was her own woman and she didn't care what anyone else
thought. She was more like her parents than they gave her
credit for.

Waltzing into the kitchen and spying Julie's sulky face and
Elle's stern one, Francesca said, 'You've told her, then? Personally,
I think you and Ralph both need to sit down and discuss this with
Diana in a friendly manner. The more you fight with her, the
more she will show her own stubborn side and you could end up
losing her altogether.'

Picking up her wine glass and taking a large gulp, Julie
nodded. 'You're both right, of course. In any other circumstances
it would be a great achievement but we aren't the most honest of

families, are we? Always ducking and diving. But it's better if I mention it to Ralph first. It will soften the blow.'

Julie was still in two minds about the situation and didn't know how to approach it. She could see Francesca and Elle's point of view, but where did Diana's loyalties lie? Would word get out she was a grass and never to be trusted? Would she ever have to visit Ralph and Tony with another officer during an investigation? What was this going to do to her family? Julie wasn't sure.

'Could I ask you not to mention this before the weekend? It's Scarlet's and Katie's opening ceremony for their hair and beauty salon and Tony has arranged a party at the club. I know it sounds selfish, but it could cause ill feeling and take the shine off their day.' Francesca felt embarrassed to ask, but needed to say it.

'Course I won't, Francesca. In fact, as far as I'm concerned, the longer I wait, the better I will feel. No. The girls have worked hard building this salon up. Let's enjoy the family party while we still have a family, eh?'

* * *

The day was upon them when Scarlet was opening her own salon, and no one yet knew the name. She had kept that very close to her chest and had had the signwriter put it up at the very last minute. This was her crowning glory, so to speak.

She had always had a talent for styling hair. Some of her styles were outlandish but that was Scarlet. Now, with her sister Katie's help, she was opening her own salon.

Scarlet had passed the entrance exams at the Elite Hair and Beauty Academy and then done an apprenticeship, where she had been held back and told to sweep floors and make coffee all day. She had been bored until the manageress had been taken ill and had been absent for a week.

The assistant manageress had no choice but to let Scarlet help. Punching the air with glee, she had felt this was the chance to prove herself. Customers had liked the styles she suggested and asked for her advice. On her return, the manageress had had no choice but to let Scarlet carry on. Scarlet was making her money and word had spread about the new stylist. Scarlet wasn't happy, though, and she'd talked to Katie about it many times, letting out all her pent-up feelings about her employer.

'I hate that old bag, Katie. She looks down on me all the time. "Make some coffee, Scarlet, sweep the floor, Scarlet. Kiss my fucking arse, Scarlet."' Sulkily, Scarlet had sat back in her seat.

'Why don't you open up your own place?' Christopher, Katie's unofficial boyfriend, had said.

'What? Look, Clark Kent, I'm talking to my sister. No one asked you to tag along. And now that you have, you can keep your nose out.'

'I asked him to tag along, Scarlet. And don't be rude. We know you've had a bad day, but you are Scarlet Lambrianu and your father is loaded. She gets a kick out of getting you to sweep the floor. To be fair to Christopher, it's a good suggestion. You've done your apprenticeship; you've passed the exams. Why not open your own salon and get someone else to sweep your floors?' Katie smiled at her to cheer her up, then gave her a wink for good measure.

'I'm a stylist, Katie! I know nothing whatsoever about running my own business.'

'I do.' Christopher had spoken up again much to Scarlet's annoyance. He calmly looked over his horn-rimmed glasses to peer at her across the table, ignoring the icy glare she shot him.

Sitting back in the chair with her arms folded and a sulky, stubborn look on her face, Scarlet challenged Christopher. 'Go on, then. Say your piece. You know you're dying to.'

Ignoring her little tantrum, Christopher carried on. 'Katie is still training but is, nonetheless, an accountant. I am a trainee bank manager who advises people on their businesses. I'm sure that would cover the business side of things. All you need are premises, money and the ambition to succeed.' His slow monotone voice pierced her ears, but he had caught her interest.

'What? You would help me do this?' Scarlet was surprised considering how she had tormented him over the last few months and had never been short of a sarcastic comment about him. She had only put up with him for Katie's sake. When he had turned up wearing a cardigan, she had told him that he looked like one of those models on an old lady's knitting pattern. But now he was talking sense and offering her advice. She had always thought she would like to run her own salon one day, just not this quickly.

'No, I wouldn't do this to help you, but I would do it to help Katie and stop you moaning.' His sarcasm matched her own. It sounded almost like a reprimand.

'Well, what do you suggest we do?' Scarlet didn't want to look too eager. She wasn't sure if he was winding her up. But then, Christopher didn't strike her as a joker!

Adjusting his horn-rimmed glasses, he looked at Katie and then back at Scarlet. 'I presume you have the money? So first you would need premises. I can keep a look out for that. But I suggest you get a mortgage. That way you can build up some credit rating. Could you ask your father to guarantee the mortgage?' Christopher felt on safer ground now. This was his line of expertise. He spent all of his working days advising people how to set up their own businesses.

Scarlet jumped forward with excitement. 'We could do it together, Katie. We have the money. You're the accountant and I'm the famous stylist.' Scarlet looked over at Christopher, who didn't seem very impressed.

'Your job, Scarlet, is to make mental notes of all the customers that like you and ask for you especially. They are your customers. You should take them with you when the time comes. Eventually, you could hand out cards. If you hate your manageress so much, the best way I have found to take revenge is by poaching their business. The last thing people like is losing money.' Again, his matter-of-fact way annoyed Scarlet.

'I'd really like to get her back for all the insults she has thrown at me. She hates me just because she knows Papa has a club and we're not short of a bob or two. I suppose I could steal her custom.' Scarlet was already making mental notes of the women that asked for her specifically. 'What else do you want me to do?'

'Nothing.' Christopher gave a slight cough and cleared his throat. 'You keep quiet about all of this. Don't start boasting and telling people your plans. We need to get premises first. Then we need to get the mortgage. So... you didn't answer my question. Who would stand as guarantor for you?'

'Mum will. She has her own money and she still owns the house.' Scarlet looked hopefully at Katie and saw her nod.

'You're right, Scarlet. Mum will stand guarantor and let us get on with it, but Dad would take over.'

'So, Chris, when do we start?' Scarlet was excited. She loved adrenalin and her whole life was based on impulse. This was her goal and with Katie and Christopher in her corner, she couldn't lose.

'Call me Christopher, Scarlet. My name is Christopher,' he stressed. 'I have to get back to work now.' He stood up and walked to the door and Katie followed him to walk him to his car. Scarlet's curiosity got the better of her and she couldn't help but sit up and watch them through the window as they said goodbye.

When she came back into the café, Katie walked up to the

counter. 'Do you want another coffee, Scarlet, or do you have to go as well?'

'Yes, I will have one, thanks.' A naughty grin appeared on her face as Katie sat down and put the cups on the table. 'Tell me, Katie, is he always as passionate as that? Not exactly shoving his tongue down your throat, was he?' Scarlet's grin widened. 'Have you and Chris done it?' Her blue eyes sparkled mischievously.

'Done what, Scarlet? I don't know what you mean.' On the contrary, Katie knew exactly what Scarlet meant, but she wasn't going to rise to it.

'You know, "it". Has Clark Kent taken his tie off and become a hot bed of passion? Underneath that boring exterior, is he a wild animal between the sheets?' The very idea made Scarlet laugh.

Slightly embarrassed, Katie looked around the café to see other people staring at them. 'Shut up, Scarlet, people are listening.' Katie's cheeks flushed, heightening the blondeness of her hair. 'I'm not discussing anything like that with you. Christopher and I are just good friends.'

Scarlet laughed at Katie's embarrassment but didn't push it any further. She was excited about the new venture they were planning.

Christopher was as good as his word. He had seen a shop that was being auctioned off down Tottenham Court Road that was central and easy to get to. It had been a barber's and so the plumbing for the sinks was already there. And the fact it already had a reputation as a hairdresser's/barber's shop made it more appealing.

The man who owned it had gone to Christopher because he was finding it hard to meet the mortgage payments. Christopher had convinced the man to sell up before getting into any more debt and the owner had agreed. The old barber's shop needed a lot of work and money investing into it to make it a going concern, but as long as they got their money back they didn't care.

'It has a flat above, too. It's unoccupied and very grubby. Students had it, I think. It also has other rooms upstairs that you could probably use for tanning booths or something like that.'

Scarlet was impressed with Christopher's cool business manner and the way he was talking to her as though talking to a client. In her own strange way, she admired him, although while he was talking to her over the telephone, she rolled her eyes with boredom. God, whatever did Katie see in him? Nothing seemed to excite him.

When they went to look at the place, it was indeed grubby. 'Couldn't you find anything better than this, Christopher?' Scarlet said, looking around the filthy place in dismay. This was not what she had hoped for.

'At this price, no. You're in the heart of the West End, for a fraction of the usual price. What did you expect? You can see for yourself now why the bank is auctioning it. The barber seemed to have given up on it. No wonder he had no customers. You could let the flat upstairs. That would generate extra income.'

'Katie, we could live here! We can't live at home forever. This would be ideal. Anyway, it would give you more privacy for Superman, here.' Scarlet couldn't help having a dig at Christopher, but shied away from her sister's blue eyes throwing daggers at her.

Within a few weeks, everything was under control. The builders were hired and Christopher and Katie had stopped Scarlet going on a mad spending spree. Christopher had negotiated a discount at the warehouse for the pink washbasins and units she wanted. Scarlet had taken a course so she could do spray tanning and they all agreed that they would hire the tanning booths for the time being. Scarlet took a back seat and let them get on with it. They had put a large deposit down and Francesca had acted as guarantor for the rest.

Francesca hated all the cloak-and-dagger stuff and keeping secrets from Tony, and insisted that Tony had to be told. She knew he would try and take over, but she promised the girls she would argue their case and let them prove themselves as efficient businesswomen.

Tony had wanted to go and look the place over, but Julie had stepped in and told him to keep his big nose out. That had been more than enough to keep him at bay.

The night before the grand opening, Scarlet was buzzing with excitement. 'Papa, do you remember when you opened your club for the very first time?'

Tony's mind wandered back to the time when he and Jake had been as excited as she was now. It all seemed like a million years ago. He could see her lips moving but he wasn't really listening. He felt sorry for being grumpy and sulky when the salon was mentioned. Now he understood. They wanted to do it for themselves, just like he had.

'Are you sure you want me to come and see it? I thought you didn't want me involved?' He winked.

'Oh, Papa, don't be like that. I want you to see it in all its glory. We want you to be proud of us, don't we, Katie?'

'I am proud of you both.' Cocking his head to one side, he looked at them. 'Anyway, you haven't said what you're calling the place. Am I not allowed to know that either?'

'All will be revealed at the opening ceremony. I'm going for a shower.' Kissing him on the cheek and walking away, she gave Katie a thumbs up.

Tony walked into his bedroom; he could hear the en-suite shower was already running. He raised his eyebrows and a smile appeared on his face as he slid the shower door open.

Francesca stood there, the water falling down her naked body. Her long wavy, auburn hair was hanging in ringlets. 'Do you have room for one more in there, Mrs Lambrianu?'

Francesca saw the familiar glint in his eye and watched him drop his towelling robe. 'Come here, Mr Lambrianu,' she said, reaching out for him, and they made love in the shower with the water pouring down on them, not dampening their passion in the slightest.

3

THE BIG REVEAL

'Thank you, everyone, for coming here today. I know you're all busy so I'll just get on with it.' Scarlet was making her well-rehearsed speech, with Katie at her side, outside of the shop. Passers-by stopped and watched. The entire family had turned up for the grand occasion.

Katie and Christopher stood at either side of the sign and pulled away the sheet to show the name, much to everyone's shock.

'Scat Katz?' said Ralph. 'That's the name of one of the clubs we own. Surely there's copyright or something?'

'You're right, Uncle Ralph, there is. It's our copyright. The newspapers always refer to us as that. Now everyone will know it's our salon.' Scarlet beamed.

'Well, as long as they don't come in for a drink and a dance with their haircut.' Ralph started clapping and congratulating them, and everyone watching nearby followed suit.

Walking into the salon, Jake gave out a low whistle. The shining modern decor was a far cry from the last time he had seen it. Giving Tony a wry smile, he looked the place over.

'Don't you think I'm clever, Mum?' Scarlet was as proud as Punch of the beautiful salon everyone was admiring.

'I think you're a very talented young woman. Of course I am proud of you. I'm proud of you no matter what you do. But let's not get carried away and forget Katie, eh?' Adamant that Scarlet wasn't going to take all the praise, Francesca lowered her voice and whispered in Scarlet's ear, 'You wouldn't have all this if it wasn't for your sister.'

The smile disappeared from Scarlet's face. She hadn't meant to take all the glory and she knew Katie wouldn't mind her boasting. 'I know, Mum. Katie and Christopher have worked really hard helping me set this up. I can't thank them enough.'

'I don't mean that, Scarlet. What I'm talking about is who wore the high-necked jumper to hide the fact that she didn't have a cleft in her chin, which is the only way people can usually tell you two apart until you open your mouth. Katie put her own future in jeopardy and sat your entrance exam into that college for you.'

'How did you know?' Scarlet's shocked look spoke volumes.

'Don't ever forget that I am your mother, Scarlet. And I'm not stupid. I'm not judging you, but when you're boasting about how clever you are, remember who got you here in the first place.'

'Well, let's see what else my daughter has up her sleeve,' said Tony, joining them both and drinking his champagne. He couldn't help but admire the very chic surroundings.

Francesca and Scarlet exchanged glances and then turned to Tony. Painting the smile back on her face, Scarlet beamed her delight. Of course, she knew her mother was right. She wouldn't have passed that exam without Katie. But how could she tell her mother it had all been Katie's idea?

'See, Papa? We've kept the Lambrianu colour scheme up. That

is our signature look. All the basins are pink and the chairs are black and chrome.' She was smiling broadly and showing everyone around excitedly. This was her and Katie's empire. Then a thought crossed her mind and she scolded herself. 'Of course, none of this would have been possible without Christopher. He masterminded everything. Thanks, Chris.'

Everyone turned to look at the young man standing beside Katie. Tony frowned.

'Not a word, love,' Francesca whispered in his ear. 'They are just friends.' Holding his hand and squeezing it to reassure him, she smiled inwardly; he couldn't help himself. He still saw them as his little girls needing his protection. It would be hard for him to let go and Francesca knew that.

'Wait till you see the apartment upstairs, everyone.' Scarlet beckoned them and ran excitedly up the stairs, pulling Tony along by his jacket sleeve.

Tony felt apprehensive about Scarlet's decision to move out. 'Tell me, Scarlet, do you really want to live here, knowing what happened here?' His voice had turned into a hushed whisper at the top of the stairs.

'You told me to get on with it, Papa.' She was whispering too, as Katie led everyone into the apartment. 'That night is over and I've been given a second chance. I will never be a victim again. Anyway,' she scoffed, 'any house you move into these days, someone has died in. It's fine, Papa, I'll have Katie with me, plus Clark Kent over there.' She laughed.

Tony looked disparagingly over the young man at Katie's side, drinking a glass of champagne. 'How long has he been on the scene?'

'Months, Papa. He's going to be a bank manager. Very boring, but he suits Katie.' She winked. 'Lighten up, you're the only man

in our lives. You sound almost jealous.' Scarlet nudged him playfully and went to join the others.

Tony stood back, trying to compose himself. Once he had, he
joined his daughters and rubbed his hands together. 'Right, now
we've seen your empire, let's all meet up at the club for a real
celebration, shall we?' He put his arms around his daughters'
shoulders, feeling proud. These were his girls and they had done
well.

* * *

Later, in the club, Scarlet moaned to Katie, and Jake's son, Jack.
'Our parents are so embarrassing. They really need to get a room,
especially at their age.' Scarlet was disgusted as she looked over
at the dance floor and watched her mother and father, locked in
each other's arms, slowly moving to the music.

Following Scarlet's stare, Jack picked up his drink and took a
large gulp. He looked almost sad as he shook his head at Scarlet's
comment. 'You two really don't know how lucky you are, do you? I
wish my parents were this embarrassing for all the right reasons.
All mine do is argue. I moved in with Bobby because I couldn't
stand it any more. I told Dad it was more convenient for work. He
was pretty sad about it, but I think Mum welcomed the fact that I
wasn't there. So you see, Scarlet, I would give anything for my
parents to openly declare their love like that.' With that, Jack
finished his drink and walked away to where their older brother,
Bobby, sat with his friends.

Exchanging glances as he left, Scarlet and Katie couldn't
understand what he was talking about. 'That's weird. Dad never
said anything about Jack moving in with Bobby. Do you think he
knows that there's trouble at t'mill?'

Scarlet shrugged. As she looked around the busy nightclub, something else caught her eye.

'Who the hell is that, Katie? He's gorgeous. Oh God, look at those pecs. He is mine, all mine. Excuse me while I go and dance with him.' Scarlet had spotted an unknown handsome young man standing alone at the other side of the room, dressed in a black tuxedo.

'Scarlet, wait. Put your tongue back in your mouth. His name is Dominic and he works for Dad on the doors,' Katie stressed. 'You're asking for trouble.' Katie shook her head as Scarlet stalked across the room like a lion to its prey.

* * *

'Oi, you two, haven't you had enough, for God's sake?' Julie poked Tony in the arm and gave him one of her stern, bored looks. 'Bloody hell, Tony, you're an old man; it's time you started realising it. Come on, Fran, drinkies.' Linking her arm through Francesca's, Julie led her away, leaving Tony looking very forlorn.

'Julie, this love-hate relationship of yours has gone on far too long. Poor Tony, look at him; he looks like a scolded schoolboy.'

'I can't help it, Fran.' Julie laughed. 'I love the fact that he hates the way I wind him up, and he falls for it every time. It's just so easy to put a little dent in his ego. You have to admit, when you see him standing with Jake at the bar, they look like Dumb and Dumber!' She burst out laughing at her own joke. Francesca couldn't stop herself from smiling. Julie was like a mean older sister to Tony and teased him mercilessly. Everyone thought he would be used to it by now, but she always found a way to trip him up when he was off his guard. If anyone was a double act, it was those two.

'Evening, Francesca, Julie.' A girlfriend of one of the men who worked for Ralph walked up to join them. She was wearing a low-cut blue ballgown with only one purpose in mind. While she was talking to Julie she was letting her hand play with the diamond necklace she was wearing, obviously waiting for admiration.

'That's a lot of glass, Avril. I didn't know you were dating a double-glazing salesman.'

'This?' Avril feigned mock surprise. 'My boyfriend thought I would appreciate it. Nice diamonds, aren't they?' Her preening and smug smile annoyed Julie to no end.

'Well, they would be nice, honey, if they were real. But, like I said, that's a lot of glass.' She enjoyed seeing the smile disappear from Avril's face. Avril stopped stroking her necklace and looked down at it. This wasn't the reaction she had expected.

Toying with her own diamond necklace, Julie held it up. 'Now this, honey, is the real thing. Keep that in mind when you're stood fingering your glass in front of your friends. Evening.' Julie led Fran away, leaving the poor woman very deflated and inspecting her own necklace even more closely.

'You're on good form tonight, Julie. First Tony and now Avril. Who's next?' Julie had really burst the young woman's balloon.

'Well, what do you expect, Fran. Trying to show off that bloody zircon. Even in this light you could see it was rubbish. My cat wears better collars than that. The bitchy cow thought she was going to make me jealous.' Julie shrugged and laughed. 'Bollocks!'

At the other side of the room, Ralph beckoned Tony over and led him to a dark corner.

'What's with all the cloak-and-dagger stuff, Ralph?' A frown crossed Tony's brow; he could see Ralph was serious and this was no joking matter.

'Someone knows about the money laundering in Paris. It needs sorting.' Ralph's business manner unnerved Tony, especially at the mention of the money laundering. Everything was as sweet as a nut as far as he was concerned and there weren't any problems.

'How would anyone know about the money laundering? We've done that for years. If they know about that, then they'll know that some of that money is Mickey Mouse money. Some excellent forgeries go through that place.'

'Inside job, I would say, Tony. We will have a proper meeting tomorrow morning. Now, let's get on and enjoy the rest of our evening, if that's possible without Julie insulting every woman in the room.' Although Ralph joked to change the subject, Tony could see that it was just a front to lighten the situation. He'd dropped his bombshell.

Tony walked over to Jake at the bar and ordered a drink.

'Do you know anything about there being trouble at the Paris casino?' he said. 'Ralph seems to think there's something up. He wants a meeting tomorrow.' Tony's mind was working overtime. It was a disturbing thought that someone knew about their money laundering. How long had Ralph known about this?

'Trouble? No, that place is a gold mine. Why should there be trouble now?' Jake was puzzled, too. But they both knew that if Ralph was bringing it to light then he must have some serious evidence. He always liked to sit back and watch a situation unfold, unlike Tony, who rushed in like a bull in a china shop. Ralph knew something, they were sure of it.

'Wait a minute, Jake. Hang on.' Something had caught Tony's eye and he wasn't best pleased. After hearing what Ralph had said and now this, he was angry.

Turning around from the bar, Jake followed Tony's gaze.

'Leave it, Tony. It's a bit of harmless fun on the dance floor. It's a busy night full of people enjoying themselves. Do you really want to cause a scene? Not now, eh?' Jake knew his words were useless, but he'd tried his best.

Marching over to where Scarlet was dancing with Dominic and blatantly flirting, Tony couldn't help himself. Grabbing hold of Dominic by his jacket and pulling him forward, he shouted, 'Just what the fuck are you doing with my daughter?'

Instantly Scarlet stopped. 'We're just dancing, Papa. What's the problem?'

'Problem? You're asking me what the problem is?' Tony's voice was loud, even above the music. 'I'll tell you what the problem is, miss. He's supposed to be working. I don't pay him to dance with you. Have some fucking self-respect. You, Dominic, get back to your post and you, Scarlet, can fuck off home.'

Walking away, Dominic left a very red-faced Scarlet on the dance floor. 'Papa, I didn't mean any harm. Sorry.'

'You're like some dog on heat. And with my employee. Is that what you need? Me to pay men to dance with you? For fuck's sake, Scarlet, the party is over, go home.' Angrily walking away, Tony went and stood at Jake's side again.

'Is it Scarlet you're angry at, Tony, or what Ralph has just said?'

'Both. I'm not paying someone to screw my daughter and if he wants to keep his job, he can bloody work for his money.'

Jake knew better than to press the situation. Everyone could see that Tony was in no mood to discuss things rationally.

Walking over to stand by Tony, Julie couldn't help but have her say. He had caused a scene when he could have waited until after the party. He always had to go in with all guns blazing. 'You know, Tony, it's a real shame someone's father didn't jump in and shout at you when you were younger. You would have had a queue around the block, you miserable sod!' She raised her eyebrows at him and gave him one of those meaningful looks of hers. But Tony ignored it. Turning to Francesca, he felt it was time to change the subject. Even he had started to regret his actions.

'Drink, Francesca? Or do you think I'm a miserable sod as well?'

Hearing the arrogance in his voice and the way he had snubbed Julie's comment, Francesca stood up. 'In a minute, Tony. Maybe we should finish our dance first, eh?' Francesca had learnt over the years how to pacify her husband. Seeing his face relax into a smile, she took his hand and led him onto the dance floor.

Feeling the warmth of Francesca's body close to him, he felt better. She was dressed in a long red mermaid dress. Her hair was up, but wisps of curls escaped and hung down the sides of her face. He was a lucky man to have such a beautiful wife.

'Have I told you that you look lovely tonight, Francesca?' He held her closer and breathed in the Chanel perfume she wore.

'No, you haven't. You were far too busy shouting at our daughter. But I do like the red bow tie you're wearing. You never fail to amaze me, Antonias. It matches my dress perfectly.' She added in a whisper, 'I think it looks quite sexy.' That seemed to appease him and she could feel his body unwind.

'How sexy?'

'Well, you'll just have to wait till we get home to find out, won't you?'

The big grin on his face showed he had forgotten everything that had just happened. Ralph's words still echoed in his mind, but that would be dealt with tomorrow.

'I'll go and see if Scarlet is okay, first, and then I think we should leave and let everyone get on with their evening, don't you?' Francesca said. 'Or you could apologise for your outburst.'

Raising her eyebrow and cocking her head to one side, Francesca waited expectantly.

'Mm, I'll speak to her tomorrow. First, I want to see what you have in store for me. Let's go.'

No sooner had Francesca got in, than she went to check on Adam who was fast asleep, and so was Elle. Then she went to her own bedroom. Tony was sprawled on the bed with his arms around the back of his head, wearing only his red silk boxer shorts and his red bow tie. A silver champagne bucket was on the bedside table and the cork had already been popped.

'Unzip your dress, Francesca, I want to look at you. Let down your hair,' he said, all the while not taking his eyes off her. He poured the champagne into flute-shaped glasses. Taking a sip, he watched her dress fall to the floor. His arousal was apparent. The red underwear she was wearing met with his approval and with his hand, he beckoned her on to the bed.

Afterwards, they lay in each other's arms, satiated and content. 'Do you think I'm getting old, Francesca?'

What Julie had said earlier about his younger days was obviously playing on his mind. He needn't have worried. The years had been more than kind to Tony Lambrianu. His full blond mane of hair remained thick, only now it had odd silver streaks, highlighting it even more against his tanned skin. Working out at the gym regularly had kept his body muscly and firm.

'If it's possible, Tony, you are better looking now. You have that air of authority and class about you. What about me? I'm not getting any younger, you know.'

'You, Francesca, look exactly the same to me as the very first night I saw you. You're never getting away from me. Not even in death. I will haunt you forever.' He laughed.

'Don't say that, Tony. It frightens me when you talk like that.'

A cold shiver ran down Francesca's spine. The very thought of Tony dying and leaving her alone made her feel sick.

'Come on, Fran. It's the only thing any of us can be sure of in life. But I'm telling you, Francesca Lambrianu...' Turning on his side and resting on his elbow to look at her face, he seemed serious. 'If I go first, I will come back for you. And if you go before me, I will be dead anyway. Two bodies, one soul, remember?' Leaning over, he kissed her gently on the lips.

4

TROUBLE BREWING

Tony was surprised the next morning when he walked into his office at the casino, to find Ralph already there, waiting.

'Ralph? You here early or am I late?' Tony looked at his watch. It was 8.30 a.m. 'Have you been here long?' Now Tony was not only curious, but the hairs on the back of his neck were standing up. Whatever Ralph was going to tell him, he knew he wouldn't like it.

'I've been here a while, Tony, thinking things over.' Ralph took a drag on his cigar and blew the smoke into the air. His thin greying hair was slicked back and he was immaculately dressed in a black suit and tie. 'In short, Tony, and there's no nice way of saying this, we're in shit. Right up to our necks in it.'

Shocked at what Ralph was saying, Tony sat down. Ralph was being very serious and, more to the point, he seemed upset. Pouring himself a coffee, Tony waited.

'As I told you last night, the Paris casino is the problem. It's just about breaking even; a few more months and it will be losing money. Which we know is bloody impossible, so somebody is creaming it off the top. We're all for the high jump if this comes to light and I don't intend spending the rest of my days behind bars.'

'How long have you known?' Tony sat forward in his chair.

'Came to light recently. We need to sort this out... now.' Pursing his lips, Ralph looked directly into Tony's eyes. He was all fired up and angry. Ralph Gold was not a man to cross.

'Wait a minute. Don't tell me you think I have anything to do with this. I haven't been there in ages. Just what the fuck are you implying? Spit it out.' Pushing his blond hair back away from his forehead, Tony stood up. He was angry too. After all these years, was Ralph Gold actually accusing him of double-crossing him?

'I wasn't sure, Tony, but your face tells a million stories and I can see now it isn't you. Sorry lad.'

'But you suspected me? How do I know it's not you and you're just covering your tracks?'

Raising his hand to stop him, Ralph nodded. 'Fair play, Tony. What do you suggest?'

'I suggest we stop sitting on our arses blaming each other and go to Paris and see for ourselves, don't you?' His blue eyes were blazing with anger and he felt insulted by Ralph's suggestions. Yes, he would bloody well sort this out, and when he did, he wanted a big fat apology!

Ralph Gold narrowed his eyes and looked at the angry man before him. A smug smile crossed his face. This was exactly what he wanted: Tony to go to Paris and find out for himself.

Jake burst in and interrupted them. He had brought a selection of sandwiches. 'Hi guys, thought you could do with something to eat. You're early, Ralph.' Even Jake was surprised at Ralph's early arrival.

Ralph looked at him with disdain. 'I will begin again. There are problems at the Paris casino. In short, somebody knows what we are doing and are ripping us off.' Ralph's mock laughter filled the air. 'How the hell it's been going on is beyond me, but now that it has come to my attention, I intend to find out.' Ralph was in charge of the situation and his air of authority filled the room.

'Ripping us off? How the bloody hell can they rip us off, Ralph? Half the money that is in there isn't even real money. Tourists come and go. We never target the local members. Half the time they are so pissed and overjoyed at winning they never even check the money. And you pour free champagne down their throats. Even the buffet is free.'

'Someone is going there, I am telling you.' Waving his hand in the air while holding his fat, Cuban cigar, Ralph pointed at both of them. 'And they are taking their winnings in cheque only. Someone has given them good advice. Someone knows what we're doing and are playing us at our own game. That is not how it is meant to be. They're not supposed to exchange their chips for cheques, even if they do have the right. Don't you understand? Once they purchase their chips and win, we are supposed to pay them in shit monopoly cash from our cash registers, plus our own laundered money, all mixed up nicely to look good. Your local tourist having a good time wants the cash. They want to feast their greedy little eyes upon it and sleep with it under their pillow, but not this lot. They are professionals, believe me. Someone is sending you to jail for forgery and laundering.'

'Us?' Tony almost shouted. 'What about you and Don Carlos?'

Ralph ignored his outburst. 'Their winning streak is unbelievable. No one is that lucky.' Ralph coughed on his cigar. 'They know the inside rules of the house. Whoever it is are fleecing us. And let's not forget, Tony, those cheques are stamped with "Lambrianu". Which means they are fleecing you.' His cold stare made Tony's blood run cold. Although Ralph's grey hair was receding and thinning and he looked a little fuller around the waistline, his distinguished suits and manner spoke volumes for him. Ralph Gold was not a man to be trifled with.

'How long has this been going on, Ralph? How many months?' Jake was intrigued by just how much Ralph knew. 'What is it that you're not telling us? I feel there's a lot more to this than meets the eye.'

Irritated, Tony looked towards Jake. 'For God's sake, Jake, this is a serious matter and all I can hear is you munching on a sausage sandwich. Put the fucking thing down, I'm trying to concentrate.' Tony was angry and disturbed by what Ralph was saying and Jake wasn't making him feel any better.

'Don Carlos is stopping any more money coming into the casino until we sort this out.' Ralph was adamant that this should be nipped in the bud for all of their sakes.

Tony sighed and ran his hands through his hair. 'Well, I will go to Paris. It's time I showed my face there, anyway.'

'You're right, I think you should go, Tony. You as well, Jake.'

'You're not coming, Ralph?' Jake looked across at Tony.

The very idea that Ralph didn't want to come disturbed Tony. Ralph always had his finger on the pulse.

'Not just now, boys. I have other things to deal with. I will stay here and keep things in order.' Ralph stood up and, without a by your leave, he left.

'He knows a lot more than he is letting on. What's his problem?' They had worked together for years and yet this time he felt Ralph was holding something back.

'You don't think he's going to let us take the rap for all of this, do you, Tony? He won't want to get his hands dirty. And, after all, it does say "Lambrianu" above the door. If this all goes wrong then it's your problem and you're the only one going to jail.'

'Thank you for stating the fucking obvious, Jake. I needed

that. No, I know Ralph. Whatever it is, he wants me to find out for myself. Well, it looks like we're going to Paris, Jake.'

'Don't you want me to stay here and keep an eye on things?'

'No, Jake. If I am going to jail, you're going to be my cellmate. Now, go home and get packed. Actually, is Graham here yet? Maybe he should come with us. After all, he has managed this casino for a very long time and I want his experienced eye. If anyone is screwing us over, he will know how.'

'Are you going to tell him everything? He is straight, Tony!'

'Do you really think he doesn't know that we're just a pair of crooks in fancy suits? No, Graham knows what's going on. He is far from stupid, Jake, and I know he will get to the bottom of this.'

* * *

'Why are you packing? Where are we going?' said Julie, as she stood in the doorway of Francesca's bedroom.

'We're not going anywhere, Julie. I have been known to go away without you. Tony called; he has to go to Paris and wanted me to pack some things for him.'

'Tony's going to Paris?' Julie watched Francesca packing. 'Did he say how long for and why? Aren't you going with him?'

'No, he didn't, Julie. I take it you're going to give him and Ralph a long list of things you want bringing back. Anyway, he never asked me to go. So I presume it's business. Hasn't Ralph said? I thought he would be going with him.'

'No.' Julie drew on her cigarette 'No, we have things to do here. A boring Paris trip I can do without right now.'

'Well, I never thought I would hear that from your lips, Julie. Since when has a Paris trip ever bored you?' Francesca laughed as she carried on packing.

'Well, we all live and learn, Fran love. I just have things to do, that's all.' Julie continued to watch Francesca packing. It was clear to her that, as always, Tony was keeping her in the dark about his real reasons for going. Walking to the en-suite bathroom and throwing her cigarette down the toilet, she said, 'I have to go, anyway, I'm meeting Ralph for lunch.' Then that familiar grin appeared on Julie's face. 'Don't forget to pack the bromide, Fran; we don't want him chafing his hand!'

5

A GAMBLE IN PARADISE

Tony turning up at the casino caused a lot of curiosity amongst the staff. He rarely went there and if he did it was usually to give someone a scolding. Those working that day looked up at him as he walked past, secretly praying it wasn't their turn to be on the receiving end of his anger.

Graham had left before them on a separate aeroplane. Tony didn't want them all travelling together; that would look too suspicious. He knew he needed to tread carefully, but for the life of him he didn't know why.

Walking into the office, Tony and Jake saw that Graham was already in there talking to the manager. 'You can leave now,' Tony said abruptly to the manager, who immediately glared at him for his rudeness. Holding out his hand to shake Graham's, Tony looked up at the manager. 'I thought I told you to leave.' Tony watched the man rise slowly from his chair and leave the room. 'Thank you for coming, Graham, at such short notice. I know it was a big ask, but I need your help. Jake, pour us all a drink.' Loosening his tie, Tony sat back in the chair and ran his hands through his hair. 'Bloody hell, where do I start?'

'What can I do to help you, Mr Lambrianu? It sounded very important on the telephone and you know I'll always help if I can.'

'There is something going on at this casino. Suddenly, it seems to be losing money. It's as though someone is stealing off us, if that is at all possible.' Glancing up at Jake as he put the drinks on the table, Tony realised he wasn't sure just how much to tell Graham.

'When you say stealing, Mr Lambrianu, what exactly do you mean?' Even Graham knew Tony well enough to know that if anyone was stealing from him, he didn't need his help to sort it out. Tony's reputation was renowned.

'We think that maybe a group of chancers are coming in on a regular basis, possibly knowing how to play the tables. But they are winning and it's too regular. I thought the house always won, Graham.' Tony gave a weak smile. He picked up his drink and waited for some kind of response.

'You mean you have a group of card counters targeting the casino?' Graham was surprised that anyone would be stupid enough to come to Lambrianu's to count cards. 'Is there any talk from the other casinos in Paris? Normally, if a gang is doing the rounds on a regular basis, all the casinos share information. Obviously, there would be CCTV footage here of the same people coming and going and those people would also be on other casinos' CCTV.'

'It is regular and monthly.' Tony didn't want to have to explain too much of what Ralph had told them, so left it at that.

'You're allowed to ban anyone entering that you think is doing this but, card counting is not actually illegal.'

Standing up and walking around to where Graham sat, Tony cupped his face in his hands and kissed him on the cheeks. 'Bloody hell, Graham. I knew I could rely on you to think straight.

Christ, Jake, we could have stayed in London and sorted all of this out from there.'

'Just how bad is this, Mr Lambrianu? It's obvious that you're not just talking about a few thousand here and there. I think the very least you can do is tell me the whole truth.'

'He's right, Tony, we can't expect him to work blindly.'

Tony took a deep breath, but before he had a chance to say anything, the office door opened and Ralph Gold walked in. 'Afternoon, boys. This is Ellis, my accountant friend. He is going to go through the books and check our losses.' Seeing the shocked looks on both Tony and Jake's faces, Ralph smiled. 'Well, Tony, you didn't really think I would leave it all up to you, did you?' Ralph let out a laugh and sat down.

Tony nodded towards Ellis, the new accountant no one had ever heard of or seen before, and offered him a chair. He was a young man, possibly in his late twenties. But how come they had never met him before?

As though reading his mind, Ralph spoke. 'Ellis is the son of my old accountant and I trust him.'

If Ralph trusted him and he was prepared to let him sit in on this meeting, then who were they to question him?

'Are you all sitting comfortably?' Ralph's manner was abrupt and business-like. He looked around the room. 'Good; then I will begin. Let's cut the crap and tell everyone the truth. That way they know what they are looking for.' Ralph was very matter of fact about everything. 'Counterfeit money is delivered here once a month, all in euros. I must say, they are excellent copies. When someone cashes in their chips, we pay out in a mix of counterfeit money and laundered money. Someone is playing our tables, and winning, then asking to be paid out in both cheque and cash. The problem is, they're winning so much that they're flooding the market with it. It's being done on purpose. Someone is out to ruin us. Shops are complaining about people with counterfeit notes. The alarm bells are ringing, boys, and the culprits are laying a paper trail that leads right back to us.' Ralph put on a silly voice. '"Ooh, where did you get that money from mister?" "Well, I got it at Lambrianu's casino!" Do you get it now, you two?' Ralph snapped. 'They are taking our real cash, via cheque payment, as well as enough counterfeit money to spread around Paris, making people talk. That is what we do not want.'

Tony and Jake watched and listened as Ralph made his speech. He must have been monitoring this for weeks, possibly months.

'Well, Ralph, you really are the dark horse, aren't you?' Tony's voice dripped with sarcasm.

'Just one more thing. I've informed the authorities that some people have been using counterfeit notes in the casino. That should keep them off our backs for now.'

'You've done what?' Tony stood up so fast, his chair flew back behind him. Standing there with his hands on his hips, he looked at Ralph incredulously. 'You fucking stupid old fool. Are you crazy?'

'Sit down, Tony, I'm sure Ralph has his reasons.' Jake needed to calm the situation, but he knew well enough that if Ralph was holding his hands up to the authorities he had a bloody good reason. The atmosphere was tense and explosive. Graham and Ellis looked on as the three gangland bosses fought it out.

'This is their country, Tony; let's not cause ripples. We need to be seen as on their side. We play it their way. Now fucking sit down, and take that look off your face when you speak to me. Remember who you're shouting at.'

Taking a deep breath, Tony sat down again. Ralph was right. It was time to remember who Ralph Gold really was. He'd been a gunrunner in Ireland, spent time in and out of prison. A thug and a murderer, Ralph had his fingers in a lot of pies. Tony knew that he and Jake were not squeaky clean. People feared them and some even thought he was a ruthless psychopath, but Ralph? Well, he was in a class of his own. He was a ruthless godfather and if he felt his home life was about to crumble, nobody was safe.

'Okay, Ralph, what do you suggest?' Tony felt calmer now. 'What do you want us to do?'

'Nothing. We watch and we wait. Ellis, go through the books and see how much money we're losing. Graham, do as Tony says and make some discreet enquiries, and see if you can spot anything on those cameras. You know what you're looking for. After all, you're the expert.'

'I would like to talk to the manager first, informally, of course, Mr Gold. Maybe he has noticed some new people coming into the casino. Also, I would like to speak to the other casinos and find out if they have had any trouble or spotted new faces. All casinos share the same information so this kind of thing doesn't happen. It's normal practice.'

The three of them nodded to each other. This was why they had brought him here; Graham knew what he was talking about.

'Right, lads, you all have hotel rooms, but remember, Graham, Ellis' – Ralph pointed his finger at them in a stern way, almost like the head teacher giving his pupils a good talking to – 'this is not a holiday, this is work. We want results, and fast.' After waiting for everyone to agree with him, Ralph stood up, satisfied that everyone knew their job, and left, leaving silence in his wake.

Graham spoke up, interrupting Tony's thoughts. 'I would like to speak to the accountants here that take your "special deliveries", Mr Lambrianu. I presume there's another set of accounts that aren't public knowledge?'

'Just do what the fuck you want, Graham. For fuck's sake,

someone wants to see me behind bars and Ralph Gold wants my fucking blood. Come on, Jake, we need to get out of here. Secrecy is the key, here, Graham.'

Tony's mind was in turmoil. It had taken him years to build up a fool proof empire and now it felt like it was crumbling. 'Don't forget, Graham, I want those bastards who are stealing off me to come back in here. I don't want them getting wind that we're onto them. I will hang the bastards out to dry.' Picking up his jacket, Tony stormed out of the office and into the casino. The staff were preparing the tables before they opened up later that day. 'Why do you all look so fucking scruffy?' Tony shouted at them all. 'Go and sort yourselves out. Or better still, fuck off the lot of you.' With that, he stormed out into the fresh air.

'Was that necessary, Tony?'

'Yes, it was, Jake. They know I would only come here if I had to. And so shouting at them to clean up their act and look respectable has put them on their toes again.'

6

BETRAYAL

'I'm not sharing a hotel room with you, Tony; I never get any sleep. All night long you're on the telephone to Francesca. It gets on my nerves. What have you got to say to each other that takes that fucking long? No, I want my own room.' Jake and Tony were standing at the hotel reception desk.

'Don't you want to talk to Sharon?'

Jake's face dropped. 'Not really. Not at the moment.' Jake picked up his room keys and bag and started walking towards the elevator.

Catching up with him, Tony frowned. 'Something wrong, Jake? Are you and Sharon having problems?'

Jake sighed and shook his head. 'Nothing more than usual.' He shrugged it off and walked into the lift.

'Jake, you can talk to me, you know. What's wrong? Menopause or something?' Tony laughed, hoping this would help lighten the mood, but he could see it wasn't working.

Tired and fed up of the interrogation, Jake said angrily, 'Look, Tony, we can't all be happy and smiling in our own cosy husband

and wife bubble. Some people have problems, okay? Now just leave it!'

It was a rarity for Jake to snap like that. Tony could see he was stressed out about the situation. He dropped the conversation immediately. Jake would tell him in his own time.

Tony had made a point of letting all the casino staff think they had left Paris, which was why it was paramount that no one saw them and they didn't leave their rooms. It was suffocating, but also necessary. No one would think of stealing from him if they thought he was in Paris.

The hotel room had been set up as an office. They trawled through mindless recordings that showed nothing but people gambling, drinking and enjoying themselves. Three days in, Jake was pacing the floor. 'For fuck's sake, Tony, there is nothing. Absolutely nothing. God, it's like painting the Forth Bridge – it never ends. We're hanging around for nothing!'

'We're hanging around here to clear our names. That's what we're doing.'

'I know. I'm just at my wits' end. We can't leave this room because you don't want anyone to know that we're here and I'm sick to my back teeth of it! What if Ralph is wrong about all of this? Have you thought of that?'

'I have, Jake, but, let's be honest, that old bastard is never wrong and he knows a lot more than he's telling us. I'm going to beat him at his own game. Why don't you go home? It sounds like you have other things to deal with.' Tony didn't want to mention Sharon, but it was apparent she was at the forefront of Jake's mind.

'Are you sure you don't need me? I can't really leave you here going stir crazy, can I?'

'You go, mate. If I need you, well, you're a couple of hours away. It's taken me longer to get across London than it has to come here. Go, Jake.'

No sooner were the words out of his mouth than Jake was packing.

Tony sat alone in his hotel room when Jake had gone. He, too, was fed up. He missed Francesca. Even though they spoke daily, it wasn't the same as seeing her. Graham had befriended every casino manager in the area and had brought more recordings for Tony and still there was nothing. Maybe Jake was right. Maybe, just maybe, Ralph was wrong and it was just a gang of chancers counting cards. Tony decided to give it a couple more days and, if there was still nothing, then it would be time to go home.

Coming out of the shower, Tony heard knocking at his door. He had ordered some room service and opened the door expecting to see a waiter. Instead, Graham stood there. Seeing that Tony was in his dressing gown and drying his hair with a towel, he realised that he had come at a bad time.

'Mr Lambrianu...' Graham said nervously. Although he had worked for Tony for years, he knew what he was about to tell him was not good news and he didn't want to be on the receiving end of Tony's wrath. In an instant, this handsome, charming man could turn into the very devil himself.

Tony invited him in and offered him a seat. 'I take it you have something for me, Graham? Do you want a drink or something?'

Shaking his head, Graham waited while Tony poured himself a drink and sat down.

The silence hung in the air as Tony waited for Graham to speak. Opening his briefcase, Graham put a video tape on the coffee table before Tony. 'It's an inside job, Mr Lambrianu.' His heart was pounding and he wished he had taken that drink now, his throat was so dry.

Tony's eyes narrowed and a frown appeared on his brow.

Graham swallowed hard. 'It's none of my business, Mr Lambrianu, but there are times when you have "special deliveries" at the casino...' Graham paused, waiting for some outburst, but none came. He could see that Tony didn't like this cat and mouse game and was losing his patience. He continued. 'There is a gang of young men that seem to come in on the very same nights that you have these special deliveries. There are two women involved. That tape shows the two women targeting certain blackjack tables.' Graham felt he had said more than enough. His job was done and he wanted to go home.

Tony picked up the tape and looked at it, weighing up what Graham had told him about the contents of the tape. 'When you say an inside job, Graham, I take it you mean members of the staff and that this tape has footage of them helping themselves to my money?'

Graham started edging towards the end of his seat nervously. Tony couldn't help but wonder why Graham was so nervous and agitated. Surely he should have been pleased that he had accomplished his mission. 'Are Ralph and Julie Gold on this tape, Graham? Is that why you're acting so nervous?' The thought had crossed his mind.

Shaking his head emphatically, Graham spoke louder than he should have. In fact, he was almost shouting. 'No. No way, Mr Lambrianu. Definitely not. Just watch the tape when I have gone; it will answer all of your questions.'

Graham stood up and left without further ado.

Tony put the recording on and waited. He saw nothing of particular interest at first, but then he spotted a group of young men come in and instantly spread out towards the card tables. Looking closely, Tony saw a woman turn around and kiss the man she was standing next to. She was adorned in furs and diamonds. It was pretty obvious she had been drinking because she was a little unsteady on her feet and using the man for support.

Suddenly feeling the bile rise in his throat, Tony wanted to be sick. Pausing the recording, he stared at the woman on the screen. Now he understood why Graham had looked so uncomfortable and nervous. His head was swimming and he felt dizzy; he ran to the bathroom and vomit spewed from his mouth. He was shaking as he bent down over the toilet. Tears were brimming in his eyes. Picking up a hand towel and wiping his mouth, he wandered back into the room and stared at the screen again. He poured a large whisky, then sat down and rested his head on the back of the sofa.

His emotions were all over the place; he felt confused and lost. For the first time in his life he didn't know what to do. He felt anger, betrayal and most of all sadness. Did he destroy the recording and forget what he had seen? Or did he show it to Ralph Gold? Tony was in turmoil. He had never had to face anything like this before.

Loyalty was a double-edged sword and he had been betrayed. His thoughts were interrupted by another knock at the door. He presumed that this time, it really would be the waiter with the food he had ordered earlier, and it was. But standing behind the waiter was Ralph Gold.

Seeing Tony's ashen face, Ralph promptly took out his wallet and tipped the waiter, then took the tray of coffee and sandwiches off him. Saying nothing, Ralph walked into the room and put the tray on the table.

Looking over at the image still paused on the screen, Ralph raised his eyebrows. 'I saw Graham leave and I thought I would give you enough time to see that. Sit down, lad, you look like you've seen a ghost.' Tony sat down and waited for Ralph to comment on the paused image on the screen.

'Shall we watch the rest of it together, Tony? After all, it's what you came for.' That was all Ralph said as he picked up the remote control and pressed play. The room was filled with nervous tension, both of them waiting for the other to speak. Feeling slightly at a disadvantage, still wearing only his bathrobe, Tony looked across at Ralph, who was immaculately turned out in suit and tie.

Sitting in silence, they watched the remainder of the recording. Sharon, Jake's wife, was standing there as clear as day, dressed in all her finery. Her arm was around some young man's waist. She was laughing and flirting whilst this young man was placing bets at the blackjack table. Eventually Tony felt it was time to break the silence. Considering what they had just witnessed, Ralph was acting very calm.

'You already knew about this, didn't you, Ralph?'

Ralph nodded. 'I did, Tony, but I wanted to wait until I had more evidence. The bottom line here is that you had to find out for yourself. You weren't just going to take my word for it. She's like a sister to you. She's Jake's wife. Why would you believe my poisonous tongue if you hadn't seen it for yourself?'

'When did you find out? Or rather, how?' Tony was intrigued. How long had Ralph known about Sharon's betrayal? Their voices were low and civil. As much as they had solved the mystery, it felt like they were mourning a loved one at a funeral.

'Julie spotted her a few weeks ago. She came to Paris on a normal shopping spree, popped in here and saw Sharon with her new boyfriend. Now, Tony, we both know Julie is not averse to someone having a boyfriend or playing away from home. She never made herself known to Sharon and left. It was only when I mentioned to her that we were losing money that she told me about Sharon and I started digging a little deeper. Was it just a woman having an affair or was it a well-informed member of our family taking us for every penny and betraying our trust? That's what I had to find out.' Lighting his cigar, Ralph blew the smoke out into the air and waited. He looked relaxed, his arm across the back of the sofa and his legs crossed. Tony wasn't quite sure what he wanted him to say. 'This new boyfriend of Sharon's is spending our money all over Paris, Tony. This two-bit nobody is suddenly driving around in a big car and wearing Rolex watches. People notice these things. Weren't you in the least bit suspicious when nothing happened all the time Jake was here? She knew he was coming to Paris.'

'Well, Francesca knew I was coming to Paris. Are you saying she is guilty also?'

'Good God, no. Francesca knows nothing of our special business deals. On the other hand, Julie knows everything. She is up to her neck in it, as much as we are. Jake has told Sharon much more than he should have, I'm sure of that.' He stabbed a finger at the screen. 'She's keeping that bastard, and on our money, Tony! Look at the face on that poor croupier. He's sweating buckets. He is doing just what she is telling him to do; the poor bastard daren't do anything else.'

Realisation of what Ralph was saying suddenly brought Tony back down to earth. He didn't want to believe it. Why would Sharon do this? She had everything she wanted. She didn't need money, she had bundles of it. Upset and unhappy, Tony could feel the bile rising in his throat again.

'Who is this man she's with, Ralph? Do we know him? Is he part of a gang we know or something?'

'I'm working on that. He's very young, mid-twenties. He has found the golden goose in Sharon. Let's be honest, it's not the first time she's shit on Jake, is it? For God's sake, Tony, she is a loose cannon. That paper trail of counterfeit money is going to lead right back to our door, and once the casino investigators come along with their police friends, who knows what they'll dig up. We are looking at a twenty-year stretch.' Still holding his cigar, Ralph pointed his finger at Tony. 'Find out if Jake knows anything about this. This is your family. You sort it... or I will.'

His words hung in the air. 'What do you propose I do about it, Ralph?' They both knew there was only one option, but Tony was shaking inside.

'Sharon is like a ticking time bomb. I don't know what her reasons are, but the answer is execution. You know that. We have to get rid of the problem and then we sell this place and never come back again. Tell people it was losing money, they don't care.' Ralph stood up to leave. He had said his piece and given Tony the option to sort it out his way or do it Ralph's way.

No sooner had Ralph left than Tony started to pack his suitcase. He was more concerned about Jake. What was he going to tell him? Thank God he had always kept Francesca out of his business dealings. That woman could take a lie detector test and pass. Julie was Ralph's partner in crime as well as life; she knew everything. But just what other information had Jake mentioned to Sharon in passing? She was involved in the club and had known their scheming ways since they started out. He took the recording and put it in his suitcase with his other things. It was time to go home and find out the full story.

_____

7

FAMILY BUSINESS

'Papa, you're home. Did you bring us anything back?' Scarlet kissed her father on the cheek and gave him a hug. That was quickly followed by a hug from Katie, and Adam squealed with excitement at seeing his father.

Tony was glad to be back in the bosom of his family. Everything seemed normal. Breakfast was on the table. Elle was cooking. As he looked around at this family scene, the horror of Sharon's betrayal flashed before him.

Francesca was waiting for him with her arms open.

'Why is it, Francesca, that yours is the first face I look for and the last one I see?' He felt safe in her arms. As he held her tightly, a thought crossed his mind. With a click of her fingers, Sharon could end all of this.

Kissing her tenderly on the lips, Tony turned and waited. Normally when he kissed Francesca in front of Scarlet and Katie there were looks of disgust and comments about their parents always kissing and being embarrassing, but none came. Katie picked up a piece of toast. 'I'm going for a shower; are you coming, Scarlet? Adam, you can play on your game for half an hour and that's it. Leave Mum and Dad alone for a few minutes.'

'Bloody hell, what happened to those two? I've only been away for a few days.' Feeling more relaxed, Tony couldn't help but laugh. He had become used to the jibes and comments.

'Sit down, Tony love, and have a proper English breakfast,' said Elle, putting his bacon and eggs on the table. 'That will be because of what Jack said at the party the other week.' Elle was making herself busy sorting out the breakfast things. She was a lot older now and a lot slower, but she still liked looking after the family.

Tony's curiosity suddenly got the better of him. 'What do you mean, Elle? What has Jack said?' Tony looked at Elle standing at the cooker with her back to him. She looked the same as she always had, only now she had grey hair.

'While you and Fran were dancing at the party, Scarlet couldn't help herself moaning about how embarrassing you were. But Jack snapped at her and said that he wished his parents were embarrassing. Jake and Sharon are always arguing these days, apparently. Has he said anything to you, Tony?' Elle was concerned. She didn't like to think Jake was unhappy.

'What are they arguing about, Elle? Do you know?'

Elle turned to face Tony. He looked tired, she noticed, and had dark shadows under his eyes. He looked as if he had the weight of the world on his shoulders. 'Oh, just one of those rough patches, I expect. They'll sort it. Come on, eat your breakfast while it's hot.' Elle may have brushed it off, but Tony's brain was in turmoil. Why hadn't Jake told him about his troubles sooner?

When Tony walked into the club the next morning the first person he saw standing behind the bar was Sharon. She was sorting out the rotas for the strippers and filling up the cash registers with their floats. She was a handsome woman, with her long blonde hair and engaging smile. 'Morning, Tony,' was all she said, and that was more than enough for Tony. His blood boiled. Knowing what he knew now, her smiling face made him feel sick. He was overwhelmed by bitterness and hate. What was it Ralph always said? Keep your friends close and your enemies closer. He knew he mustn't let her think anything had changed.

'Morning,' he said. He nodded politely then walked towards his office.

'Tony, you're back. How are things? I thought you were going to call me.' Jake looked genuinely pleased to see Tony. He was sitting at the desk, going through the receipts.

After the usual preliminaries, Tony couldn't help but ask, 'Jake, does Sharon know that I stayed on in Paris?' He knew it was an odd question but he needed to know what Jake had said to her.

'No, not under the circumstances, mate. I told her that there was nothing to report and you were just spending a few days with Fran. Thankfully, Sharon and Francesca are not that close so no one would know. Why do you ask?' Jake was puzzled. Tony was acting strangely. But then he always acted strangely.

'Nothing, Jake. Nothing really.'

'Anyway, Tony, first things first. Mark is a little upset that you had his son, Dominic, beaten up. He's asked to see you.'

'Go and get him. Let's see what he has to say.' Tony couldn't be bothered with this. In fact, he had forgotten that he had instructed his men to give Dominic a beating after dancing with Scarlet at the club.

'Boss.' Mark, an immaculately dressed tall man with dark hair and an Elvis quiff, stood before Tony. He was well-built and stout, and had worked for Tony for years, but he still felt nervous standing in front of him. Seated behind his desk in his large leather chair, wearing his suit and tie, Tony looked quite the authoritative figure. His face didn't move as Mark entered the room.

'Say what you have to say, Mark, and leave. I presume you're going to complain about twinkletoes, your son, Dominic?' His stern, bored expression said it all. 'Well, that isn't what I pay him for. He is here to mind the doors, keep the riff-raff out and help look after the cars.'

Mark was nervous, licking his lips and moving from foot to foot, but he felt he had to say something to protect his son from Tony's wrath.

'I've had a word with Dominic. He didn't know what to do, boss, when Scarlet asked him to dance. If he'd said no it would have sounded rude. But saying yes got him a real battering. They broke his jaw.' Mark looked down at the floor; he meant no disrespect to Tony, but Dominic was his son. 'He meant no harm. He's a good boy, boss.' Mark wanted to know if Tony was going to take it any further.

'I don't want a grease monkey near my daughter, got it? As long as he has learned his lesson, that is the end of it as far as I am concerned.' Tony looked down at his invoice book, which meant Mark was dismissed.

Shutting the door, Jake walked around to Tony's side. 'I didn't know you'd got them to do him over good and proper. Mark's a good guy, Tony. He wants to protect his family, that's all. You would want to protect your family; I know that for a fact.'

Not being in the mood to discuss family loyalties, Tony gave him a stern look. 'And where are your family loyalties, Jake?'

Jake was puzzled and hurt by the offensive remark. 'What's that supposed to mean?'

'Oh, nothing.' Tony couldn't take back the sarcasm, but he wished he had bitten his tongue. 'I just think Scarlet can do better than some grease monkey.'

Jake burst out laughing. 'You are taking the piss, Tony. It's not that long ago that you were a grease monkey sniffing around the ladies.'

'I'm in no mood for joking, Jake, and that was a long time ago. Plus, I didn't go messing around with my boss's daughter.'

'No, you didn't. You just screwed his fucking wife and ended up in prison for it!' Jake opened the door and left, slamming it behind him.

Tony threw down his pen, put his elbows on the desk and buried his head in his hands. He needed to have a talk with Jake, but how to approach it was a different matter. First things first, he'd telephone Ralph and iron out the details.

'Ralph, it's Tony. That matter we need to sort out; how long are you going to give me?'

'How long would you give me, Tony?' Ralph laughed on the other end of the telephone. 'Not long, that's all I can say. I have already arranged that no more money gets delivered to the casino and I am arranging for it to be put up for sale. That's how I like it, son, short and sweet.' The line went dead. When the telephone rang again, Tony presumed it was Ralph calling back, but it wasn't. It was Francesca.

'Francesca, what's the problem?'

'Does there have to be a problem for me to call you? Well, actually there is one. Rosanna has called and she wants you to call her back.'

'Why? Did she say what was wrong?' Tony sat up straight in his chair at the mention of his grandmother's housekeeper; his curiosity was roused.

'She'd just like to speak to you, that's all. I'm sure there's nothing to worry about. Although you don't keep in contact as much as you should. She is in Italy alone, Tony, trying to oversee everything since Miriam died.' Francesca knew the mention of his grandmother's name would hurt Tony, but still felt it was time to talk the subject over. It had been six months since Miriam had died, peacefully in her chapel, while taking her evening Mass. She had been an old woman and as far as Francesca and Elle were concerned, she died happy and satisfied. She had got everything she had prayed for – Antonias back, after years of searching, and great-grandchildren whom she adored.

'I'll give her a call.' The sigh Francesca heard at the other end of the telephone said it all. He didn't wish to discuss it. Not even with her.

'Why didn't you tell him, Fran?' Elle looked up from the kitchen table when the phone call had ended and waited.

'Because, well, just because. It's something he needs to talk over with Rosanna. How do I tell him that Rosanna thinks the manager of the vineyard is helping himself to all kinds of things? It's just her suspicions but, well, I don't know, Elle.' They both knew Tony would hit the roof, but maybe this was also the excuse he needed to go back to Italy and face the fact that Miriam was gone.

Sure enough, two hours later Tony was back at home, storming down the hallway all fired up. 'You knew, didn't you? She told you, didn't she?' Running his hands through his hair, he was at a loss. He felt his world was crumbling around him.

'There's no point in storming around the kitchen shouting in Italian. Yes, Rosanna mentioned something, but it's your business. Your family business, Tony, and you need to sort it. Miriam and your grandfather worked all their lives and put everything they had into that vineyard. Are you just going to turn your back on it all?'

Opening his arms, Tony welcomed the feel of Francesca within them. There was so much he wanted to tell her, but knew he couldn't. He could feel tears welling up in his eyes as he held her tightly to his chest. Miriam had died and that had broken his heart. Sharon had betrayed him and stolen from him, and then there was the subject of Jake and how to tell him all of this. He was glad of the diversion. Going to Italy to sort out the vineyard might help clear his head.

Looking into those blue eyes, Francesca could tell something was very wrong. Sliding her thumb down the cleft in his chin, she smiled. 'Come on, Mr L, my lovely Antonias. Let's go to Italy and see what's going on.'

* * *

'You're going to Italy? Tomorrow? And you didn't tell me. Bloody hell, Fran, I have packing to do and new clothes to buy.' The interrogation from Julie the next morning eased the tension in the house.

'It's more of a business visit, Julie, not particularly a holiday.'

Julie was still excited, waving her hands in the air with a big smile on her face. 'We can all go. Anyway, there is safety in numbers and misery guts Tony will be too busy throwing his weight around with that manager and then staring at his grandma's chair with that forlorn look on his face.' Rolling her eyes up at the ceiling and looking bored, Julie carried on. 'Right, I will tell Ralph we're going and I need to pack. See you tomorrow.'

Like a whirlwind, Julie picked up her bag and left.

'Does that mean we're going to Italy, Mum?' Katie asked.

'If you want, love. Can you get the time off? What about you, Scarlet? Do you want to come?'

Shaking her head, Scarlet was adamant she couldn't go. 'I've just opened the shop, I can't leave now, can I?'

'I'll come, Mum. In fact, would you mind if I asked Christopher to come with us and see the vineyard?'

'You really want Clark Kent to go to Italy with you and what, hope Papa won't notice he's there?'

'Of course you can ask your friend Christopher, Katie.' Francesca had emphasised the word 'friend' and ignored Scarlet's comments. 'I suppose Julie is right. After all, she is always right. Maybe there is safety in numbers. The more, the merrier. It may be a business trip, but your dad would feel better with his family around him. It would make things easier.'

'Does that mean Bobby and Diana are going, too? I bet Diana can't get away for the week.' Scarlet stuck her chin out and folded her arms sulkily. She obviously knew a lot more about Diana's disappearances than she had said. 'Ouch! That bloody hurt.' Scarlet bent down and started rubbing her leg where Katie had kicked her under the table.

Smiling to herself, Francesca watched them both exchanging glances. Katie's stern look said it all. It seemed they knew Diana had joined the police force. In fact, it seemed everyone knew, except Ralph, who would have to be told sooner or later. Now that really would be something to see.

* * *

'Jake, I have to go to Italy. It seems there's some trouble there I need to sort out. I will only be gone a few days. Do you think you can cope?' Tony was trying to organise things as quickly as possible.

Surprised, Jake looked up from his desk. 'Of course I can cope. Does that mean I'm not invited?' Tony had rarely gone to Italy without Jake and although he wanted to invite him, the last thing he wanted was for Jake to invite Sharon. He didn't want to hurt Jake; he knew he had enough pain to come. But now wasn't the time to discuss it.

'Of course you're invited.' Tony pasted on a weak smile. 'What about Sharon? Will she be coming?' There, he had said it, although he was silently praying Jake would decline.

Watching the relief wash over Jake's face, Tony felt sick inside. 'No, her mum is ill again. She's going to stay with her for the weekend.' Jake looked around the room, not wanting to make eye contact.

'Things not good at home?'

'Not really, mate. You know how it is. I can't do right for doing wrong.'

'Well, that's settled then.' Tony smiled and slapped him on the back. 'Bit of sun on your back to get rid of that ghostly expression and some grapes to fatten you up.'

'Who else is going?' asked Jake.

'Oh, just the family, I think. It will be a nice break. I should have gone back a while ago, but I just couldn't face going there knowing Nonna wouldn't be there. She was the only person that was part of me, my blood, and now... well, you know what I mean.' Tony sniffed and took out his handkerchief to blow his nose.

'I miss her too, Tony. But you're wrong, mate, there are other parts of you right here. You have your kids and they are your blood. Unlike me and Jack.' For what seemed an eternity, but was only a fleeting moment, they stared at each other.

'Oh, shut the fuck up, Jake. You're my brother and Julie is my ugly sister. That's family, mate. Us.' They hugged. 'Come on, we'd better stop hugging before that lot out there think we've started batting for the other side. Besides, you're just not my type.'

Seeing the broad, boyish smile appear back on Jake's face warmed Tony's heart. He was his brother, for all intents and purposes. They had travelled many journeys together and there would be more difficult roads to come.

8

GUILTY EMOTIONS

'Fran! Francesca! Cooee!' Julie was waving and shouting across the crowded airport as she and Diana walked towards them.

'Oh, God.' Tony's shoulders drooped. 'What the fuck is she doing here?'

'You know how it is, Tony. I told her we were going to Italy and she sort of invited herself along. It must have slipped my mind to mention it.' Francesca felt awkward having to explain Julie's presence. She hadn't wanted to make a big thing of it because she knew Tony hated the hustle and bustle of airports and would be in a bad enough mood already.

Breathless, Julie ran up to them and kissed Francesca on the cheek. She looked her usual immaculate self in a white designer trouser suit and with not a hair out of place. Seeing Tony's disgruntled face, she couldn't help but have a dig.

'Bloody hell, Tony, you nearly cracked a smile then. What's the matter, hasn't your Botox set in yet? Is it still giving you pain?' Stroking his face with her well-manicured hands, she pouted. 'Ahh, never mind, love. It's filled in most of the lines.' Her loud cackle filled the airport.

Tony pushed her hand away. 'I don't have Botox!' The pink blush in Tony's cheeks made Julie laugh all the more.

'No, I can see that you don't use Botox. Those lines look very deep, Tony, love. If you had, I would ask for my money back. Now, stop moaning and help Ralph with the bags.'

'Mum! Mum. Sorry we're late.' Katie, Scarlet and Christopher ran towards them, pushing their trolley full of suitcases.

'It's okay, love, I got your message. Come on, get in line, your father's just about to have another argument with Julie.' Julie and Tony were like a comedy duo. For years they had tormented each other. 'I take it you found your passport, Christopher?'

Christopher stepped forward and shook Francesca's hand. 'Yes, sorry about that, Mrs Lambrianu. I left it on the worktop in the kitchen.' He looked quite embarrassed.

'Call me Francesca, please.' She pointed to people as she introduced them. 'This is our son, Adam, and my friend, Julie. I think you know everyone else.'

Tony, Ralph and Jake joined them in the queue. Seeing Christopher, Tony turned to Francesca. 'Who the fuck is that?'

Linking her arm through Tony's and giving him a squeeze, Francesca smiled. 'Tony, love, this is Christopher, Katie's friend. Remember him from the opening of the salon? Katie has invited him to see the vineyard.'

Agitated and flustered, Tony swept his hand through his hair. 'Does anyone else want to come on the Lambrianu Vineyard tour, for fuck's sake? I bet I've bought tickets for everyone in this fucking queue!' Tony was all fired up, but he wasn't as angry as he looked; he just hated standing around. And Julie hadn't helped!

'Calm down, Tony, we'll be on the plane in a moment and you can have a drink and relax. Now, say hello to Katie's friend Christopher.'

Standing up straight, Tony examined the young man standing

before him. He wasn't happy with the idea that Katie had brought a male friend with her, but at least there was safety in numbers.

'How do you do. I'm Tony Lambrianu, Katie's father. I presume you're staying at the house with us?'

Christopher nodded and held his hand out to shake Tony's.

'Well, make sure you keep your hands to yourself and sleep in a bedroom at the other end of the landing to Katie. I will be watching you.' His calm, threatening voice spoke volumes.

Christopher still had his hand out.

'Oh, shut up, you pompous prick, and shake the boy's hand. It's okay, Christopher. He's always on the verge of blowing a fuse. It's the menopause, you know.' Julie gave the young man a wink. 'You'll get used to it.' She laughed. This prompted Tony to finally shake Christopher's hand.

Once on the aeroplane, Julie changed everyone's seating arrangements and sat beside Francesca. She nudged Francesca's arm. 'See, Fran, now he's got something else to moan about, it will take his mind off going home without Granny being there.' With that, she slipped down her eye mask and lay back in her seat as the flight carried them all to Italy.

'Antonias! Antonias! You're home, Antonias.' Rosanna suffocated Tony in hugs and looked relieved to see him. Her dark hair was grey now and her figure rounder and more matronly, but she was still full of life. Instinctively, Tony walked towards the lounge where his grandmother had always sat waiting for him. Francesca reached out for his hand and held it.

Turning to her, Tony kissed her gently on the lips. 'I don't know what I would do without you, Francesca.' No more words were needed as she gazed into those blue eyes full of love. 'Right.

Rosanna, come into the other room and tell me what has been going on.'

'Don't you want to eat first, Antonias? I have prepared some food.'

'I'll eat afterwards. Get me a glass of red and we'll go into the other room and talk.'

Wringing her hands and walking around the room, Rosanna explained what had happened in his absence. Once she had started, she couldn't stop herself and it all came flooding out. She was to the point of hysterics.

After a couple of hours, Tony and Rosanna emerged. He stormed down the hallway to the kitchen where everyone was eating.

'Do you want something to eat, Tony?' asked Francesca, even though she could see he was angry and likely in no mood for food.

He shook his head. 'We're going to the factory, Jake.' With that, he picked up his jacket.

'What, now?'

'Yes, now. So bloody hurry up and swallow that mouthful.'

Jake picked up another slice of crusty bread and followed Tony to the car.

'For Christ's sake, Jake. Do you ever stop eating? I can't believe you're a skinny bastard when you're such a fucking dustbin.'

Jake shrugged. 'Why the rush to get to the factory?'

'There's a new manager, apparently. Wormed his way in when Nonna was ill. I knew nothing about this. She trusted him and he helped her sign over management of the factory to him. In short, he is robbing us fucking blind and he has swindled an old woman in the process.'

'Wouldn't the lawyers have told you this? Hang on, do you mean he owns it?'

'No, not yet the little shit. But he has got his hands firmly in the till and is signing all kinds of contracts. And Nonna gave him the authority to do so. Bloody hell, Jake. She was old and on the verge of dementia. Why the hell didn't she tell me any of this?'

Seeing that he was upset, Jake said, 'Call it Lambrianu pride, Tony. She didn't want to bother you if she was struggling. So, are you telling me he wormed his way in and is now in charge of Lambrianu Vineyard in your absence?' Jake was amazed that this could have happened without anyone else knowing about it.

Tony was deep in thought and full of remorse. He felt he had let the family down. He should have taken over the reins earlier. Shit!

As he stormed through the factory and up to the office, Tony ignored the shocked stares of the people who worked there and knew him. His eyes were firmly fixed on the office.

He pushed the door open wide and his temper got the better of him. 'Right, you. You fat German bastard, get out of my chair and start talking.' Tony was in no mood for treading softly. He was tired and he was angry. Mostly he felt guilty. He had let down his grandmother, the only older blood relative to care about him.

The fat balding man looked up at Tony in surprise. 'And who are you, may I ask?' he said in English coloured by a deep German accent. 'I am seeing no salesmen or reps today. Please leave.'

Tony reached out and grabbed his shirt, yanking him out of the chair.

'I am Tony Lambrianu and you're sitting in my fucking chair. Now move, you fat bastard.'

The shocked expression on the man's face turned to a smug smile. He stood to one side and offered Tony his chair.

'Pack your bags and get out.' Picking up the man's jacket from the back of the chair, Tony threw it at him.

'I have rights, Mr Lambrianu. This is the twenty-first century. You cannot dismiss someone without good reason. I presume you have been listening to that maid's lies about me. She comes in and accuses me of all kinds of things, none of which she has any evidence of.' His smug expression annoyed Tony even more.

Tony clenched his fist tightly and his punch threw the man backwards. Grabbing him by the throat, Tony started to squeeze tighter and tighter. The German was struggling and trying to fight him off, and managed to loosen Tony's grip.

The man got free and stood as far away from Tony as possible. He swept back his thinning grey hair. His shirt was strained to the point where his buttons looked like they were going to pop.

'Assault and dismissal, Mr Lambrianu. There are laws against this kind of thing. Any tribunal would tell you that.' Although he was full of bravado and hiding behind his rights, inside he was shaking. He could see that this was not a man to be trifled with.

'Stop it, Tony.' Jake caught Tony's arm before he had the chance to throw another punch. 'You, Herr Schmidt, are very lucky that I am here. So take my advice and take a leave of absence, starting now.'

Knowing that Jake was right, Herr Schmidt picked up his coat and left.

'What are you doing?' said Tony. 'Are you trying to make me look a fool in front of that fat bastard?'

'No, Tony. But he's right, we have no evidence. The man is hiding behind government law. If Nonna signed anything giving him executor rights... let's find out first, shall we? We need to know where we stand, so let's play it his way for now.'

'That slippery bastard has been creaming it off the top. I should have killed him.'

'What? With a factory full of witnesses? Let's do this the right way, Tony. We'll get our revenge. But you're also to blame. After

Nonna's funeral, you walked away and left Rosanna to it. Now, let's sort this crap out.'

'Pass the Bolognese, Ralph, love, and don't forget to take your vitamins. I'll get them for you.' Julie reached over for her bag and took out the silver foil with blue tablets in. Looking up, she saw the puzzled expression on Francesca's face and gave her a wink.

Ralph swallowed the tablet that Julie gave him and carried on. 'You need an accountant, Tony. Not one from here. They are probably up to their necks in it.'

'I'll fly mine out from the club. We'll sort this, Ralph. I am so bloody angry.' Seeing Ralph taking his vitamins stopped Tony's train of thought. 'Since when did you start taking vitamins, Ralph?' Now he was curious.

'Few months now, Tony lad. Done me the world of good. I feel like a new man. You want to give them a try.'

'No! Tony won't need them. He does all that gym training and stuff. I'm sure he's full of vitamins, what with Elle's cooking and Fran to look after him.' Francesca saw the panic on Julie's face.

Thankfully they were interrupted by Christopher. 'I could do it,' he said. Everyone around the table stopped what they were doing and looked at the young man. Even Adam stopped chewing his food.

'Do what?' snapped Tony. 'Are you in the habit of listening to people's private conversations?' He was angry that this uninvited stranger had poked his nose in.

After calmly picking up his glass of water and taking a sip, then adjusting his horn-rimmed glasses, Christopher continued. 'I'm just saying, Mr Lambrianu, Katie is a qualified accountant and I am a business advisor at the bank. Maybe we could help.

And it's hardly a private conversation over the dining table, is it?'

'Piss off, you nosey bastard. You come to my house, eat my free food and then you stick your fucking nose in my business.'

'Wait!' Ralph held his hand up to stop Tony insulting this poor young man any more. 'He has a point, Tony. Why fly someone else over? Give them a chance. Where is the harm? There is nothing to hide here, is there? Only what that man may have stolen.' Tony, Jake and Ralph all exchanged glances. No, there was nothing shady here. Well, nothing that involved them, anyway. It was a legitimate company.

After weighing up the situation, Tony agreed. Although reluctant, he could see that it made sense. It would take too long to fly out someone he trusted.

* * *

'Okay, Julie. We're alone now,' said Fran, later. 'Everyone is sunning themselves and taking a break. Do you want to tell me more about Ralph's vitamins?' Francesca burst out laughing. 'I have worked in the medical profession, you know, and I know exactly what those tablets are and they are certainly not vitamins.'

'Bloody hell, Fran, we're not all married to libido man, and Ralph is older than Tony. Yes, they are Viagra. You didn't really think I was coming on holiday with no excitement, did you?' Now they both burst into laughter. Julie's secret was out. She had been buying Viagra off the internet for months and had convinced Ralph that he needed to start taking vitamins. The glint in Julie's eyes and the pink flush in her cheeks said it all. 'Bloody hell, Fran, he's been like a two-dick dog in a poodle parlour lately. Chasing me around the bedroom. It's a wonder he can pull his pants up with that thing of his on permanent standby.' Laughter filled the room. Julie never failed to amaze. She always had a plan up her sleeve.

'While we're on the subject of holidays and relaxing, maybe this would be a good time to tell Ralph about Diana. His libido is high and the environment is relaxing. Why don't we do it over a nice dinner? With everyone around the table eating and drinking, the news might go down better.' Francesca was trying to be reasonable. She knew there was never going to be a good time, but here, perhaps it wouldn't be as confrontational.

'What! You have got to be joking. Especially with Tony slamming around the place waiting to see how much that German has ripped him off. But you're right, there is never going to be a good time. Let me put some lippy on and brave it out. Maybe I should give him one of his vitamins first.'

9

THE BITTER TRUTH

Over the next few days, Tony was like a cat on hot bricks, waiting to see what Christopher and Katie were doing in his study all day. He paced up and down and even tried listening at the door.

'Do you want this, Tony?' Julie stood there with a glass in her hand, grinning. 'They say you can hear better with a glass at the door.' Turning on her heels, she burst out laughing. Each time the door opened, Tony stood up, waiting for the outcome, but Katie and Christopher were only taking loo breaks.

'Fucking hell, Jake, how long does this shit take? We know that German prick is ripping us off, so why is it taking that kid so long to figure it out?'

'Because he wants to do it properly, with evidence. No stone left unturned, eh?' Jake had just left when the door opened and Christopher appeared. He had waited for the opportunity to get Tony alone.

Standing in the doorway of the lounge, he said, 'Could I have a word with you, Mr Lambrianu?'

Tony took in the young man before him. He was surprised

that even in this warm climate he was still wearing a suit, although without the tie and the jacket.

It was the first time that Tony had actually paid him any attention. He was a few years older than Katie and quite staid in his manner. He had obviously been brought up properly. His speech and his manners were impeccable. He did have the Clark Kent look about him, Scarlet was right about that, but it seemed he also had brains.

Getting straight to the point, Tony said, 'Shut the door, Christopher, and come and sit down. What have you got to tell me?'

Christopher had folders under his arms and opened a brief-case full of papers. Adjusting his glasses and clearing his throat as though he was about to make a speech, he began.

'I speak Italian, Mr Lambrianu, as does Katie as you know, and I'm sure you will understand the paperwork,' he said, handing over receipts and invoices. 'As you can see, there are many bottles of wine, and I mean hundreds, unaccounted for. I appreciate there must be an amount of wastage, but there is no documentation that accounts for what is missing. Also, I have taken the liberty of contacting a few of the supermarkets that you supply and asking them to send over duplicate invoices, but none of them match our orders, Mr Lambrianu. It seems you are right. Your new manager has, indeed, been helping himself. I also note that there is a company in Germany, very new, and I presume not one that you have started.'

The lounge door opened and Katie walked in.

'He's started telling you the bad news, then? Well, it gets worse.'

'How the hell could it get worse? He's been ripping us off and you're both sure of it. What could be worse than that?'

Sitting down beside Christopher on the sofa, Katie began to tell Tony more of what they had found.

'We think that when the new manager was handing things to Nonna to sign, he sneaked in some papers without telling her what they were. It seems she has signed over the running of the vineyard to him. In fact, he is the executor of the vineyard. He is in charge of the day-to-day running, the payments, everything. It's legal; we've checked. Nonna signed it over without realising it.'

Katie had already discussed with Christopher that she would be the one to give her father this bad news. The accounts and receipts were one thing, but telling her father that his grandmother hadn't known what she was doing would be like a knife in his heart. Not only did he feel guilty that he hadn't taken over the reins when he should have, his beloved grandmother had been robbed of everything she loved.

Exchanging glances with Christopher, Katie waited for the explosion of anger from her father, but none came. Instead he sat there stunned, his face expressionless.

'Are you telling me that none of the vineyard is ours?' he asked, eventually. His voice was low and even wobbled slightly as the words left his mouth. He was trying his best to comprehend the situation.

'Well, the grounds and the houses are, but he is in full charge of the vineyard, it seems.' The silence was deafening. Katie half wished that he would start shouting and having one of his tantrums.

'And you say all of this is legal? How? How is it possible for her to turn all of this over without anyone knowing it? Surely lawyers must have been involved?'

Christopher felt very awkward sitting in front of this man and telling him not one grape on this land belonged to him. Adjusting his glasses and clearing his throat, he said, 'None of the lawyers involved in the takeover were Italian, Mr Lambrianu, if that's what you're thinking. Rosanna witnessed it, though I doubt she knew what she was signing. That is something you need to ask her. Maybe she will remember doing it.'

Tony was nodding his head, trying to take it all in. This German manager had been very thorough and had taken advantage of an old woman. Tony remembered being pleased when he had been told that everything was in good hands. He had never dreamt it was anything like this. This man had robbed him of his heritage.

'Thank you, both. You have been very thorough in your investigations. Would you please leave me now?' Tony stood up. He was about to shake the young man's hand when Christopher interrupted him.

'Can I just say, Mr Lambrianu, while we're on the subject? You and your family produce some very expensive wines. Excellent wines, in fact. But I feel you're missing out on a certain market.'

'Not now, Christopher. Let's leave Dad to it. He needs time to take all of this in.' Katie was steering him to the door. She knew now was not the time to talk business. Her father needed a moment to get his head around this revelation.

'No, let him speak, Katie. What else is there you want to say?' Tony waited. If it was more bad news, well, he might as well have it all in one go.

Pulling his arm away from Katie, Christopher stood face to face with Tony. 'Many people these days enjoy a glass of wine, but they can't all afford your prices. You could produce a cheaper wine for this market and it is possible that you could use another name for it which would distance you from it and avoid damaging the reputation that you have. People would just see that it came from the same vineyard. Although I doubt if any of the young people with their boxes of wine would look at the labels to see where it is made.'

Tony's face clouded over and he withdrew his hand. His voice was very calm and very steady, which Katie knew was always a bad sign. She preferred him shouting and screaming; at least that meant he was getting it off his chest. 'You have just told me that I don't have a vineyard to make any kind of wines in, so what are you talking about? My family have always produced top quality exclusive clarets, not the cheap shit you're talking about. Now, leave me in peace.' He was trying to remain calm, but Tony felt Christopher was pushing his luck too far, now. Christopher was insistent, however.

Katie closed her eyes and shook her head. 'Leave it, Christopher. Save it for another time. Please, let's go.' She pulled him again by the arm and almost pushed him out of the room. Then Christopher turned. He was on a roll and he didn't want to stop now that he had Tony's attention.

'I'm sure you will sort this matter out, Mr Lambrianu. I have no doubt about that. So, when you do, maybe you would consider what I have said. There are many vineyards out there doubling their income by doing what I have suggested.'

'Will you just fuck off and leave me in peace?' Now Tony was angry. This guy was getting on his nerves with his ideas and proposals, although he was right about one thing: he would sort this matter out. Now. Today! 'Just for the record, thank you for earning your bed and board, but that doesn't include my daughter. I take it you are sleeping alone and keeping your hands to yourself?'

Tony felt like taking him down a peg or two. He wanted to shout at somebody and this persistent upstart business advisor was just the person.

Surprisingly, Christopher stayed calm, although he blushed

slightly. 'I assure you, Mr Lambrianu, I have nothing but respect for your daughter.' After opening the door, he left the room, walking past Jake, who avoided his gaze.

Jake couldn't help laughing, even though he could see that Tony was in no laughing mood. 'I take it you have just read him the Riot Act about keeping his hands to himself. Oh, come on, Tony, you would be like a ferret up a drainpipe if a beautiful woman was alone in a bedroom just across the landing.'

Suddenly, a smile appeared on Tony's face. They burst out laughing like two schoolboys. 'Too bloody right, Jake. What she sees in him, I don't know. He is as plain as a stump fence.'

Jake shrugged. 'Well, for the record, I think he seems like a decent guy. He has brains and his conversation is okay, too. Maybe you should give him a chance and not just see him as the enemy, taking little Katie's affections from you, eh?'

'Maybe. But for now, Jake, sit down, and let's get back to business. That German bastard has taken the vineyard away from us, it seems. He has conned Nonna into signing over the vineyard to him.'

Jake's face was a picture. 'How the hell has he done that? She never said a word about handing over any rights to anyone. When did all this happen?' Jake was amazed. Not in his wildest dreams had he imagined this.

Tony looked at him sadly. 'To be honest, it's all my fault. I should have helped her more. She always seemed so strong and in control, it never occurred to me that she needed me. We have been here so many times. Shit, I even shook that guy's hand at the funeral and thanked him for looking after things. He must have been laughing his head off at me. We both knew she had a little dementia. Damn it. Why didn't I see this coming? Well, I'm going to go and see him again. Come on, let's go.'

Jake didn't move from the sofa. He was shocked. 'If you're

thinking of killing him, Tony, you can get that out of your mind right now.'

Tony picked up his jacket and made for the door.

'Stop, Tony. Think about it. This is Don Carlos' country. He is in charge here, him and his whole family. You can't go in there with all guns blazing, he will have you killed. You need his permission to kill that German bastard. He will give it, I have no doubt, but you need his blessing.'

Jake stood up and blocked the doorway. He had to make Tony see sense.

Sweeping his hand through his silvery blonde mane, Tony let out a deep sigh. 'What, then?'

'We do what we have always done. We work out a plan and see it through. We're going to scare the shit out of him and let him sign those papers back over to you of his own free will. Or something like that. Now, let's have lunch with the family. Get back on track. You're too wound up. This takes serious thought. It has to be done just as legally and as cunningly as he did it.' Jake started to smile. He knew Tony well enough to know that his mind would be working overtime now. They both knew Jake was right. Cross Don Carlos and they would both be going home in body bags. Murder the German and they could possibly still be going home in body bags.

It did cross Jake's mind to go and see Don Carlos and ask his advice. Then he thought, no, not just yet, let's wait and see what Tony comes up with first.

'Deep breath, Tony. Let's go to lunch. Smile and be happy. You're on holiday, remember?'

When they got to the dining room, lunch was already in full swing. The table was overflowing with dishes of food. Francesca and Scarlet were passing around plates. The house was full of chatter and laughter. Everyone was tanned. Adam looked as if he had put on weight and it pleased Tony to hear that Adam had begun speaking Italian. His young son looked more Italian than any of them, with his dark hair and suntan.

Surveying the room made Tony even more determined to sort this mess out. This was his family home and it was going to stay that way. 'Right, guys, what is on the menu?' he said. Slipping his arm around Francesca's waist, he kissed her on the cheek then took his place at the head of the table.

'God, I'm stuffed.' Scarlet sat back in her chair and rubbed her stomach. Thank goodness the house had air conditioning. They were all baking in the heat and now they had stuffed themselves to capacity.

'Bloody hell, Jake. Don't you ever stop eating?' said Tony. Even though everyone was full and satisfied, Jake was still eating hot crusty bread and dipping it into the lasagne sauce.

'It's lovely. Anyway, I like the bits and pieces left over; dip it here and dip it there.'

'Well, at least shut your mouth when you're eating; it's like looking into a washing machine.'

Francesca interrupted them. 'We could all stay a few more days,' she said. 'This trip has done everyone the world of good and I don't seem to have spent much time alone with you, Tony. Maybe we should get the scooters out and have a ride around the village?'

'Yes, that would be nice.' He reached over for her hand and kissed the back of it. 'I just have a few things to do first and then I'm all yours.'

'I have to get back soon, I need to keep an eye on the salon, and you will have to get back too, Diana. When do you start back at work?' Scarlet hadn't meant to say anything, it had just slipped out. 'Oh, God, sorry, Diana. I didn't mean anything.' Scarlet was blushing profusely.

Julie put her drink down and looked around the table. Suddenly everyone had gone silent and turned their heads towards Diana. A frown crossed Ralph's face. He looked from Scarlet to Diana. Obviously they had a secret that he wasn't supposed to know.

'What work, Diana? What job do you have that I don't know about?' Putting down his knife and fork, Ralph waited.

'Leave it, Ralph, love. We'll discuss it later.' Julie looked across at Fran. This wasn't how she had intended it to come out. She had been planning to tell Ralph alone, to soften the blow.

'Well? I'm waiting, Diana. Why the mystery?'

Julie was about to butt in again, but Ralph stopped her. 'She can speak for herself, Julie. It's obviously not something I would approve of or there wouldn't be such a secret. Spit it out, Diana.'

Diana could see the sea of faces all staring at her. Sticking her chin out in the same stubborn manner as Julie did, she said, 'I've joined the police force. I'm still on probation, but I've sat my exams and been accepted. There. Now you know. I knew you would disapprove or try to stick your oar in so I've changed my name. Only my immediate superior officers know that I am called Diana Gold. I'm using Mum's maiden name. I need to gain their trust before I reveal I'm the daughter of a millionaire with a shady past.'

'A shady past?' Ralph glared around the table and then back at Diana. 'What the hell is that supposed to mean? Just what have you done? And what do you mean, you've changed your name? You're a Gold. You're my daughter and I won't hear any more of this silliness. It's embarrassing. My daughter, a PC.' Ralph was angry. It was the first time anyone had seen him angry with Diana.

'It's not silly. It's a good, decent career! But thank you, Scarlet.

I suppose your big mouth is going to spill the beans about you dating that Dominic guy?'

'Dominic? You mean the guy who works for me?' Tony said. Just when he thought this day couldn't get any worse. 'Are you telling me after all I said to you that you have been seeing that bloody doorman again?'

'Will you both shut up? Listen to yourselves, for God's sake.' Julie had heard enough. These men were sitting around the table judging their children's lives. Well, she thought, it's a shame neither of them had anyone to judge theirs.

'Julie. Are you telling me that you knew about this? You don't seem very surprised.' Ralph narrowed his eyes.

'Of course I knew. I followed her, with Fran, one night. I was going to tell you. But now the cat is out of the bag. Listen to you, like two dogs fighting over a bone. Francesca, put your hands over Adam's ears.'

Reaching forward, Francesca did as she was told. She knew a barrage of bad language was going to come out of Julie's mouth. Then she had a better idea. 'Rosanna, would you mind taking Adam outside or letting him play on his PlayStation for a while?'

When Adam was out of the room, Julie continued. 'I don't like the idea of her walking the streets with drunks and druggies any more than you do, but this is her choice,' Julie said, wagging her finger in Ralph's face and giving him her glare. 'And you.' She looked across at Tony and glared at him, too. 'The quickest way to make love stronger is to oppose it. Have you never heard of Romeo and Juliet? You're both daddies who won't let go. Well, I'm someone's daughter, but it didn't stop you. And you, Tony, well, the less said, the better.' She shook her head.

'Julie,' said Ralph, 'maybe we should go back to the villa and finish the conversation there. We need to talk in private.' Ralph seemed embarrassed by the whole affair.

'In private! Since when has anyone around this table done anything in private?' She slammed her fist on the table. 'Let's face it, Ralph, this is our family. It's the only family we have had for over twenty years, so stop looking so coy.' Julie turned to Diana. 'Right, you, Miss PC... How long have you been scheming and lying behind our backs and why? Surely you knew it would come out sooner or later.'

There was silence around the table as everyone looked at Diana, waiting for an answer.

'I'm sorry about that, Mum. Dad' – Diana looked over at Ralph – 'before I told you anything I wanted to see if I would be accepted and, I suppose, if I liked it. I knew you would disapprove for all kinds of reasons and even if you did approve, you would want to buy me into a higher position. I want to be accepted by my colleagues for me, not for being Ralph and Julie Gold's daughter. I need to earn their trust and respect.' Tears were falling down Diana's face as she tried to explain herself.

'So you felt the need to change your name so you wouldn't be associated with me. Is that it? You think I'm a crook or something? Well, believe me, young lady, there are more crooks in your job then there are in mine,' said Ralph.

'I know you're not squeaky clean, Dad. I read the papers. We're old enough to know that you're some kind of gangland bosses with your rackets. But that was your choice and I love you. I love all of you. But I couldn't enter the force as a millionaire's daughter. No one would take me seriously. I talked it through with my recruiting sergeant and we both agreed this way would be for the best. Sorry.' Again, the tears rolled down her face.

'It's okay, Diana. Come on, dry your eyes.' Francesca walked around the table to where Diana sat and put her hand on her shoulder, giving her a comforting squeeze.

'Right, then, that's that in the open. Come on, Ralph, what

else do you have to say? Because once you have had your say, it's done.' Julie was adamant this should be wrapped up quickly. 'What does it matter, Ralph? She is still your daughter, isn't she? If you are going to turn your back on her, you can turn your back on me, too.' Lighting a cigarette to calm her anger, Julie blew the smoke into the air. Her lips were pursed, making her red lipstick even more prominent.

'It's not that, Julie, love.' Ralph was shocked. The very thought of losing Julie and Diana frightened him. 'For goodness' sake. There are mad men out there. She's vulnerable... and what are the papers going to make of this? I'm just shocked. Don't forget, I know a lot of the boys in blue. Does my daughter really want to be a part of that?'

'They're not all bent, Ralph. There are actually some decent coppers out there who do their jobs with dignity. The point is, Diana has already taken all of what you have just said into consideration. Well, I am proud of her. It's a good career, although of course I'm worried for her safety. There are some nutters out there with guns and knives.' Again, Julie looked around the table at Ralph, Tony and Jake. 'Maybe it's time all of you accepted that they are not children any more. Your daughters are grown women with their own lives to lead, whether you like it or not.' The ash fell off the end of Julie's cigarette and on to the tablecloth. Brushing it off with a sweep of her hand, she looked around the table again, waiting for someone to speak.

Nodding his head and looking rather sheepish, Ralph said, 'Diana, I don't like the idea that you felt you had to lie to us. We are your parents. I know you hear rumours and I wouldn't like to put you into a compromising position. If you should ever need my help, you know you only have to ask.' Ralph pushed his chair back and opened his arms. It was a very emotional scene, watching Diana in her father's arms. Wiping a tear from her own eye, Julie picked up the bottle of wine and poured herself another drink.

She had put Ralph in a very awkward position. He had no choice but to accept the situation. And accept it he would. One day, she thought to herself, he might even be proud of her!

'And what about you, Scarlet? You've had so much to say for yourself up to now, and now you're silent?' It was Francesca's turn. 'Hell, we might as well clear the whole skeleton cabinet while we're at it.'

Scarlet's face burned red, highlighting her blondeness even more. Looking at her father from under her lashes, she could see the scowl on his face. 'It's true. I have been dating Dominic,' she mumbled. 'I like him and he likes me, which is why, in case you haven't noticed, he no longer works for you.' Her voice became louder. She met Tony's stare. His puzzled look confirmed that Tony hadn't even noticed Dominic no longer worked for him. 'How come Katie's allowed to bring her boyfriend on holiday with us and I get punished for dating Dominic?'

Looking over at Christopher, Tony sighed. 'Is that what you are, Christopher? Katie's boyfriend?' He didn't sound angry, more matter of fact. After watching Ralph nearly lose his daughter, he also had to admit defeat.

'I suppose so, Mr Lambrianu.' Christopher reached out for Katie's hand and held it. She looked pleased that at last it had been said.

Contemplating the situation and seeing his daughters properly for the women they were, Tony said, 'Dominic worked for me, Scarlet. He was my employee and you were the golden goose – the boss's daughter. Not a very good start to a relationship, is it?' said Tony. 'Has he been messing around with you? Asking you to do things that you're not ready for? That randy little shit can keep his hands to himself.' Tony was indignant.

'I went to see him the day after the party to apologise. He was in an awful state and wouldn't speak to me. Or rather, he couldn't speak to me, after those gorillas of yours broke his jaw! And no, he hasn't forced me to do anything. We're not all like you.' Scarlet's voice was accusing and harsh. 'Why, Papa? That night was all my fault.'

'Tony, you didn't. Did you?' said Francesca. She looked at him, horrified. 'He's a young man; there was no need for that. Good God. By the time I was their age I'd had Bobby and had been married. People would probably say the same about me, that I was dating the boss and saw you as the golden goose, eh?'

'No, Francesca. You know that wasn't the case.' Standing up quickly and knocking his chair backwards, Tony walked over to Francesca's side and put his arms around her. 'You saw me for who I am and I love you for it. I'm sorry if you think I have been an overprotective stupid old man. Oh, God, Francesca, I love you. Don't hate me for loving our family and protecting them. That's my job.' Tony and Francesca stood holding each other. She kissed him on the lips. It had taken a lot for Tony to admit he had been wrong, but he had done it.

'When we get back, young lady, you had better ask Dominic to come for Sunday lunch. Is that okay with you, Tony?' said Francesca.

'That's just fine with me, Fran.' A faint smile crossed his face. 'Well, Ralph, it seems we're the father of grown women with strong minds of their own. Only to be expected, I suppose, with great parents like us.'

If nothing else, it broke the tension and everyone laughed. Looking across the table at Francesca, Julie closed her eyes and nodded. Maybe now their husbands would realise their children were grownups. This was the next generation and it was going to be a bumpy ride!

10

THE LAMBRIANU WAY

'Come on, Katie, let's go for a walk.' Christopher felt it was time to leave them all to it. The one thing he did know was that as much as the fathers claimed to have decided to back off and let their daughters lead their own lives without interfering, it was never going to happen. It just appeased their wives.

'This is a beautiful place, Katie, but the way you described it was nothing like this. This place is a city. A Lambrianu city.'

'I told you Grandma had a vineyard in Italy and supplied a lot of wines. What did you expect, Christopher? An allotment with a few grapes and some old women treading on them with their feet?' Katie couldn't help but laugh. But then she realised he was right. This had always just been Grandma's vineyard to her; she had never seen it for what it was in reality. She had taken it for granted.

'Don't you love the smell of the grapes and the roses mingled together? I think that's how they got the idea for rose wine,' she said, slipping her arm around his waist as they walked up a path surrounded by roses, the warm sun on their faces. 'Come on, let me show you something.' Katie walked him towards the little chapel. 'This was Grandma's favourite place in the world.' The coolness of the chapel with its stone floor was a welcome respite from the glare of the hot sun. 'She was married here and sadly she died here while taking evening Mass. Although I suspect that is what she would have wanted. Mum and Dad were married here, as well.' Katie beamed. It was lovely to be able to share her family history.

'It's beautiful, Katie. This place makes you want to whisper, it has a feeling all of its own. Maybe... erm, well maybe...' Christopher stopped short of what he was going to say, adjusted his glasses and gave a sheepish smile.

Katie waited but nothing happened. She knew she was the one who had to take the lead. It was basically now or never. 'Maybe one day we will get married here.' With that, she turned and made her way back out into the sunshine. Now it was Christopher's turn. If he felt the same way, this was his cue to say so. Sometimes people just needed a little nudge in the right direction, she thought to herself. Would he ignore what she had just said and hope it would go away? Now she suddenly felt nervous.

Catching up with her and slipping his hand into hers, he said, 'I'd like that, Katie. But I need to speak to your father first and prove to him that I could look after you.' Nothing more was said as they walked back to the house, holding hands, with smiles upon their faces.

'Where have you been?' Tony asked as they came through the door. 'I've been looking for you.'

'We've been to the chapel, Dad. I've been showing Christopher around. Why, what's the problem?'

'No, not you. Him. I've been looking for him.' He looked at Christopher. 'I need you to do something for me.'

Tony walked into the lounge, where Jake was sitting waiting

for them. Christopher had a feeling of foreboding. Was he going to get the same beating that poor Dominic had received?

'Sit down. Sit down, for God's sake.' Tony seemed agitated. 'Jake and I have had an idea and I think you can help. Did you say your brother was a lawyer?'

Confused, Christopher nodded.

'A proper lawyer, I mean. Not some kid still at school, learning?' Tony pressed him. He wanted to know the facts.

'My brother is an established lawyer and has been for years. He is older than me. My father is a barrister, so he knows the law as well.'

Tony and Jake exchanged glances.

'These papers that you say Herr Schmidt got my grandmother to sign, are they legal?'

Again, Christopher nodded, and was about to explain further when Tony interrupted him.

'What papers would be needed to overturn that decision? To hand back the vineyard, say... to me. What would I need to do or get from Herr Schmidt to reclaim ownership?' Tony and Jake waited.

'That's quite simple, really, Mr Lambrianu. You need the right paperwork, of course, but once you have that, all he has to do is sign it to hand everything back over to you and relinquish all claim.'

'How long would this paperwork take to set up? Would he need to be informed? Does he need to apply for something?' Tony fired question after question at Christopher. Everything that was going through his brain came tumbling out.

'It is usually the case that he would go and see a lawyer, but it's not necessary. As long as it is witnessed, it wouldn't matter. The paperwork could be drawn up in a couple of days.' Christopher scratched his head. 'Do you really think he would sign a gold mine like this back over to you?' He was amazed that Tony would even consider the possibility.

'Yes, I do. He will sign it one way or another, but that's no concern of yours.' Staring directly into his eyes, Tony felt this young man before him knew exactly what he meant. 'It has to be watertight, though. Not my usual lawyers; that would look suspicious. Maybe your brother would be interested in the work?' Tony at last threw down the gauntlet.

'I presume you're not implying anything untoward, Mr Lambrianu. My brother is a very respectable man. Anything he does will be legal and lawful.' Christopher cleared his throat and waited. He knew he was on icy ground, but realised this might just be the opportunity he needed to ingratiate himself with Katie's father.

'No, no, nothing illegal.' Tony winked at him and gave his most charming smile, putting Christopher at ease. 'I just wouldn't want him to be able to change his mind or find a loophole to do so. And I would need the paperwork ASAP.'

'In that case, Mr Lambrianu, I could contact my brother and have him send over the paperwork via email. It would have to be signed and stamped legally, of course, and witnessed, like your grandmother's was by Rosanna.'

'Indeed.' Tony stood up, indicating their meeting was over. 'Well, I suggest you contact your brother now. Tell him the sooner it gets here the bigger the bonus will be, for his speed and efforts.'

'It's not about money, Mr Lambrianu, although, obviously he will charge the going rate.'

'Everyone has their price, Christopher, and your brother will have his. Now, off you go. Make your calls and get on with it. Bring those papers to me directly. And, oh, Christopher, you're going to witness it. That is, if you want to continue seeing Katie. After all, this is Katie's home you're saving, isn't it?'

'Of course I will sign it, Mr Lambrianu. That is... if you and I can talk sometime soon. In private.' He blushed a little as he looked towards Jake. Tony nodded and shook his hand, while Jake stood up and opened the door for him to leave.

'What do you think he wants to talk to you about in private?' Jake looked at Tony.

'It's one of two things, or possibly even both. The way he looks at Katie, I think he wants to ask for her hand in marriage. God, he is a stuffed shirt, but at least he wants to do it properly. Secondly, he came to me with some business idea about cheap wines to sell in the supermarkets. You know, the cheap boxes of wine people have at their barbeques.'

'Hey, Tony, that's not a bad idea. The one about the vineyard, I mean.' Jake could see that the first proposition wasn't exactly to Tony's liking. 'What did you say?'

'Nothing. How can I listen to a business interest when I don't have a business to be interested in? And Katie, well... she seems to like him, so I will cross that bridge when I come to it.' He changed the topic of conversation. 'Let's go out with the family for the afternoon. That is, if any of them are talking to each other.' They both started to laugh.

'God, Tony I thought Julie was going to thump Ralph. She is one bad-tempered old bag. And Diana a copper. Well, if the worst ever came to the worst, we have the whole of the emergency services on our side. Bobby is a doctor, Jack is a fireman and Diana is a copper. Who could ask for anything more?' Again, they burst out laughing. Fate was a funny thing.

11

AUF WIEDERSEHEN

The plan was hatched. All Jake had to do was keep the German manager's teenage children out of the way for a few hours. They had photos of the children and Jake planned to meet them at the school gates and work his boyish charm. It was a gamble. Maybe they were just like their stubborn father and wouldn't go with Jake. Only time would tell.

Tony rang Jake as he was sitting in his car outside the school gates, watching everyone come out.

'Can you see them?' Tony was anxious for Jake to get it over with. The legal documents were in his breast pocket – Christopher and his brother had worked swiftly – and now it was time for him and Jake to do what they did best.

'Sure enough, Tony. Rosanna was spot on and those nice family photos he had in the office have worked a treat. They are just coming out now. Time for me to act.'

Jake got out of the car and started making his way towards the two teenagers walking out of the school gates. 'Hi, you two, how are things? Is your dad feeling any better? I heard he's taken a few days off work.'

Jake's warm friendly manner stopped them. They were uneasy, but they were curious. Exchanging glances, they realised that although they didn't know him, this man knew them.

'I'm Jake. I'm on holiday at the moment. My brother owns the vineyard. Mr Lambrianu. I suppose your father told you all about it. I recognise you from the photos he was showing us the other day.' Jake carried on chatting as though they were old friends. It put them at their ease. 'Do you two fancy an ice cream?'

The teenage boy with his bag over his shoulder looked hot and bored. The girl seemed more suspicious. 'Our father is not ill,' she said. 'He's just having a few days' holiday. Who did you say you were again?' She was going to be difficult to convince.

'I'm Jake, Mr Lambrianu's brother. We're with the family having a little holiday. Just looking over things.' Jake's nonchalant manner made them more curious.

'Yes. Go on, I will have an ice cream, if you're buying.' The boy walked towards the stall.

Breathing a sigh of relief, Jake quietly thanked God that all boys thought about their stomach first.

'You must be Kurt; your dad's told me all about you. Come on, choose what you want.' Jake waited for the girl to follow. 'You're Agnes, aren't you? Lovely name. What's your fancy?' They told him and he placed his order for the ice creams. 'Here you go then,' he said, handing them over and then taking a lick of his own. 'Have you two ever been to the vineyard?'

'We have been once,' was all Kurt said. Agnes remained tight-lipped.

'You should ask your father to take you again sometime.' Jake mopped his brow, emphasising the heat. 'Wow, it's hot today. Well, I had better be off now. Do you two need a lift anywhere?'

Agnes spoke up first. 'No, thank you. But thank you for the ice cream.' She was going to be tough nut to crack.

Jake started to walk slowly to his car. As he gave a backwards glance and a friendly wave, he could see the boy leaning over and whispering in his sister's ear.

'Wait, Mr Jake,' the boy said. 'Maybe you could give us a lift home?'

Phew! Turning on his heel, Jake smiled at them both again. It had been Tony's idea to take the bright red open-top Mercedes. All boys liked cars and, even better, driving around in them in front of their friends. 'Sure thing, guys. Hop in.' Jake smiled to himself as he opened the door. Mission accomplished!

* * *

Opening the door to his house, carrying his bags of shopping, Herr Schmidt was horrified to see Tony lounging on his sofa. 'How did you get in here?' His German accent seemed even stronger than it had the other day.

'I have my ways, Herr Schmidt.' Tony looked at the man in front of him. This overweight, sweaty lowlife had cheated and robbed his grandmother. He thought he was clever. Well, now it was time to play with the big boys.

Herr Schmidt walked over to the telephone and started to dial the emergency services.

'I wouldn't do that. Could be a bad move, or at least, a painful one.' Tony held up his mobile and showed him a picture of his son, daughter and Jake. 'Great selfie, don't you think?'

Slamming the telephone down, he snarled, 'You bastard. What have you done with my children? You have kidnapped them.' His face was red with rage.

Tony's smooth velvety voice filled the room. This time he felt on home ground. Watching this man squirm before him gave him the upper hand. 'Kidnapped? They don't even look upset. In fact, they look like they are having a great time.'

'Bring my children back home now! Or you will be sorry, Mr Lambrianu. I will have you arrested and thrown into prison for this.' Walking over to Tony, Herr Schmidt raised his hand to slap him.

Shielding himself with his elbow, Tony laughed. 'I wouldn't do that. You see, I also know how angry it makes you feel when someone takes advantage of your family and tricks them. Like you did with my grandmother. A sweet old lady who gave you a job. I also see that you encouraged her to sign over the running of things in my absence. You conning bastard!'

'It's all perfectly legitimate, Mr Lambrianu, and there is nothing you can do about it. That vineyard is mine,' Herr Schmidt replied smugly.

Trying to remain calm but seething inside, Tony took the documents from his pocket. 'You have made thousands of pounds selling wine that wasn't yours. Now you're going to sign this document and hand everything back over to me. You are going to leave Italy today, you and your kids, and never return. Whatever you have made, you can keep, and I think I am being very generous.' His pleasant manner covered the hate and bitter taste in his mouth.

'I warn you, Mr Lambrianu, I will report you. Kidnapping and threatening behaviour are taken very seriously here. You may be a fellow countryman, but the authorities will hear of this.' The smug look on the man's face angered Tony even more. His blue eyes darkened. He had heard enough.

Taking a hand grenade out of his pocket, Tony grabbed hold of the German's jaw. 'This is a black Russian. It may only be the size of a golf ball, but it can do just as much damage as a bigger one.'

Tony pulled the German forward. Herr Schmidt tried his best to escape, and suddenly they were both on the floor, Tony sitting astride him. Grabbing the man's jaw again, he pushed and pressed, breaking his front teeth in the process, until the man had no alternative but to open his mouth. Panting and trying to catch his breath, Tony was surprised just how much weight this fat bastard had behind him.

'Peace at fucking last,' shouted Tony, as he rammed the grenade into Herr Schmidt's mouth.

After sweeping his hair back, Tony reached forward and slowly took the pin out of the grenade. Hypnotised, the man watched him, and stopped struggling.

'I would keep perfectly still if I were you. You see, even though the pin is out, as long as you hold on to it tightly and keep that lever down, it won't explode.'

Standing up and wiping the blood from his mouth with the back of his hand, Tony looked down at the man with grim satisfaction. There he was, laid flat on his back with a small black hand grenade in his mouth. He didn't look so high and mighty now!

'You know, Herr Schmidt, eventually your teeth are going to ache and your jaw is going to go numb. If you pull that out, you have four seconds before it blows you and this house into oblivion. People will think you have done it yourself. Embezzlement and fraud. Some people have committed suicide for less, especially when they face a prison sentence. Well, I'm going to see what fun your children are having. I wonder if it would be so hard to shove one of these into their mouths?' Reaching into his pocket, Tony took out another grenade. Tossed it in the air and caught it again.

The wild horrified look on the German's face said it all. He raised his hand and pointed to the documents Tony had put on the table. Beads of sweat poured down his red face. He was trying his best to breathe through his nose, but it was making him pant. Saliva oozed from the sides of his mouth.

Picking up a book from the coffee table, Tony knelt beside him on the floor. He rested the document on the book and put the pen into the man's hand. Quickly Herr Schmidt signed his name three times, where Tony had marked the page with the letter 'X'.

Putting the document into his jacket pocket, Tony looked around the room. He had left nothing behind and, of course, as usual, he had worn leather gloves.

'Four seconds, now. Don't forget.' Tony waved and walked out of the door. The man on the floor was pointing to his mouth hoping Tony would do something. He was crying. His body was shaking, but he clenched his teeth tightly onto the grenade, which was making it even harder for him to breathe.

Tony had everything he wanted. Not only did he have his vineyard back, Herr Schmidt had signed over the one in Germany, too.

At last, Tony walked through the back door of his own house, where Jake was waiting.

'How did it go?' Once he saw that big grin spread across Tony's face as he waved the signed document in the air, he knew everything was okay. 'What happened to your mouth?'

'It was a struggle, Jake. That fat bastard put up a hell of a fight. Twenty stone of angry frightened man waving his arms around and struggling is a big challenge, but I managed it. This is collateral damage. I'll live. I got what I wanted and that is all that counts.' Tony put his arm around Jake's shoulders. 'Smell that, Jake. That is the smell of Lambrianu grapes. We're home again and I won't let anything like this happen ever again. Come on, let's go and see those kids and drop them off home.'

'Go and change first. There's blood on your shirt. Come on, you can tell me about it in a minute. At least you're home safe and sound.'

'Can you imagine how he's going to feel when he realises it's a dud? That's if he doesn't have a heart attack first. He could claim he was forced to sign it over through threat or blackmail, you know.' They burst out laughing as they walked up the stairs towards the bathroom. Tony took out his mobile. 'Here, I took this for you.' Tony showed Jake the picture he had taken of Herr Schmidt with the black hand grenade in his mouth. Again, they started to laugh.

'Best get rid of that SIM card, Tony. Good picture, but bad evidence. Seriously, what happens now?'

'Already got a new phone on the way back. Just couldn't resist it. I'll get cleaned up and changed, and then we'll drop the kids off.'

Standing in the bathroom, splashing cold water on to his face, Tony looked into the mirror above the basin and felt tears well up in his eyes. Not for the fight he had just gone through, but for the guilt he felt. He had been too busy going around with his eyes closed and ignoring the fact that his grandmother was an old woman who had needed his help.

'Time to take the kids home. After all, they have a lot of packing to do,' he whispered to Jake, who was standing outside the bathroom with a large whisky in his hand.

'No, let them stay a bit longer. Make the bastard sweat. If he hasn't passed out already, I would say another hour should do it,' said Jake. Chinking their glasses together, they burst out laughing.

'Another day and we can all go home. First, we have to go and pay our respects to Don Carlos and his sons. He will know we are here and he will be waiting to hear from us. Then, I'm going to appoint that old supervisor to run things around here for the time being until I can find someone else. He's a good guy and worked for Nonna for years. His nose must have been well put out of joint when that prick took over. Back to business, then.'

Jake walked ahead of Tony outside towards the two teenagers. 'Kurt, Agnes, I've called your father and told him you would be staying for dinner. That is, if you want to?' Again, Jake was full of charm. The two youngsters were having a great time. The rest of the family had returned and they hadn't expected so many people to be there. Everyone was laughing and enjoying each other's company. Julie lay on a lounger close to the porch. As Tony walked past her, she lowered her dark glasses to the end of her nose and looked up at him. 'Did you kill him?'

Surprised by her question, Tony looked at her curiously. Her voice was stern and serious.

'No,' was all he said, and he walked away to join Francesca and Adam with their new visitors. Lying back on her sun lounger, Julie seemed satisfied. She hadn't fancied taking Tony home in a body bag for breaking the rules of this country. Or of the people that ran it.

* * *

Herr Schmidt was looking up at the ceiling in a dazed state. The room was spinning and he realised he must have passed out. His head was throbbing and his jaw was numb. In fact, his whole head felt numb. Reaching up to feel the wet liquid on his throat and chest, he realised that he had been sick. His trousers were damp, and he knew he had also wet himself. Blinking hard, he saw the grenade lying at the side of him in a pool of vomit.

Fear gripped him as he stared at it, and he edged away

quickly. It was then he realised it hadn't exploded and he was still alive. It had all been a trick.

He knew next time he wouldn't be so lucky. Struggling to sit on the sofa, he rubbed his wet, stained face and looked up at the clock. Where were his children? Hours had passed since Tony Lambrianu had been there, but there was still no sign of them. Tears rolled down his face and he started to sob.

The door opened and a voice called, 'We're home, Dad.' Looking towards the hallway, relief washed over him. He couldn't believe his ears. He looked around the room at the carpet stained with vomit and the grenade in the middle of it. His back and legs ached with pins and needles, but he managed to stand. He picked up the grenade and slipped it into his pocket. There was no need for them to see that. He would have to quickly come up with an excuse to explain his own dishevelled appearance, his stained shirt and the fact that he had wet himself.

The shocked, horrified looks on his children's faces said it all. They ran towards him and sat beside him, even though the smell made them grimace. 'What happened? What's wrong?' said Kurt. His worried look convinced Herr Schmidt it was time to leave Italy for good. After all, there was nothing to stay there for. He had signed the vineyard back over to Lambrianu and the warning was more than enough to frighten the life out of him. Lambrianu was right. Just who could he report this to? Once it was investigated, he wouldn't have a leg to stand on. What was more, that grenade could have been real. He'd had a lucky escape.

'It's okay I just fell and banged my head. Nothing to worry about. It's okay.' He was trying his best to calm down Agnes, who was crying.

'Sorry we were away for so long, Dad. If we had known you were ill, we would have come straight back. We should call you an ambulance.' Looking at her guilt-ridden face made him feel worse. They were all he had in the world since his wife had died.

'No! There is no need for that. It's nothing, really, I just fell. I must have knocked myself out.' He sounded more like himself again.

'I will go and get you a drink.' Agnes stood up and made her way to the kitchen.

'Where have you been?' said Herr Schmidt.

'We've been at the vineyard. Jake and Tony are really nice guys. All of their family are there.' Kurt stopped himself short. Now he felt guilty for telling his father of the great time he had just had while his father had been ill and had needed him.

After trying his best to smile, Herr Schmidt took a sip of the cool water Agnes had brought him. Pain instantly shot through his mouth and he winced.

Agnes had also brought a bucket of soapy water to clean the floor.

'I must shower now and get cleaned up,' he said, standing up.

'Do you need help, Dad?' Kurt was already holding him up by his elbow. He could see his father was in pain and noticed his broken front teeth. 'That must have been one hell of a fall. Look, your teeth are broken.'

Herr Schmidt reached up to feel his mouth. He hadn't even realised. With Kurt's help, he hobbled towards the bathroom and let the boy run the shower. Afterwards, they would pack up straight away and leave this place for good.

12

INTRIGUE

'It's good to be home, Jake. Don't get me wrong, it's been an eventful holiday, but it's good to be back in the swing of things.' Standing at the end of the bar at the club, Tony smiled at the multicoloured lights flashing on the dance floor and people dancing and enjoying themselves. This was where he belonged. This was his empire.

'I agree, Tony. Whatever else we own, this was our first venture. This place is worth all of the others combined to me. We've grown up here.' Jake picked up his drink and looked across at his estranged wife, Sharon. She was laughing and talking and playing the hostess, handing over buckets of champagne.

'Haven't you two sat down and worked things out yet?'

'I think there is another guy on the scene and she has been having some very strange mood swings. She is always disappearing to her mother's.'

'You need to find out, Jake. If there is another guy, well, it wouldn't be the first time, would it? You need to know. You can't carry on like this.'

'Bloody hell, Tony. That was below the belt. The last time

Sharon had another guy was when she got pregnant with Jack. Why bring that up?' Jake was hurt that Tony had mentioned it. It had happened over twenty years ago. Sharon had found herself a new man and she had divorced Jake. When they remarried she was already pregnant with Jack and they'd agreed that he would never find out that Jake wasn't his real father.

'Because, Jake, I remember how hurt you were the last time and you left it too late to confront her. Maybe there isn't a guy in tow, but you need to sort it out. You look bloody miserable, mate.'

'I am, Tony. But if there is someone else, well, maybe like the last one he will leave as quick as he came.' Jake raised his glass and took another sip.

'Evening, Mr Lambrianu, Jake. How was your trip to Italy? Lovely place, I hear, although I haven't been there myself.'

Tony and Jake exchanged glances. The greedy chief inspector who had taken more than his fair share of backhanders in the past was on the scene again. Now what did he want? It was always good to have the chief of police in your back pocket, but this one always seemed to want that little bit more. Although to be fair, he had come in handy and his tip-offs had been worth the money at times.

'Chief Inspector. Nice to see you.' As usual, Tony laid on the charm. He waved at one of the barmaids to bring some drinks over. 'You're a whisky man if I remember, Inspector.' Again, Tony smiled. They didn't particularly like each other, but they had known each other for years.

Jake looked at Tony and felt like laughing. The inspector was such a scruffy bugger, Jake called him 'Columbo' after the famous TV detective. Jake made his excuses and left Tony to find out whatever was on the inspector's mind.

'Is there something I can do for you, Inspector? I didn't really have you down as a Friday night clubber. So, tell me, why are you here?'

'That's what I like about you, Tony. Straight to the point. Well, it's maybe more a case of what I can do for you. You're a very generous man, Tony. Very generous indeed.'

'Look, Inspector, if you want more money, you had better take that up with Ralph Gold. He sorts that side of things out.' Tony was about to walk away from this low life in disgust when the inspector stopped him.

'This doesn't involve Ralph Gold. It involves you. But if you're busy and want to get on with things, go ahead. You may as well while you can.' His droning monotone voice irritated Tony, but he had sparked some interest. What did this bastard know and at what price was he willing to sell it?

'I hear there is going to be a big drugs raid on a famous West End club soon.'

Smiling, Tony looked him square in the face. 'Well, that really does have nothing to do with me and it's not worth mentioning, let alone paying for.'

The inspector took a sip of his whisky. 'Nothing to do with you, you say? Well, it's your name above the door, isn't it?'

Shocked, Tony looked at him. What the hell did he mean, his name above the door? He had never been involved in drugs; they all knew this. So what was all this about?

'Why don't we go to my office, Inspector?' Tony started to move but the inspector stopped him.

'No. I don't want my superiors thinking I have quiet cosy chats in your office, now, do I?'

Tony realised this was serious. The inspector was usually only too grateful to go to his office and wait while he opened the safe to give him his money.

Tony leaned forward on the bar to whisper, 'What does this place have to do with a drugs raid?'

'Look around you. Lots of goings on in here. I see Jake's wife has made some new friends.'

The man's greasy smile annoyed Tony. He was saying a lot about nothing. Following the inspector's gaze, his eyes stopped at Sharon. She was talking to a young man and his friends. A frown crossed his brow. They weren't part of his regular crowd and he didn't recall seeing them before. The way they were dressed didn't shout money but they must have been able to pay the entrance fee and Sharon was handing over yet another silver champagne bucket.

'Seems her new friends like to hang around all the best places. I'll be in touch, Tony.' The inspector gulped back the last of his whisky.

'What's Sharon got to do with it? Why are you involving her?' Tony was trying to remain calm and not throttle him like he wanted to. He wanted answers and this cat and mouse game was getting on his nerves.

'Now, Tony, calm down. I am an officer of the law and a very influential one. Don't use that tone with me. Something is going down next week. Cinderella time. I presume it will be a club night. I will be in touch.' Turning, the inspector walked away, leaving Tony with a lot to think about.

'Oh, God, what did Columbo want?' Jake could see those blue eyes of Tony's had darkened somewhat. It was his biggest give-away. You could tell his mood just by looking into those eyes.

'Who are those guys over there that Sharon's talking to? I don't recall seeing them before. How long have they been coming in here?' Arching his eyebrows, Tony signalled to the bar staff to fill his glass again.

Jake followed Tony's stare. Tony was right. There was a new

bunch of men that he hadn't seen in there before and Sharon was laughing and sharing a glass of champagne with them.

'I don't know who they are. Why?' Looking at the happy scene made Jake feel sick. Sharon had always played a great hostess, but she actually looked like she was enjoying herself. It was the first time he had seen her laugh in ages.

'Maybe you should ask her. She looks pretty friendly with that one leaning on the bar near her. If I didn't know better, Jake, I would say she was flirting.'

'What's wrong, Tony? What has that copper said that has wound you up so much and why are you picking on Sharon? She does a good job. She laughs and talks with the punters. It's never been a problem before.' Jake was upset and he looked over at Sharon again in her black knee-length lace dress, her blonde ponytail hanging down her back, swishing around as she joked with these strangers. She looked good tonight. That was what upset him. She hadn't dressed to impress him. She probably hadn't even noticed he was there.

'Have you heard of any of the clubs around here dealing drugs? That copper seems to think a nightclub around here might be doing something like that.' Tony took another sip of his drink and glanced over again at Sharon. Something just wasn't right and he couldn't put his finger on it, which annoyed him.

'Well, what's that got to do with us? Fuck, he's a shit stirrer.'

Tony looked at his watch. 'Damn!' He always said goodnight to Adam, and it was way past his son's bedtime. 'I'm going to the office to ring Fran. I'll see you in a minute.'

Walking around the bar, Tony saw Sharon hand over another bucket of champagne. He couldn't bite his tongue any more. As he passed where Sharon stood with her new friends, he pushed his way to the front. 'You're going at it tonight, boys. Special occasion, is it?' Noticing Sharon's embarrassment, he couldn't stop himself and leaned in further. 'Your husband is over there, Sharon. Why not go and share a joke and a drink with him?' Mission accomplished. His comment had wiped the smile off her face and quietened down the laughter from the men. 'Enjoy your evening, guys.' With that, he walked towards his office. He felt a little bit better now he'd had his say. Why was she flirting in front of her husband? What kind of a woman was she? But something about the guy at the front, the main one she was talking to, made him curious. He was sure he had seen him before, but couldn't think where.

Brushing his hair back from his face, he sat down in his chair and rang Francesca. The phone was picked up almost immediately.

'Daddy, is that you?'

Adam's tired voice calmed him and made him smile to himself. He heard his son yawn.

'And just what are you doing up at this time of night young man?' He heard a giggle on the other end of the telephone. It warmed his heart and reminded him what a very lucky man he was.

'Waiting for you. I knew you'd ring. We've had pizza with Iron Man.' Adam chatted away, not leaving room for replies. '*Buona notte*, Papa.'

'*Buona notte*, Adam, *ti amo*.'

Adam passed the telephone over to Francesca.

'Sorry it's so late, Francesca. Are you okay?'

'We're fine, Tony. Adam wanted to wait up. He's been dozing on the sofa and as soon as he heard the telephone he jumped up. Well, Mr L, you have said goodnight and I love you to Adam. What about me?'

Francesca's warm laugh made Tony feel better and put him at his ease. 'You, my very sexy lady, will have to wait until tomorrow.'

After their usual flirty chat, which Tony enjoyed even more knowing that Adam was sitting beside Francesca, he hung up. He could be suggestive and teasing and sometimes downright naughty. Hearing her replies made him laugh out loud. He was still laughing to himself when the office door opened and Jake came in.

Tony gave Jake a knowing wink and a smile. Speaking to Francesca had put Tony in a better mood. Everything was okay with the world now. But it wasn't, was it?

'Jake, have you noticed anyone taking or selling drugs here? Are there any known drug dealers hanging around this place? Even outside?'

'Do you think the bouncers are supplying people? It's not unheard of. But definitely not in here, I'm sure of it. Come on, Tony, let's have a drink. It's possible that inspector was just winding you up.'

'Maybe so. But he's a rattlesnake and if he thinks he has something worth selling he won't be making jokes. Let's keep an eye on the bouncers. Question them and body search them if we have to. I don't care. This shit needs clearing up quickly.'

'Okay. Let's see to it. But I am pretty sure Sharon would have noticed something like that.'

'Really? She seemed pretty occupied to me, Jake.' Tony could have bitten his tongue. He didn't want to hurt Jake by bringing up the obvious, but he couldn't help it.

'Thanks, Tony, I needed that. Whatever you think of mine and Sharon's marriage, just leave it alone for now, will you?'

'Okay. Come on, let's have that drink and then sort out some business.' Standing up, Tony put his arm around Jake's shoulders. 'Brothers in arms, yeah?'

The schoolboy grin spread across Jake's face. 'Always, mate. Always.'

13

SUNDAY LUNCH

Tony seemed preoccupied. Francesca noticed he was being his usual charming self, but she could see there was something else on his mind. Probably business.

Elle busied herself around the kitchen. She loved these family Sundays, everyone popping in whenever they could and sharing their week over lunch.

Ralph had eaten his fill. He rubbed his stomach and sat back in his chair with his glass of wine. 'Well, Tony lad, what do you think of the police commissioner retiring? That's something I never expected.'

'Retiring? Since when?' Tony was surprised to hear this. 'I thought commissioners stayed in that job forever. After all, they don't do much, do they?' Looking across at Diana, Tony gave her a weak smile. 'Sorry, Diana, no offence. Guess we have to be nice about the boys in blue now you're one of them.'

'Don't worry about it, Uncle Tony. Everyone says the same.'

'Maybe he's just had enough and wants to retire while he can still enjoy himself,' said Ralph. 'He's having some farewell do at a hotel or something next Saturday. Do you want to come?' Ralph looked across at Jake and nodded. 'That includes you, too. Sorry, Jake, I forget to ask you sometimes, I just presume you come as a pair.'

'We're not a couple, Ralph. I do things on my own sometimes. No, I don't want to go. He's probably been kicked out, anyway. Everyone knows he's been on the take for years.' Jake looked at Tony. 'Unless you want me there?'

Nearly choking on her dinner, Julie let out a huge laugh. 'I thought you just said you weren't a couple? Sounds like it to me. Anyway, watch your mouth, eh?' Julie gave a sideways glance towards Diana.

Jake raised his eyebrows. Having Diana around meant having to choose your words more carefully. God, this was going to be more difficult than he'd thought.

'You don't have to walk on eggshells, Jake, Mum. I'm not on duty now,' Diana snapped. She was already getting fed up with the way everyone skirted around her.

Jake laughed. 'You lot are never off duty.' Raising his glass to his lips, Jake looked around the table.

'I've just had a thought, Ralph,' Tony said, ignoring the banter around the room. 'We've all known the commissioner for years. Why don't we throw him a party at the club... say, Friday night? Then he can have his official retirement party on Saturday at the hotel, which usually means he's going to get a gold watch and a gold-plated pension for all his years of hard work.'

'Good idea, Tony. I think he'd appreciate the gesture even if he didn't want to come. Yes. Let's do that. Friday, you say?' Ralph nodded his approval and smiled.

'He'll expect more than a gold watch off us.' Jake couldn't help but show his resentment for the commissioner.

'Will you be quiet, Jake? If you don't have anything constructive to say, eat another roast potato,' said Tony.

Jake's face was a picture. Leaning across, he helped himself to more food.

'Bloody hell, Jake. Do you eat on demand as well?' Julie couldn't help but have her dig at Jake, who always seemed to do as he was told. 'Anyway, you, Dominic. You don't have much to say for yourself. How long have you and Scarlet been seeing each other?' A grin spread across Julie's face as she saw a frown appear on Tony's brow.

'Not long, Mrs Gold.' Dominic felt intimidated sitting with this woman at the table.

Flamboyantly waving her hand in the air and smiling, she said, 'You can call me Julie now you're part of the family.' Julie winked at Francesca, who was giving her an icy stare, which she ignored. 'Mrs Gold makes me sound like Ralph's mother.'

Putting down his fork, Tony looked across at Dominic. 'Yes. Just how long have you been sniffing around?' Now Julie had brought it to his attention, Tony felt the need to interrogate Dominic, too.

'Papa, you know how long.' Scarlet's face flushed and she reached out for Dominic's hand.

Looking at her daughter, Francesca saw Scarlet's blue eyes shining like sapphires. She was blushing and holding on to Dominic's hand. She had seen those eyes shine before; the only difference was, they had been Tony's eyes, when he looked at her. Francesca realised then that Dominic was here to stay, whether he wanted to or not!

'And you, Christopher.' Francesca changed the subject. 'How are you?'

'Very well, thank you, Mrs Lambrianu. Thank you for inviting me.' As usual, Christopher spoke with proper respect and ignored Julie's comment about sounding like the men's mothers when he called them 'Mrs'.

Scarlet couldn't help herself blurting out her thoughts, just like her father. 'I'm going to marry Dominic,' she said.

'What?' Tony exploded. 'Where the hell did that come from?' Coughing and nearly choking on his wine, Tony held his napkin to his mouth.

Francesca patted his back and shook her head at Scarlet. God, she knew how to stir things up. The worst thing was the shocked expression on Dominic's face.

Julie laughed shrilly. This was the excitement she had hoped for.

'No. No, we're not, Mr Lambrianu.' Dominic tried to appease Tony.

Even though Tony was trying to compose himself, the daggers he threw at Scarlet said more than words could have. 'I should bloody hope not. I didn't spend all that money on private schools so that you could marry some randy mechanic.' Tony didn't realise his insult. Just like Scarlet, he had opened his mouth without thinking.

Jake was just about to remind Tony that he had been a 'randy mechanic' once when Tony threw him a stare.

'You can shut your mouth as well,' he said. He knew what Jake was going to say but didn't want to hear it.

'Papa. How could you?' Scarlet was just about to leave the table when Dominic grabbed her arm.

'No, Scarlet. Your dad is right. He wants better for you. I take home maybe eight hundred or more a month. You own your own business. I can see his point.'

Tony nodded, satisfied.

'If you feel like that, why don't you work for yourself?' Adjusting his glasses after directing the question at Dominic, Christopher waited.

'I don't have the funds, Christopher. Setting up would cost a fortune. I would need a garage and all the equipment. That alone is out of my reach.' Dominic looked embarrassed at having to admit this.

'See, now he wants you to buy him a garage! Bloody hell, you didn't wait very long, did you?' said Tony. He felt this confirmed everything he had said about Scarlet being the golden goose.

'Well, I wasn't aware Mum was a millionaire when you met her, Papa.' Snapping at her father was unusual for Scarlet, but Francesca watched as her daughter defended Dominic.

'She's right, Tony. That's how people thought of me when we met,' Francesca reminded him. She knew this would stop his outburst.

'It's different for women. Men are supposed to be the bread-winners.'

'You chauvinist prick,' Julie couldn't help but chip in.

Staying calm, Christopher carried on. 'You could start as a mobile mechanic. You would need a van and some equipment, but you could begin with small jobs. Build up a reputation. You can also apply for a small business grant.'

Flabbergasted, Tony looked around the table at the sea of faces. Everyone seemed to be smiling to themselves. Only he felt that this Christopher guy had too much to say.

Ignoring the angry looks Tony was shooting him, Christopher continued. 'Come and see me, Dominic. Maybe we could work something out. Do you have any savings?'

Again, Dominic blushed. He could see all this talk was not going down well. He had come to ingratiate himself with Tony and now he felt he had just made an enemy.

'I could help,' Scarlet said.

'No, Scarlet, you couldn't. You're not a meal ticket to me.'

'Well said, young man.' At last, Ralph, who had calmly been watching the proceedings, spoke up. 'This young Christopher seems to have a good eye for business. And young Dominic here seems to have some pride. Let's see, shall we, Tony? Now, Elle, where is your famous trifle?'

Tony realised that the conversation was over. With that, he went back to his original conversation. 'This party for the commissioner, then, Ralph. Will you suggest it to him? Friday night is always a busy night at the club but I am sure we could close for the night or use one of the VIP rooms in his honour.'

Ralph nodded, satisfied. Now he could put things into action. Looking across at Julie, Ralph smiled.

After waving everyone off and saying his goodbyes, Tony was pulled aside by Jake. 'What is all this about, Tony? You hate that slimy commissioner as much as the rest of us. Now you want to throw a party in his honour?'

'Firstly, Jake, we don't know who is taking over from him. Sometimes it's best to keep your friends close and your enemies closer, eh? Secondly, what that inspector said has unnerved me. If something is going to happen on a club night, it would be a Friday or a Saturday. He has his hotel do on Saturday, so Friday night it is. Who's going to raid a club full of coppers? We'll talk about this more tomorrow. In the meantime, keep your mouth shut.'

'What if the kind inspector is just sounding off?' Jake's voice dripped with sarcasm.

'If he is, well, we had a party for the commissioner and his friends. It doesn't hurt to keep on the right side of the law.'

Even Jake realised that Tony had a point.

As the cars sped away out of the drive, Tony looked at Elle and Francesca. 'Well, that didn't go too badly, did it?' His grin was wide and his expression full of surprise as he saw them both roll their eyes and shake their heads.

Elle walked away, leaving Tony and Francesca at the doorway.

Putting his arm around her shoulders and pulling her towards him, Tony tried again. 'Does that mean I'm still on a promise?' The schoolboy grin spread across his face in hope of the night to come.

'Well, it went better than I expected, so maybe... just maybe.' Raising her lips to his, Francesca gave him a quick peck and walked down the hallway. She stopped short when she heard Tony shout 'Yes!' and shook her head in dismay.

Francesca looked round to see Tony grinning and swaying back and forth in some form of jig. Shaking her head, she couldn't help laughing, and looked down the hallway towards Elle, who just gave her one of those exasperated looks.

'Boys will always be boys, Francesca, no matter how you dress them up.'

14

DIANA'S TURMOIL

'Oh, God, Di, do me a favour and take this to Mr High and Mighty, Terry the fat pervert.' Taking the teabag out of yet another mug, Vicki rolled her eyes.

'Why don't they get it from the canteen like all of the others? Anyway, surely taking the inspector's tea gets you noticed?'

The two young police officers stood side by side in the poky kitchenette off the incident room. It was small, airless and a total disgrace. 'Oh, yes, it gets me noticed, all right. A young blonde police officer, still on probation, accidentally getting her arse felt by the inspector. Who am I going to complain to? Please, Di, you take it.'

Diana looked down at the tray of tea-stained mugs. 'Okay, but if he touches my arse, you owe me one. What are they working on, anyway? There's loads of them in the incident room.'

'Oh, I don't know, Di, some big drugs raid or something. Knock once and if he doesn't answer, go in and put the mug on his desk, then get out of there as quick as you can.' They both burst out laughing.

Diana straightened her hat and brushed down her uniform, then picked up the tray and left the room.

After knocking on the door, she waited. No answer. She opened the door and set the mug on the desk full of folders and paperwork. As she did so, something caught her eye. There was a folder beside the computer with 'Lambrianu' written at the top. She looked around to see if anyone was about and then moved the folder aside, and saw there was another very thick folder underneath, headed 'Ralph Gold'. She felt sick. There was obviously something in these folders that all those officers in the incident room were working on. Puzzled, she was just about to open the folder out of curiosity, when she heard a cough behind her.

'Morning. Is that my tea?' Vicki had been right. The dishevelled inspector behind her was indeed fat.

'Yes, sir. And some biscuits.' Diana felt herself blush and looked down at the floor. She couldn't wait to get out of there.

'Well, off you go then.' Picking up a biscuit, the inspector dipped it in his mug of tea then put it in his mouth. Diana made a hasty exit. Once outside she breathed a sigh of relief. But she couldn't help wondering: why did the drug and fraud squad have folders on Tony and her father? As far as she knew they had never been involved in anything like that. But then she didn't know everything. She was puzzled and confused. This was the conflict of interest she had been warned about. She knew what she had to do, but she was afraid.

'Mum, can we talk? Preferably not on the telephone and the house is too far.' Diana had called Julie from one of the few telephone boxes left in the city.

'You sound nervous, Diana. Are you okay?' There was a pause on the end of the telephone that Julie didn't like. Her instincts were usually right. Something was wrong. 'Where do you want to meet?'

'The library in Streatham. And don't come all dressed up. I don't want people to recognise you. It will be nice and quiet there. I won't be in uniform.' With that, Diana put the telephone down.

Two hours later, a very different Julie walked into Streatham library. She was totally unrecognisable. Even Diana wasn't sure if it was her. Wearing old jeans, trainers and a fleecy jacket, without make-up and with her hair tied back, Julie waltzed in and sat at one of the tables.

'So, I take it this must be bad, Diana. Well, it had better be, and not just some argument you've had with a boyfriend. Bloody hell, I haven't been without make-up in years.' Julie was trying to make light of it, but could see how nervous and troubled her daughter looked.

Diana went on to tell a silent Julie the whole story. Julie's face never moved. She listened intently to what her daughter was saying. Half of her felt sad that her daughter, who was very pleased with her career choice, was compromising herself like this.

'Well, that's a revelation.' Reaching over and squeezing Diana's hand, Julie smiled to reassure her.

'Are Dad and Uncle Tony involved in drugs?' Diana whispered.

Pondering Diana's words, Julie paused. Just how much should she tell Diana? 'I don't want to lie to you Diana. Your father and I have suspicions about Sharon. The police suspect your father and Tony of embezzlement at the casino in Paris and possibly here... You know Sharon and Jake haven't been getting along lately; well, I know she has a lover. A younger man. It seems whatever her gripe is, she wants us all to suffer. For the moment, Diana, that is really all I know.'

As much as Julie wanted to scream and shout, she knew this wasn't the place. 'I know this must be very hard for you.' Julie sat back. 'You need to pack up your things and move out. Distance yourself from us completely, that way you're not involved in this.' Julie watched the shocked expression on Diana's face. 'Stay away from the club, the family and definitely me and your father. You're very clever, Diana. You used a public phone. If you ever need anything, that is the way to do it. If it's dire, you can always contact Elle. I'm sure you understand this is for the best. Give it a few months to die down, love. I'll sort it. You have a good career in front of you and I don't want this to spoil it for you. God knows, if I'd had the choice, I might have done things differently, but that's a different story. I'm going now. Leave about half an hour after me.' With that, Julie stood up. She could see the tears welling up in her daughter's eyes and didn't want to prolong their goodbye.

'Mum, does this mean you never want to see me again?'

'Don't be ridiculous, Diana. It means I'm protecting you. I don't want you dragged into any of this scandal. Let the dust settle and keep your nose clean.' With that, Julie walked away, leaving a very forlorn Diana in her wake.

Outside, Julie shouted into her mobile, angry that it had gone straight to answerphone. 'Ralph. No arguments and no excuses. Get yourself home, now.' Julie knew he was in a meeting, but once he got that message he would come straight away, and she was right.

A few hours later Ralph turned up and threw his case down in the hallway, then walked into the drawing room. He didn't know what to expect but he knew Julie wouldn't summon him unless it was urgent.

'What is it, Julie? What's wrong?'

'Pour yourself a drink, Ralph. No, pour us both one, and then I'll tell you.'

Ralph did as he was told then held a glass out to Julie and sat opposite her.

After taking a large gulp, Julie recounted the whole story of her meeting with Diana. His first reaction was anger. Anger once again that Diana had joined the police force in the first place and anger that Julie had told her everything.

'Just be bloody glad she has, Ralph. Did you know they had folders on you and Tony? No. I didn't think so. Neither did I. I never realised it was this big. A huge incident room discussing all your antics. All those police friends of yours will run a mile with an investigation like this. This has all been kept very hush-hush. They have all had their fingers in the till, but now you're on your own. God knows, Ralph, she has put everything on the line for you and don't you forget it.'

'Sorry, Julie. You're right, of course.' Taking another drink, Ralph nodded. He didn't want his daughter dragged into this mess and even he realised it would have cost him a lot of money to obtain this kind of information from some informer. In a quieter voice, he asked, 'Does she despise me?'

'Don't be silly, Ralph.' Julie put her arms around him and hugged him. She was touched that, no matter what Ralph had to face, it was what Diana thought about him that bothered him most. Julie stood up and poured herself another drink. 'The thing is, Ralph, now that you have this information, what are you going to do with it?'

'Jesus. I don't know yet.' Ralph sat back. This had really knocked the wind out of his sails. 'But you have had all day to think about this. So, what have you come up with? I know that little brain of yours. Come on, out with it.'

'I've told Diana to distance herself from the family. Don't you go contacting her.' Julie waved her finger in his face. 'She knows how to contact us if need be.'

'You've told Diana she's not a part of this family any more? For

God's sake, Julie, you can't do that.' Ralph was shocked that Julie could even suggest not seeing his daughter.

'Of course she has to distance herself from this. A bent copper is not the title she wants! Now, tell me about Tony and what he said to you in Paris.'

'Well, he's gutted, of course. Sharon, Jake and he were all kids together. They have trusted each other for decades.'

'We have to have a closed meeting. This needs nipping in the bud, now. Today.'

'I'll put the casino on the market. We need to distance ourselves from that, too.'

'Good. I don't care if you burn it to the ground. We don't need it. I do believe Sharon is more involved in this than we realise. I don't know if she is in league with the police to save her own skin or what. See if you can find out anything from those police friends of yours. They must know something.'

'I will do. Sharon is setting us all up for a fall. She is betraying us. Do you realise what this could mean for us?'

'No. I'm not even thinking about that, because I'm going to make sure we find that bitch first and see who has the last laugh then. I must admit, though, even I didn't realise it would be as big as this. Just what has been said and done, eh?'

15

SHARON

'Is everything ready?' Tony, Jake and Ralph walked around the club. All the banners and balloons were in place for a great retirement party.

'Well done, lads,' Ralph said. Although he knew this was more down to the staff than Tony and Jake, it looked amazing.

'Where's Sharon?' Normally she would be here, organising things. Sharon's absence bothered Tony, knowing what he did about her. That alone made Tony feel nervous.

'I don't know. It's not like her to miss something like this,' said Jake. He called over to the bar staff, 'Where's Sharon?'

They shrugged and then one said, 'Maybe it's her mum again. She got a call earlier and rushed off.'

Perturbed, Jake looked at Tony. 'Do you think I should give her a ring to see if her mum's okay?'

'No, leave it. We have things to do and if it's anything severe, she'll ring you.'

'Maybe that's the problem, Jake. Maybe she thinks you don't care about her family. Have you been with her to see her mother?' Ralph asked.

Jake shook his head. It wasn't for lack of wanting to support Sharon, it was more the case that he hadn't been invited.

'Maybe you should take more of an interest in Sharon's visits to her family, especially as her mother is so ill.' Ralph eyed Jake suspiciously.

'I suppose so, Ralph. But Sharon always tells me not to bother and me and her family are not on the best of terms.' Jake was loath to admit this to Ralph; he looked to Tony for help.

'Don't talk to me about in-laws.' Tony guffawed. 'We never hear from Francesca's mum. At least her brothers are okay. They visit often, work permitting, and they all have decent jobs and families of their own now.' Tony did feel sad for Francesca. Her mother had completely washed her hands of her. He felt guilty about this but there was nothing he could do. At least she had Elle and Julie.

'Ah, well, lads, let's have a drink before the wives get here and the proceedings start.' Ralph chinked his glass against theirs.

The evening seemed to be a roaring success. The commissioner was more than delighted with his party.

Ralph had invited everyone, including all his friends from the Masonic lodge, to give speeches in honour of their valued member, as well as presents. As much as the commissioner told everyone they shouldn't have bothered buying him a gift, Ralph could see he was bloody glad they had!

'What's up, Tony? You seem twitchy.' Jake was surprised at the way Tony was patrolling the room. 'Everything's going great. There are more coppers here than in the whole force. God, has every station in the country turned up for free booze and food?'

'I know, that's what I can't understand. There is just something I can't put my finger on. Maybe I'm being paranoid. Call it gut instinct, but something isn't right. I need to go and have a chat with that inspector. This jigsaw puzzle just doesn't fit.' Tony walked over and stood at the inspector's side.

'Are you having a good time, Inspector?' He flashed his most charming smile and held out his hand, but he was horrified by the reception he got.

'I am, Mr Lambrianu. The question is, are you? Well, it's not midnight yet. Enjoy it while you can.'

'Meaning?' Tony's stomach flipped and he felt sick. This hadn't been paranoia. Something was wrong. Glancing at his watch, he saw that it was just after 11 p.m. Not quite midnight.

'I had better go, Tony. Leave you to the fun and games.' He gulped back his drink. The sneering smile on the inspector's face made Tony's blood run cold.

Tony walked around the room in a panic, watching everyone, but he was at a loss. What exactly was he looking for?

'Mr Lambrianu.' One of the waitresses wanted his attention. He couldn't be bothered with their complaints. He had business to deal with.

'Mr Lambrianu,' the waitress persisted.

'What?' he snapped. 'What is it that cannot wait?'

'Sorry, sir. It's just that you were looking for Sharon earlier and I've just seen her go into one of the booths.' With that, she walked away.

Sharon was here and no one had seen her? 'Jake. Do you know where Sharon is at this moment?'

'Yes.' Jake was a little tipsy and smiled in a drunken way. 'I told you, she is with her mother. Why?'

'And you haven't seen her come in here?'

Jake shook his head.

Sweeping his hair back in his usual fashion, Tony stormed off and walked around the dance floor again. Everyone was in high spirits, dancing and laughing. He decided to check the booths. After opening the private doors, he stood in shocked horror at the sight before him.

Sharon was in there with three men. One of them he recognised as the young man she had been flirting with the other day. They had cocaine lined up on the table in front of them. Each of them had a straw and was sniffing it.

Trying to remain calm, Tony walked in and shut the door behind him. Sharon did not seem dismayed by this, but then he noticed her dilated pupils and realised she was so full of the stuff she didn't care. Now it all made sense. What had Jake said? That she'd been having mood swings?

'Mr Lambrianu!' One of the men jumped out of his seat. He was shocked at being caught in the act.

'What the fuck are you doing?' Tony said through gritted teeth. 'Don't you realise we have the whole of the Metropolitan Police Force on the other side of this door?' Tony tried his best to hold his temper. He didn't want to cause a scene or for anyone to hear him shouting.

One of the men spoke up. 'Sharon said it was okay and that you knew all about it.'

Tony looked at the four of them with white powder on their upper lips and noses. Cocaine had been spilt on the floor; it was everywhere, even on their jacket sleeves where they had leant on the table to snort it.

'Know what, Sharon?' Tony grabbed hold of her hair and pulled her head back. 'What is it he thinks I know, you fucking bitch?'

The frightened young man blurted words out, speaking more out of fear than common sense. 'We sell it here. You know that. You have known about it for months.' The man turned to look at Sharon.

'Let go of me, Tony, you're hurting me.' Sharon grabbed hold of his hand to loosen his grip on her hair. 'If you don't let go, I will shout so fucking loud, all of that lot out there will come in here and see you attacking a woman. And let's not forget all of this.' After dipping her finger into the cocaine, Sharon licked it. 'It's all bought with your money, Tony. Now, fucking let go of me and go and lick the commissioner's arse.' Sarcasm dripped from Sharon's mouth as she swayed unsteadily.

Tony was stunned and rooted to the spot. The last thing he needed was for her to scream out. The inspector had been right. They must have been watching them for months. Tony glanced at his watch. It wasn't quite midnight, but he had to work fast.

'Stay in here. Do you hear me? We'll sort this later.' Letting go of Sharon's hair, he walked out and shut the door behind him and mopped his brow. He felt sick.

Now he had to think on his feet. There was no time to plan. He walked down the hallway towards his office as calmly as he could, without attracting too much attention. He smiled at people as he passed them, then entered his office and shut the door.

As he took deep, calming breaths, he looked up at the ceiling. A thought occurred to him. It was worth a try and for now it was all he had. Pulling out the chair, he stood on it. He wobbled slightly and tried to steady himself. The last thing he needed now was to break his neck.

Taking out his lighter, he held it under the smoke alarm. Immediately, the piercing noise of the alarm filled his office. He left the room and ran down the hallway towards the party, where he smashed the glass on the fire alarm button.

All the alarms came on at once, the sound reverberating throughout the club. People stopped what they were doing and turned to look at each other. Suddenly, the sprinklers in the ceiling started spraying out cold water over everyone.

There were screams and howls as everyone ran for the exit. Some were slipping on the floor, which was now sodden, and falling to their knees. What only a few minutes ago was a bustling dance floor now looked like a swimming pool. People were scrambling over each other in panic while water rained down on them. Now it was time for Tony to act.

'Sorry, folks,' Tony shouted, trying to gain their attention. 'Can everyone slowly make their way to the exit? The staff will help you.' Looking towards the bar staff and waitresses, Tony pointed his thumb in the direction of the soaking crowd. He was drenched. Water was dripping off the end of his nose. Brushing his wet hair back, he scanned the room for Francesca. Then he spotted her running out of the toilets.

'Francesca! Francesca!' he shouted over the screaming crowd, trying to make himself heard. Seeing her look at him, he waved his arm and pointed to the exit. 'Get out. Now.'

She started pushing her way past people then bent down and took her shoes off. Her hair, which had been up, now hung wet around her shoulders, and her make-up was smudged.

'I'm not leaving you here, Antonias. Come with me,' she shouted, as she was pushed and shoved backwards. Thankfully, he saw Julie; she was wet through, and she looked at him with a curious expression, then she grabbed Francesca by the arm and pulled her away from the crowd, towards the exit.

Tony looked around at the sodden night club. His pride and joy. It was ruined. But he'd had no choice.

'What the fuck has happened?' Jake was at Tony's side, soaked to the skin.

'You play with fire, Jake, you get your fingers burnt.' Tony ignored the frown on Jake's face. Now was not the time to explain. 'Come on, let's see what's happening outside.' Looking once more around the almost empty club, Tony felt sick to his stomach. Well, at least whatever cocaine powder was around had now been washed away and that was the most important thing.

Outside, Tony could hear sirens. Everyone seemed to be shivering from the night air and the wetness of their clothes, and looking and checking for their partners to make sure they had got out safely.

The sound of sirens grew louder, and Tony looked up to see three police cars and a police van. Curious, he turned to Jake. There were more sirens in the background, which he presumed would be the fire brigade.

Police jumped out of their cars and stopped in their tracks, seeing all the people on the pavement. Then the officer in charge walked forward.

'Mr Lambrianu. We have reason to believe that you have been dealing and importing drugs into your nightclubs.' Ignoring the fracas outside, the officer in charge started to read Tony his rights.

Ralph walked towards them. 'What the hell is going on here? It's a fire alarm. Why is he under arrest?'

The commissioner approached the arresting officer, wanting to make his presence known. The officer in charge paled at the sight of him. 'What the hell are you doing? Can't you see all these people need help? Now, what is all this about?'

The commissioner was fuming. Not only had his party come to a dramatic halt, but he was soaked to the skin. His best police uniform, with all of its shiny buttons and emblems, was ruined, and now he was being accused of drug taking?

'Sorry, sir. We didn't know you were having a party here tonight, sir. But we do have good reason to believe that Mr Lambrianu has been selling drugs on these premises.'

Tony caught sight of the chief inspector, who seemed to be

there as a spectator. He had been right. 'It's okay, Commissioner. I will go with them and answer any of their questions. I have nothing to hide. Especially not in this wet suit.' Now composed, Tony turned on the charm and smiled at them all innocently.

'You will do no such thing, Mr Lambrianu. You have enough to deal with here.' The commissioner was adamant Tony was going nowhere. He looked embarrassed and horrified at his host being accused in front of all these people. Some were checking their mobile phones and taking pictures, and the newspaper journalists had turned up in their droves too. This just got worse and worse. But for Tony, it got better and better!

'Get out of here and take this farce with you,' the commissioner screamed at the arresting officer. 'I will speak to you and your superiors tomorrow.'

The red-faced woman could do nothing but walk back to her vehicle.

'My car is at your disposal, commissioner. Please, take your wife home, it's been a long night.' Ralph waved his chauffeur forward and made him give his coat to the commissioner's wife.

'Of course,' Tony shouted towards what was left of the diminishing crowd, 'any expense from damage to your clothing and personal items will be duly paid for by me. Please don't let all of this spoil your night.'

'Let's go home, Tony. It's been a hell of a night. And your suit is stuck to you like a second skin. Come on.' Francesca, who was shivering with cold, linked her arm in Tony's.

'No, you go. I have to see things are secure here.' He knew Francesca would argue the toss, so he appealed to Julie. 'Tell her, Julie.'

'Absolutely. Fran, come on, get in the car, you're shivering. He's got to see things are locked up. And don't tell him he is wet through and that his suit is sticking to him. God knows you can see through it. He probably thinks it's another kinky game.' Julie's comforting laugh put Francesca at ease and made her get into the car.

'Right, Tony, are you going to tell me what all this farce was about?' Ralph looked angry. He had kept a brave face for long enough and now he wanted to know what was going on.

'Jesus. Sharon!' Turning on his heels, Tony ran into the club. The fire crew were still in there, checking things over, and the sprinklers had been turned off. Soaked, limp food was left deserted on plates swimming in water. People had left their bags and personal possessions behind in the panic.

Running to the VIP booth, Tony opened the door. It was empty. Where the hell was she?

'Sharon? What has she got to do with this, Tony? Why would Sharon be in one of the booths? She hasn't been here all evening.' Jake was finding it very hard to comprehend Tony's actions. He seemed to be running around in circles like a cat on hot bricks.

'Run up to the apartment, Jake, and see if she's there,' he shouted. Before Jake could protest, he added, 'Just do it!'

Jake did as he was told.

'Are up going to tell me what's going on, Tony, or do I have to beat it out of you?' Looking through his damp packet of cigars, Ralph found a dry one and lit it.

'Just give me a minute, Ralph. Please, just wait.' Tony looked up as Jake came back downstairs.

'No, she's not up there. Why would she be?'

Letting out a huge sigh, Tony realised now was the time to explain. 'Find yourself somewhere dry to sit, fellas. Believe me, this is one hell of a story.'

Jake's jaw dropped to his chest as Tony told them what had

happened, while Ralph sat there, stony-faced. 'That is why I did what I did. It was the only thing I could think of that would wash that shit away. If they had come in and searched, they would have found that room with cocaine smeared everywhere and the four of them as high as kites. That's all that copper needed to throw the book at us.'

'Well.' Ralph's quiet, calm demeanour showed his displeasure. 'It seems Sharon has been having quite the time of it with her young man. Did you not suspect anything, Jake? Or, as usual, did you bury your head in the sand and hope it would go away? It's not the first time she's shit on you, is it?' His question was more of a statement.

They all sat there, sodden. The cold was starting to show on all of their faces. 'Let's go up to the apartment. We can get warm and changed up there. Let's secure this place and call it a night.' Tony was trying to sound in charge but was nervously waiting to hear Ralph's wrath.

'Okay. Good idea.' Ralph stood up and started walking towards the stairway to the apartment, then stopped short. The back exit door was ajar. 'I would say that is where Sharon and her young lover made their exit. Wouldn't you?'

Tony knew he was right. How else had Sharon got out without being noticed? He also knew that Ralph had emphasised the words 'young' and 'lover'. It was obvious that Ralph blamed Jake for this.

Turning to look at Jake, Tony could see the pain in his face. His whole world had just crumbled. His wife had a lover and she was a cocaine addict. Poor bastard. And now Ralph was blaming him.

Nothing was said once they entered the apartment. It was dry up there and each of them in turn took a hot shower. Tony made them all a hot drink to warm them up. 'Don't bother, Tony. I'll have a brandy,' said Ralph.

Tony had had enough. 'Whatever is on your mind, Ralph, I wish you would spit it out. Let's get it over with.'

Pulling his towelling robe closer around him and taking a sip of his brandy, Ralph sat down on the sofa. 'This is going to cost me a lot of money, and a lot of grovelling, making it up to the commissioner. If he hadn't been here, you would be in a police cell by now. Both of you. Drugs are not my thing, Tony, you know that.' Tony was about to say something, but Ralph held his hand up. 'You have asked me to speak, so let me speak. How have you never noticed that Sharon was passing drugs to your customers? More to the point, how was she doing it? Have none of your staff mentioned it? You've taken your eye off the ball, Tony, and it could have cost you your liberty. Find out from your staff what they know. And you, Jake. Bloody hell, man, you live with the woman. Okay, you've had your ups and downs, but nothing gave you any indication that things weren't right? I don't believe it. You just turned a blind eye to it all, hoping she would come back. Show him that bloody recording, Tony. You have had more than your fair share of time whilst you sorted things out in Italy. Now show him what that bitch is capable of.'

'Not now, Ralph. Please,' Tony said.

'Yes. Now, Tony. That woman has got to go. She is a ticking time bomb and I don't want her around to stir up any more shit. Show him.'

'What's happened?' Jake was puzzled. He couldn't understand why Ralph was shouting or why Tony was pleading with him. 'What recording? Just what is it you think you're protecting me from?'

'Sharon, mate. After you left Paris, I found out that she's been ripping us off and telling her bloke and his pals all about the money laundering. Believe me, Jake, I never wanted you to find out like this.' Leaving the room, Tony went into the bedroom to get the recording.

Jake froze as he stared at the screen. There was his wife with another man. The very woman that he loved had betrayed them all. Tears fell down his cheeks. He felt sick inside.

'Ralph. All I can say is that I'm sorry all of this shit has landed on your doorstep. You're right, I had an idea there was a new man on the scene and yes, I hoped once it was out of her system everything would return to normal. I admit that. I'm not a weak man, Ralph, you know that, but I suppose like all of us in this room, we have our weaknesses and well... Sharon was... is... mine.' Jake's shoulders shook as he started to sob. He didn't seem able to stop himself. He stood up and turned his back on them both, trying to compose himself.

'I don't know why she's done this; I can only think she's been influenced by that guy.' Tony tried sparing Jake's feelings but it was impossible. 'We need to find her. Where do you think she's gone, Jake?' Tony hadn't wanted Jake to find out like this. But Jake's bubble was well and truly burst now.

Turning around, Jake shook his head. 'I don't know. I doubt she has gone to family, knowing that's the first place we would look. We could easily trace her through her bank cards, I suppose.'

'Bollocks!' They both turned and looked at Ralph. 'Have you checked your safe, Tony?'

Daylight was dawning on Tony. He put his hands to his face and rubbed it. 'No, I haven't checked the safe or the tills, but Sharon has the keys to both. She has also had a couple of hours to go home, pack and fuck off to God knows where.'

'That money won't last forever. So, wherever she's gone, we

will find her.' Ralph was angry and determined to bring Sharon to justice, whether it hurt Jake or not.

Tony opened the door and made his way down the stairs. The cold water on his feet made him wince. Now he was warm, it felt even worse. He opened the safe in his office. Ralph was right – it was empty. Running out to the bar, Tony saw the till drawers were open. Sharon had taken everything!

16

THE FALLOUT

As he got home the next morning, Tony was greeted by Francesca.

'Tony, I've been so worried about you. How is everything? More to the point, how are you? Your beautiful club is ruined.'

'The club doesn't matter, Francesca. It's nothing that can't be fixed. It needed a make-over anyway.' Tony sounded almost nonchalant; he walked over and picked up Adam. 'How is my big guy?'

'Do they know what started it? What set off the alarms? Where was the fire, Tony?' Francesca persisted even though she could see Tony didn't want to talk about it.

'I don't know, Fran. They are looking into it. My guess is that someone was having a crafty fag somewhere and set the alarms off. Or it was some kind of practical joke. I don't know. I'm just shattered. I'm going to get my head down for an hour, if that's okay.'

'Of course. Go and get some sleep.'

After wearily climbing the stairs, Tony threw himself face down on the bed. He was physically and mentally drained.

* * *

'Oh, love, you look better. I was just going to put some food aside for you. I did come up once or twice but you were spark out.' Francesca started setting his place at the table.

'Long night, love. And now there is a lot to do. The club will be closed for a couple of weeks. It's a good excuse to have everything refurbished, anyway. Come here.' Cupping her heart-shaped face in his hands, Tony kissed her. It was a heartfelt kiss. Things could have gone so horribly wrong last night.

'Oh, get a grip, Lambrianu. Leave her alone and put her down.' Julie was sitting at the table with a bored expression on her face. 'Read this if you want something to do with your hands.' She was waving a newspaper at him.

'Yes, Dad. You have to see this. That poor commissioner is all over the headlines. God, there are going to be a lot of red-faced coppers at the station.' Katie was as eager as Julie for Tony to read the paper.

The commissioner was pasted all over the front page, outside the club. Another picture was of him face to face with the arresting officer. He looked angry and the camera had caught him just at the right angle. The snarl on his face was better than any headline they could have come up with.

'Bloody hell, Julie.' Tony flopped into a dining chair and carried on reading. Running his hand through his damp hair, Tony looked across the table towards Julie. 'Has Ralph seen this?'

'Yes, of course he has. He hasn't been sleeping all day like you, Goldilocks. He's been busy apologising and wiping the arse of that commissioner.'

'I had better go and see him. Help him out. Anyone heard from Jake?'

Julie gave Tony a sideways glance. It was pretty obvious that

Ralph had filled her in on all the details. 'No, I'm sure he's tired, like you.' Again, Julie's stare said it all. Whatever Ralph had Jake doing today, it wasn't to be discussed around the dining table in front of Francesca and the kids.

'You're probably right, Julie. Anyway, what are we eating?'

'I'm not staying. I have to see Ralph. Bye, girls.' Julie kissed Fran on the cheek and started to leave the room.

'Excuse me,' Tony barked. 'I do live here, too. Have you noticed, Francesca? She never says goodbye to me. I always have to prompt her.'

'Oh, shut up, you sulky schoolboy.' Julie walked back and planted a big kiss on his cheek, leaving a bright red imprint from her lipstick. Pouting then laughing, she said, 'Bye, Tony.'

Tony picked up the newspaper and threw it across the room towards the doorway as she was leaving. 'Bugger off!'

Julie's laughter filled the hallway as she left and slammed the door behind her.

Tony looked down at the plate of lamb casserole Elle had put in front of him. He was famished. He couldn't remember the last time he had eaten.

Everyone turned to look at each other over the dining table and smiled. Everything was back to normal. Scarlet started sniggering. 'Why do you let her get to you, Papa?'

'I'm thinking of charging her rent. She's here more often than she's at her own house. Every time I turn around, she's there. God. Even when we're in bed, Fran, I look over my shoulder in case she's stood behind me looking at my arse.'

'Tony!' Francesca held up her hand and pointed towards Adam. 'And I don't think the girls appreciate what you're saying.'

Again, Scarlet giggled; it was infectious and everyone joined in. The very thought of Tony looking over his shoulder in the bedroom was enough to make them all laugh out loud.

* * *

After dinner, Tony went into his study to call Ralph.

'You've had a busy day, sitting on your arse, Tony. But no, sorry, lad. You deserve it. Good bit of thinking, setting off the smoke alarms and the sprinklers. I like that. I have just stepped outside to take this call. I'm at the commissioner's official retirement party with his family and friends. Remember? The one I told you about. He is blowing off a lot of steam, but he's the one doing all of the apologising. Make sure he gets a nice retirement present. We'll meet up soon, Tony.' With that, Ralph ended the call.

Next, it was time for Tony to ring Jake.

'Jake, how's things? Sorry I haven't been in touch earlier. I slept late and then had dinner. Where have you been all day?'

'No worries. I've been trying to find Sharon, although I must admit I am afraid of what Ralph will do to her when I do. But she's disappeared, Tony. I've tried everyone I can think of, even Jack doesn't know where she is. She hasn't been in touch. Hell, I'm sorry, Tony.'

'Oy, shut it. This is not your fault. You're a victim here.' Tony could have bit his tongue. Victim was not the word he wanted to use. 'Look, this is nothing to do with you, and I won't have you blaming yourself. I do know, though, that if Sharon has been selling that stuff then we need to find it before the investigating fire crew do. Where the hell would she stash it?'

'I don't know, but you're right. Let's meet early and see if we can scour the place.'

'Where are you, Jake? What are you doing tonight?' Tony's concern was obvious. He didn't want Jake doing anything silly.

'I'm back at the house. Might as well; Sharon isn't coming

home anytime soon. I know we have a lot to do, but I also need some time to myself. I need to get my head around all of this.'

'Yes. Sure, mate. But if you need me and all that. Yeah, right, well, tomorrow it is.'

17

A DEALER'S DEN

'Jake, mate, I know it's early, but I wanted to get here before anyone else.' Tony got out of the car and looked around. 'We need to find where that shit is. And don't even think about complaining – I left a very warm and willing Francesca to sort this crap out. I was on a promise!'

Opening the doors, they both gagged then held their noses. 'It smells like someone has died in here.' Jake looked around the club. It was a lot worse than he had imagined it would be. Everything was still damp, and it stank.

It was dark inside and the floor still had puddles of water on it. 'How can we search for something when I can hardly see a thing?' Jake was tired and grumpy. He didn't know where to start looking. Worse still, he wasn't 100 per cent sure there was anything to look for.

'Shut up, will you, you miserable git, and get to work. Use the torch on your mobile for lighting if you have to. I know that stuff is here somewhere.' Tony walked to the other side of the room.

'Maybe her and her friends just had their own stash. Just

because they had it, it doesn't mean they were dealing it, does it?' Jake was still hopeful, but Tony knew it was useless.

'Yes, it does. Those coppers seemed damn sure this wasn't a personal thing. People have been talking. They know this is the place where they can get their drugs.' Sighing and looking at Jake's face, Tony could now understand Ralph's anger. Jake still didn't want to believe the worst of Sharon.

For a couple of hours they looked under cabinets, in the booths and even around the staging area, but nothing. Sitting on a chrome chair, Tony threw his head back in despair. Maybe Jake was right. Maybe the only stuff they had was what was on the table when he had walked in on them.

'It's just as well that water didn't touch the shelves near the champagne buckets. Those bars of soap would have made it look like a foam bath in here.' Jake laughed, pulling up a chair beside Tony.

Swiftly turning his head, Tony looked at Jake in the dimly lit room and frowned. 'Soap? Since when did we have bars of soap behind the bar? Show me.' Tony's stomach churned. This was what he had hoped for. He was sure of it.

As Jake bent down behind the bar and shone his torch on the second shelf, Tony was stunned. Kneeling down in the water, he pulled forward the blocks of 'soap'.

'You prick, Jake. That's not bars of soap. It's blocks of cocaine. You fucking idiot.' He reached to the back and pulled them out, counting as he did. There were five rectangular white blocks wrapped in cellophane.

It dawned on Tony that the night he had watched Sharon, she had been filling the buckets full of ice and bottles of champagne and handing them over the bar! Bloody hell, she had been dealing right under his nose and he had never noticed. What a bloody fool he'd been!

'This goes straight down the toilet. If those coppers had found this we would have been totally fucked! How could you not know what these are?' Fuming, Tony picked up the small blocks, pushed a couple of them into his jacket pocket and stood up with the rest in his hand.

'How the hell was I supposed to know that blocks of powdered cocaine look like bars of soap? Bloody hell, Tony, give us a break here. It seems I'm the whipping boy for everything.'

'Watch this, brother.' Picking up the knife they cut the lemons with, Tony stabbed the cellophane and held the block over a silver tray. They both stood in silence as the white powder poured out.

Jake looked at Tony. 'Shit! How much is all that worth, street value? There must be thousands there. How the hell did Sharon get all of that?'

'You mean bloody hundreds of thousands. That bloke of hers has got her so addicted to this shit she isn't thinking straight. A few soft words and a young face and that silly cow has fallen for it. Oh, for God's sake, take the hurt look off your face.' Tony shouted. His gut instinct had been right and he was angry. If the police had found this they would have had a field day. 'Let's get rid of it. Furthermore, not a fucking word about this lot to Ralph Gold. He will go apeshit!'

'Do you think there's any more?' The cold light of day was at last dawning on Jake. Sharon had set them up. She had lost all sense of reason. She would happily have denied all knowledge and let Jake and Tony take the blame. Considering the amount of cocaine there was, it would definitely have resulted in some kind of prison sentence.

'I doubt it. This was a nice convenient spot. We'll check, though, just to be on the safe side. Especially now you know what

you're looking for. God, Jake, sometimes you're as green as grass.'
He walked away, exasperated.

One by one, Tony ripped open the cellophane packages and poured the powder down the toilet. It made him shudder to think how things could have all gone so terribly wrong. Flushing the loo and watching the powder swirl away, Tony mentally agreed with Ralph. If it hadn't been for the commissioner, the place would have been searched. He had literally saved them. And if it hadn't been for that inspector putting doubt and suspicion in Tony's mind, he would never have known. How long had he been watching Sharon? How long had the police known about it, to warrant a raid on the club?

The fire investigators officially called the club catastrophe an accident. Possibly a prank. Things seemed to have settled down, even though the papers had made a meal of it for as long as they could. There was no word from Sharon over the next few weeks. She had simply disappeared off the face of the earth.

18

A DUAL PROPOSAL

The new club looked amazing. Although he'd stuck with the well-known Lambrianu pink for the interior, Tony had gone overboard with the refurbishment. To get his customers back, it had to be bigger and better than before.

All the staff had been on full pay during the closure and he had used them to do all kinds of work that they were not contracted for, to help get the place clean again. Even the strippers, who had been panicking about their lack of income, were given the choice of either getting their hands dirty and helping out or finding employment elsewhere for the time being. He knew they wouldn't want to go anywhere else. 'The quicker it's open again, ladies, the quicker you will be earning big money again. Your choice.'

Sharon's assistant had taken over the running of the club for the time being. She had learnt the ropes and, as of late, she had been doing most of the work anyway. It seemed only fair to give her a chance.

'Tony. Christopher is here to see you. Shall I let him through? He doesn't have an appointment.' Mark, Tony's driver, stood inside the office. He could see Tony didn't want to be disturbed, but this wasn't just some guy off the street wanting a loan or an appointment. This was family business.

'Is Katie with him? What does he want?' Irritated but curious, Tony looked up from his paperwork.

'Katie's not here. He's alone.'

Tony nodded. 'Show him in.'

Stretching and running his hands through his hair, Tony sat back in his leather chair and waited.

'Mr Lambrianu.' Christopher walked forward and held out his hand to shake Tony's, but there was no response so he just stood there, waiting to be invited to sit down.

Eyeing him up closely, Tony felt this clever young man had something on his mind and he knew it would include his daughter. Waving his hand at the chair on the other side of the desk, Tony waited.

'I can see you're busy, Mr Lambrianu, so I'll get straight to the point.' Although slightly intimidated, Christopher tried to be as business-like as possible. 'Firstly, you know Katie and I have been seeing each other.' Christopher waited for some response but again, there was none. Tony sat there stony-faced, those piercing blue eyes boring into the young man opposite.

Jake walked into the room and sat down, making the atmosphere even tenser for Christopher, but he carried on. 'We decided in Italy that we would like to get engaged. I love your daughter, Mr Lambrianu, and I think we're well suited. But I wouldn't do anything without your permission and Katie wouldn't accept me without your blessing.'

Stunned at this information, Tony tried composing himself. 'Have you asked her?'

'In a vague sort of fashion, but I would like your permission to do so properly.' Adjusting his glasses and swallowing, Christopher again waited for a response.

Jake cast a sideways glance at Tony; there was that humorous twinkle in his eye.

'Can I think about it?' asked Tony. 'After all, Katie is a very rich, clever woman and you haven't even told me that you're in love with her. You love her, yes, but being in love with someone is totally different. You make it sound like you have already been married for twenty years. After twenty plus years, Christopher, I am more in love with my wife than ever. When you talk of marrying my daughter, I would expect some emotion. Don't you agree?'

Blushing and adjusting his glasses again, Christopher looked down at the desk. This was obviously an embarrassing subject for him; he found it hard to declare his love to Katie's father.

'I do love her, Mr Lambrianu, and I believe she loves me. I presumed you would have realised that or else I wouldn't be asking,' Christopher said. He sat up straight and adjusted his tie.

'As I say, she is a very rich young woman. An ideal catch, you might say.' Tony was stringing it out; he cast another glance at Jake.

'She is indeed, Mr Lambrianu, and I understand your reservations. But there is never going to be a man to match up to your ideals. I may have overlooked telling you that I'm in love with Katie, but you have also overlooked the fact that she knows her own mind. She is a strong-willed young woman.'

Tony frowned. This young man seemed bent on challenging him at every turn. He was annoyed by him, but he also admired him. He had guts.

'I will have to speak to Katie first. I appreciate you wanting to do things properly.' With that, Tony held out his hand to shake

Christopher's. This meeting was over. Well, for the time being, anyway.

'There is another matter I wanted to discuss with you, Mr Lambrianu. That is, if you have the time?'

'What, now? Sit back down. What is it?' Tony was getting slightly irritated now; pursing his lips, he waited for the next instalment. He was surprised when Christopher put his briefcase on the desk and started opening it. Tony turned to look at Jake and shrugged; they were both intrigued to know what Christopher had up his sleeve.

'I have been keeping an eye on the vineyard. Although your new man in charge is doing a good job, I didn't want to let things slide again.' Christopher felt he was on safer ground talking business.

Swallowing hard and looking around the room at the two suited men staring at him, Christopher licked his lips and continued. 'As I told you once before, Mr Lambrianu, there is a bigger market to tap into when it comes to the vineyard.' He gave a wry smile to appease Tony then took out a folder and placed it on the desk. 'I've looked at the wastage figures and I think... well, I know, or I wouldn't be proposing it... that you could make a cheaper wine using the grapes that are not good enough for a claret. It would have to be a different brand and so Katie thought "Miriam's Chapel" would be a nice name, in honour of her grandmother.'

Holding his hand up to stop him, Tony said, 'Wait! You have spoken to Katie about this?' He couldn't believe his ears. 'You and my daughter have already discussed taking my vineyard off me? How dare you. Get out.'

Mark stepped forward and grabbed Christopher by the shoulders. 'You've said enough, mate. Time to get out while you can.

Come on.' Mark pulled him towards the door and marched him out.

'Can you believe it? That guy wants my vineyard. God's sake, Jake, we've saved it from one thieving bastard and now we have to do it again? The bloody cheek of it. Well, she can stop seeing him right now. I was right, he is a gold-digger.'

Jake watched Tony pace the office and slam about, waiting for his opportunity. The air was blue and Tony was tirelessly telling Jake what he should do to Christopher.

'Have you finished, Tony? Here, have a drink.' Jake poured them both a whisky and handed one to Tony. 'From where I was sitting, I never heard him say he wanted the vineyard. It sounds like him and Katie have been keeping an eye on things in your absence, knowing how close you came to losing it. It seemed more like a business proposal to me. Why not read what's in that folder and check it out? More to the point, why not talk to Katie about it?' Jake was interested. It might not be such a bad idea having a family member take the reins of the vineyard. Someone who could be trusted. And this guy did have a business brain. 'I must say, though, Tony, with his marriage proposal and his list of prospects, I thought he was going to ask *you* to marry him.' Jake burst out laughing. 'For fuck's sake, it was like something out of a Jane Austen novel. How old is that guy?'

Watching the grin spread across Tony's face, Jake knew he had said the right thing to defuse the situation. 'Bloody right, mate. It was more like a checklist than a proposal.' Tony laughed. 'Anyway, what do you know about Jane Austen, Jake? I thought you only read *Marvel* comics?' Tony's anger had passed. Jake knew just how to handle him.

'You made him squirm, you evil bastard. Still, take a look at that folder, Tony. You might find it interesting.' With that, Jake stood up, finished his drink and left the room, to give Tony time

to think about what he had said. After all, Tony was a businessman. And although he wouldn't step down from his high horse,
he was always interested in business.

Tony looked down at the folder, then picked it up and threw it
over the other side of the desk in disgust.

Unbeknown to Tony, Katie was waiting outside in the car for
Christopher. 'Well? What did he say?'

'Just as you said, Katie, interrogation and intimidation, but I
have said my piece.'

'Good. Well, now you have dropped the bombshell, it's up to
Mum, and if anyone can bring him round, she can. At least we've
tried doing it the proper way, with respect. After all, Christopher,
you didn't expect an answer from him straight away, did you?'
Katie smiled and kissed him on the cheek. She knew it would
work out, but the seed had to be dropped into her father's brain
first.

'Wait a minute. Is that Sharon over there?' As they drove
along, Katie had noticed a woman coming out of a house nearby.
She was sure it was her, but before she could get a closer look, the
woman had disappeared. It had been a month since anyone had
heard anything from Sharon.

Puzzled, Katie looked out of the car windows at either side.
Were her eyes deceiving her? It had looked like Sharon, but not
the Sharon she knew. This one looked dishevelled and unkempt,
and Sharon had always prided herself on her appearance. For the
time being, Katie decided to keep quiet about it. Maybe she was
wrong and she didn't want to cause a stir. But her gut instinct told
her it was Sharon she had glimpsed.

Katie headed for the one person she knew she could talk to in
private – her sister.

Scarlet's face was just like Tony's when she thought something was wrong. Instantly her eyes started to darken and a faint pink flush started to show in her cheeks. 'Katie, what is it?'

'Calm down, Scarlet. I just thought I saw Sharon. Have Dad or Jack mentioned anything?'

'Sharon! No. No one has heard a word since she left with that guy of hers. Are you sure it was her? Maybe you should tell Papa. Anyway, never mind about her. Did Christopher ask Papa for permission to marry you? What did he say?' Now Scarlet's blue eyes flashed like jewels. This was the kind of juicy gossip she liked.

'Yes, he did. And what do you think Dad did? Nothing more than I expected. You wait till you tell him about Dominic. He will go ape!' With that, Katie walked out of the salon. Maybe she'd been wrong about Sharon. There was no point in building up Jack's or Jake's hopes until she was sure.

* * *

'Have you had a good day love?' Tony slipped his arms around Francesca's waist as she laid the table. Burying his head in her neck and slowly sliding his hands under her top, he continued to whisper sweet nothings in her ear.

'Behave. Elle will be back soon with Adam.' Feeling his warm breath on her neck and hearing that smooth, velvety voice in her ear was enough to make her pulse race, but now was not the time.

'Mum, we're home!' Adam ran down the hallway, all excited, with Elle following. Instantly they parted and as Francesca adjusted her blouse and walked towards Adam it was obvious to Elle they had come at a bad time.

Tony beat a hasty retreat outside to get some fresh air. A few minutes later, he was back. 'Right, the pair of you.' Tony was now in full control again. 'That Christopher has been to see me. It seems he wants to marry Katie, take over the vineyard and stick his nose in. Do you know anything about this?'

The silence and the exchange of glances told Tony everything he needed to know. 'Okay. I will put it another way. What has Katie told you about it?'

'Oh, just that they intend to get married,' said Fran. 'And that they have both been keeping a close eye on the vineyard accounts. Why?'

'Well, that's a lot more than I knew. Bloody hell. Am I always the last person to hear anything around here?'

'Maybe, Tony, that is because you don't want to listen,' Elle scolded. 'You're usually so full of your own opinions, young man, that you forget you were once their age.' Elle waved her ladle at him.

'Well, what do you think of him, Elle?' he said, as he was taking his tie off.

'Let's eat, Tony. And then, if you want to listen, I will tell you.'

Elle was still the mother figure in the house and Francesca was glad to take a back seat on this one. Walking away from them both, she went to the cork board on the kitchen wall and pinned Adam's latest picture to it.

Letting out a deep sigh, Tony knew he was beaten. It was lecture time. He hadn't had one for a while. Elle had obviously let this build up and he knew he was going to get it with both barrels.

'I'm listening. Go on. You may as well come back to the table, Fran. You might have something to say about this, too. Adam, sit beside me. I need support while Granny Elle tells me off.' He was trying to make light of it.

Elle waited for Adam to get settled in beside Tony before saying, 'Okay. Well, here goes. Firstly, your daughters are young women, not children. Some of their friends are already married with kids by now. If Ralph Gold can accept that Diana is a police constable and let her get on with her life, then you can do the same. Personally, I feel the same way about Christopher as you do, which is why he gets your back up so much. He's a clever businessman and what he lacks in personality and looks, God gave him in brains. Katie loves him very much. Anyone can see that they are well suited.' Elle gave him a cold stare. 'Even if there are some of us that don't want to see it. As for the vineyard, well, someone needs to keep an eye on it. Let's be honest, Tony, if it was up to you that German chap would still be holding the reins. Now get over it. Wish them well and see what ideas that young man has. Now, let's eat.'

'Well, that's me told, Elle! You don't hold anything back, do you? What do you think, Francesca?'

'Much the same, Tony. And Elle is right. You must think he is okay or you wouldn't even be discussing it. Now, eat up and think about it.'

Francesca and Elle exchanged looks as they put the shepherd's pie on Adam's plate. No more needed to be said. Tony always listened to Elle. After all, she was the only mother he had ever really known and he trusted her judgement.

19

A GOOD INVESTMENT

Tony was surprised to see Ralph in his office when he arrived the next day. He sat down. 'Why are you here so early, Ralph?'

'Have you read this folder, Tony? Sorry, lad, but I just saw it on top of that filing cabinet and couldn't resist having a read.' Ralph looked down again and continued turning the pages in the folder.

'No, I haven't read it yet and you're being bloody nosy. What is in my office is mine, right? So, what is it you wanted to see me about? Jake should be here in a minute.'

'First things first, lad.' Ralph looked up from the folder. 'This proposal is good. In fact, it's very good. Is this from that young Christopher lad who's engaged to your Katie?'

'Yes.' Tony was annoyed that the folder he had discarded so casually had captured Ralph's interest. 'And while he may have my daughter, my vineyard is another matter.' He swept his hair back. 'So, what's this all about?' Again, Tony tried steering the conversation away, but to no avail. Ralph's attention stayed on the folder.

'He doesn't want your precious vineyard. Lambrianu Wines will remain just that. But this idea about making a cheaper wine for the other end of the market is good. You are the majority shareholder. If it makes money, then he would like you to offer 20 per cent of the shares to him. That's business, Tony. Oh, and you would have to pay him for all of his hard work, that's normal, but it's a good investment. Read it. Don't let your pride get in the way of business. Hell, I wish he'd seen Diana first. I wouldn't mind a son-in-law like him. He's as crooked as could be, but he is legally crooked and knows all the loopholes, even down to getting you a business grant.'

Picking up the folder, Tony frowned. 'You think it's that good?' Even he knew if Ralph thought it was worth a read then it must be okay. 'Maybe I will look it over. Anyway, what's the problem?'

'We both know what the problem is. What have you done about finding Sharon? I don't like this, Tony. God knows what she is saying and doing at this very moment. Time is running out.'

'I know, Ralph. But no one seems to know where she is. Don't get me wrong, people would trip up and tell me if they knew, especially if they value their lives, but there's nothing. I don't even know where to start.'

'Don Carlos is in England, I believe. He wants us to have a meeting tomorrow. This usually means he has a lot of information to share.'

They both sat there in silence until Jake walked in. 'Have I come at a bad time?'

'No, Jake. Ralph has just informed me that Don Carlos is in England and wants a meeting. God knows what he wants.'

'Well, I do,' said Jake, folding his arms in a matter-of-fact way. 'He'll want me to kill Sharon to prove myself. How the bloody hell do I do that? I don't even know where she is!' Tears mingled with snot on Jake's face. It was a sad sight to see; he was a broken man.

'Would you kill her, Jake? More to the point, could you?' asked Tony.

'I dunno. I know it's what's expected and I wouldn't bat an eyelid about anyone else... but answer me: could you kill Francesca?' Raising his head, Jake looked Tony square in the eyes.

'No. I would rather kill myself. I doubt Ralph would kill Julie, either. But I don't know what Don Carlos has up his sleeve. God knows, he would kill his own grandmother to save his skin.'

'I have no choice, do I? We both know he will kill me if I don't. I'm a dead man walking.'

The sentence hung in the air.

'If that is what the meeting is for, I will protect you as much as possible, you know that. We're brothers, Jake.'

They both stood up and hugged each other. The lump in Tony's throat was too much to bear. He could feel his own tears falling down his cheeks.

Trying to compose themselves, they sat down again.

'Promise me, Tony, if Don Carlos wants me dead, you will do it.'

'For fuck's sake Jake. No, it won't come to that. Stop being so defeatist. You sound like you're dead already.'

'Hey, boys.' Ralph interrupted them. It was as though they had forgotten he was there. 'Don't you think you're letting all of this get a little out of hand? You don't know why he's here. He may have more information. Let's not get ahead of ourselves, eh? Tomorrow.' With that, Ralph stood up to leave. 'I would have a look at that vineyard proposal, Tony. It's good.'

'Is that all he has to say?' Jake said once Ralph had gone. 'My life is on the line and that's the best he can come up with?' Jake was angry.

'No one knows what to say, Jake. But be damned sure, I will

make sure Don Carlos doesn't harm a fucking hair on your head. Let's go and see what he wants, tomorrow.'

'Welcome, gentlemen.' Don Carlos made a big show of hugging them both as a gesture of goodwill and greeting. Looking around the hotel room, Tony saw that Ralph was already there with Julie. No surprise there, then. 'You know my sons, of course.'

Tony and Jake both stepped forward and shook his sons' hands. Their reputation always preceded them. They were supposedly doing some deal with Argentina, sending money back and forth, the very same money that was going into the Paris casino. Except Don Carlos was using this so-called 'money' to pay for the campaign of a would-be president. It all seemed very deep. But Tony guessed this was why Don Carlos didn't want cages rattled.

'Don Carlos, let's have a drink and skip the pleasantries. We all know why we are here, so let's get on with it. I am sure Tony and Jake feel much the same,' said Ralph. He could see how anxious Jake was and didn't want it prolonged any further. He was also the only one in the room that could speak to Don Carlos on the same level without causing any offence.

'As you say, Ralph. Firstly, Jake, you know the problems are with you and your wife.' Don Carlos raised his hand to Tony and looked towards Ralph.

Ralph could see Tony's blood was boiling and he was going to say something out of turn. 'Let him speak, Tony. Once he has, then you can have your say. Fair?'

Tony and Jake both nodded.

'As I was saying.' Don Carlos was a very suave, distinguished Italian man. His dark hair was now greying at the sides. 'This is not just some wife cheating on her husband. This is about some woman importing kilos of cocaine with her boyfriend and selling it. Not only in your clubs and casinos, but in everybody's.' He waited for what he was saying to sink in. 'Oh, yes, gentlemen. I have been digging. This man of Sharon's is French. He is a small-time crook and drug dealer known to the police. He flattered and fucked an ageing woman and she has handed us all over to him.'

Tony looked across at Jake and saw that he was looking down at the floor. Poor bastard. He was having to sit here and listen to this.

'To impress and keep him, she has boasted that it is she who runs the clubs. With that in mind, he became even more attracted to her. This small-time crook was now sleeping with a well-known gangland boss's wife and her pillow talk was worth a fortune.' It was clear that Don Carlos was angry at Jake. 'She knows where and who makes the counterfeit money, as well as information about the deliveries.' Again, Don Carlos paused. 'My guess is that to impress this young fool she has told him all kinds of stories that he can use against any of us, at any time. If he is wise, he will have recorded it.' Don Carlos had now dropped the bombshell. No one had guessed it was this serious.

'What do you think she wants, Don Carlos? What does she hope to achieve? She knows we'll catch up with her soon enough. More to the point, why did she do it?' Ralph spoke up first. He didn't want Tony to start shouting and protecting Jake.

'That's what I was coming to next. Lorenzo, here, has put the word out that he is looking to do business with a new supplier. Of course I mean drugs, Antonias. There is a market and there is money. I am a businessman. If not from me, then they would buy from someone else. Now, that is the end of your looks of disgust. Capisce?' He waited for Tony to speak before he carried on, but nothing was said. 'Anyway, cutting a long story short. A woman contacted Lorenzo's men with a sample of goods. It was not Sharon. It was her sister...'

They all looked at each other in turn. This, indeed, was a revelation. For God's sake, just how much did he know?

'Her sister?' Jake couldn't help but ask.

'Yes, Jake. Her sister.' With a sweep of his hand, he carried on. He had everyone's attention. The room was silent. 'She was telling Lorenzo, here, about a new gangland boss. A younger one who knows the way of the world. She felt that London should be run by young men and not three ageing fools past their sell-by date. In short, Antonias, there is a plan to kill you and replace you with Sharon's boyfriend. You as well, Jake. And Ralph, well... who knows?'

'She is planning to have me murdered? Is that what you're saying?' Tony stood up and paced around the room. 'That fucking bitch wants me murdered to score points with her bloke?' He couldn't believe what he was hearing.

'What better reference could this young...' Don Carlos danced his fingers in the air, trying to remember the man's name.

'Alexandre. Alex,' said Lorenzo.

'What better reference could an upcoming boss like Alexandre have than to have murdered and got the better of the famous Antonias Lambrianu, eh? How clever that would make him look. Your enemies would admire him, Antonias. More to the point, Sharon would put him on your throne at the club and he would rule. That is what he wants and that is what she has promised him. There is more, but I won't go on. At the very least, if they fail, another way of disposing of you all is to have you put behind bars for the rest of your lives. I already have the FBI snooping around my American affairs, I don't need any more hassle. Jake, *la uccidi o lo farò.*'

'Hey, come on, guys. The only Italian I know is how to order my dinner. What the hell does that mean?' Ralph shrugged his shoulders and looked at Tony.

'It basically means, either you kill her or I will.' Jake looked across the room at Don Carlos.

'That is exactly what it means, Jake. My apologies, Ralph. But I know Jake speaks Italian and he knows I am serious. Will you do it, Jake?'

'Yes.' Jake nodded his head. 'It seems I have no choice.'

'Whoa! Wait a minute. How do we all know this is correct? How do you know it was Sharon's sister and they have made all these plans? It's just your word, Don Carlos.' Tony's eyes darkened. His face was flushed with anger and he was standing directly in front of Don Carlos.

'You doubt me, Antonias? We are brothers of the same flag. Our families have history. Have I ever wronged you? In all the business we have done together, have I ever wronged you?'

'No. *Mi dispiace.*' Tony bent down to kiss Don Carlos's hand and noticed that he still wore the diamond signet ring he'd sent him years ago.

'No apologies necessary, Antonias. Emotions are high. Julie, I will let you continue.'

Julie had sat behind Ralph listening to the conversation. Up to now she had taken everything in and remained quiet. Now she spoke. 'Sharon is back in England, so they are preparing to put their plan into action. She will be in touch soon, Jake. Take my word for it. She needs to meet up with you both. She needs to get close enough to you, Tony, to kill you and she will use Jake to do it.'

'And how do you propose she is going to get close enough to me to kill me, Julie?' Tony's cocky grin annoyed her.

'Excuse me, Don Carlos.' Julie apologised for the tirade of abuse she was going to hurl at Tony. She knew it would offend him. 'Listen to me, you blond Italian prick. She has keys to everything you fucking own. Are you telling me that while you're sat in your office that pimp of hers couldn't sneak through the back doors and put a bullet in your fucking stupid head? God knows, it wouldn't do any damage, would it? I want someone to watch your house. I will not have Francesca and little Adam put at risk. Do you hear me, Tony?' Julie could contain herself no longer. She walked up to Tony and slapped his face. The loud resounding smack seemed to echo around the room. 'You're no longer that single guy without a care in the world. You have a family and it's your duty to put them first. We are your second family. We have all fought and clawed our way to the top and I don't intend to allow some bitter ex-wife and her pimp get the better of me.'

'Stop it! Stop it now.' Ralph stood between them. Not only was Tony's face red with anger, but the mark where Julie had slapped him seemed to burn. His eyes were dark and he looked as if he was going to hit her back. 'Take a breath, son. We don't hit women. That's not what we do.'

'Well, there is a first time for everything. I will let you have that one, Julie, on the house. Don't ever do it again,' Tony spat out.

'What, like this, you mean?' Again, the sound of Julie's hand slapping Tony across the face shocked everyone. They saw Tony's fists clench. 'Francesca is innocent. She knows you're no saint but she always wants to believe the best in you, because she loves you. The only good thing you have done is keep Francesca in the dark, Tony. She could take a lie detector test and walk away. Now is the time to tell her a little of the truth. If we're all arrested it would come out in court anyway. I will protect her, but so must you.'

Nodding and stroking his cheek, Tony sat down. Julie was right. A long time ago he would have taken his chances and not given a damn, but now he had roots. A loving wife and family. Were they all in danger?

'What do you suggest, Julie?' Tony looked up at her, waiting. He knew for all her feistiness, she had his family's best interests at heart, even if she was a hard-faced bitch! He couldn't deny her loyalty.

'I know it hasn't been that long since they were there, but why not send the family to Italy for a couple of weeks? Don Carlos and his sons will be there should help be needed... right?' Julie looked across at Don Carlos. He was nodding his head. 'That is one less thing for you to worry about. I'm afraid you will have to be in London.' Julie looked towards Jake. 'You are the bait, Jake. She will contact you for two reasons. One, to see how the land lies and two, to worm her way back in. Are you prepared for that?' Julie looked around the room. Everyone had taken in what she had said. She was right. Of course she was; Julie Gold was never wrong!

'Let us all calm down and have a drink. It seems emotions are running very high.' Don Carlos nodded to one of his sons to pour them each a brandy. 'Before I forget, Antonias. I appreciate your show of respect, not killing the German who stole your vineyard. That was very wise of you. You will be pleased to know that both children are very happily living with their grandmother in Germany, where they belong. As for Herr Schmidt? He will not be stealing off anyone ever again.'

Everyone turned their heads to look at Don Carlos, stunned by his words. But no one dared ask what he had ordered to be done. It was obvious to Tony and Jake that even Ralph hadn't known about this, judging by the look on his face.

'A gesture of friendship and loyalty, Antonias,' Don Carlos continued. 'Now, I expect that gesture to be returned.' Although his voice was calm and low, it was menacing. 'I will look after your family in Italy. But you and Jake must honour your side of things.' He paused and looked to his sons. Then he stood up and held out his arms to Tony.

Tony walked towards him and hugged him. It was their way. The deal was sealed and the meeting was over.

20

SAFETY

'I'm bored! Fran, do it for me. You too, Elle. Come on. I don't ask for much.'

Elle and Francesca both burst out laughing.

'You have got to be joking, Julie. Every time you come up with a plan to escape boredom you drag me into it. Anyway, I can't. I've got too much going on here.'

Julie pouted like a sulky child. 'Please, Fran, come on holiday with me. I'm going to the villa in Italy.'

'It depends on Tony. I don't know what his plans are.' Francesca hated saying no to Julie, but this time she had to.

'You're weakening. Ha! Anyway, what has it got to do with him? He's not invited and neither is Ralph!'

'I'm not weakening, I'm trying to iron. You should try it sometime.'

'Not bloody likely. Do you know how much this manicure cost me? That is why I have staff at the house. They can do these things.' Julie started to laugh. 'I was not put on this earth to iron. Go on, Fran. Have a word with old misery guts. Tell him he's not invited and you're going on holiday with me. You too, Elle. You can tell that randy old Albert he will have to do without you for a few days. Then, when you get back you can show him your white bits!'

'Goodness me, Julie, behave! And I won't be showing Albert anything, thank you very much.'

Julie's laughter was infectious. She always seemed to bring good humour to the table, even if Tony was usually the brunt of her jokes.

'Just the man,' Julie said, swinging her legs on the high stool at the breakfast bar as she waited for Tony to come down the hallway.

'Tony what are you doing here? You only left a couple of hours ago. Have you missed me already?'

'I forgot my briefcase. It's upstairs.' Tony started to walk away, then turned back to Francesca. 'I always miss you.' Cupping her face in his hands, he kissed her tenderly on the lips.

'Oh, now we get it. Briefcase, my arse. You have come back for a bit of how's your father. For God's sake, Tony, they are going to have trouble burying you. How are they ever going to put a lid on that permanent erection?' Laughing out loud, Julie opened her cigarette case. 'Have we spoilt your morning?' She winked at him.

'I don't hear my wife complaining, Julie. Anyway, it would be a pleasure to see them put a lid over your mouth!'

'Now, children. Play nice.' Elle wagged her finger at the pair of them in a playful way.

'Fran and Elle were just discussing going on holiday to Italy, Tony. You're not invited but we're going.' Julie winked and smiled at him.

'Holiday? Since when?' Tony put on his surprised face. This had all been worked out before Julie had got there. This was part of their plan.

'I'm not going anywhere. Don't listen to her, she's bored,

which means she is going to annoy us all until she finds something else to do.'

'Seems like a good idea. In fact, it seems like a very good idea. No one had much of a holiday last time. I was going to see Katie and Christopher this afternoon. He has made some proposals about the vineyard. Maybe you could go with them and keep an eye on him.'

'Really? But what you? Wouldn't you like to come with us?' Francesca was taken aback. Of course she knew from Katie what Christopher had in mind for the vineyard, but she hadn't expected Tony to agree to any of it.

Taking her in his arms and holding her close, Tony looked over her shoulder at Julie and gave her a thumbs up. 'Go and have a look around with Katie. You can be my eyes and ears. I have things to attend to here.'

'Yessss!' Julie punched the air. 'Elle, pack up your things, we're going on holiday. Tony's paying. I'm going to leave you lovebirds now. No doubt he will want to get a few extra strokes in before you leave.' Julie's loud cackle filled the room while Elle stood there and winced.

'Are you sure you don't mind?'

'No. Go and keep an eye on that Christopher for me. Get some sun. Now, I think we should go and see if you have made the beds this morning.' A naughty, boyish grin crossed his face. 'Why waste a golden opportunity?'

* * *

'Here's hoping you all have a great holiday, girls.' Raising his glass to everyone sat at the dining table, Tony felt relieved that the people he loved most would be away from danger. It was one less thing to think about.

Wringing her hands and looking slightly worried, Elle looked around the dining table. They were having the usual family Sunday lunch and the house was full to bursting. 'I'm not sure I can go.'

'Why not?' asked Julie. 'Is Albert putting his foot down or something?' The very idea of Albert putting his foot down made them all look at each other and smile. From the very beginning it had been obvious who was boss in their house.

'No, it's just that Minnie has had a death in the family and she is very upset. And, of course, we don't know if police charges are going to be brought against her.'

Putting down his fork, Jake looked up. 'Police charges against Minnie? What the hell has she done?'

'Possible assault, I think,' said Elle, making space for yet another dish of roast potatoes.

'Assault? You have to be joking. Who the hell has she assaulted? She's a pensioner! Start from the beginning, Elle, you have totally lost me.' Tony looked around the table, confused.

Taking a seat, Elle looked at them as they waited with bated breath. Some had even put their forks down and stopped eating.

'Well, you know that old man, Pete, who lives across the road from us, who lost his wife last year?' Everyone nodded. They were still confused because no one could see where this was going. 'It seems he's been a bit lonely of late and, as Minnie is the only single woman down our street, he has taken to paying a lot of attention to her. Carrying her shopping bags and stuff,' Elle stammered.

'What, you're telling us he wants a bird after his wife has died and the best thing he could come up with is your bingo pal, Minnie? Bloody hell, she must be 100 years old!' Jake exclaimed. They all started to grin, but they didn't want Jake stopping this story. It held far too much intrigue.

'She's not that much older than me, thank you very much, Jake. And you're not too old for a clip around the ear,' snapped Elle, giving him one of her warning looks.

'Go on, Elle, tell us about Minnie, the Jezebel of your street.' Ralph sat back on his dining chair and folded his arms.

'Anyway. Minnie went home one day and, as she opened the door, there was a half-eaten bar of chocolate on the doormat. When she walked into the lounge, Butch, her thirteen-year-old Border Collie, had been sick on the rug, poor thing.' Elle waited for a reaction but there was none. Everyone had stopped what they were doing and they were listening intently. 'To make matters worse, when she went into the kitchen, poor Butch was dead on the floor. She was so upset.'

'So what has this got to do with the old man across the road wanting to see what is under Minnie's tabard?'

'Shut up, Jake!' Ralph couldn't wait to hear the punchline of this story. It all seemed very jumbled and he was trying to make sense of it. Looking around at the furrowed brows of the people at the table, he knew they felt the same.

'She saw Pete when the vet sent someone around to pick up Butch. And he asked her if she had liked the chocolate he had put through her letter box. That's when the vet and Minnie realised what had happened.' Elle folded her arms in disgust. 'That stupid old fool put a large bar of chocolate through the letter box and Butch ate it. Chocolate kills dogs and this was a bar of fruit and nut. Chocolate and raisins are the two most toxic things for a dog. Stupid old fool!'

Raising her hand to her mouth to stifle her smile, Julie looked across at Francesca. She could see the look in her eyes which meant she felt the same.

'He killed her dog? So why is she on an assault charge?' This time Tony couldn't help interrupting.

'Well, it's obvious, isn't it?' Elle snapped. 'When she realised what he had done, she punched him on the nose and started hitting him with her shopping bag, but it had a frozen leg of lamb in it. One of those special constables was walking down the street and saw everything. He had to drag Minnie off Pete. Oh, goodness, there was a real hue and cry.'

'So, what are the police going to do?' Ralph asked. This was the best bit of gossip he had heard in a long time. And it was a light relief to all their troubles.

'Well, that depends on that dog killer, Pete,' Elle spat out. 'If he wants to press charges on her for assault. But Minnie has told him she is going to give him the bill for Butch's cremation.'

The room fell silent as everyone looked around at each other. They couldn't hold it in any longer. The eruption of laughter was enough to raise the roof. Ralph brought his napkin to his eyes as tears rolled down his face. As serious and as sad as this was, they couldn't stop themselves laughing.

Elle looked on with disgust as the bad jokes were exchanged.

'Poor Pete the stud; he thought there was life in the old dog yet, giving Minnie the wink and the nod and he gets a punch on the nose,' laughed Jake.

'Yes, well,' Julie retorted, trying to catch her breath in between squeals of laughter. 'There's no life in the old dog now, is there?'

Francesca looked at Tony, who was splitting his sides laughing. He could hardly speak. It was the first time in weeks she had seen him laugh so much without a care in the world. Poor old Minnie's tale of woe about love and sadness had done the trick.

'Bring her with you, Elle. The break will do her good and we will pay any cremation bills. Tell her not to worry. Butch will have the best there is.' Julie was trying to compose herself and she still wanted Elle out of the way.

'Really, Julie? I think she would like that. It would take her mind off things.'

'You know what, Elle, if I hadn't heard it from you I wouldn't believe it. I am going to dine out on that for the next hundred years!' Shaking his head, Tony couldn't believe his ears. 'So, is it settled then? Are you all going to Italy for a break? Get old Minnie away from randy old Pete, although I would say that's cooled his ardour a bit! The only bit of leg he felt was a frozen lamb one.' Again, they all thought Minnie's plight was hilarious, but Tony saw Elle nodding.

'Yes, she will come, Tony. Thank you, Julie.' Elle looked across at Julie, who was still in hysterics, and patted her hand.

'No problem, Elle. But I have just realised, Ralph has life insurance so I might just pop down the sweet shop for a bar of chocolate.'

'Well, I can see this isn't going to stop anytime soon, so you had all better get it off your chests here and be done with it before we go on holiday.' Elle smiled. Thinking on it now, she, too, could see the funny side of things.

The banter and the laughter that filled the room was warm and genuine. Whatever was on Tony's mind these days, this had well and truly taken its place... for now, anyway. Looking around the table at her family and friends, Francesca smiled to herself, contented.

* * *

'What's wrong, Tony? What is the real reason for all of this stress?' After waking up in the middle of the night, Francesca had noticed Tony was not beside her in bed. Walking along the landing, she found him in Adam's bedroom sitting in the dark, but with the curtains open so that some moonlight shone in. Tony sat in the rocking chair beside the bed, staring into space.

'I couldn't sleep, that's all. You go back to bed. He's beautiful, isn't he?' he said, pointing at Adam

'Answer the question, Tony. I think I have been patient for long enough. You look like you have the weight of the world on your shoulders.' Sitting on the edge of the bed, Francesca reached out and held Tony's hand. 'Tell me. Whatever it is. Just tell me.' Their eyes met in the moonlit bedroom.

Letting out a long sigh, Tony nodded. 'There is trouble brewing, Francesca.' Their hushed whispers seemed to make the conversation more intense. 'I don't want to involve you, but this could all go very wrong.'

There was a long pause while Francesca waited for Tony to carry on. She could see he was troubled, almost in agony. 'Go on, Tony. I'm listening.'

'Oh, God, Fran. It's Sharon,' he blurted out. The darkness of the room made it feel like some sort of confessional.

Rolling her eyes upwards, Francesca squeezed his hand. 'You mean you know she is cheating on Jake and you feel you should tell him. Is that it?'

'What?' Tony couldn't hide his surprise. 'What do you mean?'

'Oh, I hear things, Tony, love. Like when Julie went to Paris. She popped into the casino and saw Sharon with a man. She left unnoticed and without saying anything. Is that what is troubling you?'

'Why the hell didn't you tell me?' Almost raising his voice, Tony could not hide his amazement.

'Shush! You will wake Adam. It wasn't my secret to tell. Everyone knows they are having problems. They barely spend a couple of hours in the same room together. It's not the first time Sharon has cheated on Jake, is it? I didn't tell you because I knew if I did you would tell him out of loyalty, but he wouldn't thank you for it. You would break his heart. So, getting back to the beginning, what is wrong? You're not so stressed out because Sharon is cheating on Jake. That would not cause you sleepless nights. I want the truth, Tony.'

'You will hate me, Fran. I'm not the man you think I am. I want to tell you. I need to because, if this all goes very wrong, I could end up in prison for a very long time. That's if I was ever allowed out. And Adam would be a grown man with children of his own by then.'

Fear gripped Francesca. Now she knew it was bad. Tony seemed close to tears, rubbing his face with his hands. For a few moments the only sound in the room was Adam's breathing as he slept soundly.

'I know you're not squeaky clean, Tony. I knew that when I first met you. And, as much as you have become a legitimate businessman as the years have passed, I get the feeling not everything is as legitimate as it should be. What has come out of the woodwork? I need to know what I'm facing.'

Tony took a huge breath, then, eventually, everything came out. The money laundering. Sharon's betrayal. The drugs. And the concern about what other little stories Sharon had shared with her boyfriend during pillow talk.

Stunned, Francesca sat back. Bloody hell, this was worse than she'd thought. She knew he carried a gun and was in all kinds of rackets, but she thought he had given all that up a long time ago. Francesca could feel the stress leaving Tony's body as he made his confession. It seemed like a weight had lifted off his shoulders.

'I would rather you know this now, Francesca, from me, then hear it for the first time in a whole courtroom full of people. I want you to know the truth. I have never lied to you. I just wanted to protect you.'

Wrapping her dressing gown around her and shivering slightly at the early morning breeze coming through the window, she tried keeping her voice steady. 'What are you going to do?'

Bending over and burying his head in her knees, Tony sobbed, 'I don't fucking know, Fran. My whole world is falling apart and for the first time in my life I don't know what to do.'

'Come here, Antonias.' Wrapping her arms around him, Francesca held him tightly, knowing it could be a very long time before they shared a moment like this again.

'What's that?' He raised his head quickly and looked towards the door.

'What?' Francesca asked, but Tony was already up and walking towards the bedroom door. Opening it, he saw no one on the landing. Every door was closed. Tony stood staring out into the empty space as though waiting for something or someone.

Standing behind him, Francesca followed his stare. 'What is it? There's no one there.'

'I heard someone, I know I did. Someone was out there listening to us. The only question is, who?'

'Houses like this creak all the time, Tony. You're just a little on edge. It could be the wind or something. Let's go back to bed... or do you want a drink of something to help you sleep?'

Steering him downstairs, Francesca knew he wasn't paying attention to her. His eyes were scouring the landing for some trace of anyone that had been listening to his confessions.

She handed Tony a glass of brandy and poured one for herself. She felt she needed one after tonight. 'If anyone was out there, Tony, I am sure they will say something in the morning. Anyway, we never heard a door close. No one could hear us, we were whispering, and the door was shut.'

It seemed to satisfy him. 'Do you hate me, Francesca? Have I disappointed you?'

'No, my lovely Antonias. I could never hate you. But I agree, this needs sorting out. We'll discuss it tomorrow. Come on, let's get some sleep and start again in the morning.' Taking him by the hand, Francesca waited while he gulped back the last of his brandy, then led him up the stairs.

21

REVENGE

'Dad. Mum's been in touch. She asked me to pass a message on.' Jack stood in the club beside Jake with a piece of paper in his hands, looking rather sheepish.

'Your mum called? Did she ask about me?' Although Jake knew what she had done, he couldn't help but wonder about her.

'She didn't have time, Dad. She was busy going somewhere. But she wants you to call her as soon as possible.'

Taking the piece of paper with Sharon's telephone number on it, Jake put it in his pocket. 'Okay, Jack, don't fret son. I will give her a call.'

Jack left the club feeling as though he had betrayed his father by speaking to his mother after everything she had done to him.

'Well, Tony, I hate to say it but Julie was right. God, I hate that woman. Doesn't she ever get fed up of being right?' Jake slumped into his chair. 'Sharon wants me to call her. What do you think she wants?'

'Well, she doesn't want to kiss and fucking make up, does she? She wants to put her plan into action. Go on, ring her.'

They both sat staring at the phone as Jake dialled the number. Instantly, Sharon answered. She sounded flustered.

'Jake, hi. Thanks for ringing.'

'Not a problem, Sharon.' Looking up at Tony, he put the phone on loudspeaker. 'So, what is it you want to talk about?'

'Us, Jake. I need to see you and we need to sort out where we go from here. I have made a lot of mistakes and I'm sorry, love. I really am. I suppose Tony is pissed off with me?'

Tony and Jake frowned. Pissed off? It wasn't the expression they would have used. This was also not the conversation they had expected.

'So, do you want to meet up so we can talk properly?' she said, when Jake didn't reply.

Tony gave Jake a thumbs up.

'Yes, I'd like that, Sharon. What time?'

'How about tomorrow night? What about that little restaurant you like on the South Bank, around 8 p.m.? I don't want this to be public knowledge Jake. This is between you and me.'

Jake felt sick. At any other time he would have welcomed this 'date' with his wife. But there were so many strings attached to this he felt like Pinocchio.

'I'll be there, Sharon. See you then.'

He ended the call and both men breathed a sigh of relief. Tony hadn't dared cough or breathe while the phone was on loudspeaker.

'Sounds like a romantic cosy meeting. She's trying to make out she wants to get back with you, Jake, when we know full well that is not the bloody case.' Tony pointed his finger at Jake in warning. 'Don't you dare go all sentimental and start falling for it. Remember what she has done. Most of all, remember what you have to do.' Tony looked down at the floor. He hadn't wanted to bring it up yet, but he didn't want Jake raising his hopes and falling for Sharon's sob story, either.

'I know, I know. You all want me to kill my fucking wife,' snapped Jake, and left the office.

Tony didn't go after him. Poor bastard; as if he didn't have enough to cope with. This was truly a double-edged sword and either way, Jake couldn't win.

* * *

After arriving at the restaurant early, Jake was surprised to see that Sharon was already there. She sat at the table, large as life, waving to catch his attention. He could feel the butterflies in his stomach as he sat at the candlelit table. It had been a long time since she had made any kind of effort for him, but tonight she looked amazing in a red halter dress which complimented her blonde hair perfectly.

'Thanks for coming, Jake. I ordered you a drink.' Her smile was warm and friendly.

To Jake it felt surreal. This beautiful smiling woman before him was the very same woman who was ruining all of their lives. Looking down at the drink, Jake felt suspicious. He didn't know why but felt he shouldn't drink it.

'I'll have a fresh one of those, please, and another one for the lady,' Jake said to the waiter. 'You don't mind, do you?' he said to Sharon. 'The ice seems to have melted in that one.' He put on a fake smile. 'Shall we order?'

Neither of them was very hungry, but they ordered anyway. While they waited for their food, they made polite small talk. It was like a game of cat and mouse.

Suddenly a woman caught Jake's eye. It was one of the waitresses. He looked across at her in her uniform. For a moment he thought his mind was playing tricks on him. No, it couldn't be, he thought to himself, but the woman turned, smiled at him and walked into the kitchen.

'Don't you think she looks like...?' Jake stopped himself. He wasn't sure, even though his gut instinct told him he was right.

'What?' Sharon snapped. 'Why are you looking around the room when we're trying to talk!' She was starting to sweat and Jake noticed she looked on edge. It was clear even in the dimly lit restaurant that Sharon didn't look as stunning as he'd first thought. There were dark rings under her eyes, even though she had very skilfully applied her make-up. Her hair didn't shine like it used to and she looked old. Much older than her years. Looking over Sharon's shoulder again to where he had seen the waitress, he saw she had gone. No, it definitely couldn't be who he thought it was.

'So, what is it you wanted to talk about, Sharon?' Jake asked after the food had arrived and they'd spent a few awkward minutes picking at it. 'We've been here for half an hour and you haven't said much, apart from the usual pleasantries. You haven't even asked about your son.'

'Let's go somewhere a bit quieter. I need some fresh air, anyway.'

Jake agreed; this was no place for a slanging match. 'I'm going to go and pay first.'

As he walked back towards the table, Jake stopped short. In a far corner of the restaurant was Sharon's boyfriend. He was sitting at a table on his own. Jake's first instincts were to go over there and beat him to a pulp, but he didn't. Did she really need to bring her boyfriend with her? What the hell was he doing here anyway?

'Right, Sharon. You got everything?' Doing his best to sound nonchalant and helping Sharon with her coat, he watched as she looked over her shoulder and exchanged glances with her boyfriend. He pretended not to notice.

'Do you feel like a walk, Jake? Along the riverbank. Maybe we could talk properly then.'

'Sure. Why not.' It wasn't what he had planned but he needed to hear what she had to say and maybe it was for the best. There were still things he wanted to know about their marriage, that he felt was his own business.

Just after leaving the restaurant, Jake turned back. 'Hang on a minute, I think I've left my wallet,' he said. Leaving Sharon on the pavement, Jake ran back in. He saw Sharon's boyfriend standing up and walking towards the door. So this was going to be some kind of ambush, was it? How many of his friends were hiding round the corner?

Jake bumped into the man on purpose; he could see that the man was shocked to see him back in the restaurant. 'Oops, sorry, mate,' Jake said. Then he leaned in towards the man's ear and hissed, 'Get the fuck out of here while you still can, or I am going to break both of your legs, and my friend in here' – Jake slightly opened his jacket to show his gun in its holster under his arm – 'is going to blow your fucking head off.' Jake's threatening whisper made the man do as he was told. Taking his mobile phone out of his pocket, Jake rang the chauffeur. 'Sharon's boyfriend is in the restaurant. We're going for a walk up the South Bank; watch the front doors for a young kid, brown suit, dark hair.'

He trotted back to where Sharon was waiting. 'Hey, sorry about that, Sharon. Bloody fool I am, I dropped it on the floor.' Jake's smile was broad, even though inside he felt sick. Reaching out for Sharon's hand brought a lump to Jake's throat. It was a clear moonlit night. Perfect for lovers.

Hand in hand, they started walking, both looking straight

ahead of them. It seemed neither of them wanted to make eye contact.

'Jake, it's been a nice evening but we both know it's over.'

'Am I allowed to ask why?' Feeling the gun inside his jacket pocket rub against his chest he knew what he had to do, but he needed some sort of closure first. Had she ever loved him? He felt sad and crushed as they walked side by side, with the moon shining on the Thames.

'I did love you, Jake, but I want my own life now.' Her words stabbed Jake's heart. She was being matter of fact about it. As though she was just discarding an old pair of shoes. The woman he loved wasn't there any more. This one was bitter and heartless.

'Well, if you walk away, you walk away a very wealthy woman and will be able to start afresh.' He was trying to sound reasonable to this shrew.

Pulling him into a side alley, Sharon laughed. 'Do you really think I am going to walk away with just a few quid in my pocket? Think again, Jake. I want it all. Why not? I've earned it. You and Mr High and Mighty Tony think there is nothing and no one that can knock you off your pedestal. Well, I have, Jake. Game, set and match, eh?'

Trying to keep his voice steady, Jake tried again. 'It wouldn't just be a few quid, Sharon. We're talking millions, not thousands. I know what you've done. You've betrayed us all. Is that what would make you happy, seeing us all behind bars?'

'I would be the architect of it all, Jake, and I wouldn't have had to do half of the things you have. Do the others know? No.' She shook her head. 'That was a stupid question, of course they do. I'm sure they all want me to keep my mouth shut. Well, Jake, I have a contingency plan. The police will be all over you and Tony like flies around shit if anything happens to me.' Even in the darkness Jake could see the sneer on her face. Her pupils seemed dilated and he realised she must have taken a lot of cocaine before this meeting. This was not his Sharon. She seemed glad he knew what she had done and was proud of her achievement. What a bitch.

As they stood in the darkness of the alley, lit only by moonlight, Jake felt he had to ask, 'When did you stop loving me, Sharon? What happened?'

'Years ago, Jake. I am sick of being "good old Sharon", one of the boys. Tony never looked at me once. Instead, he fell for that slut stripper who I gave a job to.'

Jake felt stunned by this confession. 'Tony? What has he got to do with it? He has only ever treated you well. We're family. Don't be nasty about Francesca, she has nothing to do with any of this.'

'The only person Tony loves is himself. Or rather, it was, until that stupid slut turned up.' Sharon's fake laughter rang out. 'Well, he came from the gutter and that was the best he could get.'

Ignoring her comments, Jake carried on. 'Why do you have such a grudge against Tony? He has worked bloody hard to make us all rich. He bought us our first house, Sharon. Tony has been more than generous.' Jake was confused.

'Not once did he look at me like a woman. He would fuck anything with a pulse, but not me. How the hell do you think that made me feel, Jake?'

Jake couldn't believe his ears. 'You fancied Tony? Is that what you're telling me? All this is a woman scorned?' As crazy as the situation was, Jake felt like laughing. He now felt no reservations about what he had to do. He had his answers.

'Oh, Jake, love.' Sharon stroked his face. 'You only see what you want to see. I loved him for years. He could have given me children. I married you again because I needed a father for Jack and I could be close to him, still. He needed me, if only to run his club. But I don't need him or you any more. Alex is younger and more powerful. You, Tony and Ralph are past it now.' Her shrill laughter filled the air. 'Old pensioners playing cops and robbers. I'm not walking away from anything, Jake. You are.'

'You really are a nasty piece of work, Sharon.' Jake shoved her against the wall, banging her head against it.

A shot rang out into the night air and Jake fell to the ground on his knees. His lifeless body, with just one bullet hole to his head where Sharon had shot him, lay in a crumpled heap.

'I'll not take your crumbs, Jake. I want it all,' Sharon spat out as she looked down at his dead body on the ground. She felt no remorse. Then she saw the gun in his pocket. Stunned, she peered at it more closely; he had been going to kill her.

Hearing a noise, she looked up and saw a figure standing in the shadows. 'You took your fucking time,' she said. 'He was going to kill me, the bastard. We need to leave now.'

A woman emerged from the shadows. Taken aback, Sharon said, 'What the fuck are you doing here? Where's Alex?'

Raising her gun, the woman pointed it at Sharon.

'You haven't got the guts!' Sharon spat out, reaching for her own gun. A shot fired and Sharon collapsed on top of Jake's lifeless body. Blood poured from her a wound in her stomach.

Walking up to her, the woman pointed the gun at her once more. 'That was for the family. This one is for Jake.' Again, the woman pressed the trigger and shot Sharon in the head. She looked at their dead bodies lying on top of each other in the darkness of the side alley, highlighted by a touch of moonlight; they made a pitiful sight.

At the top of the alley, the woman gingerly stepped over another dead body with a bullet hole in it as she walked towards the main road. Sharon's lover, Alex. Thankfully, the silencer had muffled the sound as she had shot him in the back. She was sorry that she had got there too late to save Jake, but it couldn't be helped. Maybe it was for the best. This way she had saved him from tormenting himself for years and feeling guilty about Sharon's death.

Looking up, she saw an orange light coming towards her. 'Taxi!' she shouted, as she held her arm out. The black cab slowed down and stopped. Turning her head for one last look towards the alleyway, she opened the door and got in.

22

DEVASTATION

'Tony, it's me. Has Jack been in touch yet?' Francesca's voice quivered as she spoke. How she wished she wasn't stuck in Italy.

Yawning, Tony sat up in his bed and rubbed his face. Looking at the clock, he saw that it was 3 a.m. 'What's wrong? Francesca, are you all right?' Instantly he shook himself awake.

'We're all okay, but have you heard from Jack?'

'Francesca, you're crying, what the hell is wrong? No. In answer to your question, Jack hasn't contacted me. Why should he?' A cold sense of foreboding passed through Tony's mind. He knew what Francesca was going to tell him. Sharon was dead. He had expected that, but why hadn't Jake called him?

He heard a scuffle on the other end of the phone and Julie's voice in the background; he waited. 'Give me that phone,' he heard Julie say.

'Tony, it's Julie. Jack has rung us. He probably forgot we were in Italy. Sharon is dead. But worst of all, Tony...' Julie paused.

'What! For Christ's sake, spit it out. What's happened?' He felt the panic rise in him; he knew something had gone terribly wrong.

'Jake is dead, too. They've both been found by a man walking his dog on the South Bank. I am going to arrange flights home as soon as possible. Get in touch with Jack, obviously he's distraught. Apparently the police contacted him. I don't know the rest of it. I am going to call Ralph. Ring me back when you get hold of Jack.'

Julie waited. She knew Tony was still on the line, but there was silence.

'Are you there, Tony? Speak to me,' Julie prompted him in her most authoritative voice. She knew this would knock the wind out of his sails and no one had expected this. 'Answer me!' she shouted.

'I'm here. Jake can't be dead, Julie. He can't be.' The lump in Tony's throat rose and he could feel the tears rolling down his cheeks. He was shocked into silence. 'Jack must have got it wrong.' The sob left his throat and Julie could hear him crying.

'Listen to me. Wipe your fucking eyes and contact Jack. Both his parents have died tonight. Now, do as you're told. I'm going to ring Ralph.' Julie started shouting at him to bring him out of his shocked state, but she had to get through to him. 'Are you listening to me, Tony?'

'Yes. Yes. I hear you.' Tony's voice was barely above a whisper. His heart was pounding and he felt dizzy. Sitting on the edge of the bed, he wiped his face with his hands and tried composing himself. 'I'll ring Jack now and call you when I can.'

'You call Jack and I will call you in one hour. Do you think I am hanging around here for you to ring me? No. Do what you have to do. We'll get some flights. Try and hold it together.' With that, Julie ended the call. Tony was in a state. She wouldn't have expected anything else.

'I just can't believe it. Jake is dead. How? Why?' Francesca fell into Julie's arms and sobbed. It was pretty obvious to Julie she would have to take charge here. First things first, she had to get them both a stiff drink, then she would call Ralph. She sat Francesca down in a chair.

'Drink this, it will do you good,' she said moments later, handing a brandy to Francesca. She gulped her own straight down. Dear God, she needed it. Her mind was all over the place. What the hell had gone wrong?

* * *

'Thanks for coming, Uncle Tony. I didn't want to go and identify the bodies without you.' Throwing his arms around Tony, Jack tried composing himself in front of the police officers at the station.

Ralph had already contacted Tony and put him on the alert. He knew, now the news was out, there would probably be the odd journalist sneaking around, so warned him to be on his guard.

As much as Tony felt like breaking down and crying himself, he knew he had to be strong for Jack. The next few minutes were going to be the worst of his life and something he would remember forever.

'Are you ready, Mr Sinclair?' The detective looked at Tony and then back at Jack. 'We have a car waiting. This won't take long, but if you would rather wait...' Her voice trailed off. She had been in this job for years and she knew there was never a good time to identify a body, but it had to be done.

'No, I'll come now.' Then Jack faltered. 'Is it okay if my uncle Tony comes as well?' His eyes were filling with tears and he wiped them with his sleeve.

The female detective was an older woman, possibly in her late fifties. She had obviously been dragged out of bed for this. Her brown hair was pulled back with a scrunchie and she had a tracksuit on. She had known about Tony Lambrianu and Jake Sinclair for years, but the very idea of this grown man saying 'Uncle Tony' nearly made her smile. The most notorious gangster in London was 'Uncle Tony'. It sounded almost laughable.

'Yes. Of course. Just take your time, Jack, there's no rush. Whenever you're ready... okay?' She led the way to the car and Tony and Jack followed.

Police officers stood in the mortuary watching and waiting as the attendant pulled back the white sheets from Sharon and Jake's bodies in turn.

Almost collapsing onto Tony, Jack cried out and burst into tears. This huge young man clung to Tony like a baby as he cried. Holding him, Tony looked over his shoulder at the officer in charge and nodded.

'What happened?' Tony asked as he tried remaining calm– although it was pretty clear from the bullet holes.

'We're not sure, Mr Lambrianu. It's still early days. A passer-by found them while walking his dog and called the police. There is a lot of investigating to do, but first we had to officially identify the bodies.'

'They are not bodies!' Jack turned and screamed at her. 'That's my mum and dad!' He was distraught and upset.

The female detective looked down at the floor and then back up at Jack. 'Yes. Of course. Sorry, Mr Sinclair. Maybe we should leave now.' She walked to the door and opened it for them both.

Tony had his arm around Jack's waist and steered him towards the door, and then he turned back and looked at Jake. His beloved brother. Maybe not biologically, but by God they were brothers in every possible way. Lying there on that cold slab was his partner and friend. One of the few people he had trusted all his life.

Then he looked at Sharon. Hate filled him. He half wished she were alive so that he could kill her himself!

Emotions were at an all-time high. Tony felt numb. How on earth had Jake ended up on a slab in the mortuary beside her?

Eventually, all cried out and with a few whiskies down him, Jack fell asleep out of exhaustion and drunkenness.

Sweeping his hair back, Tony at last had time to breathe and think. It had only been a short while, a couple of hours at most, but it seemed like an eternity.

Looking around the apartment where he had shared so many good times with Jake, he felt sick. Never again would he see his brother's boyish smile, or tease him for always looking in the fridge for something to eat. His voice of reason had left his side; Jake always saw the other person's point of view. Running to the bathroom, Tony threw up. Alone, he sat curled up on the floor and cried. He thought he would never stop.

* * *

After walking into the apartment, Ralph looked around. Seeing the half-empty whisky bottle on the coffee table, he walked to the bedroom. Jack was lying on his back, snoring, still dressed. Then he heard a noise and walked to the bathroom. The door was shut but he could hear muffled sounds through it. He knew it was Tony. 'You in there, Tony? It's me, Ralph,' he said, as he knocked on the door.

Pressing his head closer to the door, Ralph could hear Tony was crying. What else did he expect? This poor bastard had just lost the other half of himself. 'I'm going to make some coffee.'

At last Tony came into the lounge where Ralph was sitting. His face was red and his eyes were swollen, but Ralph said nothing. 'Get that down you. We need to talk.' Trying to be matter of fact, Ralph carried on. 'There is more to this than we know, Tony. I've been doing some digging with a few friends of mine and it seems there were three people killed last night.'

Raising his head, Tony looked at Ralph, shocked. Forgetting his sorrow for a moment, he asked in disbelief, 'Three bodies? Who was the other one?' His voice was croaky. After clearing his throat, he spoke again. 'Ralph?' He knew he looked shocking but he really didn't care.

Smacking his lips together and throwing his hands up in the air, Ralph looked bewildered. 'At a guess, I think it was Sharon's boyfriend, but I'm not sure. As far as I can gather, Sharon shot Jake. Forensics have told the police that the bullet that killed Jake came from the gun that Sharon was holding. It has her fingerprints all over it. I don't for the bloody life of me know who killed Sharon or the boyfriend. Believe me, Tony, I really don't know.'

Tony frowned, then looked up as a thought crossed his mind. 'Was it that bloody Don Carlos? Did he set this up?' Standing up, Tony started stomping around the room. Why hadn't he thought of this before? Don Carlos had done this. He was desperate for Sharon to die, no matter what.

'Sit down, lad! No, it wasn't him. He is as shocked as all of us, believe me. It's a bloody mystery, Tony. No one knows who it was. I did wonder if you had anything to do with it.'

'Me? You think I would kill Jake? You bastard!' Tony went to slap Ralph, but Ralph held his arm up and stopped him. He took no offence; he knew Tony was just lashing out.

'No, you bloody fool. Sharon! Look, just sit down. You will wake Jack up in the other room and we don't need that right now.'

Looking across at the bedroom door, Tony nodded. 'Hand on heart, Ralph, you really don't know?'

'Hand on heart, Tony, I swear I really don't know.' Ralph shook his head.

'Then we'll do some digging and find out who was behind this.'

Ralph had no doubts about that and he would do his best to help, but even he was confused. 'Julie and the family will be back home this afternoon. You need to stay strong, Tony. Elle is in a pretty bad way, by all accounts. I'll do whatever I can. I'm not Jake, but I'm here. Do you hear me?'

'Elle! Oh, my God, I had forgotten about her. Shit, Ralph, I should ring her.' Putting his head in his hands, Tony felt a stab of guilt. Elle had never even crossed his mind. Dear God, how could he be so selfish?

'Leave it for now, Tony. You can't think of everything. We'll sort it. Julie and Francesca are with her. So are the rest of the family.'

'What am I going to say to her, Ralph? Jake was her son. He lived with her long before I did. She had him as a young boy. Fuck's sake, how could I be so thoughtless.' Tears filled Tony's eyes again while Ralph sat there and looked on. There was nothing he could do or say to make him feel better. Jake had been a part of them both for years. And now he was dead.

23

CUCKOOS IN THE NEST

'How is Elle doing?' Julie looked around at the kitchen which had always been so full of life, but was now empty. 'It's been a week, Francesca, and we're no further on.'

'She's doing okay. She has Albert and Tony. The girls are popping in, but you know Elle. She is waiting for them to release the body. She keeps saying she needs Jake to rest in peace. I don't know how long that is going to take. Their investigations are taking them nowhere. Tony is working himself into a frazzle, and Jack hasn't said much.' Fran felt deflated. Ever since they had got back from Italy there seemed to be a dark cloud over the house. The worst thing of all was that there were no answers.

'It will get better, Fran. Everyone grieves in their own way. You have to let them get on with it. Let's be honest, there has been no time to grieve. It's all over the newspapers. "Gangland boss shot dead by wife". Fucking hell, they are making a meal of it.' Julie tried to laugh to break the tension but she could see Fran was beside herself with worry.

'I don't know how this will affect Tony. He has never been without Jake. Bloody hell, Julie, I saw Tony looking at photos the other day. Photos I have never seen before. They are of him and Jake at the beach with Elle, school photos they had taken together. Can you believe that? Tony's school photos. Now, the newspapers would love to see those.' Smiling, Francesca squeezed Julie's hand. As usual, Julie had taken the reins and looked after everyone.

'I heard Sharon's family are all in mourning for her. I couldn't give a shit! And that sister of hers, badmouthing Jake as a bad husband, hasn't helped matters. You know what, Francesca? I have already made my mind up that when this all dies down, that bitch is going to get what is coming to her. They hadn't seen each other for years. Even Sharon had no real love for her. She only turned up when she wanted something, but now she is playing the mournful sister. It's a fucking joke Fran.' Julie couldn't stop ranting; it was her way of letting off steam.

'Stop it, Julie. Don't you think there's enough bad feeling and death around at the moment? I feel sorry for Jack. He is being pulled in every direction and Sharon's family are trying to make him choose a side. It's disgusting.'

'No, they are trying to make money out of this. I presume, unless she has stated otherwise, that Jack will get her share, plus Jake's. Wow. That makes the fireman an even better prospect for that greedy family.'

'Actually, Julie, you have a point.' Francesca agreed with her friend; none of this had even occurred to her. 'Jack will be a very rich man and someone they will want on their side.'

'The question is Fran... can they poison Jack's mind against his father?'

'I hope not.' The sadness in Francesca's voice said it all. Jake had been a good father and had adored Jack. The last thing Francesca wanted was to have his memory tainted. 'I don't want Jack to have to choose. He has to be able to make his own mind up, Julie. He knows we're here for him, and Bobby is looking after him, but whatever he decides I will go along with.'

'No, you bloody won't!' Julie was adamant. 'He is a part of our family. How many fucking Christmas and birthday cards did he get off that lot? Christ, he hasn't met half of them. They are like cockroaches coming out of the woodwork all waiting for their handout. There is no choice, Francesca. He is our family and you have been a mother to him. He belongs here with us. Well, you,' Julie corrected herself and poured another glass of wine. 'No, Fran, love. There is no contest. Jack is our family. Fuck them all, especially that sister of Sharon's!'

'Mum! Are you in?' Bobby walked down the hallway with Jack. 'Ah, there you are. Hi, Julie, how are you?' After walking over and kissing her on the cheek, Bobby turned and kissed Francesca. Jack sat at the table.

After lighting a cigarette, Julie blew the smoke into the air, crossed her arms and looked at Bobby. 'What's up, guys?' Julie eyed them suspiciously.

'Well, it's Uncle Tony,' said Jack. 'The police have been in touch; they want to come and see me, but Uncle Tony wants us to have the meeting here. I would rather be here with you all, too, if that's all right with you.'

'Of course it is.' Francesca put her arms around him. Within minutes, Tony was walking through the door.

'Ah, good, lads, you're here.' Tony rubbed his hands together. 'The police should be here anytime.'

'I'll put the kettle on. Is anyone hungry?' Francesca looked around the kitchen. No one wanted anything to eat. They were far too interested in what the police wanted and finally the buzzer went on the intercom for the gates to be opened.

The two detectives sat down. They asked Jack how he was and told them all that they were releasing Jake and Sharon's bodies.

'Is that it? Is there no update?' asked Tony.

'The truth is, Mr Lambrianu, we are investigating this but half of it seems to already be solved.' The female detective looked across at Jack. 'Sorry, Jack, but we both know that your mum shot your dad. Forensics have been over everything with a fine-tooth comb. Your father was also carrying a gun, but it was still in its holster. So as for who shot your mum, Jack, there are no leads. We will carry on investigating it, of course. But there are no eye witnesses. The other man who was found dead, we believe was your mum's boyfriend. We traced him back to a bed and breakfast where he and your mum had been staying.' The detective paused to allow her words to sink in, before saying, 'Do you want your mum and dad sent to any particular funeral parlour? We can arrange that.'

'I've been in touch with a funeral director.' Tony took a card out of his wallet and handed it over to the detective. 'This is for Jake and Jake only. I don't give a fuck what you do with her body.'

'Tony. Stop it.' Standing beside Jack, Francesca put her arm on his shoulder. 'Whatever you think of Sharon, she was Jack's mum. Have some respect.'

'Respect! Are you fucking crazy, Francesca? You are talking about a woman that murdered my brother and robbed that lad of his father. That slut had already left everyone behind.' Tony's eyes darkened and his face flushed pink.

'You shut the fuck up, Tony. And don't you ever speak to Fran like that again.' Julie had had enough of this squabbling. 'Sit down.' Her authoritative voice filled the room. 'Now then. Jack, what do you want to do? Come on, cards on the table. The officer is waiting. We know where your dad is going, but what about your mum?'

Jack glanced across at Tony.

'Don't bother looking at him; these are your parents. We'll do what you want to do.' Julie gave Tony a sharp look. He nodded. She was right. It was Jack's decision.

'I don't want them to be together,' Jack began. 'For whatever reasons, Mum shot Dad. So, no, I can't have them together. I think it would be for the best if Mum's family organised her funeral. I am fully prepared to pay for it, but I think they should organise it.'

Tony breathed a sigh of relief. It seemed Jack had made his choice. This was his family.

'Very well, then. Are you sure, Jack, that you want your mum's family to take over her arrangements?' Julie asked. She wanted him to be absolutely sure.

'Yes, Aunty Julie. She made Dad sad. He loved her and I don't know why she didn't love him back. He was a good man and I want to do right by him... if that's okay with everyone. Also,' Jack stammered. He looked embarrassed.

'Go on.' Julie was curious as to what he was going to say.

'Did you know, Uncle Tony, that my dad wasn't my real dad?' Jack looked across at Tony.

Glancing around the room and pursing his lips, Tony wasn't sure how to answer. But he decided now was the time to tell the truth. 'Yes, I did, Jack. But then, he was not my real brother. You're talking biology, Jack. That doesn't make a family. Love does. I'm not Bobby's father, you all know that, but to all intents and purposes I am. I'm the man that bought him his first pint of lager. I took him to football matches. As far as I'm concerned, I'm his dad.' Tony looked up at Bobby.

'You forgot to mention, you taught me how to cheat at poker.' Bobby laughed. 'Yeah, you're my dad. You're the only dad I have ever known, same as Jack here with Jake.'

The police officers glanced across at each other and decided it was time for them to leave. 'If you need anything, Mr Sinclair, here is my card. We will be in touch with Mrs Sinclair's family to make arrangements with them.'

'Thank you. You have all been very kind.' Jack stood up and shook their hands before they left.

'So, who told you, Jack?' Tony couldn't help but ask. Why now, after all these years, did someone feel the need to tell him that Jake wasn't his real dad?

'Grandma.' Jack's voice was barely a whisper. 'She said she felt I should know. We're not blood-related at all, Tony. In any way. I am the son of some guy I don't know about. Did you know him?' Jack waited.

'Not really, mate. Think he got a job elsewhere and left. As far as I'm aware, he didn't know you were on the way. Why are you so worried about blood and family, Jack?'

'Well. I don't really belong, do I? I'm like a cuckoo. I don't belong anywhere. Now Dad... erm, Jake, is dead, I don't belong here, either.' Tears rolled down Jack's cheeks.

Everyone expected Tony to start throwing a tantrum but he surprised them all. He reached out and pulled Jack towards him and hugged him. 'We don't do blood in this family, Jack. We're all bloody cuckoos. Your dad was my brother and I am your uncle Tony. Got it? Lambrianu and Sinclair. That's how it's always been. Blood or not, eh?' Tony held him tightly.

24

GAME, SET AND MATCH

Elle handed Tony his coffee and stood there waiting. She wanted to speak to him, but knew he wouldn't see her side of things.

'Well, Elle, I can see you're waiting for something so you might as well get it over with.'

'It's Sharon's funeral today. I want to go.' Elle was serious. She felt better now all was resolved with Jake, and his funeral was going to be a lavish affair. Horse-drawn carriages would bring London to a standstill. Everyone had agreed to close their shops and pubs for the day out of respect. Reporters were on standby and it would be splashed all over the local news.

Sharon's funeral was going to be a much smaller affair.

'Why the hell do you want to go and see her, Elle?' Tony couldn't believe his ears.

'Because Jake was and is my son. I want the chance to see the woman who killed him, for the very last time.'

Tony knew there was no point in arguing. 'Okay, I will have a word with Jack. I'll go with you to the funeral parlour; make sure none of her screaming banshee sisters are there.'

'I don't care if they are, Tony, love. I can look them in the face. Can they look at me, knowing their sister is a cold-blooded killer?'

Tony could see there was no way of changing her mind.

* * *

Elle walked into the room. Sharon looked beautiful, almost as though she were asleep. Tony looked up at the ceiling; he couldn't bear to look at her. Jack and Tony were both curious and confused when Elle stood by the open coffin and stroked Sharon's hair.

'I used to think, Sharon, you were the best thing that happened to Jake, but I was wrong. The more he loved you, the more you hurt him.' Elle's voice was soft and soothing, as if she were talking to a child.

Tony and Jack stood mesmerised by this strange scene. 'You held a sword of guilt over his head, forever reminding him that he couldn't give you children. Once you had Jack, you held that over his head, too. He knew if you left him you would take him away. Oh, yes, Sharon, he told me many times about your threats to take Jack away. Now Jake has gone, I can do the one thing I've always wanted to do.' Elle raised her arm and, with one mighty sweep, she slapped Sharon hard across the face, although it made no impact. She was about to do it again when Tony grabbed her arm.

'Enough, Elle.'

'I've wanted to do that for a very long time.' Elle pulled her coat together and walked out of the room.

'What was that all about, Elle?' Tony asked later, after they'd dropped Jack off at Bobby's.

'Justice, Tony. It was something I've always wanted to do and that was my one and only chance. I did it partly for Jake, but mostly for myself. I will always protect my boys. And you and Jake are my boys.'

25

THE LAST WORD

'What's all this then?' Looking around the room at the whole family gathered together, Tony was surprised. It seemed they were waiting for him. 'If it's a family meeting, it must be bad.' Tony sat down on the huge leather sofa, brushed his silvery blond hair from his face and sighed. 'Well, let's have it. More bad news, I presume?'

'It's not bad news, Dad. We've decided to support you the way you have always supported us.' Scarlet was taking the lead as spokesperson.

'Do you know anything about this, Francesca?' He frowned. He really didn't need to play games at a time like this.

'I do now, darling. Listen to Scarlet and Katie. Hear them out; it's not all bad news.' Her warm smile convinced him it would be okay, but he was curious.

'Go on, then, I'm listening.' Getting comfy and folding his arms, Tony waited.

'Everyone who works at the club is being paid still, even though the club's been shut for ages. Katie and I have been talking. I know you can afford it, but, nevertheless, it's bad business.

You have to open up the club again.' Pausing, Scarlet waited for his protests, but none came. 'I'm going to help run the club. Take over where Sharon left off. Sharon's assistant is doing a good job, but she is not a Lambrianu. Katie and Chris have ideas about taking on the vineyard and running it as a Lambrianu legacy, as you know. We think you should let us. We also think that you and Mum should take a well-deserved break from all of this. Go away on holiday.'

Looking around the room at the sea of faces, Tony wanted to laugh. His young daughters thought they could run his businesses. They were kids. What did they know? He appreciated the gesture but it was laughable.

'That's really nice of you, Scarlet.' He turned towards Katie. 'It's nice of both of you, but there is a lot you haven't taken into consideration. What do you know about running a club? More to the point, a pole-dancing club. And besides, what about Adam?' Tony shook his head. He didn't want to crush Scarlet's good intentions.

'I bet I know more about the club business than you did when you started.' Scarlet stuck out her chin stubbornly and looked him squarely in the face. 'We've been brought up with it and what I don't know, I'll learn. It's the same with Katie. She has been brought up going to the vineyard. She and Chris have some good ideas. Fresh, new ideas. And as for Adam, there are enough of us to look after him. Elle is more than happy to live in, I've already spoken to her. It will give her something to do as well. Losing Uncle Jake has wiped her out. Now she has another little boy to look after.' Scarlet winced at mentioning Jake's name, but they had to talk about him sooner or later. 'We're going to reopen the club with our engagement parties.' Stopping him with her hand again, Scarlet spoke a little louder this time. Her confidence had grown somewhat and she felt braver. 'Yes, Papa, we're going to marry these two guys, and I think this family needs something to celebrate. We will start sorting things out after Jake's funeral.'

'Well, they have been busy, haven't they, Ralph. I always thought someone might want to steal off me, but bloody hell. These two want the lot. Lock, stock and barrel. What do you say?' Tony laughed. The very idea seemed absurd.

'Personally, Tony, I think they have some valid points, and where would we all be if no one had given us a break, eh? They have more back-up than we ever did,' said Ralph, giving him that knowing look.

Tony thought it was ridiculous. 'Thanks, girls, but no thanks.'

Christopher interrupted. 'Probationary period, Mr Lambrianu.' Much to Tony's annoyance, he was sitting in on this family meeting, as was Dominic.

Tony narrowed his eyes. 'What has all of this got to do with you two?'

Very calmly and unintimidated, Christopher said, 'It's inevitable that we are going to marry your daughters. Everyone else knows it. You haven't even asked how Dominic is getting on with his garage. I have invested with Dominic and it's a going concern. No one is trying to steal anything from you. You cannot be in Italy and over here. You don't have any confidence in us, I understand. So why don't you make it a probationary period of say, three months?'

'Okay, I will think about it.' Tony held up his hands in submission. He felt browbeaten. Everyone seemed to have an answer to each objection he made. 'I am making no decisions until after Jake's funeral.' Sitting back in his chair and sweeping his hand through his hair, he let out a deep sigh.

Ralph gave a little cough. 'Erm, talking of Jake's funeral, Tony, I would like a word with you. Can we have a talk in private?' Ralph looked serious, but he also looked embarrassed.

'Sure, Ralph.' Tony was glad of the excuse to leave the meeting behind. 'Let's pop down to the games room now.' He stood up and walked away with Ralph.

'Jake loved this place.' A smile crossed Tony's face as he looked towards the leather sofa in the corner that still had Jake's games controller on the arm.

'I had a telephone call from an undertaker today. Apparently, they have tried contacting you, but you haven't got back to them, so they called me.'

Tony waited while Ralph took the tops off two bottles of lager and handed him one. 'Oh, you mean that undertakers in town. Yes.' Tony nodded. 'They've left a few messages for me to call them but they just want to offer some kind of deal, I suppose. They are after selling me something.'

'Well, you're wrong, Tony, which is why they probably decided to contact me. I popped in to see them and they gave me this.' Ralph handed over an envelope.

Tentatively, Tony reached out to take it, all the while curiously looking at Ralph. After first taking a gulp from the bottle of lager, he opened the official-looking envelope and read the letter within.

Suddenly, Tony burst out laughing. He was belly laughing so much, tears streamed down his face. Waving the letter under Ralph's nose, he said, 'Have you seen what that cheeky bastard has done? Jake has fucked us all. Oh, my God, he's amazing, Ralph. Read that. That little brother of mine had to have the last word.'

Ralph picked up the letter and, as he read it, a faint smile appeared on his face. This is what it had taken to bring Tony back into the land of the living. This was closure for Tony, hearing from Jake again. It read:

Tony, mate, if you're reading this then I'm dead. We both knew it would happen someday. Don't be sorry. Fuck, we had a few scrapes in our time. I'm surprised we lasted this long.

Right, so after all these years I can have my say without you bloody interrupting. I've organised my funeral the way I want it. I don't want your posh suits and mourning. I am going to make you suffer, brother. You support Chelsea and I love West Ham. Possibly the only thing we ever disagreed about. If you want to do right by me, follow my instructions and do this for me. I'm so pleased I'm going to be there in spirit only, cos you'd fucking kill me anyway!

I want everyone in full football kit. West Ham colours, claret and blue. I want it done with horses and cart. Not cos it's posh, but I am not having you hide and squirm behind tinted windows in your car, you arsehole! You always said I wasted my money on my season ticket, but this is going to be worth its weight in gold.

I ain't leaving you, Tony. I'm still gonna be around watching your back. I'm your wingman, always will be.

On a sentimental note, I love you, mate. You have always been my idol and the best brother ever. Look after Elle and Jack for me. I trust you with the two people I love the most. Give my love to the family. Carry on, Tony. You're doing this for 'us', as always. See you in hell, mate. (Not too soon, I hope.)

Jake

P.S. Thank your lucky stars, mate. I did think about having a Marvel funeral and having you stood there as Iron Man!!!

Ralph handed the letter back to Tony. Although he was smiling, Tony noticed the date and then looked up at Ralph. A deep frown crossed his brow. 'This was written last month. Do you think he knew he was going to die?'

'Who knows, son. The bottom line is, he was prepared for it and he had enough foresight to send you a message from the grave. Thank your lucky stars for that, too, Tony.' Ralph started to grin. 'Or not, as it may be. He's forcing you to wear his football colours. And he knows you can't refuse his last wish. That's blackmail. I like his style.' Ralph burst out laughing.

'That cheeky bastard! He had already sorted his life out. Or rather, the end of it. Well, Ralph, we had better go and see these guys. Come on.' Bouncing up the stairs in a much better mood than he had come down in, Tony was laughing. 'Let's go and see what else he has planned for me.'

Hearing the commotion as Tony ran up the stairs, Francesca and Julie walked into the hallway. Seeing Tony's flushed face, Francesca was worried. 'Are you okay, Tony? What's happened?'

'Everything is just fine, Francesca. Isn't it, Ralph?' Tony was waving a piece of paper in the air and smiling. 'We won't be long.' After kissing her on the cheek, Tony almost ran out of the front door.

'Where are they going?' Julie muttered under her breath. Shrugging her shoulders, she turned and walked back into the lounge. 'Well, you lot.' Julie picked up her gold cigarette case and flicked it open. Taking a cigarette out and putting it in her holder, she picked up her gold lighter and lit it. Standing there in her red trouser suit, blonde bob and full make-up, she looked quite the authoritative figure. 'It looks like you're going to have to wait a little longer before you get your sticky paws on the empire.'

'We're trying to help, Julie, not get our hands on anything.' Scarlet was adamant, but the sly grin on Julie's face spoke volumes.

* * *

'Are you ready, Tony?' Francesca couldn't help smiling at the figure before her. She didn't want to burst out laughing, but she had to admit Jake had left a legacy and taken the sadness out of the occasion. Tony's mourning had changed to moaning! Kissing him on the cheek, Francesca was pleased to see some of her old Tony back.

'Well? When are you going to take that bloody coat off? You look a right idiot. Come on, Tony, let's see those famous knees of yours. Actually, it's just occurred to me.' Julie tapped her finger on her chin as though pondering. 'Do you realise, Tony, I must be the only woman in London that hasn't seen you undressed!' Julie wasn't as tactful, but seeing Tony standing there in his long, camel coat, bare legs and trainers made her burst out laughing.

'That's your claim to fame, is it? Tony Lambrianu didn't fancy an old bag like you! What the hell are you laughing at, anyway? Have you seen that fascinator with those feathers? God, you look worse than the horses.' Tony had to have his usual jibe as Julie stood there in her satin football shirt and shorts that Jake had asked for, having added some of her own style to it.

Everyone else walked into the room; they were all having one last toast to Jake.

After unbuttoning his coat slowly, Tony removed it and threw it on the chair. 'Well? Are you happy now? There are my knees; that's the closest you will ever get to them!'

Julie's loud cackle filled the room. The feathers in her white fascinator shook and bent as she held her stomach. 'You're never going to live this down, you know.'

Everyone's football shirt had their name on it, including Jake's, as he had insisted on being buried in his football kit. Only Elle was allowed a tracksuit in the same colours.

'Bollocks! Come on, the horses and carriages are waiting.'

Tony led the way with the funeral director, who was also stifling a smile.

'You do know that I'm a Chelsea supporter, don't you?' Tony raised his eyebrow and looked at the funeral director, who was sporting claret and blue plumes in his black hat. Stepping out into the street and seeing the horses gave Tony a warm feeling inside. They had done a good job. Nothing had been left to chance. Every detail had been carefully taken into consideration. He shook his head and smiled, realising they were all going to ride through the whole of the East End wearing West Ham football team colours, which would please them enormously. But knowing Tony was a Chelsea supporter would please them even more. Jake had had his last laugh! He would have loved it.

26

DECISION TIME

Ralph had summoned Tony to a meeting in the office at the closed club. It was time to discuss business. Both dressed in their suits and ties, even though no one was around to see them, they sat on either side of the desk.

'I'm surprised you haven't asked me how things are, Tony. It seems you have forgotten there is a huge investigation going on.' Seeing Tony's sheepish look, Ralph carried on. 'Don't you care what happens to the rest of your family? Well, I do, and I have been very busy while you have been wallowing.'

'So, Ralph, where do we stand with this investigation now?'

'Those detectives still have files on us. And they still want to make a huge arrest, which will help their promotion prospects, no doubt. But we have had a close shave and I don't intend taking chances like that again. It's time to keep our noses clean. We're not getting any younger and, personally, I think you're a lucky bastard.' Ralph shook his head and laughed. 'You have been offered a lifeline. The kids. Or rather, your kids, want to lighten the load. Take their offer, Tony. It's fresh faces with fresh ideas. More to the point, there are no files on them.'

Taking a drink and gathering his thoughts, Ralph continued. 'Obviously I have done a lot on my own and Don Carlos has helped. I think we all feel a little guilty about the outcome. This tragedy was never meant to happen.' Looking up, Ralph saw Tony's mask fall for a moment. The sadness behind his eyes said it all.

'Firstly, I have it on good authority that the investigation is going nowhere. As we speak, they are packing away that incident room and all its files. Although we both know they will keep them... just in case.'

Tony looked at Ralph curiously. The investigation was over? That seemed incredible. This couldn't be right. He knew Ralph was a 'fixer', but this went beyond even his reach. 'Tell me, Ralph.' Tony's velvety voice was calm and steady.

Feeling on more solid ground, Ralph smiled and spread his hands wide, almost spilling his whisky. 'How can there be an investigation without their star witness? Oh, yes, Sharon had sung like a bird. About the money, our lifestyle and, of course, the dead bodies we left in our wake.' Ralph paused.

'They have pages and pages of statements from Sharon. Possibly even things we haven't done. My guess is, if it all went tits up she wanted into the witness protection programme. Tell me, Tony, what court would believe a drugged up, bitter ex-wife who turned out to be a cold-hearted murderer? The very thing she was saying about us.' Laughing to himself then taking a drink, Ralph smacked his lips and carried on. 'Let's be honest, Tony, that would not stand up in court. After all, she was a cheat and a con woman and she was a killer.' Ralph saw Tony wince a little, but felt this had to be said.

'But what about the casino and the money laundering? She will have left them a paper trail leading to all of our doors. What about that boyfriend of hers? What had he told his mates? No, Ralph, this will never be over.'

'Oh, shut up, Tony,' snapped Ralph. 'Do you really think I would be telling you it was all over if it wasn't? Get real. The bottom line is this: we have had a warning, and a very big one at that.'

Tony looked at Ralph apologetically. 'I'm sorry, Ralph, I never meant to question you, but even you have to admit it seems impossible.' After reaching over to pour Ralph another drink and pushing the cigar box towards him, Tony waited.

'Sharon's boyfriend.' Ralph nodded as he lit his long Cuban cigar. 'I presume he knew a lot but he isn't going to be telling anyone soon, is he?' Ralph held up his hand to stop Tony interrupting. 'Before you ask, I haven't found out who killed that man. There is no gossip and no trace. His friends that he had with him in the casino that we saw on the recordings have each come to a sticky end.' Ralph looked Tony squarely in the eyes. 'Don Carlos. He's a clever bastard, if ever there was one.' Shaking his head and blowing out thick smoke from the cigar, he sat back and began to explain how Don Carlos had his men hand over a bag of money to these young friends of Sharon's boyfriend, including her sister, who had been in on it all, stating that it was from Sharon. The instructions were simple: they were to cover all the local casinos and play the tables. If they won, they won, and if not, it wasn't a problem. There was plenty more cash where that had come from.

All of the casinos in the area reported that forged money was being passed over the tables and all the time these young fools were being recorded. Of course they were all arrested.

Now Don Carlos had them off the streets and rounded up, he needed to silence them once and for all. While in custody they were each in turn given a present by one of the guards: a packet of their favourite drug – laced with a deadly dose of rat poison! The guard had watched the four young men in custody happily and gratefully snort this lethal concoction and then he had left. The morning shift would find them. It was nothing unusual in prison. It happened all the time.

'As for Sharon's sister.' Ralph gave Tony a knowing look. They both knew the things Don Carlos was capable of. 'All I have heard is that some woman slit her throat. The point is, as far as the police are concerned, there is no evidence and so no case.' Ralph grinned and let out a huge sigh of relief.

'He even covered your tracks, Tony.' Ralph raised his eyebrows. 'Jake's driver...?' Ralph shook his head and tutted.

'He was a lazy bastard!' Tony shouted. His face flushed with anger. 'We both know he was having a sleep while Jake was lying dead on the ground. Where was he, Ralph? When he never heard from Jake and time was passing, where the fuck was he?' Tony's anger raged.

'Yes, and we both know that you made him put the hose in the exhaust of his car then sat in the garage with a gas mask on while you watched him die. For fuck's sake, Tony, I know you were upset, but was that necessary?' Looking disgusted, Ralph shook his head.

Tony stood up and paced around the room. Punching his hand with his fist, he said, 'He could have saved him, Ralph. Don't you see he could have saved him? What did he say to me when I asked him why he hadn't gone looking for Jake? He said as Jake hadn't contacted him, he presumed – yes, *presumed* – that they had gone off to spend the night together! That lazy worthless bastard will never let anyone down again. A stranger walking his dog found my brother!'

'I know, Tony. Believe me, I know. But don't you think it will look strange that Jake's driver suddenly committed suicide? Don Carlos and I felt it was best if it was known that he wasn't driving

Jake that night and Jake had used another driver without your knowledge. The best we could come up with at short notice was, erm...' Ralph paused. This was an awkward situation given the circumstances but Tony had to know everything.

'Who? Who was supposed to be driving Jake?' Curious, Tony turned on Ralph. Who would put themselves in that position with the police and admit to being the driver? 'I told the police who the driver was, Ralph. They already know!'

'No, you told them who you thought was driving Jake. Then a nice young man popped up and admitted he had driven Jake that night because the regular driver had begged this nice young man to stand in for him.'

Shocked, Tony sat down. This indeed was news. 'Who, Ralph? Who would perjure themselves like that?'

'Dominic. Scarlet's boyfriend, or whatever they call themselves these days,' said Ralph, waving his hand in the air nonchalantly.

'Dominic? Why?'

'Listen to me, you stupid bastard. He is Mark's son, and Mark has loyalty to you. Whether it be loyalty to his father or to Scarlet, that boy got you out of a scrape, and so did Don Carlos and I.' The heated discussion between them was leaving Ralph feeling quite breathless. 'It's over now, Tony. Jake's dead. Sharon can rot in her own grave, but we have to carry on. I've given you enough to think about; it's time I left.' He stood up and walked out.

Sitting at his desk alone, Tony looked across at the empty leather chair at the other side of the room. 'Well, Jake. What do you think?' Smiling, Tony nodded at the chair. 'Yes, that's what I think, too.'

27

THINKING TIME

'Well, where is he? You know, the man we all love to hate?' Laughing, Julie picked up her coffee cup and took a sip, leaving her red lipstick mark on the rim. She was curious because she knew Ralph had left Tony at the club hours ago.

'You mean the man you love to hate, Julie.'

Julie's warm infectious laugh filled the room, making Francesca and Elle smile.

'Well? Have you heard from him? What's he doing?'

'He will be doing some sort of business. You know me, I never get involved. Although I do agree he usually texts or phones at this time of day, so it must be something important.' Glancing towards Elle, who had at last joined the fold again, a frown appeared on her brow. Why was Julie so interested in Tony's whereabouts? 'Isn't he with Ralph?'

'No, Ralph has gone to see the doctor; he hasn't been feeling too well lately so he is getting checked out.'

'Probably all those vitamins you've been giving him.' Elle gave Julie a knowing look.

'I knew you would bring that up. Well, for your information, I haven't given him any in a couple of weeks. I just don't have the energy. God, he turns into a rampant old devil.'

'Serves you right, you little minx. Anyway, are you staying for dinner?' Francesca asked.

'Probably not. I suppose I had better go and see what's wrong with Ralph. Probably that bloody "man flu", which means he is going to moan for the next few days and milk it for attention.' Rolling her eyes to the ceiling, Julie looked bored at the thought.

Elle and Fran loved these coffee mornings with Julie, which usually spread throughout the day. All the bitchy gossip about who was sleeping with who came out.

'Maybe you should try some of those "vitamins" on old Albert, Elle. Give him a new lease of life and put a smile on your face,' said Julie, giving Elle a cheeky wink.

'Don't you even think of slipping something into his tea, young lady.' Elle playfully threw her tea towel at her, which made Julie laugh even more. 'Have you heard from Diana?'

'Yes. You know I have. She's got some house share with another couple of female coppers. She likes it. She seems happy enough and that's all that matters, really, isn't it, Elle?' It made her sad not having her daughter around as much and she knew it hurt Ralph immensely, even though it was for her own good. 'Well, I had better go and listen to Ralph moaning. I'll ring you later with the diagnosis.' Julie picked up her bag, kissed them both on the cheek and left.

'She doesn't seem her usual self today, Fran. I know Julie puts on a good front, but today she seemed a bit down. Do you think she's okay?'

'Julie's always okay and, between you and me, she is more worried about Ralph than she cracks on. I wonder where Tony is?'

As if by magic, the telephone rang. Francesca could see that it was Tony and answered it with a smile on her face.

'Francesca.' Those velvety tones on the other end of the line made the hairs stand up on the back of her neck.

'How are you, Tony? I wondered where you were.'

'I'm at the club. It's closed, it's quiet and I have been thinking. It's been a long time since I just sat and thought about things, without interruptions.'

'Are you okay?'

Tony was never one to think things through and this bothered Francesca. He always jumped in feet first and thought later.

'I'm fine, darling,' he reassured her. 'I've telephoned Scarlet and Katie; they are coming to dinner tonight. I want everyone there. Bobby is trying to change his shift, but it's short notice so I'm not sure about him.'

'Really? You want a family meeting in the middle of the week?' Francesca couldn't contain her surprise. This had to be something important.

'Yes. I've told them all to be there around seven. I'll see you later, okay.'

The line went dead and Francesca stood there, still holding the phone. Something was definitely wrong.

'Was that Tony? You look worried, love, what's wrong?' Elle couldn't help but notice the look on Francesca's face.

'I don't know, Elle. Tony has asked everyone to come here tonight for dinner. He didn't say why, but he sounded kind of strange.'

'Well, time will tell. Come on, you pick up Adam and I will put something in the oven. It seems there is going to be a feast to make with everyone coming for dinner.'

* * *

One by one, everyone turned up. 'So, what does Papa want to see us all about?' Scarlet asked and it seemed to Francesca he hadn't told her anything, either.

'Didn't he say when he phoned you?'

'No, he just said he wanted to speak to us all. That was it and then he put the telephone down.'

'Well, we will all find out soon enough, Scarlet. There's his car pulling up in the driveway.' Elle was matter of fact. It seemed she had some kind of idea what this was all about but, as usual, she kept her cards close to her chest.

Tony came through the door like a whirlwind, picking up Adam, who had run down the hallway to meet him.

'How's my boy? Did you have a good day?'

To Francesca's surprise, Tony seemed in a buoyant mood. This wasn't what she had expected; to see him all smiles made quite a change from recent events.

Elle started laying the tureens of vegetables on the table and gave Tony a sideways glance. That convinced Francesca she knew what all of this was about. He had obviously spoken to her at some point in the afternoon and told her of his plans.

Clapping his hands and rubbing them together, Tony announced they should all eat first and then they would talk properly. Looking around the huge dining table at his family talking and laughing about their day while they ate convinced Tony he had made the right decision. This was his family and it seemed to him for the last few years he had let things slide. His business had taken up most of his time and he hadn't really been 'there' amongst them, as he should have been.

Looking at Francesca, his heart skipped a beat. She was always at his side, through the good and the bad. He could never express how much he loved her. Words just didn't seem to say what he felt. Her long auburn wavy hair hung around her shoulders and down her back. Her eyes still shone when she looked at him. She had never lost her girlish figure. Her laughter was warm and genuine. This was his wife and these people around the table were his family. He had been blessed.

'Right then,' he began, breaking up the laughter and chatter. 'I have kept you all waiting long enough. I suppose you're curious as to why I wanted you here on a work night.' Firstly, Tony turned to Katie and Christopher. 'I have decided you can take over the running of the vineyard if you want to.' The pleased, shocked expressions on their faces made him smile.

'Really, Dad? That would be great.' Katie hugged Christopher.

'I won't let you down, Mr Lambrianu. I promise you that.' Christopher was more business-like about the proposal.

'I know,' said Tony, reaching over and shaking his hand in a gesture of goodwill. 'I hold 60 per cent of it. It is still my vineyard. The rest is to be split between you. Of course, Christopher, you will get a wage on top of that for all of your hard work. A percentage of the profits, if that is acceptable.'

'That is more than generous, Mr Lambrianu. As I say, I will not let you down.'

That seemed to satisfy Tony.

'You, Scarlet. You can help with the running of the club. That is, if still think you're up to it. I am in charge and any madcap ideas you have must be run past me first, okay?'

Scarlet's eyes shone like sapphires as she stood up and walked around the table to give Tony a hug and a kiss. 'It won't interrupt with the salon. I can alternate my days. Everything is going splendidly there. Thank you for giving me the chance, Papa.'

Tony pushed her arms off him. He hadn't finished yet. Remembering what Ralph had told him, he turned to Dominic. 'You know about the running of the club, Dominic. Your father also knows about what goes on there. I appreciate you have to run your own business, but I would like you to be involved in it also.'

Astonished at being involved in the family meeting, Dominic looked up at Tony. 'I would like that, Mr Lambrianu. And yes, I will help wherever I can.' He could almost feel a lump in his throat at this acceptance. He knew it was a big offer of friendship for Tony to do this and so followed Christopher's lead by calling him 'Mr Lambrianu', giving him the proper respect he deserved.

'It's time we opened the club again and I don't know of a better way of doing it than announcing your engagements and throwing a huge party to celebrate.' Again, the pleased expressions on all of their faces confirmed he had made the right choice. He realised he had been a stubborn old fool and spending time alone this afternoon, thinking it through, he had realised he needed them as much as they needed him. What would have happened to everything if he had gone to prison? It was time to hand over some of the reins to the people he loved and trusted, if they wanted it.

Francesca reached over and squeezed his hand. She knew it was hard for Tony to let go. The club was his baby. The vineyard was his heritage.

'You all realise that, my finger is still well and truly on the button and all decisions go through me first. Everyone is getting a fair crack of the whip and now it is time to prove yourselves.'

Everyone nodded in acceptance.

'What about you, Bobby? What do you want?' Tony asked.

'Nothing really, Dad. Just for things to run as smoothly as they always have and for everyone to be happy. Of course, I will be sorry to see Katie leave and live in Italy...' Then he stopped himself and turned to Katie. 'I presume you will be living in Italy?'

'Yes, Bobby.' Taking hold of Christopher's hand, she nodded.

'That is exactly our plan. Another Lambrianu bringing up their family on Lambrianu land.'

'For some reason I always thought it would be Scarlet moving to Italy, not you. Don't ask me why. As I say, I will miss you. But good luck. And no, Dad, in answer to your question, I don't need anything. I have everything right here around this table. Something you cannot buy: love and security.'

Tony nodded and turned to Jack. 'What about you, Jack? You already have your father's share in the club. Is there anything else you want or need?'

'No, Uncle Tony. Well, yes,' he stammered. 'Like my dad I want a feeling of belonging. I've been disowned by Mum's family since I didn't open my chequebook. I realise I am not a Lambrianu or a member of the family, since Dad died. But I would like to think I still have you all.'

'What the hell are you saying? You're my brother's son. You are a member of this family, Jack, and don't you ever forget it.' Tony was quite upset at the thought that Jack felt alone. That he thought he had been deserted. 'You will be expected to be around this table regularly, eating and drinking with us all. This is your home. Got it?'

Jack nodded. 'Thanks, Uncle Tony.'

'Right, then, it seems everything is sorted out. I suppose you'd better start making the plans for this engagement party of yours. Congratulations.' Tony stood up and shook the hands of both men that were to marry his daughters. Now he felt settled. Everyone knew their lot in life. The rest was up to them.

After they had all gone to bed and Tony had swallowed the fact that Dominic and Christopher had gone into the same bedrooms as his daughters, it was time to speak to Francesca.

They both checked on Adam, who was sleeping soundly. Tony always made a point of kissing him goodnight, even if Adam was asleep and didn't know it. It made him feel better. How often, as a child, he'd wished that someone had loved him and done that. This made him more determined to show his little boy how much he was loved.

Looking at him sometimes he remembered being that age and the horrors he had encountered. This was not the life for Adam. He would guard him and love him with every fibre of his being.

'You have been doing a lot of thinking, today, Tony, and I'm proud of you. But tell me, and please tell me the truth, are you sorting things out because you won't be here?' Francesca's voice was barely above a whisper. Tears brimmed on her lashes. Was this Tony's way of saying goodbye? Did he need to sort out his affairs and get them in order before everything went wrong?

'No, love.' Tony put his arms around her reassuringly and kissed the end of her nose. 'This is my way of accepting we have a grown-up family with lives of their own. All that other stuff I told you about... well, it's over, Francesca. Sharon did us all a favour in more ways than one. Telling the police and ripping us off like she did has only made her look like a bitter ex-wife. Jake took the bullet for us that cleared our names and got us out of a scrape. Sad but true. He knew I would have done the same if the boot was on the other foot. Sharon also made me realise that if anyone was going to take my empire from me it would be my own family, and with my blessing, not stolen by her or her boyfriend. That still nags at me, though. Who did kill her boyfriend, Fran? There is no trail. Maybe one day, eh?' Tony was puzzled. This was one of those mysteries that would never be solved...

'I know, darling. I know how close you and Jake were. I thought I was going to lose you.'

'You're never getting rid of me, Francesca. Anyway, on a

lighter note, I have something for you.' A mischievous glint came into Tony's eye followed by that charming smile.

'Well, I wonder what that could be.' Laughing, Francesca reached up and ran her hand through Tony's hair. Standing toe to toe with him like this, in their lamplit bedroom, made her feel warm and loved.

Bending down and whispering in her ear, he said, 'Undress me. Take off my tie and then undo my shirt.' The warmth of his breath on her ear gave her goosebumps. Slowly, she did as she was told while he stood before her smiling. After unbuttoning his shirt with a slow seductive motion, Francesca looked up into those famous blue eyes of his. 'What's this?'

'It's for you.' Undoing his shirt, button by button, had revealed a diamond necklace Tony had bought her earlier on. 'Isn't this better than some old box? Are you going to try it on?'

'No, not yet. I want to make love to you tonight while looking at two beautiful things.' Trailing her hand along the diamond necklace that rested on the golden hairs of his chest created a deep stirring inside of her. As it shone and sparkled against his tanned muscular body, Francesca put her arms around his neck and trailed her tongue along the cleft in his chin. Emotions were high. Tonight, there was a need for each other. Things could have gone so badly wrong and they would have been parted forever. 'I love you, Antonias,' she whispered, as Tony swept her up in his arms and carried her towards the bed.

28

A NEW PARTNER IN CRIME

'Right, it's been weeks. Is everything ready for the engagement party on Saturday? It's time that bloody club was opened and making money again. And for God's sake, don't let Scarlet change one more thing!' Julie was tutting and moaning from her usual place at the kitchen table as Elle and Francesca looked on.

'You know Tony has been showing her how the club runs, how to do the ordering and getting her acquainted with things first. If she is going to help him run the club she has to start with the basics. While the club is closed it seemed like the perfect time,' said Francesca for the hundredth time.

They were going about their daily chores while Julie sat there contemplating what she was going to wear for the evening. 'I need a change, Fran. What do you think?'

'I think you always look beautiful, Julie. Here I am in my jeans and a silk blouse and you're wearing a designer Chanel suit and it's only 1 p.m. What sort of look are you thinking of?'

'Dunno. I might have a word with Scarlet to see if she can do something with my hair. I've had it like this for ages.' Julie's bored expression as she drummed her long fingernails on the table told Francesca there was something else on her mind.

'By the way, Julie, you never did say what the doctor said about Ralph. Is everything okay?'

'Mmm. Yeah, he's okay,' said Julie, avoiding Francesca's eyes and making a point of checking her nail polish.

Francesca tried pushing it a little further, but Julie wasn't saying anything more. Something was definitely wrong. Julie would tell them in her own good time, but whatever it was, it was making her feel unsettled.

'I think I will go and see Scarlet. What are you wearing on Saturday, Fran?' Julie stood up to leave.

'Not sure yet. I suppose I had better have a look around the shops. Fancy a shopping spree tomorrow?'

'Yes, I will give you a ring and we will sort out a time later.'

As Julie left, Francesca and Elle looked at each other. Something was definitely wrong with Ralph.

* * *

'Mark! Mark!' Tony sat in his office trying to look over his own accounts. The noise from outside was driving him crazy.

'What's up, boss?'

'What the hell is that bloody racket? All I can hear is Scarlet stomping around barking orders; she is driving me crazy!'

Standing in the doorway in his black suit, Mark raised his eyebrows and rolled his eyes. 'I think it's just Scarlet putting her stamp on things.' He was trying to be polite but it was chaos in the club.

'Get her in here. I want to know what's going on.' Tony took off his gold-rimmed glasses, sat back in his chair and let out a huge sigh. 'Give the woman an inch and she's gone power crazy. Get her in here before she's a laughing stock.'

The wry grin on Mark's face spoke volumes. Narrowing his eyes and looking up at Mark, Tony could tell there were things going on that he wasn't aware of.

'What? What is it? What has she done, Mark? God, at this rate we will have a mutiny on our hands. Come in and sit down; I want to hear it all.'

'Well...' Smacking his lips, Mark was unsure what to say. He knew Tony had a short fuse and he was beginning to learn that Scarlet was just like her father. 'You know the doormen are terrified of her, after what she did to Ryan.'

'What she did? What the hell is that supposed to mean? What could a young girl in her twenties do to a gorilla like him?'

'She burnt his dick, Tony. Stubbed her cigarette out on it.' Mark hesitated. This was a touchy subject and he knew it.

'Burnt his dick? What the bloody hell are you talking about? How did she get close enough to do that?' Tony's anger was rising. The faint pink flush in his cheeks was beginning to appear.

'From what I gather, he was flirting with her and thought she felt the same. So Scarlet coaxed him to take his dick out while she had a cigarette in her hand. She grabbed it and stubbed her cigarette out on it while squeezing it. The howl he made was deafening. Believe me, that is a man's worst nightmare.' Mark grimaced at the thought.

Tony had heard enough. 'Get her in here. I want to hear this from her. Go. Go on, now!' For the last couple of weeks all Tony had heard was Scarlet's high heels stomping up and down the corridor. He had tried his best to keep out of it and wanted to keep his word about letting her run things, but this was a step too far. Although he was angry, he was trying to remain calm for the family's sake.

'What's wrong, Papa? Mark said you wanted to see me.' Sitting down before him, Scarlet waited.

Tony looked at his daughter. She had changed enormously over the last few weeks. Wearing a pink skirt suit and with her blonde hair tied up in a chignon, she looked like a business-woman, not his young daughter.

'I hear we're short of ashtrays, Scarlet, and you have nowhere to stub out your cigarettes.' Tony's blue eyes flashed knowingly at her own.

'Yes. And I will do it again if I have to.' Scarlet's eyes flashed back at him. She stuck her chin out in the same stubborn way as he did.

'Do you want to tell me about it?' He realised shouting at her would do no good, so he sat back in his chair and waited for an explanation.

'If I must. But I don't see why. That Ryan guy thought I was just some bimbo blonde he could hit on. Well, did he get a shock. He'd gone out the back for a smoke or something but he was taking far too long so I went to see where he had disappeared to. There was only me and him out there and suddenly the flirting began.' Scarlet laughed. But it wasn't her usual warm laugh. It was sarcastic and determined. 'You of all people, Papa, know that I have had my fill of employees flirting with me, thinking just because I am a young female I must be "up for it". I take it you remember the builder at the salon? Well, I will never – *never* – be put in that position again.' Scarlet raised her voice and slapped the desk.

'I remember that night, Scarlet, only too well, but I presumed you had let it go. It seems I was wrong in my estimation.'

'I will never forget that night. The more I think of it, the more it haunts me. Yes, that guy would have raped me, but then what? It would have been easy to dispose of me with all the building works going on. I shudder to think. I will never let any man think it's okay to flirt and play games with me again.'

Scarlet's words stung him. Maybe he had overlooked her feelings in this matter. His face softened and he reached his hand over the desk to take hers but she shrugged it off.

'I don't want sympathy, Papa. It's over and done with. But this lot have to learn I won't be messed around with. I have to put my stamp on things. They think I am Tony Lambrianu's daughter pissing around at running a club. Well, no. I am your daughter, but in all the right ways. I will not let them take the piss out of me and, slowly but surely, they are learning that.'

Pursing his lips and looking across at this confident, self-assured woman, he pondered the situation. 'And what about all this stomping around and barking orders at everyone. What's that all about? All I hear is your voice these days down the corridor.'

Nonchalantly, she threw her hands in the air. 'When this club is open properly again, Papa, I want everything to be in order. Things have been overlooked and let slide. I appreciate you have been busy and Sharon's assistant has done her best. But this is supposed to be the best club in town and that is just what it will be. The best.'

'Are you saying I've done a bad job, Scarlet, and that I couldn't survive without you?' Scarlet's slight had annoyed him.

'No, Papa.' She smiled apologetically. 'I'm just saying while you were busy sorting other things, they staff have taken advantage. Well, it's time they remembered that to work here is a privilege and they can soon be replaced. Vicky does a good job, don't get me wrong, but she doesn't carry the same weight as a Lambrianu. Or indeed, Sharon Sinclair.' Scarlet almost stopped herself from mentioning Sharon's name, but it had to be said. Sharon had kept on top of things and kept everyone in order, until she had discovered the wonders of cocaine.

'I won't let them ride roughshod all over me, Papa. I am Scarlet Lambrianu.' Indignant, she pointed to her chest. 'And they can bloody like it or lump it. Or better still, sod off and find employment elsewhere.' She had said her piece and stood up to leave. Then a thought crossed her mind. It was something she had been finding the right time to bring up, and it seemed as they were clearing the air, now was the time.

'I think it would be better, Papa, if while I am here at the club, I call you Tony.' She held her hand up to stop his protests. 'It sounds more business-like. Saying Papa makes me sound like a schoolgirl and this lot have to realise that is just what I am not. Anywhere else, you're my papa and I love you. But here, it has to be business.' Then she faltered. 'Is that okay?'

'Mm, I see your point. Why don't we give it a try?'

Nodding, she left the room, walking past Mark as he was entering it. Shutting the door, he stood in front of Tony. 'Chip off the old block, eh, Tony.'

They both burst out laughing. He was proud of his daughter's determination to make a go of things. And he liked the way she wasn't afraid to speak her mind. 'Bloody hell, Mark, she scares me and I'm her father.'

'She's doing a good job, though. All the bar staff have new uniforms and everything is spit and polished for the engagement party.'

'Thank God she's on our side, eh, Mark. Look, I want you to keep an eye on her and report back to me. I don't want her to think I'm undermining her. Let's see how this goes.'

'Sure thing, Tony, but I think it will work out just fine. She has Dominic by her side, and us. Although she doesn't need anyone. The one person she does rely on for her strength, funnily enough, is Katie.'

'Katie?' Tony was surprised at this. 'I always thought it was the other way around.' Tony had always seen Katie as the peace-maker, the quiet one who went along with things. He was learning new things about his family that he had missed or overlooked.

'Oh, yes, hard as nails that one, but she gives the impression she is as sweet as candy. Whenever Scarlet isn't sure about something, that's who she calls. Two sides of the same coin, Tony.'

Tony raised his eyebrows. 'Katie as hard as nails, Mark. I find that hard to believe; she wouldn't hurt a fly.'

'Wouldn't she? I'm not so sure. The only thing is, she doesn't make a song and dance about it. She is more logical and thinks things through. That is the worst kind of enemy.'

* * *

'Well, the engagement party went well. Everyone seemed to have a good time. But I have to say, Julie, with that new hairstyle of yours, you really did steal the show.' Francesca kicked off her shoes and walked around the stool Julie sat on, admiring Julie's new hairstyle from different angles. She truly looked amazing.

'She did a good job, didn't she?' Julie smiled. 'I warned Scarlet if she messed it up I would shave her head. Especially when she went on about my age and how I should soften the peroxide blonde into an ash blonde. And when she suggested getting rid of my lifelong bob I nearly had a heart attack. So she covered the mirror in the salon and I smoked a hundred fags as I watched my hair falling on the floor!'

Julie's blonde hair *was* now a warm ash blonde. It was long on the top, giving her more height, and cut deep into her neck at the back. The fashion magazines that had turned up to take photos of the engagement party couldn't help themselves when they saw Julie Gold's new hairstyle. The lights on their cameras flashed away like some movie premiere, as she made her way from the car to the club entrance.

'Oh, I can still turn a few heads, Fran, and now everyone knows that Scarlet did it, she will be busier than ever!'

'Why was Ralph wearing that silk sling for his arm? You never said he'd sprained it or anything?'

'Oh, it's nothing. You know Ralph, he banged it or something, but he likes to be the centre of attention.' Julie brushed it off, but Francesca wasn't having it this time.

'You never did tell me what the doctor said about Ralph when he went for his check-up. Is he okay?'

'Yes, sort of. He just has to take things easy. He has to slow down. All those cigars and whisky don't help, either.' Julie brushed it off yet again, but Francesca wasn't convinced. This was becoming more mysterious by the day.

'Well, I presume the girls will be dancing the night away until the early hours. It was nice to see Diana with her boyfriend in tow. Very handsome. He's a sergeant or something, isn't he?'

Julie's face broke into a smile at the mention of Diana. Now things had settled down a little she didn't have to be quite so secretive about their meetings, although she enjoyed living in town with her new friends and so had decided to stay there.

'They make a nice couple. He seemed friendly enough, so I presume she has decided to come out of the closet, Fran, and by this time tomorrow everyone will know she is Ralph Gold's daughter.' Shrugging, Julie lit a cigarette. 'Well, it had to come out sometime. You can't keep something like that a secret forever.'

'I suppose we had better go downstairs and see what's happening. I only came up to the apartment to change my shoes. Come on, Julie.' Fran paused while Julie stubbed out her cigarette and stood up to leave. 'When you're ready to tell me what's wrong with Ralph, you know I am always here to listen. That's all I'm saying on the matter.'

'Oh, don't go on, Fran,' Julie snapped. 'It's nothing. Come on, let's go and drink some of that free booze that's on offer.' Then her voice softened. 'But thank you. Some other time, eh?'

This convinced Francesca that something was truly wrong. She would ask Tony later; maybe he could shed some light on it.

By the time they got downstairs, Ralph was dancing with Diana. He was truly delighted his daughter was back in the fold. That was when Francesca noticed how much weight Ralph had lost.

'That Wendy is a bitch!' Scarlet was losing no time in telling them that the daughter of one of the guests her father had invited had insulted her. 'She told me my dress didn't suit my colouring. It's red, for God's sake, and I'm blonde!' Her face was flushed and she was sweating from dancing. Sitting beside Julie and Francesca, she picked up her champagne glass and took a huge gulp. 'She said she liked my "little diamond ring".' Scarlet held up her hand to show them the three-stone diamond ring on her finger. They had both seen it a hundred times. 'She deserves a slap and I am just the person to give her one. Then, can you believe it, Mum, she said Dominic was the hired help and that was the best I could get.'

Julie burst out laughing. 'Bloody hell, Scarlet, it's not like you to sit back and take it. How come you haven't already slapped her?'

'Katie. She reminded me it was her engagement party as well and wouldn't have it spoilt. Then Christopher said it would only confirm Papa's decision that I was too young for the job.' Folding her arms and wearing a sulky expression, Scarlet sat back on the pink sofa. The disco lights flashed and the music blared out, and everyone was in high spirits apart from Scarlet. It seemed Wendy had achieved her goal.

'Is she still sulking, Mum?' Katie walked over in her blue ball gown and sat down. 'You know, Scarlet,' said Katie. She had the same velvety voice as Tony. It was calm and soothing as she reached her hand out to hold her sister's. 'There is more than one way to skin a cat, and nothing would please Wendy more than to cause a scene at your engagement party. Dominic is handsome. I bet she wouldn't throw him out of bed.' Her reassuring smile seemed to bring Scarlet back to life.

'You're right, Kat. Have you seen that ugly thing she has on her arm? God, I wouldn't screw him with yours!'

'Nicely put, Scarlet.' Julie cackled that famous laugh of hers. 'Oh, look, here comes Rebecca. My turn, Scarlet. You fuck off and dance with that man of yours before he changes his mind.' Brushing the girls off with her hand, Julie waited for the sting.

'Julie, your hair looks lovely,' she gushed. 'It makes you look younger than ever.' Then came the famous sarcasm. 'I suppose it must be hard keeping up with the younger models.' Her false smile made Francesca wince. She knew what was coming. Hadn't these women learnt over the years that Julie's sharp tongue was always on form?

'You're right, darling. My hair does make me look younger. That is exactly what your husband's mistress said earlier.' Julie watched the smug satisfaction fall from Rebecca's face. 'Oh, there she is, in the black dress, standing in the corner with your husband. Those earrings really suit her – I wonder where she got them from...'

Rebecca's face reddened as she looked in the direction Julie was pointing to see her husband fawning all over a young woman. Julie smiled her sweetest smile. Poor Rebecca turned and fled to the bathroom. Julie wet her finger and pointed it upwards.

'I would say that's one to me. Wouldn't you, Fran?' Julie shook with laughter and nudged Francesca. 'Come on, Fran. She was asking for it, smug bitch. Everyone knows he's been cheating on her for months. Did she really think I didn't know?' They both burst out laughing. There wasn't a woman in there that was a match for Julie's sarcastic wit.

'Oh, God.' Julie put on her bored expression. 'Here comes Casanova and his erection.' She looked up as Tony was walking over to join them and laughed again.

29

RALPH

'Cut the bullshit, doctor. I know what's wrong. My mother had it, and I watched her deteriorate slowly. So, let's have it.' Ralph sat across the desk from the doctor. All his nightmares had come true.

'Well, Mr Gold, you do show symptoms of Parkinson's disease, but I would have to do more tests. It's not a death sentence. You could live for another ten, maybe twenty years.'

Ralph nodded. This doctor just didn't understand. 'My mother developed memory loss leading to dementia. Of course, that was in the later stages, but I watched her while she became a stranger. I cannot die like that. I have to go out with all guns blazing, not be remembered as a pathetic old man who couldn't feed himself.'

'You're talking a long way off into the future, Mr Gold. Parkinson's is not a death sentence, as I say, but it can develop into the kind of symptoms you describe. I would like you in for more tests just to be on the positive side. How long have you been like this?'

'A while, doctor. My hands shake and I am having posture trouble. It's advanced, I know that. I will come for your tests just to put my mind at rest, but I think we both know the truth. I am an old man, I have lived a great life and I will not, do you hear me, *not* be a pathetic man where people that respect me now look at me with pity. That is not how I planned things for my ending.'

'Very well, Mr Gold. Come in tomorrow and we will do more tests. I understand your concerns, but there are lots of medications around and times have changed; medicine is more advanced now.'

'Thank you, doctor. I will see you in the morning.' Ralph stood up and shook the doctor's hand. There was nothing more to say. His mind was in turmoil. He needed to sort things out the way Tony had. He knew Julie suspected what was wrong. She, too, had seen his mother in the nursing home. Both of them were in denial. Neither of them wanted to discuss it, but now it had to be talked about.

* * *

'Ralph, where the hell have you been? I've been calling you.' Tony looked towards Ralph as he walked into the office. He was pretty pissed off.

'I need to talk to you, Tony.' Ralph had gone straight there from the doctor's surgery. His original plan had been to speak to Julie, but business came first.

Seeing the solemn seriousness in Ralph's face, Tony felt his anger subside. Something was wrong, he could see that.

'What I am about to tell you stays in this room, okay?'

'Of course, Ralph. What is it?' Tony's mind was working overtime. He couldn't think what was so serious that it would take the smile off Ralph's face.

'I have Parkinson's disease.' Ralph held his hand up to stop Tony interrupting. 'I know it's not the end of the world, but I also know the symptoms and I'm not a young man. I have to go into hospital for some tests to confirm it so I am letting you know first. I won't be around as much and I expect you to take the reins. You and that daughter of yours.' Ralph managed a smile.

Now knowing what else to do, Tony put his arms around Ralph and hugged him.

'You have been like sons to me, you and Jake. You will look after Julie for me Tony... if things get bad I mean?'

Parting, Tony smiled. 'Look after Julie? She looks after all of us.' Tony laughed. 'But seriously Ralph.' Tony's voice softened. 'That goes without saying. Julie and Diana will always be loved and cared for. You are like the father I never had. If there is anything I can do for you Ralph, tell me'. Tony could almost feel tears brimming in his eyes. 'You are a man to be envied, you have done it all. Ralph Gold the legend. You've got another twenty years in you yet, I'd say.' Not knowing what else to do, Tony quickly brushed away his tears and poured them both a drink. Handing Ralph his, he chinked his glass against it. 'Do you miss the good old days? Wheeling and dealing without a penny to scratch your arse with?'

Ralph sat down. 'Sometimes son, sometimes. You never knew what was coming did you? And I never thought this would be my ending. I expected it to be with a bullet in my head, not an old man's disease. My mother had it you know. It's a family thing.'

Tony didn't want to discuss it; it stabbed at his heart. He'd lost Jake; he couldn't lose Ralph as well. They were silent for a moment. Raising his glass, Tony toasted, 'Here's to you Ralph Gold. My hero.'

'And here's to you Tony Lambrianu, my son and my friend.' Gulping back their drinks, they nodded to each other.

Swallowing hard, Tony laughed, wanting to break the sombre mood. 'You know what, Ralph? Sometimes I do miss the old days.

Fighting for survival and trying to be one step ahead of everyone else all the time.' Letting out a deep sigh, Tony sat up. 'They always seem like the good old days when you look back, but at the time they were a nightmare.'

A faint smile crossed Ralph's face. 'We lived on adrenalin then and we didn't have a care in the world.'

Tony returned his smile. 'It may not be as bad as you think, Ralph.'

'The best way to fight this Tony, is to face it head on. If they don't get you one way, they get you another, eh?' Ralph got up from his chair to leave. 'Now I had better go and tell Julie.'

Watching Ralph walk away saddened Tony. Surely this wasn't going to be the end of Ralph Gold?

30

A TIME TO CELEBRATE

'Well, I want a double wedding. Think of it, Katie, it will be great. You and I going down the aisle together. Papa in his element. The newspapers will go crazy for it.' Scarlet was so excited she was nearly shouting.

'Calm down, girls, please.' Francesca tried stopping what was going to be an argument. 'For God's sake, you're worse than Adam.' She looked towards Elle then threw her hands up in the air. 'I give up, Elle.'

'If that's what you want, Scarlet. Personally, I want the wedding brought forward a bit.'

Raising an eyebrow and giving Katie a peculiar look, Scarlet said, 'Why?'

Francesca, Julie and Elle exchanged glances. They waited for Katie's answer, but none came.

'For God's sake, Katie, how many months are you?' Julie gave a bored look, implying that she'd known all the time, which, of course, she hadn't.

Blushing and slightly stammering, Katie said, 'Only about six weeks, but I would rather be married before the baby is born and not look pregnant on my wedding photos.' Her voice seemed to drop to a whisper as she looked across at Francesca's stunned face. 'Sorry, Mum.'

'Oh, my God. You mean you and Clark Kent have done it?' Scarlet laughed out loud. 'Did he keep his tie on? I bet he said, "Do you mind if I come now, Katie?"' Again, Scarlet was beside herself with laughter. What Katie had just revealed didn't seem to bother her. The thought that Christopher and Katie had had sex seemed much more interesting.

'I need to sit down.' Francesca did, then asked the usual questions. 'How long have you known? Was it an accident? I thought you were on contraception?'

'Oi, Mrs. Shit happens,' snapped Julie. 'Personally I agree with Scarlet. I didn't think he had it in him. Obviously there is more to him than meets the eye.' Julie winked at Katie to make her feel more at ease. 'Don't worry, Katie. You wouldn't be the first woman to be pregnant while taking her vows, would she, Francesca?' Casting her a knowing look, Julie remembered when Francesca and Tony had got married in Italy and she, too, was in the very early days of pregnancy. 'All you've got to do now is tell Tony he is going to be a grandfather.' The very thought of that made Julie laugh. 'Grandpa Tony. Oh, please' – Julie put her hands together in prayer – 'please let me be the one to tell him.'

'Julie, stop it! This isn't funny.' The very idea of Tony blowing his top at this and going all self-righteous made Francesca feel sick. He had only just got used to the idea of them being engaged.

'It bloody is, you know.' Julie wiped a tear from her eye. 'Grandpa Tony. Fuck, he'll be suicidal!'

'Does Christopher know?' As usual, Elle was the voice of reason.

Katie nodded. 'He knows, Elle. It's still early days and I don't want to jinx it, but we're both happy about it now that it has happened. It was an accident, but most babies are.'

'Oh, for Christ's sake, Francesca, stop looking so worried,' Julie snapped again. 'She's having a baby. It's about time we had some good news around here for a change.'

'Of course. Sorry, I was just a bit stunned, that's all.' Standing up and taking her daughter in her arms, Francesca hugged her. 'Julie's right. It's lovely news. Congratulations.'

'If you're going to bring the wedding forward, it can be done in a couple of months. I have arranged weddings in less time, haven't I, Francesca?'

Julie had fast-tracked her wedding to Tony so much her head had spun.

'As for Tony, we don't fucking tell him. He'll never notice. He's a bloke. He will just think you're getting fat. Anyway, you won't be showing in a couple of months. That's the best way, Katie. It's not worth the hassle; let him find out afterwards. Let's say...' Julie thought for a moment. 'You're bringing the wedding forward because you're going to Italy soon to live. Sounds okay to me.' Looking around the room at the stunned faces before her, Julie shrugged. It all seemed perfectly simple to her, if they wanted to avoid another one of Tony's tantrums.

'What about you, Scarlet?' Katie looked at her sister, who was beaming at the news. 'Why don't you have your own wedding in your own good time? When you're ready.'

'I'm ready now, and if Julie can fix it, like we all know she can, then let's go for it. Yes, the sooner I am married to Dominic, the better. Why wait?'

'Okay. Are we all agreed, then? Operation Let's Get Married is now about to begin. I'll get a wedding planner. Don't look so worried, Katie love. We're doing this to save you the ear ache from Grandpa!' Julie burst out laughing. The very thought of it made her laugh. That really would dampen Tony's ego if he realised he was going to be a grandpa.

'Oh, here's Ralph.' Julie saw the car coming through the gates on the security monitors.

'Are you okay with this, Katie?' Scarlet held her sister's hand. She could see she was nervous.

'If you are, Scarlet. Although I would have liked to have got married in Italy. In that lovely chapel, like Mum did.'

'If that is what you want, Katie, then Italy it is.' Although Scarlet had set her heart on a celebrity wedding, she was prepared to go along with her sister's wishes.

'No, Scarlet. If it can be done and I don't look like a beached whale, let's have your celebrity wedding. I'm sure Dad would want it here, too. He can invite the world! I can always have a blessing in Miriam's Chapel.'

'Just one thing, young ladies.' Elle shook her ladle at them. 'Don't you think you should tell those young men of yours they are getting married?'

'Only when we have a date, Elle. All they need to know is what time to turn up and, of course, when they can have their stag night.' Scarlet hugged her sister again. This was turning out to be a great day!

* * *

'Julie, we have to talk sometime, you know. I've been in hospital, I'm having treatment and still you won't discuss it. Today is Scarlet and Katie's wedding day. You did say that after all the planning, we would sit and talk.' Ralph was at his wits' end. The more he tried to talk to Julie, the less she seemed to want to listen.

'Well, today isn't the day, is it, Ralph? It's the wedding and you still have to get dressed.' Julie was busying herself packing her bag to go to the hotel to have her hair done. Noticing Ralph's crushed expression, Julie paused. 'Ralph, I promise you, love. We will have that talk, but there's no rush.'

'All right, this can wait. Tony's as nervous as can be. You would think this was his wedding day.' They avoided each other's eyes. Denial was their only defence.

The church was packed to the hilt. Everyone was dressed up to the nines, trying to outdo each other in clothes and jewellery. Not only had Julie masterminded this day very quickly, she had put her head together with Elle and realised that two months from the day they decided to arrange the wedding was Tony's birthday!

Scarlet had chosen the biggest and most expensive dress she could find. It had so many underskirts everyone was concerned whether she would actually fit into the car. She had encouraged Katie to have the same design, saying that it would help hide her 'bump'. Diamante crystals had been sewn into the white satin gowns, with their bodice tops. The veils alone were nine feet long and were to trail behind them up the aisle.

Scarlet and Katie had already had many photos taken, standing at the top of the hotel's winding staircase with their veils trailing down behind them on every step. They looked beautiful.

The newspapers loved it. Tony Lambrianu's beautiful twin daughters in identical wedding gowns. This was indeed the event of the year. And, as father of the brides, he would walk them both up the aisle. One on each arm.

Dressed in their grey morning suits and top hats, all the men looked just as glamorous. Tony standing in between his two daughters made a picture indeed. Three blondes. All identical, it seemed. That would definitely be the front page of the glossy magazine that had asked Julie if they could have exclusive photos and paid a hefty price for the pleasure.

Julie wore a gold ball gown, and with her new ash blonde hairstyle she made quite the statement. Preceding them, were Francesca and Adam dressed in his morning suit, too. He had been practicing for weeks how to walk slowly up the aisle with Francesca. 'Right foot, together. Left foot together,' Francesca had heard him whisper to himself.

The pink and cream theme suited everyone to perfection. It was the Lambrianu signature colour. Even the wedding cars were pink, including the huge Rolls Royce that took the brides and their father to the church.

Julie had arranged a Catholic wedding, so before they began the priest gave Mass. It was all very formal and, according to Julie, long-winded, but Tony enjoyed it. This was the best birthday present ever. Julie and Francesca had also organised balloons to be placed in the hotel dining room saying 'Happy birthday Tony'. He would never forget this day.

'You have done a beautiful job, Julie,' said Francesca. 'Everything looks fantastic. But then, I don't know why I am so surprised.'

'Oh, shut up.' Julie held her hand up for the waiter to pour more champagne into her glass and gave a wry smile. 'It has been great fun spending Tony's money. He must have been having a heart attack when all the bills came rolling in.' She was a little tipsy and her laughter seemed even louder than usual.

'Well, I've done my bit.' Tony at last joined Francesca at the table. 'I have danced with each bride, the mothers of the grooms, Elle, and even been dragged around by Julie. Now it is time I danced with the most beautiful woman in the room.'

'Happy birthday, Tony,' Francesca whispered in his ear, as she stood up. She took his hand to join him on the dance floor.

Taking her head off his shoulder as they danced slowly, Francesca looked at Tony and realised he was wearing a purple cravat, and then she looked across at Ralph and saw that he was wearing a gold one. Each male member of the family was wearing the exact same coloured cravat as their partner's dress. Nice touch. Even Adam's was purple!

31

SCARLET'S TIME TO SHINE

'Scarlet, why don't you go on a honeymoon like other couple's do?' Tony had welcomed the idea of Scarlet not being at the club, but she had insisted that the honeymoon could wait.

'Dominic is busy. Katie and Christopher have their own plans and will soon be on a permanent holiday in Italy. I want to see things through here. Is there a problem?'

'No, no problem, but you are a newlywed and business should take a back seat. Anyway, I need to see Angus. It seems one of the restaurant owners doesn't want to pay his dues for security. I need to sort it out.'

'Is there anything I can do to help?'

Tony let out a sigh. 'I know you mean well, but these guys can turn nasty when you catch up with them. What are you going to do, eh?'

'Well, we won't find out until you try me, will we?' Scarlet was adamant. This was her chance to become more than the tolerated hired help.

'Fuck it.' Tony wrote down the address and threw the piece of paper at her. 'Get on with it and when it goes tits up don't come back crying. Then I'll send in the boys who know what they're doing.' He had lost his patience. He couldn't be bothered any more. It seemed he was doing everyone's work. Ralph was only there in between hospital appointments and there was no Jake. Shit, there were only so many directions he could be pulled in!

Scooping up the paper, Scarlet smiled. 'I will bring back your money.' With that, she stormed out of the office.

Walking into the restaurant, Scarlet could see it was busy. There was no hardship here and no reason why they couldn't pay for protection. The place was overflowing with customers.

After walking up to the bar and ordering a drink, she looked at the piece of paper again. 'Is the manager around, please?'

The barman looked at her and smiled. He seemed to presume she was after a waitressing job or something. 'Come through.' Feeling pleased that she had actually obtained access without force or argument, she followed the barman to a little cubbyhole out the back.

Looking around the kitchen area made her feel sick. The walls were greasy. There was steam everywhere and plates piled up waiting to be put in the dishwasher. This place looked great from the front, but behind the scenes, it was a shithole.

'Sit down, love. What do you want? I am a busy man.' A man in a white apron spoke.

'I'm Scarlet Lambrianu. I believe you owe me some money.' Now she put her business face on. She had this man at a disadvantage. If anything, he had presumed men would go in there looking for him. Never in his wildest dreams did he think a young woman would go to the collect money.

Eyeing her while smoking his cigarette, he smiled. 'So, this is the best of it, is it, sweetie? Daddy sending his kids to do his dirty work.' Mocking her, he stubbed his cigarette out and got up to walk away.

Scarlet followed him. Her face was flushed and she was trying hard to contain her anger, nearly slipping on the greasy floor in the process.

'There's no need for insults, James. Just pay what you owe and I will leave, thank you.'

Ignoring her, the manager went about his business, making sure the huge fat fryers were ready for the chips and the temperatures were right. There were other people in the kitchen. Some were peeling potatoes and others were grilling steaks. They all seemed to be deliberately ignoring her.

Scarlet tried again. 'You know why I am here. Surely it's better you deal with me than have anyone else coming here to collect what you owe.' She spoke as calmly as possible.

'Look, sweetie, why don't you just take that pretty blonde arse of yours and get out.' He slapped her backside for good measure. A red mist appeared before her eyes and she could feel herself beginning to tremble with anger.

'You have nice hands. Strong hands.' Her voice was smooth and velvety, just like her father's. An idea popped into her head. She would show this bastard!

'You like my hands, blondie?' A sick twisted smile appeared on his face and for the first time he looked at her properly. Running his tongue over his bottom lip he leered at this pretty young woman in his kitchen.

Reaching out seductively, she held his hands and brushed one over her lips and smiled. Then, before he could react, she forced them into the boiling fat fryer. James's howls were loud and piercing as she held them in for as long as she could without burning herself. Hot oil boiled over onto the floor and onto his feet, making him howl even louder.

A man came rushing in from the fire exit door. Scarlet was shocked as he pushed her out of the way, grabbed James's red, burnt hands and pushed them under the cold tap. Cold water poured over them but they could all see the damage had been done. James's red hands were already blistering and the skin was peeling.

'Somebody call an ambulance,' the man shouted. 'You.' He turned to one of the kitchen staff. 'Close that bloody door so the customers can't hear him.'

Weeping and wailing, with tears streaming down his face, James cried out, 'Lambrianu! She's from Lambrianu.'

Panic and mayhem erupted in the kitchen. The staff were trying their best to avoid the burning hot oil on the floor. Some even ran out through the fire exit. They were shocked and horrified at what they had witnessed.

'Are you telling me that you didn't pay him? You didn't pay what we owed? You bloody fool.' The man looked towards Scarlet. 'Who the fuck *are* you?'

'More to the point, mister, who the fuck are you?' Scarlet smiled. She felt a rush of sadistic pleasure in watching this maimed man scream before her eyes.

'I'm his brother. We own this place together,' he said, looking at her with horror and disgust.

Scarlet focused on what she had come for. She was at ease and felt a strange calm within herself. This feeling of power was better than sex.

'Here.' The man reached into his pocket and threw his keys at her. 'The safe is in that room. Now take what is owed and fuck off or I will call the police as well.'

Taking the keys, Scarlet walked back into the little cubbyhole-cum-office and spied the safe in the corner. Trying each of the three keys on the key ring in turn, she opened it and took out a large sum of money. She wasn't sure what the amount she was supposed to collect was; her father hadn't said. He obviously hadn't believed she would get this far. Well, he had been wrong.

Walking calmly back into the kitchen, she picked up a tea towel and wiped her fingerprints off the keyring. Hearing the sirens of the ambulance, she realised now was the time to leave.

'If you'd had protection, shit like this wouldn't have happened. Next time, I will come with a gun and blow both of your brains out. Don't forget, now. The name is Scarlet. Scarlet Lambrianu... and I will be back.' With that, she walked back into the restaurant. It was nearly empty. What had been a thriving place when she had walked in was almost deserted now. Obviously, the screams from the kitchen had put people off their food and they had hastily left. Only the curiosity of some had made them stay to see what was going on.

After pushing past the paramedics as they rushed in, Scarlet walked to her car and got in. For some reason she couldn't stop herself; she burst out laughing. She enjoyed the power. This was just the beginning.

* * *

The next morning, before going to the club, Scarlet went to her salon. She felt different today. There was something in the air. Every time she thought of the previous night, a smile crossed her face.

She checked the salon appointment list, which seemed to be overflowing with famous names. She smiled. Then she swept her fingers across the leather chairs and looked at them. Dust! There was dust on the chairs. On closer inspection, she noticed the floor had not been cleaned properly. This needed to be nipped in the bud, quick smart.

After putting on the coffee machine, she waited for her manageress to come in.

'Hi, Scarlet. I didn't expect to see you here so early. I thought you had things to do at the club.' She was friendly and carefree as she waltzed in with a smile on her face, holding two pints of milk for the fridge.

'I'm sure you didn't,' Scarlet drawled, narrowing her eyes.

'What's up? You don't seem yourself today. Is something wrong?'

'Too bloody right it is, lady. I come in here, there is hair on the floor, it hasn't been washed and there is dust on the cutting chairs. This is a deluxe salon and it looks like a shithole. I want it cleaned from top to bottom. That is what I pay you for.' Walking up to the manageress, Scarlet grabbed her jaw. The snarl on her face frightened the life out of the manageress and brought tears to her eyes. 'If you don't want this job, honey, there are a million hairdressers out there who do. Sort it.' With that, she let go and walked out, leaving a very frightened and upset manageress in her wake.

Next, she decided to visit this Angus guy. All night long, while she had listened to Dominic snoring his head off, she had been planning the day ahead. Her father seemed to think a lot of Angus. Personally, she thought he sounded like an idiot. It was time to go and see for herself.

She introduced herself to man with all the sweetness and charm she could muster, and was satisfied. Angus was an oaf, but her father was right – all was in order on that side of the Thames.

Angus was a tall red-haired oaf, although his hair was thinning somewhat, and he had a broad Scottish accent. Being introduced to his wife was another matter. This short woman ruled Angus with a rod of iron, barking orders at him to get out her best china for such an important visitor. Looking around while Elsie barked her orders at Angus, Scarlet spotted a man. He was everything she would need. He was magnificent.

Coming in to see Angus and get his orders for the day was an almost seven-foot-tall man. He was nearly seven feet wide, too, but she could see it was all muscle. By no means was he handsome. Her father always insisted that his male employees wore good black suits and ties and that was what he was wearing, only he looked as though he had got dressed in the dark. He was unkempt and even smelt a bit. Yet there was something about him.

His stern face never moved as he sat down at the table. Then something strange caught her eye. Although it was warm, he was wearing black leather gloves and didn't attempt to take them off. Angus's wife caught her looking his way. 'This is Knuckles, lassie. He doesn't say much.'

Proffering her hand and giving him her most enchanting smile, Scarlet waited for a smile or something in return. But nothing came. He just nodded his head in her presence.

'He won't shake your hand, love. Too many complaints. But he's working on it.' Elsie gave her a wink and poured the tea.

Scarlet's curiosity rose. What was the story behind this fearsome man, Knuckles? His very presence set your teeth on edge. 'Well...' She proffered her hand again. 'There won't be any complaints if you shake my hand, err... Knuckles, was it?' She smiled.

Surprised, Knuckles held out his gloved hand and shook Scarlet's. She winced in pain. Doing her best not to show it, she smiled through gritted teeth, not wanting to offend him. 'Well, thanks for the tea. I have to be going now. It was nice meeting you all.' Mesmerised by this strange man sitting at the table, Scarlet gave him one last look. He seemed to blush slightly under her gaze. Rubbing her hand from the fierce grip she had just encountered, she left. An idea was forming in her head.

32

KNUCKLES

Walking into her father's office, Scarlet stood in front of Tony and put the money she had taken from the restaurant safe on his desk. 'Morning, Tony.' Scarlet still faltered when she called her father by his name.

Immaculately dressed in his grey suit and pink tie, Tony looked down at the pile of money before him. Then he looked up at Scarlet, ignoring her greeting. Nonchalantly, he looked down at the money again and moved some of it aside.

'There is more here than what was owed,' he answered, showing no pleasure in her proud moment. She wanted to show off and he knew it. He wasn't going to rise to it.

Scarlet's blue eyes met Tony's own. She had expected some kind of praise. 'Well, the rest will go towards next month's, won't it. Or at least some new shoes for me. God, that place is a greasy shithole,' she snapped. She was determined to stand her ground.

'Mm. Thank you,' was all he said as he scooped it up.

'Is that all you have to say? Aren't you even the least bit curious as to how I got it?'

'I know how you got it, Scarlet.' Tony's calm voice filled the air as he got up and put the money in his safe. 'Believe me, Scarlet, I know. That man's fingers are stuck together. Is that what you want to hear? And you want to thank your lucky stars he is not pressing charges. But then again, he might. What you did is GBH.'

She stuck out her chin in a stubborn way and her eyes flashed at him as he turned to face her. 'I pushed him off me when he slapped my arse. Ask the other people in the kitchen. That floor is so greasy and dirty, he slipped, and when he tried to steady himself with his hands, they went into the fat fryer.'

This time Tony smiled and nodded. 'And that's your story and you're sticking to it, eh, Scarlet? Well, it wasn't just his hands. When the burning oil flowed over, it went down his legs. They have done their best at the hospital and cut his trousers off him without peeling too much of the skin away in the process.' Tony pointed at her in a stern way. 'Don't ever think I don't know what is going on, young lady. And never forget, what was given can just as easily be taken away.'

She looked down at the floor, embarrassed. The day had started well and now she felt like a child again. 'Is he going to the police?' she asked.

'He's already made his statement. But it's good you already have your own story firmly fixed in your head. You play with fire, Scarlet, then you get your fingers burnt. Or hot oil, in your case.' Tony almost laughed at his own joke, but now was not the time for frivolity. 'The police have been in touch. They want you to go down the station and make your own statement.' He waved his hand towards her, indicating that she was dismissed. 'Go on, then. Off you go.'

As she turned to leave, a thought crossed her mind. If she was going to mention it, now was the time. 'When I come out of this unscathed, and I will, I would like a favour for all my hard work,' she snapped.

Looking up at her again and realising she was not going to apologise or back down on this, Tony waited.

'I need a driver. And I need my own wingman. You have Mark and you had Jake. I would like Knuckles,' she blurted out.

Tony looked at her, amazed. 'Knuckles?' This indeed was a revelation. 'How on earth have you met Knuckles?' Throwing his pen down on his desk and sitting back, he grinned. 'You have been to visit Angus. Well, you have been busy. I'm impressed.' Tony nodded and smirked at her. 'You do know that Knuckles has been sectioned and is certified insane? One gang member cut his hand off and, to prove he didn't care and wasn't afraid, Knuckles shouted and screamed at them to hack the other one off, as well. Do you hear me, Scarlet? The guy is nuts!'

'If he's so bad, why do you let him work for you?' She was determined to get her own way on this and the more he told her about this man, the more he intrigued her.

'I employ that emotionless nutcase because he's brilliant at his job. I don't deny that. But he's as ugly as sin. Shit, Scarlet, Knuckles didn't evolve. He's a fucking ape.' Tony despaired at his daughter's choice of driver. He had expected her to want some young, handsome man by her side, or even Dominic, not this animal of a man without fear or conscience. He was a killing machine.

'Well, when I walk away from the police station a free woman, with my reputation intact...' She smiled. 'Can I have him as my driver?' She was adamant she wanted this magnificent giant by her side.

Tony looked at her. She had done well to get his money that was owed. Secretly, he was proud of her. If she had been his son, he would be full of congratulations, but this was his daughter.

Tony stood up and walked around the room and swept his hands through his golden hair. There were some advantages, he argued mentally with himself, trying to weigh up the positives of Scarlet's request. Scarlet would always be safe with Knuckles by her side to protect her. He welcomed that. Against his better judgement, he pursed his lips together. 'Okay then.' He nodded. 'If you manage to walk away from the police station unscathed, Knuckles is yours,' he heard himself say.

'I will, Papa. I don't want a lawyer to go with me. That will only make me look guilty of something. Believe me, I have everything sorted. Thank you.' Scarlet kissed Tony on the cheek.

'You will need a lawyer, Scarlet. I will take care of things.'

'No!' she shouted. 'No, I will take care of this. I am Scarlet Lambrianu and I will clean up my own mess.' She left Tony open-mouthed as she hastily left the room.

Before going to the police station Scarlet drove back to South London. A plan had already crossed her mind. It might not work, but it was worth a try. She waited outside Angus's to see if Knuckles was still hanging around. She had almost given up and was about to drive off when she saw him coming down the street.

'Hi, it's Knuckles, isn't it? I'm Scarlet; we met at Angus's place.' Standing there, she could see he had no real recognition of her. It had only been a few hours but he seemed to have already let it disappear from his mind. Damn it! 'Well, I won't shake your hand this time.' She laughed, and suddenly she saw the recognition spark in his eyes. Thank God for that. The lightbulb had turned on and he nodded. He was about to walk on when she stopped him again. There was no playing games with Knuckles, she realised, you had to get straight to the point to let it sink into his brain.

'I'm looking for a driver. I don't suppose you would consider it, would you?'

The nonchalant shrug he gave didn't give her much encouragement. Here was her moment and she was going to grab it with both hands. 'Well, if all goes well when I make my statement at the police station, I will need a driver, and I thought you might like to do it. You're so big and strong, you could protect me.' Squeezing a tear from her eye for good measure, Scarlet waited, but there was nothing... Oh well, it had been worth a try.

'Why you going to cop shop?' He narrowed his eyes at her and she could see he was interested. That had been the hook to catch the fish.

Scarlet told him her fake version of the story and then dropped the bombshell of what hospital James was in.

'What about your dad?' His conversation was short, but she could see she was getting through to him. This helpless female act was working its way into his brain.

'That's why I'm going to the police station. He wants me to tell them the truth about what happened. Though God knows what lies that man is saying about me,' she half sobbed. 'Oh, well, nice meeting you again. Bye.' Scarlet smiled; she had said her piece and now was the time to leave. It was a gamble but anything was worth a try, given the predicament she was in.

James, the restaurateur, lay in the Burns Unit. His hands were in plastic bags to keep them from infection. He was sedated, but he opened his eyes when he sensed someone come into his room.

Knuckles stood there eating an ice lolly, totally oblivious to the situation. 'You telling lies about Miss Scarlet, trying to get her into trouble.'

James shook his head. 'That bitch did this to me and she is going to pay for it.' His words were laboured, in his dazed state.

'No, she's not. You're a pervert and she's a young girl.' There was no emotion in Knuckles' voice. 'Time to eat your words and say no more.'

James's eyes widened with fear. Suddenly he was awake from his dazed state and watched this giant lean forward and grab his jaw. The pain was worse than the pain in his hands. He was helpless; he couldn't fight him off. Knuckles shoved two fingers down his throat, making him gag. Having no feeling in his hands, Knuckles wasn't sure how hard he pushed, but he could see the man was choking and about to vomit so he took his hand away, leaving James gasping for breath and spewing all over the bed sheet and down his face.

'Change your statement or I will be back.' His low threatening voice echoed in James's ears. He nodded as best he could. Satisfied, Knuckles took another lick of his ice lolly, which he'd held in his mouth momentarily. Paying no attention to James's distress, Knuckles walked out of the room. On his way out he saw a nurse. 'You better go in, he's been sick,' was all he said, then he left.

* * *

After the interrogation at the police station, Scarlet had gone back to the salon. She'd been like a cat on hot bricks all day. Her heart sank when she saw two policemen come through the door. They asked to speak to her in private.

Her hands felt clammy and she was nervous. But, as they spoke, she realised her plan had worked. Knuckles had come up trumps. Relief spread through her as the police informed her there were no charges. James had told them he had made the whole thing up because he didn't want his wife to know what he'd done. He'd confessed everything and took all the blame. She was off the hook!

An hour after they had left, Scarlet was in the back room when one of the stylists walked through. 'There is a brick wall with a suit on in the shop asking for you, Scarlet.'

Puzzled, she followed her out and there was Knuckles. He had come to claim his prize as her driver. 'Knuckles, how lovely to see you,' she said. She smiled and greeted him like an old friend.

Ignoring her greeting, he got straight to the point. 'When do I start, Miss Scarlet?'

'You start when I have cut and styled your hair; then we will go shopping and buy you a new suit, one fitting for my driver.' Linking her arm through his, she led him to one of the basins. She could see everyone grimacing as Knuckles tried his best to squeeze himself into the chair.

Standing behind him, spraying his hair with warm water and massaging the shampoo in, Scarlet smiled. This was the beginning of a wonderful relationship.

33

SUSPICION

'Sorry to come and see you on a night like this, Mr Lambrianu. I didn't know you were having a party.' Norman stood in front of Tony's desk. He had done a lot of lucrative business with Tony over the years.

'I have another four black cabs now, Mr Lambrianu, and they will all want parking spaces. So... how much do you want?' He was friendly and jovial. There was no ill will between him and Tony. Money exchanged hands and his fares were guaranteed.

'As it's you, Norman, the usual for each cab. I will lengthen the taxi rank at the front for you, as always. Good luck.' Standing up, Tony reached out and shook his hand. 'Come and have an orange juice. It's my daughter's leaving party. She and her husband are going to live in Italy.'

Black cabs always parked outside the club in the hope of picking someone up. It was a good opportunity. Norman had approached Tony many years ago. His business proposal was simple. He wanted to always be at the front of the rank and, Tony always contacted Norman when a taxi was needed.

It had been a good proposal and it had worked. Slowly, over

time, Norman had bought another cab and then another. Tony had set up his own rank outside and the bouncers were to walk a customer to one of Norman's cabs, irrespective of who had been waiting in line first.

'Thank you, Mr Lambrianu. Don't mind if I do.' Norman followed Tony's lead into the club. It was buzzing. 'Could be a good night for me and my cabs tonight.' Norman rubbed his hands together and laughed.

'Give Norman what he wants to drink,' Tony shouted across the bar. Looking around the room while waiting for the barmaid to hand Norman his drink, Tony spotted his family. Soon Katie would be leaving the fold. It was what she wanted and he was willing to go along with it, but he was sad to see her go.

'Phew! I hope she wants a taxi tonight.' Norman nodded in the direction of one of the booths. 'She's a good tipper. Remember her well, I do.'

Tony followed his gaze and looked across to where Norman was looking. All he could see were Julie, Scarlet, Francesca and Katie.

'They rarely use cabs, Norman. Are you sure you have the right women?' Picking up his own glass of whisky, Tony looked across at the four of them again.

'Too right I am. That one there.' Norman indicated again. 'She gave me a fifty-quid tip. You don't forget that in a hurry, Mr Lambrianu. Never seen her since, not until tonight.'

Tony couldn't help his curiosity. Why would a member of his family give a fifty-pound tip to a cabbie? Why hadn't they just called for one of the cars to pick them up?

'When was that? You see, I know those women and they all have chauffeurs when they are out and about. They drive themselves occasionally, but I have never known them use a black cab... no offence, Norman.' Minding his manners and not wanting to offend, Tony held up his hands and smiled.

'No offence taken, Mr Lambrianu, but it was definitely that one there. God, was she in a hurry on the South Bank that night.'

'The South Bank? You picked her up on the South Bank? Are you sure?' Stunned, Tony turned to look at them again. He couldn't believe his ears. 'When was that? Can you remember?'

Scratching his head, Norman pondered the question. 'It was that night Mr Jake... well, you know. The night he died.' Embarrassed and realising he had brought up the night of Jake's tragic death, Norman could have bitten off his tongue.

'Who else have you mentioned this to, Norman? A hefty tip like that deserves a lot of boasting.' He was laughing and trying to make a joke of it, but Tony felt sick inside. He was stunned.

'Mentioned what to who?' Norman shrugged. He obviously had no idea what he was saying. 'I picked up a woman on the South Bank and she heavily tipped me. It was my guess she'd had some argument with some fella, the hurry she was in.'

Finishing his drink, Norman shook Tony's hand again and left. It was such an innocent conversation. Norman had no idea what he had just said. Tony's mind was in overdrive as he walked over to join the four women in question.

'How are my favourite ladies enjoying themselves?' Tony was all smiles and charm as he looked at the women around him. But this time he looked at them differently. One of these women had killed Sharon. And they had also let Jake die. What is it they say? Keep your friends close and your enemies closer. Well, one of these women had watched Jake walk to his death. They had mourned him and gone to his funeral. They knew Tony had tortured himself, wondering what had happened to Jake that night, and yet they had said nothing.

His mouth felt dry, although he could feel bile rising in his throat. He wanted to shout and ask all the questions that had gone through his mind about that night. But he didn't. He wanted to gather his thoughts first.

Francesca linked her arm through his and smiled, then frowned as she looked at Tony's ashen face. 'Are you okay, love?' she said.

'I'm fine, Francesca. It's just hot in here. I think I'll pop out the back for some air.'

'Do you want me to come with you? You don't look well at all.' Concerned, Francesca stroked his face and moved to walk with him.

'No, you stay here.' He gave a faint smile. 'I'll just be a minute.' Desperate to get away, Tony walked on. He could feel beads of sweat on his brow. His head was swimming. He needed to compose himself.

* * *

'Tony, come back to bed. What's wrong? I know Katie is leaving the nest but I thought you were okay with it.' Standing in the kitchen, Francesca put her arm on Tony's shoulder. Since they had got back from the party he had been quiet. Then he had tossed and turned in bed until he had eventually sneaked out of the room in the darkness and gone downstairs. After waiting a while for his return, she had got up. She knew Katie leaving seemed like the end of an era. But kids grow up. They move on.

'I just can't sleep, love. You go back to bed.' Tony reached out and kissed her hand, then sipped his whisky and just stared at the walls.

'No. What is it? Is there more trouble? Is there anything I should know about tonight?' Wrapping her dressing gown around her and sitting at the table, Francesca waited for the worst.

'No, that's all over and done with now. I've just been thinking about Jake. He would have loved tonight. I still can't believe he's gone. It's still on my mind who killed Sharon and left them both there in an alley to be found by strangers. No one seems to know anything about it. Even the police have given up on it. It's all very strange.' Tony looked up at Francesca. Did she know anything?

Looking at him blankly, Francesca shrugged. 'That is a mystery, Tony. There is no point in torturing yourself about it. We might never know how or why it happened.' She looked genuinely sad. He realised there and then she knew absolutely nothing about it.

'What about Julie?' He pushed a little further. Maybe Julie had said something that had seemed irrelevant at the time but now meant something.

Surprised, Francesca sat back. 'You don't think Julie had anything to do with it? She was as shocked as the rest of us. Anyway, you know Julie, she was never one to shirk from the truth. She would have admitted it. Told you point blank.' A wry smile crossed her face at Tony's absurd thinking.

'Yes, you're right,' he had to admit. Julie would have shouted it from the rooftops. She wouldn't have given a damn and she wouldn't have let him wallow the way he had. There were only two other people it could have been. Scarlet and Katie. The very idea of either of his daughters killing someone in cold blood disturbed him.

What on earth was he supposed to do? He needed to know and the only way to do that was to confront them both. But what if Norman had made a mistake? That would mean he would be accusing his daughters of murder without good reason. It could cause a real rift in the family. He could lose them forever. Damn it! He wished he had never had that conversation with Norman.

'Come up when you're ready.' Tony was so wrapped up in his own thoughts he didn't hear Francesca leave the room.

* * *

'Come on, everyone, wave them off.' Francesca hugged her daughter again. Tears rolled down her face. Her baby was leaving them.

'Mum, it's a couple of hours on a plane. You've done it millions of times. Be honest, it's taken us longer to cross from one side of London to the other, in traffic,' laughed Katie.

'Yes, I know, love, but I don't like the idea of you being on your own. Especially in your condition.'

'I'm not alone, Mum. I have Christopher, Rosanna and the internet.'

'Your father said he would come home early; I don't know where he has got to.' Worried and upset, Francesca looked towards Julie and Elle.

'Simple, Fran. He has said his goodbyes and doesn't want us all to see him blubbing. Come on, let the girl go, she has a plane to catch.' As usual, Julie was very matter of fact, even though deep down she was sorry to see Katie go.

'Right, no more goodbyes. I want no one at the airport, this is hard enough as it is.' Katie got into the car and watched as they all waved her off with tears in their eyes.

'Come on, Christopher, let's start our new life.' Squeezing his hand, she turned and took one last look at her family home and all the wonderful memories it held.

* * *

'I thought you would have gone to see Katie off. She leaves soon, doesn't she?' Ralph looked at his watch; he was surprised to see Tony in his office. This wasn't the time for work. This was family time.

'We have said all we have to, Ralph. I don't like long goodbyes. We will visit her soon enough, it's just a bit raw, eh?' A lump rose in his throat. This is exactly what he didn't want to happen. 'She's just a kid, Ralph. What does she know about life? I won't be there when she needs me.' Feeling slightly embarrassed, Tony looked down at his books, avoiding Ralph's eyes.

'You underestimate her, son. Katie and Scarlet are as hard as nails. Both of them are good businesswomen and have their heads firmly screwed on. You and Francesca have brought them up well.'

'I think I know who killed Sharon, Ralph. Would you believe me if I said it was one of my own daughters?' There, Tony had said it out loud, and to the only person he knew he could say it to. He rubbed his chin and looked at Ralph for answers.

Ralph put his drink down on the desk. There was a silent pause between them as they exchanged glances. 'Do you have anything to back that up, Tony? That's a strong accusation.'

'Call it gut instinct, Ralph, but I know one of them did.'

Ralph's response confirmed Tony's suspicions; Ralph Gold knew nothing about it. 'Well, son, you have a choice. You either let it haunt you for the rest of your life or you go to the airport now and confront them. Sharon got what she deserved, no matter who did it, so don't let this come between you, Tony. Find out the truth. This may be the last proper chance you get.'

Realising Ralph was right, Tony stood up and grabbed his jacket. 'I have to go. I won't be long.'

Running through the airport packed with people and suit-cases, Tony could feel his heart pounding in his chest. He was looking up and scanning the monitors to see what check-in they would be at, when he saw them: Katie, Scarlet and Christopher were standing together having a coffee.

Out of breath and panting, Tony stopped.

'Dad! What are you doing here?' Katie smiled and walked towards him.

Still winded, Tony looked past Katie. His face was flushed, but he knew it was now or never. He pointed at Scarlet. 'It was you, wasn't it? You killed Sharon,' he blurted out. Scarlet had become cold and calculating. Why hadn't he seen it before? This was one of the reasons Katie was leaving. She couldn't keep Scarlet's secret any more. All his emotions came pouring out. He was angry and frustrated.

'You're driving your sister away. Tell me. Tell me now!'

34

MYSTERY SOLVED

'It was me.' Katie's calm, matter-of-fact voice shocked him.

He looked at her and shook his head. 'No, Katie. This is one time that you're not going to stand up for her and take the blame. Tell me the truth, Scarlet.' He looked at Scarlet and paused. He wanted to hear her say the words.

'It was me, Dad. I killed Sharon. Scarlet doesn't know anything about it.' Katie looked him squarely in the face. This time he knew she wasn't bluffing. Stunned, he stared at her. This couldn't be true.

'You? You killed Sharon? How? Why?' Words tumbled out of his mouth. He hadn't been prepared for this. Katie was always the quiet peacemaker. She wasn't a killer. Christopher stepped forward and took Katie's hand.

'You're going to tell him, then? It's for the best, Katie. We're starting a new life. Let's not start it with skeletons in the closet.'

'You knew? You knew what she had done?' Tony was amazed. His legs felt weak.

'Come and sit down, Mr Lambrianu,' said Christopher. 'Scarlet, go and fetch your dad a coffee. We all need to talk.'

Tony's hands felt clammy. His breathing had become erratic and he could hardly draw breath as he stared at them. His chest felt crushed and the room was spinning. He was close to a panic attack.

Christopher saw a discarded brown paper bag from a take-away in one of the bins. Quickly, he grabbed it. 'Breathe into this, Tony. Very slowly, in and out. Come on, you can do it.' He held it to Tony's mouth and waited for him to follow his instructions; Tony began to breathe into the bag.

Scarlet put the coffee by Tony's side and the three of them waited until his breathing returned to some form of normality.

'Are you feeling a little better now, Dad?' Concerned, Katie sat beside him and put her arm around his shoulder.

He nodded. 'Tell me, Katie. Was it really you?'

'Yes, Dad. It was me. I'm surprised it's taken you so long to work it out. What did you think? It was Miss Scarlet, in the broom cupboard, with a candlestick? No, Dad, it's not Cluedo. It was cold, calculating Katie, in the alleyway, with a gun.'

Tony was horrified at the easy way his daughter shrugged and joked about it. 'Why did you leave Jake there, dying on the ground? After everything he had done for you, you turned your back on him and left him to die.' Tears started to roll down his face.

'Let's start from the beginning, shall we? It's all very long-winded but I'll try to keep it short. We have an hour before our flight and Christopher is right, we need to be honest.' Katie took a deep breath, then began. 'I thought I'd seen Sharon and her bloke a few weeks before Sharon and Jake's meeting. I wasn't sure so I drove past the place a few times and discovered I was right. She looked haggard. A real mess. The place they were staying in said one thing and one thing only: they were broke. Everyone thought she was out of the country... even Jack. I was going to tell you, but then Jack said that Sharon had been in touch and wanted to meet Jake. He thought maybe, just maybe, Sharon wanted to mend their marriage.

'Funnily enough, it was Jack who told me where they were meeting. I know that restaurant, Dad. I've done the accounts for them. It's one of the few restaurants that has two entrances. I followed them. I knew Jake had to kill Sharon, but to be honest, I didn't think he would be able to go through with it.'

Tony raised his eyebrows in shock. 'How the hell do you know that? What makes you think Jake was going to kill her?'

'I thought we weren't playing games, Dad? You wanted the truth and here it is.'

Tony nodded. 'You're right, I'm sorry. Carry on.'

She sat down again. 'I was going to go in the back door when I saw some of the staff through a side entrance. It's where they take deliveries and it's also where the staff take their breaks and have a fag. I still had my black suit on that I wear for work, so I took off the jacket and walked through the staff entrance. Let's be honest, Dad, how many restaurants have you been in where you could describe the waitress who served you?' She half laughed. It was true.

'Jake saw me. He probably thought you had sent me to keep an eye on him. He maybe even thought I was Scarlet. That's when I noticed Sharon's boyfriend sitting in a corner. Jake also saw him. Then Jake and Sharon decided to go for a walk. Sharon's boyfriend left out the back. It was all very well thought out and planned perfectly.'

'Why didn't you warn him, Katie? Why didn't you save him?' Tony could feel the tears brimming again. Surely she could have saved him.

Letting out a huge sigh, Katie waited and looked at them all. 'That's the sixty-million-dollar question, Dad. I took a wrong turn but, thankfully, I fell upon that boyfriend of hers hiding in a side alley, watching them. I shot him. When I walked further up to the end of the alley, Jake was already lying on the ground. Sharon still had her gun in her hand. He was dead, Dad. Not dying. Dead.' Katie emphasised the words. She didn't want her father thinking that she left Jake there on his own to die.

'Sharon was pretty shocked when she saw me.' Katie smiled. 'That bitch mocked me and said I didn't have the guts, so I showed her point blank that I did and shot her, twice. One was for Jake and the other one was for my family. I am a Lambrianu. I have your blood running through my veins. Whatever else we have, we have family loyalty.' Katie felt justified in her actions.

'Where did you get the gun from?' Tony's sadness turned to intrigue.

'You look, Dad, but you don't see. You're the best dad in the world and I love you, but not once have you ever asked how Christopher and I met.'

Tony frowned. He had checked up on Christopher. He came from a good family. They weren't short of money and he had a good job. What more was there to know?

Katie smiled and let out a little laugh. 'You were so busy protecting us you never asked the obvious questions, you silly thing.' She nudged him playfully with her elbow and saw a faint smile cross his face. 'Christopher and I met at Don Carlos's wedding anniversary party in Italy. Then we met up again in England. Christopher is Don Carlos's great-nephew!'

Tony's jaw dropped. This was beyond believable. That explained how Don Carlos knew so much about what was going on.

'Christopher sorted out all your accounts with the vineyard and got it back for you. He has helped Dominic with his business to make it easier for you to accept him as a son-in-law. Don

Carlos got me the gun. He didn't think Jake would kill Sharon. He felt there was no way he could live with the guilt of killing Jack's mother, whatever she had done. Sooner or later Jake would have confessed or, worse still...' Katie paused. Dare she say it? 'He might have killed himself, Dad. Don't you find it strange that he had arranged his funeral in advance? He knew he was going to die, one way or another.' Tears rolled down Katie's face and she wiped them away with the back of her hand. 'She threatened my family, Dad. You thought you were going to prison for the rest of your life. You were going to leave Mum and that would have killed her. Our whole family would have been in tatters because of Sharon. I wasn't going to let that happen. If she wanted to run off with a younger man, then she could go with our blessing. She could fuck off! But not at our expense.'

'How do you know about that? Me going to prison, I mean?' Then Tony looked up at Christopher. 'Ah, I see, Don Carlos's spy told you.' Tony's voice dripped with sarcasm.

'No, Dad, you did. You were in Adam's bedroom one night, telling Mum all about it.'

Tony thought back to the night he had confessed everything to Francesca. 'I knew there was someone on the staircase,' he said.

'You were right, Dad. I had got up and, dare I say it...' She smiled, trying to hide her embarrassment. 'I was going to Christopher's room.' She held her hands up to this confession. 'I heard you whispering in Adam's room, so I stopped and listened. My strong, powerful Dad's world was crumbling. Everything he had fought for and risked his life for was now going to come to an abrupt end, because Sharon wanted to impress her new man. I decided there and then that if I could help, I would. I told Christopher and he found out the rest. Well, what can I say, Dad?

You know everything now.' She looked towards Scarlet who was still speechless.

She took a sip of her father's coffee and sighed. She had always expected to tell him, but not at an airport! 'Think what you like of me, but remember. I am like you. I will do anything to keep my family safe.'

Although he had found it all hard to take in, he accepted it. Katie had done what he would have done in the circumstances. More to the point, she had saved them, and possibly even Jake. He didn't want to admit it, but even he had wondered if Jake could have gone through the rest of his life knowing what he had done. Could he have ever looked Jack in the eyes again? It was time to let sleeping dogs lie. He had his answers; there was no more to say.

They were all woken from their shock by the announcement from the airport that it was time for Katie and Christopher to board their plane. Reaching out, he hugged her and held her tightly.

Shaking Christopher's hand, he said, 'You look after her. Do you hear me?' He added a warm, friendly smile to the warning.

'Look after them, you mean. Yes, I will, Mr Lambrianu. We're going home and we will make you proud.'

'Them?' Now Tony was confused.

Reaching out and taking her father's hand, then laying it on her stomach, Katie laughed. 'Yes, Dad, I am taking Antonias home. Where he has always belonged. Like I said, you look but you don't see. Bye, Dad.' Kissing him on the cheek, she started to walk away.

'Katie! Does your mother know?'

'Of course she does. Why do you think we brought the wedding forward?' With that, Katie and Christopher disappeared through security to start their new lives together, leaving Tony and Scarlet standing there with their arms around each other's waists.

'How come no one ever tells me what is fucking going on in this family?' Tony was feeling quite himself again now. 'Are you pregnant as well? God knows, you do everything else together.'

Scarlet laughed out loud. 'Good God, no. Anyway, I think you have had enough shocks for one day, don't you, Papa? Oh, by the way, thanks for the accusation. Is that what you think of me?' Raising her eyebrows, she looked at him playfully.

'Sorry, Scarlet. But if anyone was going to commit murder, I would have put money on you. Come on, we have a club to run.'

35

THE BITTER END

Five years later...

'Happy anniversary, Fran. I hope stingy is taking you somewhere nice tonight.'

'Julie, your compliments are like a double-edged sword. Yes, he is, actually. We're going for dinner at that new Italian restaurant. And before you ask, I have my dress and everything sorted out to make it a lovely anniversary.' Exchanging glances with Elle, Francesca knew only too well that Julie would want to poke her nose in.

'Ralph's Parkinson's getting worse. He is so full of pills he rattles when he walks! His age is against him, Fran. Now he is terrified he is going to end up like his mother. We hardly mention it.'

Although Ralph had carried on as normal these past few years and things were okay, Julie was tired of keeping a brave face on. Nothing was going to get any better. If anything, it was going to get much worse, and both she and Ralph knew that.

'What happened to Ralph's mother? He never mentions her. I know she is dead, but what happened?'

Francesca and Elle sat in their normal seats in the kitchen and listened to Julie pour her heart out.

'She had it, but back in the days when they didn't know much about it. Eventually, she got dementia. You start forgetting things and that's what Ralph has started doing. He put her in the biggest, most expensive care home there was, but she didn't know the difference. It could have been a cardboard box. Eventually, she didn't even know who he was. Poor bastard, it broke his heart. Every week he went to see her and she showed no recognition of who he was. In the end I felt it was best for both of them if he stopped going.'

Fran and Elle shared a glance.

'It frightens him, Fran. He doesn't want to end up like that.' Julie's worried, stressed face surprised Francesca and Elle. She was letting her mask slide. She burst into tears. 'I don't know how to help him. The doctors say he could go on for years, but the very idea scares him. Who would have thought it? Ralph Gold terrified!' Julie tried to smile, but she couldn't.

Elle handed her handkerchief. There was nothing any of them could say that would really help. They offered the usual words of comfort, but Francesca and Elle knew it was little consolation.

'Well, if it got to that stage, Julie, at least he's had a full and happy life. He got the chance to be father of the bride with Diana. It was a lovely wedding and he has seen his grandson. It's not much, but we all know it meant the world to him,' Francesca said, trying to lighten the mood.

'You're right, Fran.'

'And, talking of grandchildren, did I tell you Katie is pregnant again?' Francesca smiled. 'I spoke to her today and everything is confirmed.'

"Three kids in five years. Bloody hell, what is that Christopher, a sperm bank?' Wiping her face, Julie laughed. She'd had her moment, now it was time to get back to normal.

'Yes, she has little Antonias, Miriam, and now a new baby on the way. It's lovely, isn't it? We're going to see them next week; why don't you and Ralph come? Get away from it all, have some sunshine.'

'Mm, sounds good. Yes, I might just do that.'

The door flew open and in walked Scarlet. 'Happy anniversary!' She walked up to Francesca, gave her a kiss on the cheek and handed her a bouquet of flowers.

'Bloody hell, are you alone? Where's Shrek?' Julie couldn't contain herself. At last she had someone else to pick on.

'If you mean Knuckles, he's outside in the car. We've just taken Adam to the football match.' With that, Adam came running in wearing his football scarf.

'Oh, come on, Scarlet, I appreciate you have done your best, but he is still a forty-year-old monster. He treats you like a Barbie doll and you treat him as a lapdog.' Not able to contain herself, Julie laughed out loud.

'And that is just how I like him. If it ain't broken, Julie, why fix it? He knows he can stop being my driver whenever he pleases. He can walk away tomorrow if he wants.'

Standing there in her blue cashmere dress, matching shoes and full-length mink coat, she made quite the statement these days. 'We work well together. He protects me.'

'From what I have heard, you don't need protection, Scarlet.' Julie gave her a knowing look. Scarlet had created quite a reputation for herself. She was cold and heartless and with Knuckles by her side, she was frightening.

'So, when are you going to join the baby club, then, and give Dominic a child?' Again Julie pushed Scarlet. It made her laugh. She was so much like Tony it was unbelievable. Her fuse was always ready to blow.

'Oh, what's the rush? I'll leave that to Katie. After all, I have Adam.' Scarlet loved Adam. She was like a second mother to him.

Ruffling his hair with her hands and straightening his football scarf, Scarlet made her usual fuss of him.

'You spoil him, Scarlet.' Smiling, Francesca poured a cup of coffee for each of them.

'He's my beautiful baby brother, why shouldn't I spoil him? Anyway, I must dash, Mum. Have a lovely evening with Papa.'

Francesca and Julie walked Scarlet to the door to wave her off. 'Go on, there's Shrek standing with the door open. Don't keep him waiting, now.'

Sitting in the back seat, Scarlet opened her briefcase. 'Right, Knuckles, back to business. We'll go to the salon first and sort the takings out then we'll—' Scarlet stopped short as, without taking his eyes off the road, Knuckles held up a string of pearls and handed them over to the back seat.

'Pearls? For me? Oh, Knuckles, I've told you before, you shouldn't spend your money on me.' Taking hold of the string of pearls, Scarlet marvelled at their beauty.

'Didn't.' Knuckles' conversation hadn't improved over the years, but Scarlet had got used to it.

'You didn't what, Knuckles?' Looking into the rear-view mirror, Scarlet looked at his face.

'Stole them. Couldn't get the box,' was all he said.

Scarlet's heart sank. This wasn't the first time he had done something like this. Maybe Julie was right. You couldn't make a silk purse out of a sow's ear. And old habits die hard.

'Knuckles, we have discussed this before. You have more than enough money. And you don't have to get me presents.' As much as Scarlet was flattered, she felt she had to say something. Although, she secretly loved the fact that every now and again Knuckles would turn up with an unexpected gift.

Taking hold of each end of the string of pearls and rubbing them across her mouth, as though flossing, she asked the obvious question. 'Are they real?' A big grin spread across her face as she saw him nod.

'Do you like them, Miss Scarlet?'

'They are absolutely beautiful Knuckles. Thank you.' Reaching forward to the driver's seat, she squeezed his shoulder, then proceeded to put the string of pearls around her neck. His stony expression never changed, although she saw him glance up at the mirror. She thought she saw the glimmer of a smile, but then knowing Knuckles, it was probably wind!

* * *

'Good, Scarlet, you're here. What's this about you charging the strippers to work here? I keep getting earache about it.' Sometimes Tony despaired of her. 'You can leave, Knuckles, you're not needed here.'

Tony's anger rose as he saw Knuckles turn towards Scarlet. 'What the fuck are you waiting for? Her permission to leave? Get out, you fucking oaf. I pay the wages around here.'

'It's okay, Knuckles.' Scarlet touched his arm. 'I'm just going to have a quiet word with Papa.'

'What the hell is going on with you two? He does my head in. No wonder you and Dominic are always arguing about him. If he defies me again, Scarlet, I will put a bullet in his head or I will take him off you completely and put him back working on the doors. Do you hear me?'

Wincing at the mention of Dominic, she felt her cheeks burn. Dominic was always complaining these days. He had said he felt he had to make an appointment with Knuckles to speak to his wife. 'He's just got used to following my instructions, Papa. He doesn't mean any harm.' As much as Scarlet always defended Knuckles, she realised now was not the time to appeal to her father's better nature. 'Anyway, I saw Mum today. She is really looking forward to tonight. What have you bought her?'

Tony opened his desk drawer and took out a red velvet box. In it was a gold bangle with two heart-shaped rubies. The inscription read: 'Two hearts, one soul.'

'It's lovely, Papa. She will love it, you old romantic.' She kissed him on the cheek. She marvelled at the rubies and made a mental note that she must get Knuckles to steal her one just like it.

'So, you have softened me up, Scarlet. Now tell me about the strippers.' Tony was determined that he wasn't going to let this go.

'It's business, Tony. This club is one of the most elite pole dancing clubs there is, if not the best. It's a privilege for them to work here. They get a wage and yet they are still all fighting over the best shifts. I have solved that problem. If they want the best shifts, then they pay a commission for them.'

Tony couldn't help smiling. Scarlet was a good business-woman and over the last few years had become as cunning and as crafty as a fox. 'I like your style, Scarlet.'

'Have a good night tonight.' Scarlet winked at him and went out into the club, where Knuckles was waiting for her.

36

A TRAGIC END

Tony was waiting at the bar of the restaurant as Francesca walked in. She looked beautiful. Her long wavy, auburn hair trailed down her back, highlighting the white, spangled, tasselled cocktail dress she wore.

'You look beautiful. Happy anniversary, darling.' He gently kissed her on the lips and then waited for the waiter to show them to their table. They laughed and they flirted with each other.

'You know, I've been thinking about my mother today.' Tony's eyes saddened at the thought. 'It's strange, I haven't thought about her for years, but today I couldn't get her out of my mind.'

Puzzled, Francesca looked over at him. He never mentioned his mother. 'Really? And what were you thinking about, darling?' She could see that he was troubled and wanted to talk about it.

'Oh, nothing.' He tried brushing it off as a whim. 'Just how the girls reminded me of the women in my life.' He smiled. 'Katie reminds me of Miriam. She sees everything and says nothing. Scarlet lives the life my mother always dreamed of. It seemed the higher she aimed, the lower she sank.'

The candlelit romantic evening was everything it should be, and then Tony reached into his jacket pocket.

'Damn it,' he cursed. 'Your present. I've left it on the desk in my office.'

'It doesn't matter, we can get it tomorrow. What was it?' Francesca smiled lovingly at him.

'It's a bracelet. I wanted to give it to you tonight. I left it there when I showed it to Scarlet. We'll stop by the club on the way home and get it.'

'Tony, don't worry about it. We can pick it up tomorrow. Let's enjoy our evening and go home. Adam's having a sleepover and the house is ours to make as much noise in as we like.' She tried to make light of his forgetfulness but she could see it disturbed him.

'It's your anniversary present. I want you to see it. I had it made especially for you.'

'Okay, Tony. We'll stop by the club and pick it up. Now, let's finish our meal and stop worrying, darling. Another hour isn't going to make any difference.'

* * *

'I'll just be a minute; I know where it is.' Tony got out of the car and then turned back to Francesca. 'Unless you fancy a nightcap.'

'Mm, that would be nice, and I could say hello to Scarlet while I'm here.'

Tony went down to his office while Francesca made her way to the bar, where Scarlet sat on her stool with Knuckles at her side.

'Mum, sit down and have a drink. Where is Papa?'

'Gone down to the office. He forgot to pick up my anniversary present. I think he thinks it's spoilt the evening.'

'It's beautiful, Mum, I've seen it. He's probably more excited about it than you are. What's that?' Something had captured Scarlet's attention. There was a noise coming from the foyer. 'Knuckles, go and see what's going on. Probably some drunk, but find out where the doormen are.' She was angry at the thought that her father was here and there was trouble. She needed to sort it – fast! Excusing herself, she followed Knuckles. Francesca followed Scarlet. She was surprised her daughter could hear anything with the music as loud as it was. If it was some drunken upset it would be sorted soon enough. It wouldn't be the first time. People got drunk and they argued. That was a part of club life.

There was a man in the foyer shouting at a man and a woman. He was threatening the woman.

'What the hell is going on here?' Scarlet walked up to the doorman. 'Get that fucking drunk out of my foyer, now.'

Feeling embarrassed, the doorman felt he had to explain. 'That's his wife with another bloke, Scarlet. He's just caught them together.'

'I don't care if that's his wife with a monkey. Get them out of here. You!' Scarlet shouted at the couple. 'You have five minutes to take your domestics and fuck off.'

Tony walked down the corridor from his office. Hearing the noise, he started walking faster and headed to the foyer. He saw the man take out a gun and wave it around aimlessly. He pointed it at the couple. 'You bitch. I'm going to kill you. You've been cheating on me with that piece of shit!' In his other hand he was holding a bottle of whisky and he took a drink. Everyone stood back at the sight of the gun. He started turning around in a half circle, pointing the gun and shouting threats at everyone there.

Tony saw the man's finger on the trigger and ran towards Francesca.

The gun went off.

Everything seemed to go into slow motion.

Francesca turned, just as Tony reached her to push her out of the way. Then he slumped into her arms.

'Tony?' His dead weight pulled her down on to her knees. She removed her hand from his back and saw blood. Kneeling beside him, she grabbed his head. 'Tony! Tony! Speak to me,' she shouted. Fear and panic gripped her. This couldn't be happening. She kissed his face and saw his eyes flicker.

'I'll come back for you,' he whispered, with his last breath. His lifeless body lay on the floor.

Francesca's once-white dress was now drenched in blood. Her hands were covered in it and her face was smeared with it. Everyone from the nightclub had run into the foyer to see what had happened. They all stood there in shock. Tony Lambrianu was dead.

Francesca pulled Tony's head on to her lap and held it. Throwing her head back, she let out a deafening howl. It seemed to go on forever.

The police came running through the doors and stopped when they saw the sight before them. Looking around, they saw a man face down on the floor with his hands behind his back. One of the doormen was sitting on him.

They walked up to Francesca. She was a pitiful sight, covered in blood. Even her long hair was matted with it.

Trying her best to gather her thoughts, Scarlet stepped forward and pointed to the man. 'That bastard has just shot my father when he should have shot her.' She pointed to the woman cowering in the corner. 'Knuckles, go and ring Julie. Tell her what's happened.'

Now handcuffed and on his feet, the drunk gunman stood in shock. He was trembling and tears were rolling down his face as he looked at Tony's dead body and Francesca crouched over him, holding him tightly to her.

Then Francesca looked up and saw him. Standing up, she ran towards him like a wildcat. Reaching out her hands like an animal, she scratched her fingernails down his face. Then she started slapping him and hitting him until the police pulled her back.

'Mum. Come here.' Scarlet reached out for her mother but Francesca pulled away and went and knelt beside Tony again, stroking his hair back from his face.

Tears rolled down Scarlet's face. She felt helpless and turned to Knuckles, who opened his arms and held her while she sobbed.

'Leave him. Leave him alone,' Francesca shouted at the paramedics, as they checked Tony's pulse. They knew it was futile but they had a job to do.

'Mrs Lambrianu, we need to take his body with us.' They were being as tactful and as polite as possible, given the circumstances, but Francesca wouldn't let go of him. She knelt there beside him, rocking back and forth, tears streaming down her face as she said his name over and over again. It was heart-breaking to watch.

In the end Scarlet walked up to her and gently pulled her away. 'He's gone, Mum. Let them do their job.'

After what seemed an eternity, Francesca released him.

'We'll take good care of him, Mrs Lambrianu,' said the paramedic. He put a blanket over her shoulders. He could see her trembling shaky body. She was in a state of shock.

'Are you coming in the ambulance with your mother?' asked the paramedic, on hearing who she was.

'Yes. Will you stay, Knuckles, and sort things out here?'

He nodded.

* * *

Julie burst through the hospital doors, frantically looking for Scarlet and Francesca. 'They've sedated her, Julie.' She was so pleased to see Julie she couldn't help but sob.

'It's okay, love, I'm here now. Tell me what happened, Scarlet.' Julie listened to Scarlet's tearful rendition of the events. It all seemed so pointless. A ridiculous tragic accident. A drunken chancer waving a gun around at his cheating wife had ended Tony's life. Tony had run in front of Francesca to save her and ended up dying himself. 'Who have you called, Scarlet?'

'I haven't rung anyone yet. Mum went berserk when they were going to take him down to the morgue, shouting and screaming. They had to restrain her. In the end they injected her with something to make her sleep.'

'This is going to be all over the news in hours. Don't let the family find out like that. Go, get on your phone and let them know what has happened.'

Scarlet nodded. 'I'll go outside and make the calls.'

It was one of the hardest jobs Scarlet had ever had to do, but she knew Julie was right. First, she rang Elle. She felt numb as she said the words, but she had to think about Adam. Then she rang Katie. Going back into the hospital, she looked around, but Julie was nowhere to be seen. After making a few enquiries she walked into the room her mother was in, fast asleep. Where else would Julie be but at her mother's side?

'I'm staying with her until she wakes up. I've told the nurse to bring me some warm water and a towel so I can wash some of that blood off her face.'

'Elle's really upset but she's going to spread the word and be there for Adam in the morning. There is no point in getting him out of bed. Poor little sod. Katie is trying to get the next flight out. What are we going to do, Julie? Without him, I mean.' Scarlet broke down; she felt she would never stop crying.

One by one, the family came. The mood was solemn and no one spoke as they sat around Francesca's bed. After repeating the story of the evening's events time and time again, Scarlet felt exhausted. Darkness turned to daylight. This nightmare seemed like a million years ago. Any moment now she expected Tony to waltz through the doors with that charming smile on his face.

The doors opened and everyone looked up. It was Ralph; he took in the scene before him and beckoned Scarlet outside into the corridor.

'The police are here,' he whispered. 'They want to talk to you. They will also want to talk to your mother when she wakes up. I've already given them my statement.' Ralph was very matter of fact about the whole situation.

'Statement?' Scarlet was puzzled. 'What statement did you have to give them? You weren't even there.'

'That's what I wanted to talk to you about, Scarlet. Yes, I was there. Do you understand me? I was in the back office, that's why your mother never saw me.' Ralph's look was stern and authoritative.

Taking the lead and following instructions, Scarlet nodded. Ralph obviously had something up his sleeve. 'Yes, I know you were there. We had a couple of drinks and then you went to make some phone calls in the office. Isn't that right?' Watching the grin on Ralph's face, she knew she had said the right thing. The police interrupted any further conversation. Scarlet agreed to make her statement later that day.

'Let's get a coffee, Scarlet.' Ralph took her hand and walked with her to the vending machine. Coughing and clearing his throat, he waited till Scarlet sat beside him with her coffee. 'There is never going to be a right time for what I have to say, and I want you to think on it carefully.' He could see she was tired and drawn but he needed to say his piece. 'Already, the vultures will be circling. People will be in a state of panic. Your father ran a tight ship but now...' He looked down at the tiled floor. He, too, was sad, but business was business. 'Now there is no captain at the helm. Someone will already have it in their mind to take his place. They are probably already planning on visiting the pubs and restaurants to inform them that they will be collecting their dues. There is no protection out there, Scarlet. It's going to be a free-for-all.' Ralph's words were harsh, he knew that, but he had to get his point across. 'There is money to be had and they will want it. The club is safe for the time being, it's a crime scene swarming with police. The question is, what happens next? What do you intend to do?' Ralph sighed and waited. He realised he must have sounded heartless.

'I don't know, Ralph. I really don't know. I feel lost without him. But what about you? Won't you be taking over and carrying on?'

'I'll be there, Scarlet, but it's not my name above the door of the club.' Ralph had his own reasons for not wanting to be in charge. Time was definitely not on his side. 'If you want to sell up and live in domestic bliss with Dominic, now is the time to do it. Now is the time to make the decision, and quick,' he warned, and he stood up and walked away, leaving Scarlet behind to ponder on his words.

Dominic came down the corridor. 'Scarlet, oh God, Scarlet, I'm so sorry. I've just heard. Are you okay?'

Standing up, Scarlet held on to him. She was pleased to see him. 'Oh, Dominic, what are we going to do without him?'

As he held her closely to him, his warm breath filled her ears. 'It's the end of an era, Scarlet. We have to move on. We can have our babies and get on with our lives without clubs and hassle. I'll take care of you, love.'

She was sure he meant well, but this was exactly what she didn't need to hear right now.

'Move on?' Pushing him away, Scarlet couldn't believe her ears. End of an era. That was her father he was talking about and he wasn't even cold yet!

'Get out! Get the fuck out of here. This sounds more like a blessing to you. Has it ever occurred to you that I like the *hassle*? That I like the clubs? That I don't want to turn into Mrs Doubtfire?'

'I know you're upset, Scarlet. I'm just trying to give you some-thing positive to think about.'

'You know what, Dominic?' Scarlet's mind was made up. 'You're right. We have to move on.' Leaving Dominic standing there, she walked back to the room her mother was in.

'Ralph, can I have a word?' she said. She felt stronger now, although she knew she must have looked a fright. Her make-up had gone and her eyes were swollen from the tears.

Ralph knew what was coming, based on the look on Scarlet's face. 'What is it, Scarlet?'

'We need to let these people know that nothing's changed. Tony's dead, but I am very much alive and I will not let his legacy die with him. I need your help, Ralph. Where do I start?'

'By giving them a choice, Scarlet. You need a meeting with all the people that worked for your dad. If they want to stay on board and work for a woman, good. If not, they can leave and find employment elsewhere. Once they have made that choice they have to stand by their decision. But you give them the choice.'

'Where can we have this meeting? The club is closed.'

'The casino. You will also need to make the rounds and visit some of the pubs and people who paid for protection. They need to know where they stand. It's not going to be easy, Scarlet. People don't like change and you're going to take a lot of shit. But I believe you can do it and so did your father. This wasn't all just handed to him on a plate, you know. He had to fight for it and prove himself first, just like you will. The king is dead, eh?' Ralph smiled and reached out his hand to shake hers. 'Long live the queen.'

'Just one more thing, Ralph. Why are you telling the police you were there when he was shot?'

'Good question. I want to be on the inside looking out. Not the outside looking in. If I am part of the investigation, I will find out more and not just get snippets. Your Knuckles did well, ringing me before Julie. I take it he's your wingman?'

'Yes. I trust him with my life.'

'Well, personally, I wouldn't trust him to look after my granny's false teeth, the light-fingered bastard.' Ralph laughed. 'But he's been loyal all these years and he's good to have on your side.'

Scarlet nodded.

'What about Dominic?' Ralph was curious that Scarlet's husband never came into the equation.

'Dominic wants his dinner on the table at five and a house full of kids to keep me at home. He's changed a lot, but then so have I, although he knew that was never what I intended to be. No. Knuckles is my wingman.' She didn't want to admit that things between her and Dominic had been rough lately. Dominic was always complaining she was home late. Even when she made a special effort to be there for him, he wasn't satisfied. She knew why. It hurt his ego. He didn't want her involved in the clubs, full stop. It surprised her, really; she thought if anyone would have understood, he would have. But his macho sexist ways insisted that it was no place for a woman. Well, it seemed she had a lot to prove to a lot of people, including her own husband.

37

THE END OF AN ERA

'London has more or less come to a standstill, Julie. The pavements are packed with people wanting to show their last respects.' Katie looked up at Julie in despair. The last few months had been hard. At least now they could have the funeral. It was some kind of closure. The worst was still yet to come. The court case.

'Is your mum still on those bloody happy pills?'

'Yes, she hardly speaks these days. You can hear her crying every night. I don't know how to help her.' Katie was at her wits' end with worry. 'Elle is trying to be strong for everyone, but she's lost both her sons.'

'Well, the pills stop today, after the funeral. It's time she woke up and realised he has gone.'

Julie felt she had tiptoed around Francesca for long enough. She looked a mess these days and Julie knew she was drinking brandy at night to help her sleep, along with taking those pills of hers. She had gone along with it up until now, but it had to stop.

'Let's get today over with first. I'll go and see if she's getting ready.' Julie went up the stairs with a heavy heart. She knew

Francesca had lost interest in everything and stayed in her room most days.

'Time to get showered and dressed, Francesca. The least you can do is say goodbye to your husband properly.'

'I'm not going. I'm not going to say goodbye. He said he would come back for me and I believe him.' Francesca lay in bed. She didn't have the energy or the inclination to get up.

Julie had had enough. It was time for a different approach.

'You selfish bitch!' she shouted, pulling the duvet off Francesca. 'You have a young son down there who has lost his father and you don't give a shit. You say you love Tony. Well, that's his son and you don't give a fig about him. His father is dead and his mother may as well be. Well, I hope Tony isn't looking down on you today; he would be heartbroken and disgusted. Go on. Wallow in your grief! Take more of your pills. In fact, take the fucking lot, no one would notice.' Julie threw the black dress at Francesca and walked down the stairs.

'What did she say?' Katie had heard the shouting. She didn't know what to do. Adam sat by her side in his black suit and squeezed her hand.

'Time will tell, Katie. In the meantime, we have things to do.' As brave as Julie felt, she didn't know what was going to happen. All she knew was they had to go through with the funeral. 'Adam, go upstairs and see if your mother is getting ready.'

The two of them watched Adam leave the room. His sunken shoulders as he walked away said it all. He was upset and afraid.

What seemed a lifetime was in fact only forty minutes. Francesca came downstairs dressed in black. Julie heaved a sigh of relief and walked with her to the car. Everyone knew it was going to be a long and stressful day.

'Wait a minute.' Francesca looked up as they reached the church. There was a lone woman standing in the distance. She thought she recognised her but couldn't see her properly through the long black veil she was wearing over her hat. After slowly walking up to the woman, she lifted her veil. 'Roxy? Is that you?'

Roxy had been Tony's casual girlfriend when they had first met. The women had been enemies, once, but Roxy had finally accepted the fact that she was never going to be Tony's wife, and moved on.

Looking slightly embarrassed, Roxy looked up. 'Sorry to come, Francesca, but I felt I had to say goodbye. I didn't mean to interrupt your grief.'

'Are you coming into the church?' Francesca asked. Roxy shook her head and turned away. 'Come on.' Francesca linked her arm through Roxy's and led her into the church. 'You need to say goodbye properly.' It gave Francesca a warm feeling inside knowing she had come after all these years.

'Fucking hell. Have you seen how many women are in the churchyard, sobbing? I thought that long procession was bad enough with people throwing flowers in front of the car, but this is fucking crazy. It's more like a parade, Ralph.' Julie nearly laughed out loud, but tried her best to contain it.

Ralph waited while Julie linked her arm through his. He, too, found it amusing. 'He was a well-loved man, Julie. Admired by a lot of people. Even though it was mostly women.' Ralph turned and smiled at her. 'Do you think this many women will come to my funeral?' Ralph tried lightening the sombre mood. Looking round the churchyard, Ralph saw the 'soldiers' he had organised to stop the newspapers making a farce of it.

'Don Carlos.' Ralph hugged him in the Italian way that was expected. 'Thank you for coming.'

'Ralph, Julie.' Don Carlos nodded at them. 'Antonias should not be here. He should be flown home to his own country.'

'Francesca needs his grave here, Don Carlos. She needs to be able to visit it regularly. The only other option would have been for Francesca to go and live in Italy.' Ralph tried stressing the point, but he knew it was useless. Don Carlos wanted Antonias home.

'Will you be coming to the court hearing?' Ralph wanted to change the subject.

'Yes. I will be there. That is, if there is anything left of that man to hold a hearing with. Antonias's family was my family. And you know how it is, Ralph. Once you're in our circle, you never get out.'

Ralph's blood ran cold. Don Carlos was a good man, and an even better businessman, but he took Tony's death personally. After all, he was Italian.

'Bloody hell, Ralph. Has he brought his enforcers to dig Tony up after we've left? He wants him back in Italy bad enough to do so.' Julie saw the weak smile on Ralph's lips.

'Wouldn't surprise me, Julie. Come on, let's go in.'

Taking the reins, Ralph made a speech about Tony and his life. He was trying to crack a few jokes, but could see it wasn't working. He was struggling. To Ralph's surprise, the undertaker tapped him on the shoulder.

'Mr Gold, we had our instructions not to do this until this very moment.' Undertakers came out holding a projector screen. Everyone turned to look at each other in surprise. 'Go and take your seat, Mr Gold. Mr Lambrianu has his own words to say.' Arching his brow and looking towards Julie and Francesca, Ralph shrugged his shoulders and walked away from the podium and sat down. No one knew what to expect as the undertakers busied themselves setting everything up.

Pressing the button on the machine, the undertakers stood aside and let the recording Tony had made at some point play.

Tony was standing at the front of the church. His usual

charming grin and piercing blue eyes filled the room for one last time. Francesca removed her veil to see more clearly.

Dressed in his grey suit and pink shirt, and running his hands through his mane of blond hair, he was laughing.

'Well, none of you expected this, did you? Jake gave me the idea and, as always, I was going to do it better. I've had a great life and spent most of it with the love of my life. You, Francesca.' The church had fallen into silence as they watched the recording. 'Francesca, this is for you, wherever you are. And for you lot thinking you had seen the back of me. Well, you couldn't have been more wrong, could you? I felt this song and the photos you are going to see summed up my life pretty much. I want you all to listen to this and think about the words. It sums up my zest for life. Take it away, Barbra Streisand.'

A drumbeat, and the voice of Barbra Streisand, filled the room as 'Don't Rain On My Parade' started to play. Julie held onto Francesca's hand and Francesca followed suit and held onto Elle's, as she sat beside her. The first photo was sad. It was just a photo of a young woman. It was the only photo Tony had of his mother; it had been in her locket and he had kept it. He was the spitting image of her, with her blonde hair and blue eyes.

The song indeed spoke volumes of how Tony had lived his life. And the pictures that followed were happy ones. School photos of him and Jake. The pair of them in the club, hugging each other, their heads thrown back in laughter. Photos of Tony holding the twins as babies. Selfies with Adam, family Christmases with Ralph, Julie and the whole family sitting around the table with their Christmas jumpers on. Suddenly, in the midst of all the sadness, people were tapping their feet and clapping in time to the music, and smiling – even laughing.

The next song he had chosen by Barbra Streisand was 'The Way We Were'. This one accompanied photos of the family with

Miriam at the vineyard. The rest were of himself and Francesca dancing closely, with their arms around each other at the club as they looked into each other's eyes. Tony then appeared again as the photos finished. 'Great fun, wasn't it?' He threw his head back and laughed. 'Don't feel sorry for me, folks, by my reckoning I should have been dead years ago. Don't forget, Francesca, I will be back. In fact, I've never left. I love you, Francesca. Two hearts, one soul, remember?' Tony's eyebrow was arched as his smile filled the screen. '*Questo non è un addio.*' (This is not goodbye.) With that, he blew them a kiss. 'Just one more thing, folks. I had to get my own back one day. I've waited a long time for this. And shit, I would never have done this while I was alive. Although there were times I was tempted.' He was laughing out loud and shaking his head. 'This is for you, Julie Gold. God, I wish I was here to see this.' How he had got hold of this picture was anyone's guess. But the very last photo was of Julie.

It was early morning and Julie had no make-up on. The mascara she had worn from the night before was smeared around her eyes. She looked hungover. Her hair was stood up on end and looked a mess. To make it worse, she was sitting on the loo with a cigarette in one hand and her mobile in the other.

'That bastard!' Julie shouted. 'I'm going to fucking kill him.' Julie's voice filled the church.

'Too late, Julie,' said Ralph, laughing, 'he's already dead.' Ralph nudged her in the ribs and laughed. Even Francesca laughed. This was the Julie Gold that no one ever saw. Everyone stood up and applauded.

As always, Tony Lambrianu had done it in his own unique style, with class and humour.

38

SCARLET'S REIGN

'Here she comes, Daddy's little princess. Look at Barbie, with that fucking ape by her side. She doesn't fool me, silly cow. Who does she think she is?' Tim was one of the drivers. He was a horrible man in his fifties. He thought of himself as a leader and caused trouble where he could. He was standing in a circle with some of the other drivers, watching Scarlet get out of the car and walk towards the club.

She looked quite the grown woman now, in her pink cashmere dress and mink coat. She had grown up and was now taking all the worries of the family on her shoulders.

The club was no longer a crime scene and she was getting it cleaned up and sorted out for reopening. She wasn't sure anyone would come, but Ralph assured her they would, even if at first it was just the ghoulish weirdos wanting to see where Tony had been killed.

'Shut up, Tim. She'll hear you. You know what a bad-tempered cow she is.' One of the drivers who had previously been on the wrong end of Scarlet's wrath threw his cigarette on the ground and stubbed it out with his foot, then walked away.

'I'm not scared of her. She's a jumped-up tart trying to be like her father,' Tim joked with his friends.

'Morning, Tim.' Scarlet smiled. She hated him. Whenever there was trouble, his name was at the forefront. She had wanted to sack him, but Ralph had told her to 'keep her friends close and her enemies closer'. She knew what he said behind her back but Ralph had also told her it was going to be tough and assured her the same comments were made about him and Tony. 'No work today? I don't pay you to stand idle.' She stood in front of him and glared at him.

'Just getting off, Scarlet. Having a smoke and going.' He smiled through gritted teeth. He hated answering to a woman and he resented the way she had taken over. Most of them had stayed with her and accepted it. Some had decided it was time to retire, with no hard feelings. But Tim had stayed on for the money.

As she walked into the club, Scarlet had to bite her tongue. Tim's surly manner made her angry. If he worked at the local supermarket he would have some respect for his boss who paid his wages.

Thinking she was out of earshot, Tim laughed with his circle of friends. 'How can she fuck that fucking ape? There is no accounting for taste, eh, lads? I could give her a good shag. That's what she needs to bring her down a peg or two. Her mother was a stripper, you know. She was a slag, too. Best Tony could get, though.' The nasty venom poured out of his mouth as he boasted and tried to make himself look good in front of the other drivers. He was laughing in his own cocky manner until he saw Scarlet standing beside him.

Her face was flushed and she was angry. Her blue eyes darkened, just as her father's used to. 'Anything else to say, Tim?

Surely you're not going to stop now when you can say it to my face.'

'Just a joke, Scarlet. Can't you take a joke?' His nervous smile and furtive look to the other drivers didn't assuage her anger. He was trying to cover his tracks; he knew he had gone too far. 'Anyway, I had better get on.' It was time to make a hasty retreat. He knew that look on her face. He had seen it many times over the years.

'You think it's a joke to call my mother a slag?' Anger rose in her but she kept her composure. Her deadly calm seemed to unnerve Tim. She didn't shout and scream like other women. There was more than one way to skin a cat. She had watched and learnt from her father. His calm, steady voice had people on edge. They hadn't known which way to take him.

'Well, I am sick and tired of your jokes. You can leave, you know. I didn't want you here in the first place.' Scarlet felt satisfied that she had achieved her goal. Tim stood looking down at the ground like a schoolboy, blushing. Scarlet turned to the other men, her eyes flashing angrily. 'Do you lot have anything to add to Tim's statement about me or my family?' They all stood in silence and shook their heads, lowering their eyes.

'Good.' Turning to where Knuckles was standing behind her, Scarlet coldly and calmly gave her order. 'Let's shut his mouth for good. Break his neck and dump him somewhere, that way we don't have to hear his jokes again. And the rest of you will watch your tongues in the future. Now, either get on with your work or fuck off.'

Shocked horror filled Tim. His eyes widened and he looked at his friends for back-up, but there was none. He turned back to Scarlet. 'Sorry, Scarlet,' he stammered, 'I didn't mean no harm.' He was trying to think on his feet and save his own skin. He was pleading with her. 'It's just me shooting off my big mouth. Mates, eh?'

Scarlet nodded at Knuckles. The other men winced as they heard the crack of Tim's neck under the force of Knuckles' hands.

'I'm sorry, too. Anyone else got something to say?' Scarlet looked around at the horrified sea of faces, then down at the ground where Knuckles had let Tim drop. With that, she turned on her heels and went into the club. Taking a deep breath, she walked into the office and sat down. She was shaking slightly but she knew that would pass. It wasn't the first time she'd had to resort to the extreme over the last few weeks to get her point across.

She had never fully realised just what her father had gone through on a daily basis, dealing with people like Tim. Now she appreciated the fact that you had to forever prove who was in charge and keep ahead of the game. Fear was the key. She knew Knuckles would dump Tim somewhere where he wouldn't be found for a very long time. That was the end of that. Now, back to business.

Her main concern was the forthcoming court case and her mother's sanity. Day and night, her mother had played the recording Tony had made for his funeral.

Francesca visited his grave every day, sitting there for hours, reading the newspaper to him and talking about the old days. The doctor had said it was just a grieving period, but with the looming court case and having to relive it all, Scarlet wasn't sure she would cope.

'Oh, Papa, I wish you were here.' Burying her head in her hands, Scarlet sobbed.

39

THE COURT CASE

'The court case begins next week, Julie. Francesca will be called as a witness. Personally, I'm not sure she's up to it. Maybe she should do one of those video links?'

Ralph too, was going to be a witness of sorts, if needed. The police treated it as an accident, but they also wanted to know if Tony had known the man and whether it had been some sort of revenge. Being gangland, they always had their suspicions.

'I don't know, Ralph. I really don't know. What do you have in mind?' Julie knew something was forming in Ralph's mind or he wouldn't have mentioned it.

'Just an idea. You're just getting Francesca back on her feet and now she has to relive it all over again. It will send her over the edge. And we both know that son of a bitch is going to walk away with a minimum sentence.' Ralph was sick to the stomach.

'Let's find out who the judge is, shall we? My guess is we'll know him,' said Julie. She was damned sure of it and over the next few days the answer fell into her lap. It was a judge from Manchester who they had known who used to be a member of the 'men's club'. And if he was a member there, then Julie was sure he had a skeleton in the cupboard. Most of them did.

Sitting in their outlandish mansion, Julie felt nervous. She had done Ralph's bidding, but Ralph's plan was so far-fetched even she felt it was impossible.

'So, Ralph, we know who it is but we also know he is bound by the rules for sentencing. He can only give what the law allows. Now what?' Sitting there stony-faced, putting her cigarette into its long gold holder, she waited.

'Now, Julie, we need to have that talk we should have had long ago about my illness. I want to go out in a blaze of glory, just like Tony did. I don't intend to die a crippled old man in my bed. Sit down, love. I have a plan.' Silence hung in the air as Ralph sat opposite her and poured them both a whisky.

* * *

People were camping outside to claim their seat in the court and the fact that it was high profile meant the police were on standby and took extra precautions. Everyone was checked and scanned. They forced a woman with water in a glass bottle to pour it over her hands to make sure it wasn't acid. People were talking of nothing else. The newspapers were full of it. Francesca tried shielding Adam from it as much as possible, but he could hear and he could watch the television.

Francesca had wanted to go but Julie explained that she couldn't sit in the court and listen as she was a witness, but promised that she would have her chance to look her husband's killer in the eyes soon enough. It was going to be a pretty short case because everyone knew that the man who had killed Tony had given a guilty plea. It would all be over in a few days. Katie had flown back from Italy especially for it and joined the rest of the family.

Julie waited outside the court as planned with Ralph and saw the judge. Yes, she knew him – and his tastes. Accidentally on purpose bumping into him through fair means and foul, she had got to meet him. He had hurriedly taken her to his chambers. He couldn't be seen with Julie Gold. Quickly getting to the point, Julie explained Ralph's plan. The judge was astonished at the very idea of it. He was also on edge in case anyone came in and saw him with Julie.

'I have an old video tape here.' Julie took out the tape and waved it in the air for good measure as she sat in his chambers. 'I wonder if your respectable wife would like to see how you like the Thai men you visit? It must have been hard for you, being in the closet all these years and playing the respectable husband. I understand. But I doubt the papers would.'

'That's blackmail,' he shot back at her.

'True. But I don't have a reputation to lose, like you.' Julie's expression said it all. She wasn't bluffing.

'What you're asking is impossible. I could go to prison for this. Do you know how they treat judges inside those places?'

'Okay, just a thought. I'll drop this off on my way home. Nice to see you again.'

Standing up slowly, Julie waited. The judge was pacing the room and wringing his hands. Rubbing his chin and in a state of panic, he looked at the tape in Julie's hand. 'I could try, but I couldn't guarantee anything. Everyone is checked. You're asking the impossible, Julie. You must see that,' he pleaded.

'Everyone but the judge is checked, John. The judge just waltzes in.' Julie smiled. 'Here, take the tape, I have copies. Take a look and see what the journalists would make of it.' Opening the door wide, Julie mentally counted to three in her head and smiled when John called her back.

'Okay. I will do my best, but I want any copies you have and I also want to walk away from this a free man.'

'Done. I will send you all I have after the event and no sooner.' A wide grin spread over Julie's face. 'I'll see myself out. I know the way.'

Sick, and with a heavy heart, Julie went to see Francesca. The house seemed to have lost its laughter but she had to keep up the momentum. 'Hi, ladies, I hope that kettle's on, I'm parched.'

'Of course it is. Since when did you know me not to have the coffee boiling?' Elle smiled.

'How's Ralph? We haven't seen him lately.' Francesca's concern was apparent. Julie had looked after everyone but herself. Ralph was ill and yet Julie hardly mentioned it.

'Oh,' Julie sighed, 'same old Ralph. He's not getting any better, if that's what you mean. He looks like shit and is a shadow of his former self. Tony was like a son to him, Francesca. Yes.' Julie nodded at them both. 'It's time someone stopped pussyfooting around and mentioned Tony's name.'

Wincing slightly, Francesca nodded.

'How do you feel about giving your statement in court, Fran? You're their number one witness. Everyone is waiting for you to take the stand.' Everyone wanted to see and hear Francesca pour her heart out about that night. It was sickening.

'My statement doesn't count for anything, Julie. Tony's dead. What difference will it make, reliving that night? It won't bring him back, will it?'

'No, but you may feel better if you get justice.'

'Nothing will make me feel better. And what is justice?' Francesca's eyes clouded over. She seemed disinterested in it.

'Okay.' Julie was fishing and she had her answers. Maybe

Ralph had a point, but it didn't make it right. 'Thanks for the coffee, Elle. Now, if you don't mind, I will leave you.'

Her next step was to go and report back to Ralph about her meeting with the judge. She had a heavy heart, but she had made Ralph a promise and she couldn't go back on that. He was deteriorating and he hated it. His hands and feet shook constantly and, worse still, he was forgetting things. For now, he still had his faculties but even she wondered how long that would last.

'Do you think everything will go as planned, Ralph?' Even Julie was unsure. It seemed a little far-fetched given the circumstances. She felt nervous but didn't want to show it.

'I'll make damned sure it does, Julie. I know this is hard for you, but it's for the best, believe me. Either way, the outcome would be the same. Only this way is better.'

'Everything else is arranged.' She reached out and held his trembling hand. 'I have never said this often enough, but I'm saying it now. I love you, Ralph Gold.' She felt tears well up in her eyes, but sniffed and blinked hard to keep them at bay.

'I know that, Julie. I love you, too. You are the only person in the world that I trust. This is for all of us. Most of all, for me and for Tony. Thank you.'

Julie rested her head on his shoulder. Sitting in silence and holding each other, it seemed like the deal was sealed. There was nothing more to say.

40

PURE GOLD

'Is everything in place for Mr Gold?' The judge sat in his chambers, drinking a cup of coffee and talking to his clerk. 'Make sure he is called first. If he is not a well man, we can't have him hanging around all day.' Brusque and business-like, he gave his orders. 'Has the courtroom been checked?'

'Yes, sir, everything is in place.' The clerk proceeded to put the judge's red robes around his shoulders. 'Although we don't need Mr Gold in court. There's nothing he could add to the proceedings.'

Brushing his clerk away from him, the judge looked at the man. 'It's not our affair, Mr Jones. The point is, Mr Gold was one of the last people to talk to Mr Lambrianu in private. Had Mr Lambrianu seen the man when he came in? Did he mention anything to Mr Gold? That is why he is taking the stand.'

The judge just wanted today to be over. Julie had met up with him again in secret and slowly given him his orders. She had been very matter of fact about it all. She made it sound so simple.

Ralph Gold was to be called into the witness box. As he entered, he looked up and saw Julie sitting there in her white trouser suit. She had gone to extreme efforts so that she would stand out in the crowd.

Everyone was expectant and excited at the prospect of seeing Ralph Gold in the flesh. They had read about him and seen his photo in the papers many times. Now it was time for the real thing.

People looked on in awe. They had heard about Ralph Gold, but this ageing, thin man wasn't what they had expected. Halfway through his speech, he coughed and held his chest. He leaned forward slightly, supposedly to catch his breath. The judge asked someone to get Ralph a glass of water. While bending forward slightly, Ralph felt for the gun, which he hoped had been taped underneath the chair he was sitting on, as planned. This was his only chance. He quickly pulled at the tape, which gave way easily. He was surprised the weapon hadn't fallen on the floor as it hadn't been secured well, but now he had it in his hands.

Pointing it directly at the man in the secure dock, who had shot Tony, he fired three times in quick succession.

Mayhem and panic filled the courtroom as the shots rang out. Some people were running for the doors and others were crouching down beneath the benches for protection.

Two policemen in the far corner instantly got on their radios to ask for assistance as they ran towards Ralph. Shouts and screams filled the courtroom. Only Julie remained in her seat, in stony silence, as people pushed past her to get out.

The doors burst open and more police ran in. 'Put the gun down!' they shouted. They didn't go any further because Ralph pointed the gun towards them.

'You want it? Then come and get it,' he shouted at them. Glimpsing over at the man who had shot Tony, Ralph felt satisfied. He was dead. Justice was served. His hands shook slightly as he held the gun, but he continued waving it around and then he pointed it at the judge.

'You. You bastard. You were going to let that prick walk with a minimum sentence. Dressed in your fine red robes, you don't give a shit about Tony. You probably felt he deserved it,' Ralph snarled. 'Stay back, you lot, or I will shoot him,' he shouted at the police. They stood back a little and tried talking to him, asking him again and again to lower his weapon.

The doors burst open and armed police ran in and shouted their orders. Their own guns were firmly fixed on Ralph. They knew Ralph had already killed one man.

Julie and Ralph quickly exchanged glances. Putting her fingers to her lips, she blew him a kiss. This is what he had wanted. This would make him a legend. He wanted to be remembered and talked about in a manner that befitted his reputation. He was going to go out in a shootout and a blaze of glory!

'This is for you, judge.' Ralph aimed higher than the judge, just slightly above his head. 'Fuck you, arsehole,' he shouted, and pulled the trigger.

'Fire!' was the last word he heard as the police fired their guns. It was over. Ralph slumped in the witness box. He was dead.

Tears slowly ran down Julie's cheeks. Now she knew how Francesca must have felt. But Julie had had the chance to say goodbye. Ralph had planned and wanted this and had relied on Julie one last time to help him. It was his dying wish.

Brushing away her tears, she stood up. She looked over at the judge and gave a slight nod and made to leave. Tired and weary, she made her way home and poured herself a large whisky. 'This one's for you, Ralph, love.' She held her drink up in salute then gulped it down in one.

After switching on the television, she watched as the news showed footage of the scene outside the court. Blue lights from police cars and vans with their sirens blaring out were everywhere, and people were running around in panic. Some had been interviewed, giving their tearful stories about what had happened.

The telephone interrupted her thoughts. She had a fair idea who it would be.

'Julie! I have been trying to get hold of you for hours. Where the hell have you been?' Francesca shouted down the telephone.

Julie told Francesca what had happened, even though she knew most of it from the news. They had a long conversation, which drew to an end when Diana ran through the door.

As predicted, Diana was distraught. After comforting her as best she could, Julie sat in the bath. She welcomed the warm soapy water. For once she was tired of being the strong one. Bursting into tears, she sobbed.

Half of her thought Ralph had been selfish, the other half of her agreed with him. Ralph had been dying, they all knew that. How he chose to die was up to him. She would have to inform their son, Josh. He was still in Japan; God knew what time it was there.

Paparazzi were already gathering at Julie's door and over the next few days the police were constant visitors. Francesca had begged her to go and stay with her and so she had. Julie felt numb, but she had to remain in control.

On the day of the funeral, she smiled to herself. The procession of people paying their last respects was long and just what Ralph had wanted. His hearse was a vintage Rolls Royce, his favourite. The pavements were full of people waving at the car. At the churchyard, she secretly smiled to herself. There weren't half as many women as there had been at Tony's funeral!

As promised, she had sent any recordings she had of the judge to his house. He had done his job well.

The police knew it had to be an inside job. How else would a gun get under the chair? The problem here was that Ralph knew and had befriended so many police commissioners and detectives that a thorough investigation could open up a can of worms, and nobody wanted that. They all had secrets they didn't want uncovered. Thankfully, they had all argued the case that no civilians were hurt apart from the accused. And, since Ralph was now dead and couldn't be arrested, it had been swept under the carpet, just as Ralph had predicted.

41

A MATCH MADE IN HEAVEN

'You're getting fat.' Filling the doorway of Scarlet's office, Knuckles sucked on his lolly and stated the obvious.

'No, I'm not getting fat, Knuckles. I'm having a baby!' Scarlet threw her hands up in the air and looked across at Mark. 'You were saying, Mark. So, we have some new kids on the block who think just because I am a woman they can do without our protection. Is that right?'

'In short, Scarlet, yes. They are making a noise and badmouthing you. Do you want me to send a couple of the boys round?'

Scarlet shook her head. 'No. If they are badmouthing me or my name, I'll go.'

'You're six months pregnant, Scarlet! You can't go. What if they get rough?' Mark had been amazed by her spirit these last few years, but even he thought this was a recipe for disaster.

'Get my coat, Knuckles, we're going out.' Scarlet stood up.

'Scarlet!' Mark was desperate to make her see sense. 'These guys you're going to see will put up a fight, you know that.' Mark was worried. It didn't seem right that a pregnant woman should go and face her enemies.

'I am in charge here, Mark. And if there is trouble in the camp, it's my job to go and sort it out and let them know who's boss.'

'You remind me so much of Tony. That is, without the bump.' Mark laughed. Scarlet showed no fear. She was ruthless. Behind her back they called her 'the Ice Queen', although she probably knew it.

'Just out of curiosity, Scarlet, I know that's not my grandchild. It's been a couple of years since you and Dominic divorced, but who's the lucky guy?'

Everyone seemed curious about this. There was no man on the scene and Scarlet kept her business very close to her chest.

'Have you never heard of the Virgin Mary, Mark? Anyway, what about you and Julie? Word is that you're more of a companion to her than her new driver.' Seeing him blush slightly, Scarlet felt she had said enough. Mark was a good man and it was good to know they could still be friends. 'I have to go. Knuckles is waiting.' Scarlet had started to walk away when she stopped and turned back to him. 'It's good to know that you're still loyal to the Lambrianu firm. Thank you.' After kissing him on the cheek, she walked away.

'Right, Knuckles,' she said, when she was in the car. 'I have a plan and I'll tell you about it on the way. Let's go and see these hard men, shall we?' Knuckles pulled away and she gave him her instructions as he drove through the streets.

It was early evening and most of the shops were closed. This fitted in nicely with Scarlet's plans. The fewer witnesses, the better. Walking in, she turned the sign on the door around to 'closed'.

'Are you the owner?' Scarlet was all smiles and charm. 'My

name is Scarlet Lambrianu and I believe you're having trouble paying your protection money.' Putting her finger to her chin and looking up to the ceiling, as though deep in thought, she carried on. 'Oh, yes. That's right. You don't need protection from a silly pregnant woman, do you?'

'Get out, missus, and turn my fucking sign around. Leave while you can.' The owner turned to shout through the back room. 'Come and see this. It's that Lambrianu witch coming to threaten us, with a bun in the oven.' He was laughing and mocking her, but still she remained calm. Over the years she had faced many situations like this and they made her smile. All these owners started out with bravado and insults and they all said the same things. 'Just what the fuck are you going to do?'

'Me?' Scarlet looked shocked. 'I'm not going to do anything. As you say, I'm a pregnant woman. What could I possibly do?' Turning around and noticing a little stool which she presumed they used to stand on to get to the high shelves, she sat down. 'But he will.'

The owner turned around and his face paled as he stared at Knuckles, who stood in the doorway behind him.

'Mick!' the owner shouted. 'Get through here.'

'He can't. He's unconscious. He's breathing, though.' Knuckles seemed pleased that he had done it right, just as Scarlet had instructed him.

Opening her handbag, Scarlet took out her nail file and started filing her nails. 'Show him what happens when your store isn't protected from thugs and burglars, Knuckles.' She was wearing her well-practiced bored face.

'Get out or I will call the police.' The once brave owner had suddenly become a quivering mess. He became hysterical when he saw Knuckles sweep everything off his shelves on to the floor and take his lighter out.

'I pay the police, love,' said Scarlet. 'Believe me, they will drive very slowly to get here. And by the time they do, everything will be burnt to a crisp. Including you.' Her voice became more threatening. 'Now. Do you need protection from an overweight pregnant woman or not?'

'Please don't do this. This is everything I have.'

Knuckles set fire to the newspapers and magazines on the shelf.

'Please don't. Yes. Yes, I need your protection.'

'Open the till, honey. Let's see what's in there.' Scarlet watched as the owner opened the till. It didn't have much in it. After all, most people paid by card these days. 'I will take that now and the boys will be around in a couple of days for the rest. Or would you like me to send Knuckles back? Now, are we going to be friends or are you going to carry on badmouthing me?'

The owner was jumping up and down, trying to stamp out the fire. Looking in the far corner, where the fire was starting to take hold, Scarlet decided it was time to leave.

After opening her handbag, Scarlet took out her gun. 'Just in case you think I need protection and someone to fight my battles, I don't. You wouldn't be the first shop owner to have a bullet in him. Come on, Knuckles, let's go.'

The owner stood there, hypnotised by the gun Scarlet held.

'If I were you, I'd get my fire extinguisher. Or ring the fire brigade.' With that, she turned the sign around on the shop door. 'See you soon. Come on, Knuckles.' Scarlet left, shutting the door behind her.

Inside the car, she started to cough. She opened the window. 'For God's sake, Knuckles, was it really necessary to steal a bar of chocolate as well?'

'I like chocolate.' Knuckles opened the wrapper and proceeded to eat his ill-gotten gains as he drove off.

A thought crossed Scarlet's mind that she had been wondering about for some time. 'Do you remember what happened at Christmas when you stayed at my mum's?' After her disastrous marriage to Dominic, the very last post she had received on Christmas Eve had been her decree absolute; she'd known it was coming, but seeing confirmation that her marriage had ended in black and white had saddened her.

She had gone through the motions on Christmas Day at her mum's, but during the night she had wanted to feel needed. She had gone to Knuckles' bedroom, across the landing, and was surprised that he was still awake. He had pulled up the duvet and, without a word spoken between them, she had got in beside him and welcomed the warmth of those big arms enveloping her.

Of course, one thing had led to another. She had been surprised that for such a big man, Knuckles had been a gentle, caring lover. Shy, even. She had left early in the morning, and gone back to her own bedroom. Knuckles had never mentioned that night, and he had never tried repeating it.

A few months later, when she realised that Knuckles' little tadpoles had found a home, she had accepted her fate. Everyone was speculating about who the father could be. Not once did they guess Knuckles.

He now joined her for the Sunday dinners and Christmases at her mum's. He looked a lot smarter these days. His made-to-measure suits and his hair, which was always washed and styled, had given him a new lease of life. Knuckles' voice brought her back to reality.

'Yes. It was nice, Miss Scarlet.'

Scarlet hadn't expected fireworks from Knuckles but this was an understatement. A little more enthusiasm would have been appreciated.

'Well, just so you know, this baby of mine is the product of that night. I don't expect anything from you. I just thought you should know the truth.' There, she had said it. Expecting some kind of response, Scarlet waited.

'Okay,' was all he said.

* * *

A couple of days later, Knuckles walked into her office pushing a pram. It was a grey, deluxe model, absolutely beautiful and something she would have chosen herself.

'What's this, Knuckles?'

'It's for that.' Knuckles nodded to her stomach as she sat at her desk.

'You bought me a pram, Knuckles?' A smile crossed her face as she stood up to admire it, until she saw Knuckles lower his head in a sheepish fashion and blush slightly.

'You stole it, didn't you? How the hell did you walk out of a shop with a pram without anyone noticing?' This beggared belief.

'Practice, Miss Scarlet. Got this as well. I've been practicing.' Leaning forward, Knuckles took a baby-sized doll out of the pram.

'Practicing? Practicing what?' Baffled, Scarlet stood there stunned. She was still wondering how he had walked out of a shop with a pram.

'Holding it.' Knuckles cradled the baby in his arms.

Looking at this sight, Scarlet had to bite her bottom lip. Then she frowned. She noticed something peculiar about the doll. 'Knuckles, it's only got one arm. Surely if you can walk out of a shop with a pram like this, you could pinch a better doll than that.'

Again, that sheepish look crossed his face and he looked down at the floor. 'It fell off. Squeezed it too tight.'

For a fleeting moment, Scarlet thought about Tony and Jake. They would have laughed their heads off at this revelation. She almost felt like bursting out laughing herself, but she realised it was a serious moment and meant a lot to Knuckles.

'Well, Knuckles. You have a few months yet. Maybe you just need a little more practice.' She squeezed his arm and smiled to show her appreciation.

Knuckles seemed satisfied with that. He put the doll back in the pram and carried on as normal.

A warm feeling filled Scarlet as she watched him leave and a smile crossed her face. Putting her hands on the pram handle, she felt content. Knuckles was doing his best to support her in the only way he knew how. And for now, that was more than good enough.

42

THE NEXT GENERATION

'Happy birthday!' Everyone burst into song around the dining table. Today was Adam's eighteen birthday. Time had moved on and a lot had happened in the intervening years.

'Elle would have loved this, Julie.' Francesca couldn't help feeling sad, although it was a happy day.

'I know, love. She loved those boys of hers and protected them all her life. She knew a lot more about their dirty dealings than she cracked on.'

The whole house seemed empty without Elle, but she had been in her nineties and had gone peacefully in her sleep.

'Scarlet's bought him a car for his birthday, you know. There is no competing with that.' Francesca looked at her presents for Adam. The one thing she really wanted to give him was Tony's vintage Rolex. She hoped that would mean a lot to him. Julie, in her unique fashion, had bought him socks and underpants!

'For God's sake, Fran, I got bugger all for my eighteenth. Did you get a car for your birthday?'

Francesca laughed. 'I don't even remember mine. As for Adam, Katie paid for all the driving lessons and the boys took him on a wild weekend in Amsterdam. I don't even want to think about what might have gone on.' Some of the things they had got up to had slipped out, and none of it was for the faint-hearted.

'Come on, Adam, cut the cake, Teddy is gagging for some,' shouted Scarlet above all the singing and laughter.

'Bloody Teddy! What a fucking name! Can't that idiot say her name?' Julie couldn't help having a dig at Knuckles. He had taken Tony's place when it came to her sarcastic digs. But he didn't rise to it and so it wasn't as much fun.

Scarlet had given birth to twins, a boy and a girl. As Katie had called her son Antonias, Scarlet had called her son Jake. The brothers reunited. The most unusual thing was that Scarlet had called her daughter Annette, after Tony's mother, saying that she felt Tony's mum deserved a second chance and that Tony would have liked it.

Knuckles had decided that Annette looked like a little cuddly teddy bear and had called her that. Weirdly, it had stuck, and so everyone called her Teddy now.

'You can call her whatever you like, Julie,' exclaimed Scarlet. 'But now her initials are TL, just like Papa's. Anyway, isn't Mark coming to the party?' Scarlet had found her own way of getting Julie back for her sarcasm.

'Why would he be?' Julie gave her an icy stare. 'He's my driver, Scarlet. Mind your own business.'

'Really, Julie? Since when do you need a driver in the middle of the night?'

'Don't push it, Scarlet. Better people than you have tried to get one over on me and failed miserably. I've been a widow for years. Now and again it's nice to have a plus one and a little male companionship. Just like you and Shrek.'

'Stop it, both of you. Not today. And definitely not in front of the children.' Francesca felt it was time to step in. She reached over and took out some headache tablets and put them in her mouth.

'Are you still getting those headaches?' Julie was concerned.

'Yes, every now and again. It comes and goes. Just aches and pains. None of us are getting any younger.'

'Well, I am making you a doctor's appointment for next week. It's been going on too long.'

'I'm fine, Julie. Now, let's join the others and celebrate my little boy's birthday, eh?'

'You okay, Mum?' Katie stood beside Francesca. Her concern was touching. They all constantly made journeys back and forth to Italy. Sometimes if felt like she had never left home.

It was a lovely sight to see Katie's son, Antonias, with his blond hair and blue eyes, running around the vineyard, playing. Francesca wished Tony could have seen him. But, she decided it would have probably made him sad. Little Antonias was living the life that he should have led, without a care in the world and with a loving family.

Christopher had been as good as his word and had moved Lambrianu Vineyards forward, making it even more successful. Scarlet was more than established in running the organisation in London and had gained the respect and admiration of her employees. She even had Adam working for her.

She made him work in the kitchens, behind the bar and on the doors, claiming that he needed to know every aspect of how the club worked. And now he was facing his biggest challenge.

When he had first seen the strippers at the club, like any young man he had been gobsmacked. He had been flattered and made to feel important when they had made a fuss of him. Scarlet knew that he had sampled a few of them and she had accepted that. He was a very handsome young man. She had even encouraged his flirtations. Being surrounded by the strippers on a daily basis would soon lose its attraction. Now, he could walk into the club without even noticing the girls dancing.

'I'm okay, Katie love. Just tired, that's all.' Smiling, Francesca wanted to put her at her ease. Her headaches seemed to be more regular these days but otherwise, she was okay. Just tired.

'Have you seen the painting Scarlet has had put up in the foyer of the club? It's a six-foot oil painting of Dad that she took from one of his photos. It's beautiful. Here, I took a photo.'

Francesca hadn't been to the club since the night Tony had been killed there.

'That is beautiful.' The full-length oil painting was of Tony smiling, dressed in his grey suit and pink tie; to have him there like that overlooking the club seemed very apt. Whoever had painted this had caught him to perfection. It oozed charm and sophistication.

'Will you be staying long, Katie, or is it just a flying visit for Adam's birthday?' Francesca was desperate to change the subject. The very mention of Tony still felt like a dagger to her heart.

'Well, we're staying for the anniversary of Dad's death and I want to be here to go to the cemetery with you all.' Katie knew this wasn't the right time to bring it up, but someone had to mention it. 'And Scarlet wants Christopher to show Adam how to do the accounts. He has a good head for business and is excellent at mathematics. Dad would be proud. All he lacks is experience, but Scarlet is teaching him well.'

'That would be nice if you can stay. And Katie, for the record, your father would be proud of you all, no matter what.'

They put their arms around each other.

'Hey! You two. Stop looking so bloody miserable and get over here. If I have to stand and watch Shrek eat half a cake by himself, I'm not doing it alone!' Julie's voice was loud over the chatter and excitement of Adam unwrapping his presents.

'Oh, hang on, I've left my present upstairs. Back in a minute, you lot.' Francesca ran into her bedroom and opened one of the drawers on Tony's side of the room. Rummaging through to find Tony's Rolex, she came across another red velvet box. A cold shudder ran through her. It was the anniversary present Tony was going to give her the night he was killed. She had never opened it. At one point she was so angry that the present had led Tony to his death she had thrown it in the bin. Someone must have found it, possibly Julie, and put it away.

Something compelled her to open it. Tentatively opening the box, she stared at the thick gold bangle. It had two ruby hearts in it, and the inscription read, 'Two hearts, one soul.' The tears welled up in her eyes.

'Come on, Mum. Adam's waiting,' Bobby shouted up the stairs. Brushing away the tears from her eyes and putting the bangle back in the drawer, Francesca picked up the Rolex and went downstairs.

'Here you are, darling. Sorry, I forgot where I had put it. Here, wear it with pride. Your father loved that watch.'

'Oh, Mum, are you sure?' Adam asked. He knew how much it meant to her. 'Oh, God, this is the best present, Mum.' Beaming with happiness, he put the watch on his wrist and admired it, then held it up for all to see.

'Hey, what about my car?' Scarlet butted in to lighten the mood. 'And, of course, there are Julie's very expensive socks!' Everyone burst out laughing. It was a good birthday and a good day with all of the family there, reunited as one.

43

A HAPPY ENDING

'Are you all set to come to the cemetery, Mum? The cars are ready and filled with flowers.' Katie held Francesca's hand. The anniversary of Tony's death was a hard day for all of them.

'If you don't mind, Katie love, I'd rather go on my own later. It's a beautiful sunny day and I thought I'd just potter around in the garden. It's been pretty neglected lately.' Seeing the worried look on Katie's face, Francesca smiled to reassure her. 'I'm okay, Katie. Really, I am. I just want to be alone for now. Where's Adam?'

'Where he always is. With Scarlet.' Rolling her eyes up to the ceiling, Katie sighed. 'No offence, Mum, but sometimes I wonder who his mother is.'

'Don't be silly, Katie. Lay a yellow rose on your father's grave for me.' Francesca couldn't wait for them to leave. For the last couple of weeks she'd had a yearning to look back into the little velvet box with the gold bangle inside.

Watching the cars leave from the window, Francesca breathed a sigh of relief. After going upstairs and opening the drawer, she took out the box and opened it. It was beautiful.

Looking out at her own private little garden, she felt guilty. Things needed pruning. Her border plants had been neglected and had died. There were so many happy memories in this little garden, including conceiving Adam there on a day just like this.

She went outside and felt like a naughty schoolgirl wearing her ruby bangle while turning over the compost. Her head pounded and ached. Maybe she should have gone to the doctor's after all. Tears started to flow and fall down her cheeks. 'Oh, God, Tony. I need you. Where are you?' she shouted out.

'I'm here.' That smooth velvety voice filled her ears once more and stopped her short. Slowly looking up, her eyes took in the sight of the man before her. Standing there in his suit and with that familiar smile on his face, was Tony. He looked younger. Raising her hand to shield her eyes from the sun, she noticed her own hands looked younger and felt smoother. Francesca shook her head. It felt like a dream. But there was no mistaking it. As she continued to look up, her eyes met with Tony's blue ones. 'I told you I would come back for you, Francesca. Two hearts, one soul, remember?'

Francesca walked towards him. Tears fell down her cheeks. 'I've missed you, Tony.'

'I have missed you. But I didn't want to come here and make our beautiful son an orphan.' He took her hand in his and held her arm up to look at the ruby bangle. 'You took your time wearing that.' He smiled and kissed the back of her hand. 'Come here,' he said, opening his arms wide. She stepped into them and he held her tightly.

Suddenly, Francesca could hear a commotion behind her. 'What's that noise? What's going on, Tony?'

'Don't turn around, Francesca. Look at me.' Brushing aside her long auburn hair and cupping her face in his hands, he gently kissed her.

Swiftly turning around to see what the noise was, she could see her whole family behind her. They must have come back from the cemetery. But lying amongst the bedding plants, still holding the trowel in her hand, was a woman resembling herself.

Scarlet was shouting and screaming to the paramedics. 'Do something for fuck's sake! Oh, God, Mum. Come on, open your eyes.' She was crying. They were all standing in a circle watching the paramedics trying to waken their unconscious mother.

Katie fell to her knees. 'Oh, Mum, please don't leave us. She's having a seizure. What's happened, Julie? We've only been gone for a few hours.'

'How the hell do I know? I've been with you,' Julie snapped, as she watched the panic and mayhem before her. Everyone fell to their knees, shouting for Francesca to wake up.

'Get the defibrillator,' said the paramedic to his colleague. He was on his knees and about to start CPR.

'Stop!' Julie stood there stony-faced and held her hand up. 'Don't do that. If she is going to wake up, let her do it naturally. Your mum had one of those do not resuscitate agreements in place. She did it ages ago.'

'Why would she do that?' Scarlet looked up at Julie and then at the paramedics.

'Scarlet, this was her wish,' Julie replied

Everyone carried on crying and shouting for the paramedics to do something. Only Julie stood still, calmly looking down at Francesca's body as it lay there.

Turning her head to look at Tony again, Francesca met his eyes and smiled. She had missed him so much. Now, no one would ever take him away from her again.

'Do you want to go back, Francesca? You can if you want to.' His hushed whisper filled her ears and made her smile.

'No, I want to be with you.'

Leaning forward and holding her tightly in his arms, Tony kissed her, inhaling the very last breath from her. 'Come on, Francesca. Take my hand.'

'She's gone,' said the paramedic, looking at his watch. 'Recording time of death: 3.54 p.m. Agreed?' He looked at his colleague for confirmation of the time and saw him nod.

Bobby was on his knees, holding Francesca's hand.

'Why didn't you save her?' Scarlet shouted. 'You're a fucking doctor!'

Katie grabbed hold of her sister.

'No one could have saved her Scarlet. It's my professional guess that she's had a brain bleed. Maybe that was the reason for all of those headaches. Didn't she go and see a doctor, Julie?' Everyone turned around to look at Julie. They needed someone to blame.

'No, I don't think so. She said it was nothing to worry about.'

'Why didn't you force her? You're supposed to be her friend,' shouted Scarlet.

'Your mother was not my friend. She was, is, my family. My sister. I love your mum, which is why, as sad as I am, I know she is happy. She's with your father now. Look. She's wearing the bangle he bought her for their anniversary the night he died. He always said he would come back for her and she hung on to that for all of these years. Let her go, love.'

Of course they knew Julie was right. Each in turn dried their eyes and exchanged glances with each other. The mood was sombre. There was nothing more to say. Francesca was dead.

* * *

'The cars are here, Julie.' Falling into Julie's arms, Katie sobbed. Everyone had tried to be so strong lately, but Julie had held them all together, as usual. 'It's a nice thought, you putting her in Dad's plot. Now they are together again.'

Julie held back her tears and drew on her cigarette. 'We talked one night, your mum and me, a while ago. I'm only doing the things your mother asked me to do.'

The funeral was a small affair. Family only, even though many people who had been touched by Francesca's kindness sent flowers. The blazing hot sun shone, as they all stood there in their black funeral clothes.

'Your mum wrote this poem,' Julie said. 'She wanted me or someone to read it, so here goes.' Taking out a piece of paper, Julie stood there and read Francesca's poem.

'There is a thinly veiled curtain between life and death and only love has the power to reach up and part it, reuniting us with the ones we love. Love is like the eighth day of the week. It is not recognised scientifically, but it hovers over everyone, deep in our hearts. It's the one thing we all yearn for. To love and be loved in return. Like I love you, Antonias Lambrianu.'

Wiping away a tear from her eye, Julie felt a cool wind blow across her arm, blowing her veil and hair slightly. She felt goosebumps on her face and the hairs on the back of her neck stood up. Looking around at everyone, she could see there was no breeze. No one else had felt it.

Smiling to herself, she stroked her cheek. She could have sworn she'd felt Francesca kiss her cheek and stroke her arm, letting her know that all was well.

Everyone made their way back to the cars that were waiting for them. Julie threw a yellow rose into the plot.

Walking slowly back to her car, Julie was just about to get in when she looked back at the graveside. The sun was playing tricks with her eyes, because for one fleeting moment she thought she saw Tony standing beside Francesca with his arm around her waist.

Blowing a kiss before she got into the car, she said, 'Bye, my beautiful Francesca.' Then suddenly something popped into her mind, making her smile. She remembered how Tony always complained when she never said goodbye to him. She laughed to herself.

'Goodbye, Tony Lambrianu. You take good care of her, now.'

EPILOGUE

Scarlet sat behind her desk in her father's leather chair. It had seen better days, but she drew comfort and strength from it. 'Knuckles, go and get Adam for me. Tell him I want to see him.'

'Scat, what do you want? I haven't done anything wrong.' Adam stood in the doorway. He usually came under fire for his reckless behaviour with the ladies. But then again, Julie had reminded Scarlet of her father's behaviour before he had married. It seemed they were like two peas in a pod.

'Here. These are for you.' She handed over a bunch of keys.

Adam was unsure what they were for.

'It's the keys to Papa's apartment, upstairs. You need a bachelor pad and I know you use it. So, it's yours. You're twenty-one, now. You know how to do the accounts. You know how to fire a gun. You know how to run the casinos and, if I may say so myself, Knuckles has taught you how to fight and defend yourself very well. Your training is over.'

'Really, Scarlet? You're giving me the apartment?' A wide grin spread across his face. With their father's blue eyes and the cleft in his chin, combined with their mother's wavy auburn hair,

Adam could talk the knickers off a nun! He had become quite the confident club manager now and asserted his authority well.

'It's time for you to take your seat beside me. You are Adam Antonias Lambrianu. The only male in the family with Papa's blood. It's time you took your seat in the office and ran the clubs alongside me.'

'Thanks, Scarlet. I will make you proud of me, I promise you that.'

Scarlet smiled at Adam, satisfied that Tony Lambrianu's legacy was in safe hands. Katie and Christopher had the vineyard. Scarlet and Adam ruled the streets and the clubs. This was their own family firm, built up by their father and Jake.

'I am proud of you, Adam. This is going to be your empire now.' Scarlet's voice was soft but authoritative. She wasn't a woman to cross.

'Are you thinking of leaving, Scarlet? Surely not. You run these places with an iron fist. Some even say you're worse than Dad.' Adam tried to make a joke of it, but it was true. When people spoke about Scarlet now, it was with respect.

'Not in a million years, Adam. This is my turf and I will continue running it, but with you beside me.'

'Hey, Scarlet, I have just had a thought. You know how people call you and Katie Scat Katz? Well, if they mix our names together they will call us Scam! Sounds about right to me.' They both burst out laughing.

'You're right. Who would have thought it? A Lambrianu running one big scam. Close the door, Mr Lambrianu. We have work to do.'

ACKNOWLEDGMENTS

To all the readers, for their much appreciated support, thank you. Many thanks to Avril, for all of her encouragement. Thank you to Emily Ruston, my tireless editor, who always has my back and helps me through the writing process, and to the rest of Boldwood Books for all of their support.

MORE FROM GILLIAN GODDEN

We hope you enjoyed reading *Dirty Dealings*. If you did, please leave a review.

If you'd like to gift a copy, this book is also available as an ebook, digital audio download and audiobook CD.

Sign up to Gillian Godden's mailing list for news, competitions and updates on future books.

http://bit.ly/GillianGoddenNewsletter

Dangerous Games, another gripping gangland thriller by Gillian Godden is available to order now.

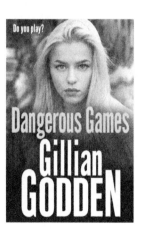

ABOUT THE AUTHOR

Gillian Godden is a Northern-born medical secretary for NHS England. She spent thirty years of her life in the East End of London, hearing stories about the local striptease pubs. Now in Yorkshire, she is an avid reader who lives with her dog, Susie.

Follow Gillian on social media:

 facebook.com/gilliangoddenauthor
twitter.com/GGodden

Boldw**oo**d

Boldwood Books is an award-winning fiction publishing company seeking out the best stories from around the world.

Find out more at www.boldwoodbooks.com

Join our reader community for brilliant books, competitions and offers!

Follow us
@BoldwoodBooks
@BookandTonic

Sign up to our weekly deals newsletter

https://bit.ly/BoldwoodBNewsletter

Printed in Great Britain
by Amazon

50391358R00195